BOX 88

By Charles Cumming

THE THOMAS KELL SERIES
A Foreign Country
A Colder War
A Divided Spy

THE ALEC MILIUS SERIES
A Spy by Nature
The Spanish Game

OTHER WORKS
The Hidden Man
Typhoon
The Trinity Six
The Man Between
(published in the United States as *The Moroccan Girl*)

BOX 88

CHARLES CUMMING

THE MYSTERIOUS PRESS
NEW YORK

BOX 88

Mysterious Press
An Imprint of Penzler Publishers
58 Warren Street
New York, N.Y. 10007

Copyright © 2020 by Charles Cumming

JAN 1 2 2022
First Mysterious Press edition January 2022

Interior design by Charles Perry

First published in the UK by HarperCollins*Publishers*

Lyrics from 'Disco 2000' by Pulp (written by Jarvis Cocker, Nick Banks, Steve Mackey, Russell Senior, Candida Doyle and Mark Webber) reprinted with permission. All rights reserved.

Library of Congress Control Number: 2021919426

ISBN: 978-1-61316-273-6
eBook ISBN: 978-1-61316-274-3

10 9 8 7 6 5 4 3 2 1

Printed in the United States of America
Distributed by W. W. Norton & Company

for Harriette

Index of Characters

The Kite family:

Lachlan Kite ('Lockie'), intelligence officer
Isobel Paulsen, Lachlan's Swedish-American wife, a doctor
Cheryl Kite (née Chapman), Lachlan's mother
Patrick Kite ('Paddy'), Lachlan's father (d. 1982)

The Bonnard family:

Xavier Bonnard, Kite's childhood friend
Luc Bonnard, Xavier's father
Rosamund Bonnard (née Penley), Xavier's mother
Jacqueline Ward ('Jacqui'), Xavier's younger sister

BOX 88:

Michael Strawson, veteran CIA officer and co-founder of BOX 88
Rita Ayinde, senior officer (UK)
Jason Franks, head of Black Ops (a 'Closer')
Carl Fowler, surveillance officer (a 'Falcon')
Freddie Lane, computer analyst (a 'Turing')
Ward Hansell, senior officer (US)
James ('Jock') and Eleanor ('Miss Ellie') Carpmael, office managers at 'The Cathedral'
The Reverend Anthony Childs, a vicar

Alford College:

Lionel Jones-Lewis, Kite's housemaster, known by the initials 'LJL'
Cosmo de Paul, joined Alford in the same year as Kite
William 'Billy' Peele, history teacher

The Security Service (MI5):

Robert Vosse, leader of MI5 investigation into BOX 88
Cara Jannaway, intelligence officer
Matt Tomkins, intelligence officer

Other Characters:

Ali Eskandarian, an Iranian
Abbas Karrubi, bodyguard to Ali Eskandarian
Hana Dufour, a friend of Ali Eskandarian
Ramin Torabi, an Iranian businessman
Martha Raine, a schoolfriend of Jacqueline Ward
Zoltan Pavkov, a Serb
Bijan Vaziri, an Iranian exile

'We have as many personalities as we have friends'
Ralph Waldo Emerson

21 December 1988

They were just another American family heading home for the holidays.

A taxi had been booked to take them from their house in Pimlico, little Gaby facing backwards on the fold-down chair, her legs not yet long enough to reach the floor, every inch of the cab crammed with suitcases and boxes and Harrod's carrier bags full of presents wrapped for Christmas. Mommy and Daddy were facing her, side by side on the back seat, her giant Hamleys' teddy bear wedged between them. Whenever the driver braked, Gaby could feel herself pulled backwards and then forwards, weightless for an instant, like the feeling of being on the swings in Battersea Park and wanting to fly off into the afternoon sky. Her mother said: 'Careful, sweetie,' but there was no way she was going to fall, not with the suitcases to steady her and the handle on the door to hold onto. She loved the growl of the taxi's engine, the Christmas lights receding in the back window, her father's voice as he pointed out the Italian restaurant they had been to for Grandpa's birthday, then the home of the Martins in Chelsea, the other American family they knew in London with their golden retriever, Montana, who licked Gaby's face whenever she gave him a hug.

Mommy had told her that there were only three more bedtimes until Christmas Eve. One tonight, on the aeroplane which was taking them across the ocean to New York, then two in her bedroom at the house in Stamford. Gaby felt giddy with excitement. She would miss her friends from school—Claire and JenJen,

Billy and Pi—but they had promised to stay in touch and write postcards to one another from wherever they were going.

Soon the taxi started going faster and they were on the freeway heading out to Heathrow. At the airport, the driver found a trolley. Gaby watched her parents pile the suitcases one on top of the other until Daddy insisted Mommy fetch a second trolley to cope with all the bags. He had given the driver thirty pounds saying: 'Keep the change.' The driver's name was Barry. When he asked where they were going, Gaby told him: 'New York. Pan Am flight number 103. Have you ever been to New York?'

''Fraid not,' Barry replied. 'You have a safe trip, sweetheart, lovely Christmas.'

There was a tree with tinsel but no lights near the desk where they queued with the trolleys. Afterwards Gaby showed her passport to a man wearing a turban who wished her a happy Christmas. She had to walk through a special door that detected metal while her rucksack and teddy bear went through the X-ray machine. A boy beside her was crying. Gaby couldn't understand why someone would be crying when there were only three more bedtimes until Christmas.

Eventually, after Mommy had taken her to the bathroom and bought some earplugs in a pharmacy inside the terminal, they walked down a long corridor to a big room where the other passengers were waiting to board the aeroplane. Gaby heard American accents, lots of them, saw older children listening to music on Walkmans, a woman lying asleep, sprawled across three chairs. There was a family of Indians sitting in the corner of the lounge. The mother had a red spot in the centre of her forehead.

'Flight's on time,' her daddy whispered, pointing outside to the waiting aircraft. 'That's the cockpit. Can you read that, sweetie?'

Words had been painted on the front of the plane, right beneath where the captain was sitting. Gaby could see him through the window, flicking switches above his head.

BOX 88

'That's easy,' she said. 'It says *Clipper Maid of the Seas.*'

They were allowed to board first because Gaby was part of a family. There were other children behind her, but no sign of the boy who had been crying when they walked past the X-ray machine. It was cold in the tunnel. There was a colour photograph on the wall of the Statue of Liberty and the Hudson River, the Twin Towers behind them glinting in the sun. A tall stewardess wearing red lipstick and a pretty blue skirt said: 'Hi there! Love your teddy bear! He's huge!' as Gaby walked through the big open door, right behind where the captain was sitting in the cockpit. It was dark now and the sound of the airport was deafening, but as soon as she entered the cabin and started following her father towards her seat, the noise seemed to fade away, as if Gaby had put in her mommy's new earplugs.

They were seated towards the front of the plane. The stewardess strapped her in and gave her a set of headphones, explaining that a film would start playing once the plane was airborne over Scotland.

'Scotland?' Daddy asked. He sounded surprised.

'Weather diversion,' the stewardess replied. 'Little bumpy tonight over Ireland.'

That was when she told Gaby that Teddy was so big he was going to have to go in a cupboard until after take-off. The cupboards were full of cases and handbags; it looked as though he was going to be squashed in there. Gaby felt like crying but she wanted to seem grown-up in front of the other passengers. The stewardess said she would give her candy to make her feel better.

'You know they call candy "sweets" in London,' Gaby told her.

'Is that right?' the stewardess replied, looking sideways at Mommy. 'Sweets, huh?' She had a pretty smile and very white teeth. 'So does Santa Claus know where you're going to be on Christmas Eve, honey? Have you told him?'

'I don't believe in Santa Claus. My friend Billy says it's just my daddy dressed up with a beard.'

'News to me,' said Daddy, and secured his seat belt as the stewardess walked off. She was smiling.

Gaby owned a yellow Swatch. She looked at it as the plane took off; it said twenty-five past six. Mommy hated flying so she always sat between them, Daddy holding her right hand, Gaby holding her left. Mommy closed her eyes as the aeroplane climbed through the sky. It was a better feeling even than the swings in Battersea Park, the noise and the rattle and the power of the big plane taking them up towards the moon.

'Set your watch to New York time, honey,' said her father, reaching across and touching her wrist. 'We're going home.'

Beneath them, in the chill of the hold, was the luggage Gaby's parents had checked in at Heathrow a little more than an hour earlier: clothes, toiletries, Christmas presents. Close by, secured inside a brown Samsonite suitcase loaded onto a feeder flight at Malta airport that morning, was a timer-activated bomb constructed with the odourless plastic explosive Semtex and hidden inside a Toshiba cassette recorder by agents working on behalf of the Libyan government.

Gaby and her parents and the more than 250 souls on board Pan Am 103 would never reach New York City, never return to their families for Christmas. At three minutes past seven, as the aircraft was passing over the small Scottish town of Lockerbie, the bomb exploded. Those sitting towards the front of the plane were killed instantly. Others fell for over five miles, some still strapped in their seats, thrown free of the fuselage yet conscious for up to three minutes as they plunged to the ground. The wreckage of the obliterated plane, scattered over an area of 850 square miles, destroyed twenty-one houses and killed eleven residents of Lockerbie. In an instant the *Clipper Maid of the Seas* had been transformed into a flight of angels, violated by terror.

London, the present day

1

It was Martha, of all people, who rang Kite to tell him that Xavier Bonnard had killed himself.

The call, logged to Kite's mobile at 11.24 GMT, transcripted by GCHQ before midday and copied to Thames House, was traced to a cell phone in the New York metropolitan area registered to 'Martha Felicity Raine' of 127 Verona Street, Brooklyn. The take quality was considered moderate, but a recording had been automatically archived. An analyst in Cheltenham was able to provide a full account of the brief conversation.

LACHLAN KITE (LK): Hello?
MARTHA RAINE (MR): Lockie. It's me.
LK: Martha. God. What a surprise.
MR: Yes.
       [break, 1 second]
LK: Is everything all right? Are you OK?
MR: I'm afraid it's something awful.
LK: What's happened? Are the children all right?
MR: You're sweet. They're fine. They're both well. No, something else.
LK: What is it?

MR: It's Xavier. He's gone. Xavier has died.

[break, 2 seconds]

I thought you would want to know. Perhaps you already do.

LK: No. I didn't. I didn't know.

[break, 1 second]

I appreciate you ringing. Must be early there.

MR: I only just found out. Thought I should ring straight away.

LK: Yes. What happened? What . . .

MR [overlapping]: They think it was suicide. They're not 100 per cent sure. He was in Paris. In an apartment. Not his father's place, somebody else's.

LK: Who's 'they'?

MR: Jacqui. She rang me. She's in Singapore these days.

LK: What about Lena? Were they still together?

MR: I think so, yes. Just about. Living in London. They still have the Onslow Square house. I don't know where the children are.

LK: (Inaudible)

[break, 2 seconds]

MR: Are you there? Are you all right, Lockie?

LK: I'm fine. I'm in the country. Sussex. We have a cottage here.

MR: We?

LK: Yes. I met somebody. I got married.

[break, 1 second]

MR: Right. Yes, I did hear that. On the grapevine. I'm happy for you. Finally settling down. What's her name? What does she do?

LK: She's a doctor. Isobel.

[break, 2 seconds]

MR: And what about everything else? Are you still doing those things you used to do? That life?

BOX 88

LK: I'll tell you when I see you. We can talk about it then.

MR: Of course. Silly of me to ask. Must be beautiful there. Lovely England. I never get back . . .

LK: Killed himself *how?*

MR: They think an overdose. I didn't want to pry. Jacqui didn't go into details. Obviously she was very upset.

LK: Yes, of course. Christ . . .

MR: I'm sorry, Lock. I have to go. The kids . . .

LK: Of course. School run? They must be big now.

MR: Gigantic. Are you sure you're OK?

LK: I'm fine. I'll be absolutely fine. You?

MR: Yes. Just makes me think of the old days, you know. He was such a lovely man, such a mess. A lost soul.

LK: Yes. He was all of those things.
[break, 1 second]
Thank you for telling me, Martha. I really appreciate it. It's been good to hear your voice, if nothing else.

MR: Yours too. I don't think I'm going to be able to get to the funeral if it's next week. There's just too much on here. Jonas is going away, he has work. My au pair just quit . . .

LK: I'm sure the Bonnards will understand. There'll be lots of people there.

MR: Everybody from that time.

LK: Yes. Everybody.

The four members of the MI5 team gathered around an IKEA kitchen table in a damp, under-hoovered safe flat in Acton, read the transcript and, later, listened to the recording of the conversation several times. One excerpt in particular—the question *Are you still doing those things you used to do?*—gave team leader Robert Vosse the shot of operational adrenaline he had been craving ever since his investigation into BOX 88 had begun. Like a detective happening upon the clue that at last placed his suspect at the scene of the crime, Vosse—a big-boned, amiable man of forty-one with outsized features who wore thick-rimmed glasses and clothes from Marks & Spencer—was convinced that Martha Raine had provided concrete evidence that Lachlan Kite was a spy.

'We've been digging into every nook and cranny of Kite's existence for the past three weeks and come up with precisely sweet Fanny Adams. Nothing recorded against, not even a parking fine or a speeding ticket. A six-person surveillance team—the best of the best—has been following him around like Rain Man waiting for Kite to pop his head into Vauxhall Cross or catch a flight to Langley. Has he done that? Has he bollocks. Here is a man we are told is the operational commander of a secret Anglo-American spy unit that's been running off the books for almost forty years, but the most Lachlan Kite has done this month is get himself a haircut and book a weekend break to Florence. Now, finally, he takes a phone call. A woman from his past says, "Are you still doing the things you used to do?" What did she mean by that? What else could she *possibly* have meant other than "Are you still operational as a spy?"'

Vosse was a man who liked to pace around as he spoke. His underlings, all of whom were as mystified by BOX 88 as their boss, variously stared at surveillance photographs of Kite, copies of the GCHQ transcript, half-eaten bars of Chunky Kit-Kat. Their investigation had come about as a result of a private conversation between the director general of MI5 and a disgruntled former MI6 officer who claimed that Kite had been recruited by BOX 88 as a teenager.

'"Are you still doing those things you used to do?"' Vosse muttered. 'What is "that life" if not the life we are investigating? What could this Martha Raine possibly have been referring to if not our man's thirty-year career as an industrial-strength spy? Drug-pushing? Is that it? Was he secretly a crack dealer? No.

BOX 88

Lachlan Kite was running his own little Mission: Impossible unit without any of us knowing.'

'Allegedly.'

This from Tessa Swinburn, at thirty-nine a contemporary of Vosse, in every way his operational and intellectual equal, who had nevertheless been overlooked for promotion due to fears within Personnel that she would soon become pregnant by her new husband and likely spend at least eighteen of the next thirty-six months on maternity leave.

'What's that supposed to mean?' Vosse asked.

'It means we still don't have proof. It means we still have to keep following him around. It means until we can actually catch Lachlan Kite in the act of spying, we can't do anything about it. We can't arrest him. We can't interrogate him. We certainly can't prove the existence of BOX 88.'

'How do you *catch* somebody in the act of spying?' Vosse asked, a question which, given their vocation and operational remit, took all of the team by surprise. 'He's not going to sit on a bench in Gorky Park and share a cigarette with Edward Snowden. We're not going to film him orchestrating a spy swap on the Glienicke Bridge.'

'Then why are we here, doing what we're doing?' Tessa asked.

'Because we're assembling evidence. Following leads. Building a case against a man, bit by bit, step by step.'

'Exactly,' said Matt Tomkins.

Tomkins, who always liked to agree with Vosse, had been employed by the Security Service for almost six years. The Kite operation was the first job that had taken him permanently away from Thames House. He was one of only five employees who knew about BOX 88; the DG didn't want to look like a fool if the investigation proved to be a wild goose chase. Socially withdrawn, but clever and ambitious, Tomkins spent an hour every evening pumping weights at a gym in Hammersmith, another three on weekends throwing people onto crash mats at a ju-jitsu class in Barnes. Though not yet thirty, his hair had already started to recede at the crown, giving him the look of a particularly humourless and unpleasant trainee monk.

'If the men say so,' Tessa sighed.

She looked out onto Acton High Street. She had always been suspicious that the MI6 whistle-blower was a fantasist. It seemed implausible that BOX had existed for almost four decades without anyone knowing. Who was paying their bills, for a start? Where was it based? Was it a rogue unit or—as the DG feared—an arm of the Deep State operating with the tacit approval of Washington and Downing Street? The one-bedroom flat was situated two floors above a dry-cleaner's. Tessa could see a clump of teenagers in school uniform on the top deck of a bus. They were gathered around the screen of a mobile phone in a way that made her think of families in pre-war London huddled in front of the wireless listening to speeches by Neville Chamberlain. She looked at her watch. It wasn't even two o'clock. Why weren't they in school?

'So here's what we're going to do,' Vosse announced. 'Matt, you're going to find out everything you can about this Martha Felicity Raine. Sounds posh. What's a nice, well-brought-up English girl doing in New York, besides marrying a Yank called Jonas and walking her kids to school? Are they Kite's kids? What does she do for a living? Housewife? Art dealer? Spy? How does she know our man? How far back does their relationship go? Sounded to me like she was pining for the old days, jealous of Dr Isobel and our man's comfortable life in Sussex.'

Tomkins nodded, agreeing, writing everything down.

'Tess,' Vosse continued, pivoting towards Tessa Swinburn. 'If you can tear yourself away from gazing at the splendours of Acton High Street, spend the rest of the afternoon on the corpse. Get onto Paris. Get the coroner's report. Overdose or foul play? Furthermore: who, what, when, why and where is

BOX 88

"Lena"? If she owns a house in Onslow Square, that says money to me, lots and lots of money. Any link to Kite? Also "Jacqui". Who she? Sounds like a relative of the poor bloke who topped himself. What's she doing in Singapore? I want the whole Bonnard family tree, dead and alive. I want *detail*. Don't give me a trunk and a couple of branches. I want it to look like one of those big healthy sycamores you see in ads for health insurance. *Massive*. Now what's left?'

Vosse briefly consulted the transcript. He had long, thick fingers and tufts of black hair on the backs of his hands.

'Funeral,' came a voice.

Cara Jannaway was standing in the doorway to the kitchen. She was twenty-six and new to MI5 and already unremittingly bored by the job. Hadn't anticipated the sheer mundanity of keeping tabs on the same target, day after day, moving rumours around a room, mousing files on a computer, lying to her friends about working at the Ministry of Defence, telling boys on Tinder and Bumble she was a chef, a make-up artist, a personal trainer.

'What's that?' said Vosse.

'Somebody should keep an eye on ATLANTIC BIRD at the funeral. See who he talks to.' ATLANTIC BIRD was Kite's operational codename, typically shortened to BIRD. 'Maybe Martha will find a new au pair and fly over from New York. Maybe I could talk to her, find out what she meant.'

'Meant by what?' said Tessa. She was still looking out of the window and only half paying attention.

'Are you still doing those things you used to do?' Cara replied. 'What did she mean by that? What does she know about Kite's past that she could tell us?'

Vosse looked up. He had found a true believer. There was a smudge on one of the lenses of his thick-rimmed spectacles.

'You got a black dress, Miss Jannaway?'

'Sure.'

'Pair of sunglasses?'

'Lots.'

'Good. Then dust them down, pick out a pair of heels.' He examined a tea towel of dubious hygiene and laid it out on the windowsill. 'It's your lucky day, Cara. No office drudgery for you. You're going to a funeral.'

2

Lachlan Kite woke at sunrise, crept out of bed, changed into a pair of shorts and running shoes and set out on a four-mile loop around the hills encircling the cottage in Sussex. The news of Xavier's death had hit him as hard as anything he could recall since the sudden loss of Michael Strawson, his mentor and father figure, to a cancer of the liver which had ripped through him in the space of a few months. Though he had seen Xavier only fitfully over the previous ten years, Kite felt a personal sense of responsibility for his death which was as inescapable as it was illogical and undeserved. Usually, pounding the paths around the cottage, feeling the soft winter ground beneath his feet, he could switch the world off and gain respite from whatever problems or challenges might face him upon his return. Kite had run throughout his adult life—in Voronezh and Houston, in Edinburgh and Shanghai—for just this reason: not simply to stay fit and to burn off the pasta and the pints, but for his own peace of mind, his psychological well-being.

It was different today, just as it had been on the afternoon of Martha's call when Kite had immediately left the cottage and run for seven unbroken miles, memories of Xavier erupting with every passing stride. The stillness of the morning was the stillness of dawn at the Bonnard villa in France, thirty years earlier, the eighteen-year-old Kite sneaking back to bed after a stolen night with Martha to find Xavier passed out in his room, a bottle of Smirnoff tipped over beside him, a cigarette burned down to the filter in his hand. The rising sun was a memory of Ali Eskandarian smoking a Cuban cigar in the gardens of the house, laughing uproariously as Xavier lost to him once again at backgammon. The pain in Kite's lungs was Strawson and Billy Peele in the safe house in Mougins, master spies urging Kite to greater and greater acts of treachery against his friend. No matter how hard he tried, whatever tricks of mental discipline he summoned, Kite could not shake off the memories. They were as clear to him as home movies projected onto the Sussex hills and the English sky. He was suddenly a prisoner of a summer three decades earlier when his life, and that of Xavier Bonnard, had been inverted by BOX 88.

Kite jogged home, showered and changed into a dark lounge suit, slipping a black wool tie into the side pocket of the jacket. He had only one pair of black shoes in the cottage and they were scuffed and dirty. He spat on the leather, rubbing the shoes with the sweat-soaked T-shirt he had worn on the run before drying them with an old handkerchief he had found in the pocket of the trousers.

'Classy,' said Isobel, kissing the top of his head as she passed him on the stairs. She was already dressed, the bump of her pregnancy visible beneath a blue cotton dress.

'Old army trick,' Kite replied, remembering his father polishing his shoes in the pantry at the hotel in Scotland, telling tall stories about a deranged sergeant-major at Sandhurst.

'You were never *in* the army, were you?'

'Dad was. They kicked him out.'

'What for? Having dirty shoes?'

'Something like that.'

Patrick Kite had died when Kite was eleven years old. Hearing the note change in her husband's voice, Isobel turned at the

BOX 88

bottom of the stairs and smiled up at him with the look of quiet understanding she employed whenever they were confronted by the myriad complications of his past. She knew that when it came to Kite's father, 'something like that' could mean anything—fighting, drinking, even desertion—but did not press him for details. Kite's long life in the secret world was a place as mysterious and concealed to her as her own background was to him. They had met six years earlier at a party in Stockholm and fallen in love with the tacit understanding that they should avoid mentioning the past as much as possible. For Kite, this was a simple matter of Official Secrecy: he was forbidden to disclose the existence of BOX 88. For Isobel, there were elements of her past—former lovers, former selves, betrayals and mistakes—of which she was ashamed. It made sense that they should both want a clean slate. Isobel had been vetted and cleared to know that Lachlan Kite was an intelligence officer, supposedly working for MI6. Her file sat on a computer, but Kite had never accessed it, both out of respect for Isobel's privacy and because he did not want to think of her as just another source or asset. They had built a life together separate from the secret world, a life that was as precious to him as the child now growing inside her.

'Want some breakfast?' she called out from the kitchen.

'Don't worry,' Kite replied, walking in moments later. 'I'll get something on the train. You go to work. You'll be late.'

'Sure?'

'I'm sure.'

He stood behind her and kissed the back of her neck, his hand resting on her stomach.

'Rambo just kicked,' she said. 'You missed it.'

'Really?' Kite dropped to his knees in a pantomime of frustration, pressing his ear against Isobel's belly. He turned to address his unborn child. 'Hello? Are you there? Do it again!'

Isobel laughed as Kite stood up and grabbed an apple from

a bowl. She looked down at her stomach and continued the conversation.

'Your daddy is crazy,' she said. 'But he looks very sexy in his suit.'

'My whole life was designed so that I don't have to wear one of these things,' he said, briefly wrapping his arms around the suit as if it were a straitjacket. He took a carton of grapefruit juice from the fridge and set it on the counter.

'How was your run?' she asked.

'Strange.' As Kite poured the juice into a glass, biting into the apple, he thought again of Strawson and Eskandarian, of the long-ago summer in France. 'Whatever the opposite of Zen is, that's how I'm feeling. It's the funeral. Can't get used to the idea that Xav's gone.'

'You haven't told me much about him,' Isobel replied, picking up her car keys. 'He was at school with you?'

'Yes. For a long time he was my closest friend. He was around when I was recruited.'

'OK.'

Ordinarily, that would have been the end of the conversation, but Kite wanted to tell Isobel at least something about their relationship.

'The nature of the job took me away from him. Xav went to university, and I was travelling in my twenties. He got into rave, Ecstasy, all that Gen X stuff. Like most of the wealthier boys at Alford, he had a trust fund. Half a million on his twenty-first birthday, a flat in Chelsea, an Audi Quattro for the residents' parking. No need to work or to prove himself. He just wanted to have a good time. He was wild and he lived well. People loved being around him. From eighteen onwards he was basically an addict spending most of his money on coke, vodka, parties— whatever would make the pain go away. None of us were wise enough to be able to persuade him out of it. He was having too much fun.'

BOX 88

Kite was circling around the truth. He was looking at the woman he loved, trying to explain what had happened, but holding back key facts. To tell the story of the life of Xavier Bonnard was to tell the story of Xavier's father, Luc, and of Ali Eskandarian, the Iranian businessman who had come between them. Kite could not and would not do this because the story belonged to BOX 88. It was all in the files. One day—when they were old and grey and nodding by the fire—he would tell Isobel the whole story. There were times when he wanted her to know everything about him; others when he wanted never to speak of the past again.

'Sounds like a classic fucked-up posh boy.'

'He was definitely that.'

'Too much money. Too little love.'

'Exactly.'

'That school,' she said, sounding exasperated. 'One part Hogwarts, one part Colditz. What did that writer in the *Guardian* call it? "A gateway drug for the Bullingdon." Why do the Brits send their kids to these places?'

'I've been asking myself that question for thirty years.'

'No way Rambo's going there. No way, José.' Kite met her eyes. Though her father was American, Isobel had been born and raised in Sweden, where only diplomatic brats and royalty went to boarding schools. She said: 'I can come with you today if it's going to be difficult.'

He touched the side of her face. 'You're kind. There's no need. You have work.'

'When will you be home?'

The funeral was at eleven. Kite was due at a gallery in Mayfair at four where his usual dealer had a Riopelle he wanted him to look at. If the Eastbourne train was on time, he would be home to make dinner.

'Eight?' he said. 'Shouldn't be any later than that. If I run into problems, I'll call you.'

3

Robert Vosse had given instructions that the Kite cottage wasn't to be touched.

'No car or van or drone or pushbike is to come within half a mile of the place. Get too close on foot surveillance and Kite will smell a rat. Follow his car for more than a couple of miles and we might as well put stickers on the headlights saying *MI5 Is Following You*. If Lachlan Kite is even half as experienced and thorough as we've been led to believe, he'll sniff out a microphone or a camera in less time than it took Matt to make my cup of tea this morning.'

Vosse was addressing the troops at the Acton safe flat. It was a Tuesday afternoon. They had spent the day poring over the various reports the team had assembled on the Bonnard family and Martha Raine.

'Kite's hardly likely to blab about BOX 88 within earshot of his pregnant wife,' said Vosse with a nod of agreement from Matt Tomkins. 'He's a thirty-year veteran of the intelligence world, hard-wired for secrecy and discretion. Man like that gets wind we've rigged his love nest for sight and sound, he'll do a Lucan. Let him go for his jogs unmolested. Let him have his lunches

20

BOX 88

at the Dog and Duck. The funeral's all we need. Cara's going to pop him in her pocket, aren't you, love?'

* * *

It wasn't quite how things worked out.

Just to be on the safe side, on the day of the funeral Vosse positioned a two-man team outside Lewes station in a plain-clothes Vauxhall Astra. Officer Kieran Dean followed Kite onto the London service while Tessa Swinburn drove ahead and boarded the same train twenty minutes later at Hayward's Heath. Dean disembarked and picked up the Astra as Swinburn settled in a carriage adjacent to Kite and tracked him to Victoria station. After buying a pain au chocolat and a double espresso at Caffè Nero under the watchful eye of Matt Tomkins, BIRD was observed boarding a District line train to South Kensington. By eleven o'clock, Lachlan Kite was standing outside the Brompton Oratory surrounded by the great and the good of the European elite on a cold February morning blessed by clear blue skies. Wearing Nina Ricci sunglasses and a long black overcoat (both sourced on expenses from TK Maxx), Cara Jannaway approached the mourners from a starting position outside Harrods. Watching her grudgingly from a patisserie across the road, Matt Tomkins told Vosse by phone that Cara certainly looked the part, but was 'too tall, and too striking, for effective surveillance work'.

'You think?'

Vosse had finely tuned antennae both for the toadying of ambitious junior officers and for any carefully worded slights against colleagues. He liked Cara, always had, and didn't want to hear a bad word against her, especially when she wasn't around to defend herself. Vosse had known from day one that Matt Tomkins was a triple-dyed shit of outsized ego, possessed of boundless tenacity and cunning. Such characteristics were always an asset to any team, but he hoped that Tomkins would be smart enough to learn when to talk and when to keep his mouth shut.

'I just think she's standing out a bit too much,' he said. 'Needs to talk to somebody, sir. Needs to blend in.'

'She'll be all right,' said Vosse, and hung up.

* * *

Kite had given up smoking on his fortieth birthday and nowadays lit up only when he needed to for cover. Standing amid the Bonnard mourners on the steps of the Brompton Oratory, he caught the smell of a cigarette on the morning air and walked towards its source.

'You couldn't spare one of those, could you?'

The man holding the cigarette was at least six foot six and heavily bearded. Kite did not recognise him, though he had spotted several of Xavier's friends and former colleagues in the crowd.

'Sure.' The accent was American, the cigarettes a brand Kite didn't know. The packet was mercifully clear of gruesome images of babies on ventilators, of lungs and throats decimated by cancer. Kite took a long, deep drag.

'Thank you,' he said. 'Needed that.'

'Me too. Bad day. You knew Xav a long time?'

'From thirteen. We were at school together.'

'What's that, the famous place? Alford? Students go around in tailcoats, like they're dressed for a wedding the whole time?'

'That's the one.'

'Fifty-six prime ministers and counting? Every prince and king of England since 1066?'

'Pretty sure Prince Charles went to Gordonstoun, and hated it, but otherwise you're right.'

The American suppressed a broad grin, as though it would be tasteless to be seen enjoying himself on the steps of a funeral.

'How about you?' Kite asked. 'How did you know Xavier?'

'AA,' the American replied, and tested Kite's reaction with his eyes. 'Did time together in Arizona. Dried out in South Africa. Attended meetings in London, New York, Paris. We

BOX 88

were what you might call a travelling double-act. They should put up one of those blue plaques in the Priory.'

That explains the unmarked cigarettes, Kite thought. Bought by the carton in Cape Town or Phoenix duty-free.

'Had you seen him recently?' he asked.

The American shook his head. 'Not for a year or so. I met a girl, moved back home. Xav kind of vanished, like he always did. No way he took his own life though. Not a guy with that much spirit. Must have been accidental. You?'

'I hadn't seen him for a long time.'

Kite looked out among the gathering crowds, the stiff-backed grandees and the poleaxed mourners. He was sure that his friend had taken his own life but didn't want to explore that theory with a stranger who knew things about Xavier from therapy that Kite himself had never been privy to. One day he would get to the truth of what had happened, but not today. A tall woman in a long black overcoat was walking towards the church beside a short, bullish man in a pinstriped suit. With a thud of irritation, Kite recognised him as Cosmo de Paul. From Alford to Edinburgh, from MI6 to Royal Dutch Shell, de Paul had been a malign presence in Kite's life and a consistent thorn in the side of BOX 88. Kite doubted that de Paul had spent more than fifteen minutes in Xavier's company since the turn of the century. That he should attend his funeral merely demonstrated that he valued the opportunity to network more than he valued his friendship with the deceased.

'Who's the girl?' asked the American, indicating the tall woman in the long black overcoat. She was wearing a pair of oversized Jackie O sunglasses, drawing attention to her own grief while at the same time challenging anyone to speak to her. If she was de Paul's latest wife or mistress, Kite sent his condolences. If she was a friend of Xavier's, it was the first time he had set eyes on her.

'No idea,' he said. 'Time to go in. Thanks for the cigarette.'
'Don't mention it.'

Cara's basic cover, agreed with Vosse, was to role-play a friend from Cape Town who had got to know 'Xav' while he was drying out at a clinic in Plettenberg Bay. Research carried out by Tessa Swinburn had shown that Bonnard had enjoyed two separate stints at rehabilitation centres in South Africa, most recently in Mpumalanga. It was plausible that he had befriended 'Emma', an English teacher from East London, while passing through Cape Town. Cara hoped that by referring obliquely to Bonnard's struggles with narcotics and alcohol, she would prevent anyone she happened to speak to from testing her legend too closely.

She was aware, of course, that Xavier had been to Alford College, a place she knew only as the school which had produced at least three of the Conservative politicians who had done so much to damage British public life in the previous decade. Looking around, she saw men in their mid-to-late forties whom she assumed were Bonnard's contemporaries. Some of them, with their signet rings and their Thomas Pink shirts, looked like dyed-in-the-wool Tory whack jobs pining for the halcyon days of Agincourt and Joan Hunter Dunn; others seemed no different to the bland, blameless middle-aged men who haunted the corridors and conference rooms of Thames House and Vauxhall Cross. Cara had never fully understood the widespread British prejudice against public schoolboys. It wasn't exactly their fault that at the age of eight, their parents had seen fit to pack them off to boarding school with not much more than a tuck box and a thermal vest. To Cara, who had grown up in a happy two-parent, two-sibling house in Ipswich, attending the local grammar and partying on weekends like Gianluca Vacchi, spending five years at Alford sounded like a prison sentence.

'Hello there.'

BOX 88

She looked down. A squat, vain-looking man with a cut-glass accent was introducing himself.

'Hello,' she said.

'You look a bit lost.'

If there was one thing designed to instil in Cara Jannaway a prejudice against posh, entitled ex-public schoolboys, it was being told by this silver-spooned creep that she looked 'lost'.

'I'm fine,' she said. 'I was just about to go in.'

'Me too,' the man replied. 'I'm Cosmo. Cosmo de Paul.'

'Emma.'

They shook hands. Was it a set-up? Had Lachlan Kite become suspicious and sent him over to check her out?

'Are you a friend? Family?'

'Friend,' Cara replied, grateful for her sunglasses as she looked around for BIRD. She hadn't been able to spot him among the dense crowds moving into the Oratory and wondered if he was ahead of her, in all senses. 'You?'

'Xavier and I were at school together.'

'And where was that, Alford?'

'That's right.'

'Ah. Good for you.'

Cara found herself walking alongside de Paul, making halting small talk about London and the weather. She was glad to be free of the miserable, drip-drip inertia of the Acton safe flat but didn't like it that a stranger had latched onto her in this way. She had heard that a certain type of man preyed on a certain type of woman at funerals, hoping to usher hysteria and grief into the bedroom; if this little runt with his snub-nose and Rees-Mogg pinstripe tried it on, she'd push his face into the baptism font.

'Are you here alone?' he asked.

'Yeah. I don't know anybody here. Just came to pay my respects.'

All around her, middle-aged men and women in scarves and

overcoats were embracing one another, recognising faces from yesteryear and nodding respectfully. It was as if the funeral of Xavier Bonnard was not merely an occasion of great solemnity, but also a reunion of sorts for a generation of men and women, schooled at St Paul's and Roedean and Oxbridge, whose paths had diverged some thirty years earlier, only to be brought back together by the sudden, tragic death of a mutual friend. Like the posh weddings Cara had occasionally attended, impeccably mannered ushers in morning coats were handing out the Order of Service and shepherding older members of the congregation to their seats. She fancied that she could spot the addicts and party boys among them: they were the ones with unruly hair and the Peter Pan glint in their eyes, the hand-me-down tweed suits and look-at-me patterned socks. That was the thing about upper-class druggies: they had the money to go on and on. Get hooked on smack in Ipswich and chances are you'd wind up dead. Get addicted to coke on an Alford trust fund and you could afford to get addicted all over again, just as soon as Mummy and Daddy had checked you out of rehab.

'How did you meet Xavier?' de Paul asked, accepting an Order of Service from a good-looking man in his twenties who looked as though he'd walked straight off the set of *Four Weddings and a Funeral*.

'Out in South Africa,' she said.

'I see,' he replied, absorbing the euphemism.

One of the mourners passed de Paul and touched him on the back, saying only: 'Cosmo' in a low murmur before settling into a pew. Cara told de Paul that she would prefer to be alone 'at this difficult time' and was glad to see him take the hint.

'Of course. It was charming to meet you.'

'Likewise,' she said, and moved quickly along the nave.

She was staggered by the opulence of the church. Tessa's research into the Bonnard family had revealed that Xavier's mother, Rosamund, was the daughter of a duke whose family

BOX 88

appeared to have owned, at one time or another, most of the land between Cambridge and Northampton. Perhaps it took that kind of old school clout to secure the entirety of Brompton Oratory for a midweek funeral. Certainly it looked as though the church was going to be three-quarters full. There were already at least four hundred people filling the pews and many more still shuffling in through the entrance. Cara stopped halfway along the aisle and turned to look for Kite. To her astonishment she saw him immediately, standing no more than ten feet away beneath a sculpture of St Matthew. It was the first time that anyone on the team had been that close to BIRD. She was struck by how easily she recognised him from surveillance photographs: the dark hair, greying slightly at the temples; the narrow blue eyes, catching light from a window in the southern facade; a face at rest, giving nothing away, but with the faintest hint of mischief in the lines around his mouth. Not a noticeably handsome man, but striking and undeniably attractive. Cara had a habit of comparing people to animals. If Robert Vosse was a cow, plodding and decent, Matt Tomkins was a vulture, circling for carrion. If Cosmo de Paul was a weasel, sly and opportunistic, Lachlan Kite was not the bird of his codename, but rather a leopard, lean and prowling and solitary.

She sat at the end of a vacant pew, removed the sunglasses and immediately took out her mobile phone.

He's here, she typed to Vosse, glancing up at Kite as she accidentally pressed 'Send' too early on WhatsApp. To her horror, she realised that Kite was looking directly at her. Cara returned to the message, her heart beating so fast that her hand began to shake as she held the phone. *Dark grey suit, tailored. Slim. Six foot max. Appears to be alone.*

The service was scheduled to begin in five minutes. Cara decided to return Kite's gaze. If she could forge a connection with him, however briefly, it was more probable that he might talk to her in the aftermath of the funeral. That was the Holy

Grail as far as Vosse was concerned: to get alongside BIRD and to cultivate a relationship with him.

She put the phone back in her coat pocket, composing herself. But when she turned and looked back towards the statue of St Matthew, Kite had disappeared.

Walking into the church, Kite was suddenly confronted by the sight of Martha talking with a crowd of university friends. He had not expected her to make the trip from New York. His heart thumped as she turned around—and he realised that he had been mistaken. It was just a trick of the light. The desire to see her, of which Kite had barely been conscious, had momentarily scrambled his senses.

Looking up at the vast, vaulted ceiling, the grandeur of the Oratory reminded him of the great chapel at Alford, religion on a scale Kite had never before experienced as a bewildered thirteen-year-old boy, arriving from the wilds of Scotland in an ill-fitting suit in the late summer of 1984. That first year at his new school had thrust him into a world of privilege and wealth with which at first Kite had struggled to come to terms. More than thirty-five years later, every second face in the Oratory was a pupil from those days or a friend of Xavier's whom Kite recalled from the 1990s. The intervening years had not been kind to most of them. Kite was blessed with a photographic memory, but some were barely recognisable. The eyes remained constant, but the features, like his own, had been bullied by time. Everywhere he looked Kite saw slackened skin, thin, greying hair, bodies warped by age and fat. To his left, Leander Saltash, once a lean, aggressive opening batsman, now a bald, stooped television director with a BAFTA to his name; to his right, a man he took to be the diminutive, acne-ridden Henry Urlwin, now transformed into a six-foot beanpole with a chalky beard. Even Cosmo de Paul, that creature of the yoga retreat and the dyeing salon, looked washed out and slightly

BOX 88

overweight, as if no vitamin supplement or exercise regime could reverse the inevitable decline of middle age.

'Tell me. Did I fire six shots or only five?'

Kite felt two fingers pressed into his lower back, a hand clamped on his shoulder. It was a voice he hadn't heard in years, a voice he had hoped, in all honesty, never to hear again. The voice of Christopher Towey.

'Chris. How are you?'

Years ago, at Alford, Towey had obsessively watched the films of Clint Eastwood, quoting *ad nauseam* from the Harry Callaghan series to anyone who would listen. Every time Kite saw him, Towey made the same joke. He did so again in response to Kite's reply.

'Well, Lachlan, to tell you the truth, I've forgotten myself in all this excitement.'

Kite was in a bleak, uncooperative mood, thinking of Martha and Xavier. He didn't recognise the quote and smiled as best he could, hoping they could skirt around *Dirty Harry* and *Sudden Impact* and talk like grown men.

'It's good to see you.'

'You too, mate,' Towey replied. 'Christ, doesn't everybody look so bloody old?'

'Very.'

'Age has withered us,' he said. With dismay, Kite remembered that they had studied *Antony and Cleopatra* together for A level. Towey was still locked in the classroom, a man of forty-eight stalled for ever in his school days. 'Custom has staled our infinite variety.'

'It's not *that* bad,' Kite felt obliged to say, and suddenly wished that he had taken Isobel up on her offer to come with him. 'People are probably happier now than they were twenty years ago. There's a lot to be said for not being young. Fewer choices, less pressure. You look great, Chris. How's married life?'

'Divorced life nowadays.'

'I'm sorry to hear that.'

'Don't be. I'm bonking like a madman. Best-kept secret in London. If you're a moderately well-financed middle-aged man with a British passport and some shower gel, the world's your oyster. Poles, Brazilians, Uzbeks. Some days I can hardly walk.'

'I'll bear that in mind.'

'So what have you been up to lately, eh? Last time I saw you, you were working in Mayfair. Oil or something.'

'That's right.' Shortly after the attacks of 9/11, BOX 88 had been mothballed. Kite had taken a long sabbatical, then worked in the oil business for a small private company financing exploratory research in Africa.

'Still doing that?'

'Still doing that,' Kite replied.

It was a lie, of course. Kite and Jean Lorenzo, his opposite number in the United States, had revived BOX 88 in 2016. In one of his final acts as president, Barack Obama had approved intelligence budgets totalling more than $90 billion, 7 per cent of which was diverted to 'Overseas Contingency Operations', a euphemism for BOX 88. Kite was now director of European operations working out of the Agency's headquarters in Canary Wharf.

'Tell you who thinks you're a man of mystery. Remember Bill Begley? Always reckoned you were a spy.'

Kite had lived so long with the triplicate lives of the secret world, never settling down, always packing a bag and moving on, working one day in London, the next in Damascus, that people from time to time had suggested to his face that he was a spy. He had a well-honed response for such occasions which he used on Towey now.

'I confess,' he said, raising both hands in mock surrender. 'Get the cuffs.'

Towey, never the brightest button in the Alford box, looked confused.

BOX 88

'To be honest, I wish I *had* gone into that life,' Kite added. 'Lot more interesting than the work I've been doing the last ten years. But from what I understand, it doesn't earn you any money. Foreign Office pays peanuts. Are you still in the City?'

Towey confirmed that he was indeed 'making investments on behalf of private clients' but was soon drawn into a separate conversation with a married couple whom Kite did not know. He grabbed the chance to leave. As he crossed the aisle, Xavier's children, Olivier and Brigitte, walked in front of him. Kite had not seen them in years and was staggered by Olivier's likeness to his father; it was as if the seventeen-year-old Xavier had walked past and failed to recognise him. Nearby, Kite spotted a senior French diplomat talking to a member of the Bonnard family; Kite knew that MI6 had recruited his number two in Brussels as part of the broad intelligence attack on EU officials during the Brexit negotiations. Two pews beyond them, Lena—Xavier's long-suffering wife, herself a recovering heroin addict—looked at Kite as she sat down. He had written a letter of condolence to her within hours of Martha's call, but could not tell from her reaction if she had read it. He raised a hand in greeting and Lena nodded back. She looked shattered.

A sudden silence settled on the congregation, punctured by organ music. Kite felt eyes on him. He looked up to find the woman he had seen walking alongside de Paul—still wearing oversized sunglasses and the black overcoat—staring in his direction. Had she recognised him? She sat down and began texting on a mobile phone.

'Lachlan?'

Xavier's younger sister, Jacqui, was gesturing at him from some distance away. The woman in the long overcoat removed her sunglasses and briefly looked at Kite a second time. He had never seen her face before—mid-twenties, alert and attractive— and wondered what had become of de Paul.

'Communing with the tax collector?' Jacqui asked.

She made her way towards him and they embraced. Kite felt the dampness of tears on her cheek as she kissed him.

'What's that?'

'St Matthew,' she said. 'You're standing underneath his statue. He was a tax collector. And here they are, the Catholic Church selling candles at fifty pence a pop.'

Jacqui indicated a box of candles nearby. She was uncharacteristically wired and jumpy. Kite assumed she was running on Valium and beta blockers.

'I'm so sorry about Xav,' he said, aware that there was nothing he could do or say to make the situation any better. 'Did you get my letter?'

'I got it,' she replied. 'You were very kind to write. Nobody knew Xavier like you did, Lachlan.'

The remark served only to stir up those same feelings of guilt which had dogged Kite since Martha's phone call. His friend's suicide had become a set of nails drawing down the blackboard of his conscience; he wished that he could be free of remorse, but could not shake the idea that what had happened in 1989 had shaped the entire corrupted course of Xavier's life.

'A better friend would have protected him,' he said.

'Nobody can save anybody,' she replied. 'Xav was the only person who could protect Xav.'

'Maybe so.'

The service was due to start. Jacqui indicated that she should take her seat and they said farewell. Kite moved towards the centre of the church as Jacqui joined her family in the front row. A few seats away from his own sat Richard Duff-Surtees, an old Alfordian of towering arrogance and sadism who had called Kite a 'pleb' and spat on him in his first week at the school. Eighteen months later, seven inches taller and almost three stone heavier, the fifteen-year-old Kite had knocked him out cold with a clean right hook on the rugby field and been threatened with expulsion for his efforts. Duff-Surtees caught his eye during 'Abide with

BOX 88

Me' and looked quickly away. It was the only pleasing moment in an otherwise heartbreaking hour of tears and remembrance. The family had asked for a High Mass and much of the service, to Kite's frustration, was conducted in Latin. An agnostic from a young age, he loathed the smoke and mirrors voodoo of Catholicism, felt that Xavier would have insisted on something much lighter and more celebratory. Why was it that the upper classes, when confronted by emotional turbulence of any kind, retreated behind ceremony and the stiff upper lip? Kite was all for strength of character, but he had no doubt that Rosamund Bonnard and her waxwork friends would have grieved more openly for a Jack Russell or Labrador than for the death of their own child.

Singing the final hymn—the inevitable 'Jerusalem'—he looked around the church and decided to skip the wake. Better to stick twenty pounds in the collection box and slip away rather than risk another Eastwood quote from Chris Towey or, worse, a face-off with Cosmo de Paul. To that end, Kite waited in his seat until the church was almost empty, then walked out through a door in the south-eastern corner, wondering where he could grab lunch in South Kensington before setting off for the gallery.

Matt Tomkins told Vosse that Cara had panicked. As the service drew to a close, Kite had remained in his seat. Obliged to stand up to allow the mourners in her row the opportunity to leave, Cara had bottled it and gone with them, fearing that Kite would turn and notice that she was hanging around. Finding herself caught in a tide of Sloane Rangers shunting out of the Oratory, Jannaway had consequently lost sight of the target and been buttonholed by Cosmo de Paul on the steps of the Oratory.

'So where is she now?' Vosse asked.

'Still talking to the man she was with before. Said his name was Cosmo de Paul. Pinstripe suit. It's obvious he's chatting her up, sir. I told you she was too attractive for surveillance work.'

'Don't talk crap,' said Vosse, who was sitting in the Acton safe flat. He had high hopes for Cara but was worried that Kite was going to slip away yet again. Three times they had followed BIRD in central London. Three times he had vanished without trace.

'It's not crap, sir. I just call it as I see it.'

Tomkins had been sitting at the patisserie watching the traffic go by when Cara texted, telling him to get to the Oratory as fast as possible to help in the search for Kite. He had requested the bill—an eye-watering £18.75 for two cappuccinos and a slice of chocolate cake—and strolled across Brompton Road as the mourners continued to pour out of the church. He knew from Cara's texts that Kite was wearing a tailored grey suit and black wool tie, but so were at least fifty of the other middle-aged men standing in clumps outside the church.

'Head to HTB,' Vosse told him on the phone.

'What's that?' said Tomkins. He knew the answer to his own question the instant that he asked it; for the past hour he had been staring across the street at two signs next door to the Oratory bearing the letters 'HTB'. But it was too late.

'Holy Trinity Brompton,' Vosse replied impatiently. 'Pay attention. Protestant church round the back of the Oratory. Brainwashed evangelical Christians claiming to be possessed by the Holy Spirit. Posters advertising the Alpha Course and a better life with Bear Grylls and Jesus. You can't miss it.'

Vosse had obviously done his homework, walking the ground the night before. Tomkins looked for a side door into the Oratory but couldn't spot one. There was no sign of Kite. Black cabs were pulling up outside the church all the time. BIRD could easily have ducked into one and driven off while Cara was looking the other way.

'Hello?'

She was on the phone again.

'Yes?' Tomkins replied.

BOX 88

'Any luck?'

He looked over and saw Cara standing beside de Paul. She might as well have been holding a placard above her head emblazoned with the words: *Have YOU seen Lachlan Kite?* Vosse would have a field day when he found out.

'Not yet, no,' Tomkins replied. 'I'm not really dressed for a funeral. If I come any closer, I'll stick out as much as you do.'

'Fuck's sake,' said Cara, looking up at the sky in dismay. 'Just walk past or sit in a fucking bus stop. There are more people in Knightsbridge who look like you than there are people who look like me. Wait—'

Tomkins could tell by the note-change in her voice that she'd spotted Kite.

'My days,' she said. 'I've got eyes on BIRD. He's over by the wall.'

'Another smoke?' said the American, offering Kite a cigarette as the forecourt in front of the church slowly began to empty. The congregation was heading for a residential square to the west of the Oratory where drinks and snacks had been laid on in a hall reserved for mourners. Kite had stopped to check a message on his phone and liked the idea of a quick cigarette before lunch.

'Would love one,' he replied, wondering if the American had been targeted against him. 'I never got your name.'

'John,' he said. 'And you?'

'Lachlan.'

Alcoholics Anonymous was decent cover for a phoney relationship with Xavier: most people wouldn't pry into a stranger's struggles with addiction, nor would anyone at the funeral know very much about Xavier's experiences in the programme. Kite decided to probe a little deeper.

'What did you make of Xav?' he asked. 'When he was down, could you bring him out of it? Did you ever have any success talking to him about his depression?'

35

It was a trick question. Xavier had been wild and unpredict-able, but had consistently hidden his gloom from even his closest friends. Kite had never known him to complain, to cry on a shoulder, to lament the path his life had taken nor to despair over his addictions. He was, in his own particular way, every bit as stoic and uncomplaining as his mother. Outward displays of failure or self-pity were not in the gene pool.

'Funny,' John replied without hesitation. 'I never knew him to be like that. Even in meetings he was always upbeat, always trying to find a way to make people laugh, to think more deeply when it came to their own situations.' John appeared to have passed the test. 'A lot of us were pretty down a lot of the time, present company included. Xav didn't go in for that stuff. That's why I can't believe he did what they say he did. Had to be an accident, sex game or something.'

Xavier had been found in the bathroom of a Paris Airbnb, hanged by the neck. Unless somebody had staged the killing, it was suicide, pure and simple.

'Maybe you're right,' Kite replied.

'I'm sorry for your loss, man.' John put his hand on Kite's shoulder, his long, thick beard and the bright sunlight on his back momentarily giving him the look of an Old Testament prophet.

'Yours too,' Kite replied. 'The world was a better place for having Xavier in it. We're going to miss him.'

'Lachlan?'

Kite turned. A striking man of Middle Eastern appearance had approached him from the western edge of the enclosure. He was wearing a dark grey lounge suit with a black tie and a crisp white shirt. A navy blue handkerchief protruded from the breast pocket of his jacket. Kite did not recognise him.

'Yes?'

'Excuse me.' The man acknowledged the American, tipping his head apologetically. An expensive-looking watch caught the

BOX 88

sun on his left wrist. 'I don't think you will remember me. I was at Alford, several years after you. My name is Jahan Fariba.'

Kite immediately recognised the name. Xavier had spoken about Fariba on one of the last occasions they had met. He was a businessman, British-born, his parents having fled Iran shortly after the revolution. Xavier had done business with him in a context Kite could not recall. He remembered that his friend had spoken fondly of him, on both a professional as well as personal basis.

'Jahan. Yes. Xav talked about you. How did you recognise me?'

'I'll leave you guys to talk,' John interjected, shaking Kite's hand and moving off. Kite thanked him for the cigarettes. Fariba tipped his head respectfully at the American's departure.

'Jacqui told me who you were,' he said, nodding in the direction of the church. 'She pointed you out. I wanted to introduce myself.'

'I'm glad you did.'

Fariba was in his late thirties. Fit and tanned, he resembled a recently retired professional athlete who still worked out twice a day, eschewed alcohol and went to bed at sunset six nights a week. It was late February and rare to see someone looking so vibrantly healthy.

'Xav spoke of you, too. He was always going on about his old friend Lachlan.'

'He was?'

Kite never liked hearing that. Xavier had known too much about his life in the secret world. The wrong word to the wrong person was an existential threat to his cover. He preferred to be anonymous: at worst the enigma at the back of the room; at best unnoticed and forgotten.

'Yes. He was a great admirer of yours. I always wanted to meet you. I thought this would be a good opportunity. Are you going to the drinks now?'

Fariba's accent was located somewhere between Tehran and Harvard Business School: an Americanised English characteristic of the international jet-set. He gestured towards the square.

'Sadly not,' Kite replied, indicating that he was short of time.

'Me neither. I don't feel like it. I didn't know many of Xavier's friends. What's happened is awful. Just a terrible day.'

'It really is.' Beneath the slick, executive exterior Kite glimpsed a softness in Fariba. 'When did you last see him?'

'This is what I wanted to talk to you about.' Fariba lowered his voice to a confessional whisper which was almost drowned out by the noise of a passing bus. 'I was with him less than two weeks ago, in Paris, the night before he died.'

Cara had worked up a possible pitch with Vosse. The drug addict friend from South Africa was too risky to play on Kite, who had known Xavier well and would quickly smell a rat. Instead she would play the art card. They knew from the MI6 whistle-blower that Kite had an interest in collecting paintings. He'd been seen at the Frieze fair back in October and had exchanged emails with several dealers. Cara had briefly studied Fine Art at university before switching to Politics and knew how to talk shit about painters and paintings. She could say she'd had a temp job at one of the galleries exhibiting at Frieze and had recognised Kite as a prospective buyer. That would be enough to start a conversation, perhaps even to lead to an exchange of numbers. Vosse had joked that he wanted Cara to get to know Kite so well that he would ask her to be the au pair for Isobel's baby when it was born in the summer. Cara preferred to think that Kite would try to recruit her into BOX 88.

But when to approach him? Outside the Oratory, Kite had been trapped in two conversations: the first with the tall, bearded man who had offered him cigarettes; the second with a good-looking businessman, possibly of Arab descent, wearing thousand-dollar shoes and an expensive suit. After what had

BOX 88

happened before the service, Cara reckoned she could bump Kite and take her chances with an open pitch.

'What's going on?'

Matt Tomkins was on the phone again, calling for no good reason other than to make her afternoon more difficult than it already was.

'What's going on is that you're making me answer the phone when what I want to be doing is getting on with my job. What do you want?'

'Just to let you know, Eve and Villanelle are outside Smallbone in the Astra.'

'Eve' was the codename for Tessa Swinburn, 'Villanelle' was Kieran Dean. Vosse had a penchant for naming team members after characters in television shows. Cara looked across the busy street. There was a branch of Smallbone of Devizes on the corner of Thurloe Place. She couldn't see the Vauxhall Astra but assumed it was parked nearby.

'Great. Can I go now?' she said.

'I guess,' Tomkins replied.

'Thank you, Matthew. Always nice to chat.'

She hung up. Kite was heading back into the church. It was time to make her move.

'Do you have time to talk?' Fariba asked.

Kite was keen to learn about Paris. It was obvious that Fariba knew something of Xavier's state of mind in the hours leading up to his death. He looked at his phone. It was not yet half-past twelve. He wasn't due at the gallery until four.

'Or we can do it another time,' Fariba suggested, misinterpreting Kite's reaction. 'You may not feel like talking today. We are all still in shock.'

'No, it sounds like a good idea. I'd appreciate that. It would be helpful to find out what was going on. I hadn't seen Xav for at least a year. If you could explain what he was going through . . .'

'Of course.' Fariba adjusted the sleeve of his jacket. His movements were clean and precise, as if life were a martial art he had taken years to perfect. 'I can try to help as much as I can.'

Kite looked up to see Cosmo de Paul scuttling away from the funeral, hailing a cab which did a U-turn opposite Smallbone of Devizes. Doubtless he had lunch at White's in the diary or a pressing engagement with a Russian woman half his age charging £300 per hour. Looking back along Brompton Road, Kite saw the woman in the long black coat standing alone outside the enclosure. She was talking on the phone. There was something about her that didn't sit well. For thirty years Kite had been at risk from surveillance and his antennae were finely tuned. It was possible that a team had been put on him at the funeral.

'You have a family?' Fariba asked.

'One on the way,' Kite replied.

'Wonderful. Congratulations.'

'And you?'

Fariba held up his right hand and showed Kite four splayed fingers.

'Jesus. You've been busy.'

'Not me. My wife does all the hard work. When is your child due?'

'Late summer.'

Kite had forgotten to put money in the collection and explained that he was going back inside. While there, he looked quickly at Facebook on his phone and searched for Xavier's profile. Jahan Fariba's photograph came up as one of Xavier's contacts. He put a twenty-pound note in the collection box and went back outside.

To his surprise, the woman in the long black overcoat was waiting for him on the steps.

'Excuse me. It's been driving me mad,' she said. 'Have we met before?'

She removed her sunglasses. Kite ran her features—soft brown eyes, a button nose, peroxide blonde hair and a wide, singer's

BOX 88

mouth—through a memory palace of names and faces, but turned up nothing.

'I don't think so,' he replied. 'Did we meet through Xav?'

'No. Definitely not.' The woman stared at Kite intently. 'I'm Emma,' she said, offering a hand to shake. Her skin was soft and cold to the touch. 'It's the weirdest thing. Your face is so familiar.'

If she was a friend or colleague of de Paul's, it was possible she knew of him by reputation, but Kite didn't want to establish the link.

'I know!' she said, suddenly remembering. Her face was overcome with relief. 'I was working for one of the galleries at Frieze. You came in and chatted to my colleague. I think you were interested in buying something.'

'Really? What a good memory you have.'

'Never lets me down,' she said, tapping the side of her head. 'I just couldn't place you.'

She had a sharp south-eastern accent, London or Essex or Kent. The fact that she had made no effort to soften its edges made Kite think that she wasn't interested in blending into Xavier's rarefied world. She was dressed like a model or fashion designer but, on closer inspection, the coat and black leather boots were off-the-peg.

'Which gallery were you working for?' he asked.

'Karoo,' she replied. 'Based in New York. We were mostly displaying Sarah Lucas, Gavin Turk, Marc Quinn.'

That was all Kite needed to know that 'Emma' was not who she was pretending to be. In thirty years of collecting and selling paintings, he had never had a conversation with a New York gallerist about Sarah Lucas, Gavin Turk or Marc Quinn. Several collectors he knew had piled into the Cool Britannia crowd in the 1990s and made small fortunes as a result, but to Kite a lot of the work by the Young British Artists of that period was soulless Groucho bullshit. For the second time in less than half an hour he was obliged to set a trap for a stranger.

'Are you sure that was at Frieze?' he said as though still searching the recesses of his mind for some distant recollection of the encounter.

'Yeah,' she said. 'Frieze.'

Whoever Emma was, she hadn't done her homework. Karoo would have been selling Turks and Quinns at 'Frieze Masters', a parallel exhibition dedicated to older works of art located in a separate area of Regent's Park. So who was she and what was she trying to achieve by speaking to him?

'Well, it's amazing you remembered,' he said. 'I don't think I ended up buying anything last year. Are you still in that world?'

'Nah. It was a temp job. Didn't fancy making it permanent. Didn't do it for me.'

'I see.' In his peripheral vision, Kite could see Fariba waiting for their conversation to finish. 'Look, I'm going to be rude and take off,' he said. 'I'm sorry we can't chat more, but I've got a meeting to go to.'

The woman looked crestfallen. 'Oh. OK.'

'Do you have a card?'

'Me?' she said. 'Afraid not.' Looking up hopefully, she added: 'You?'

Kite was carrying a business card in his own name with an address, email and phone number which would flag as soon as anyone tried to use them. By sunset BOX 88 would know exactly who Emma was working for.

'Lachlan,' she said, holding the card in both hands. She pronounced the name in the correct way, making 'Lach' sound like 'Lock', and bowed slightly as she studied the text. 'Well, at least I had the right person.'

'You did,' Kite replied with false enthusiasm. 'I'm really sorry, but you've caught me at a bad time. Thanks for coming over. I wish I had your memory for faces.'

BOX 88

He walked back towards Fariba, trying to assess what was going on. If MI5 were investigating BOX 88, Xavier's funeral would be a natural place to mount a surveillance operation against him and to make a pitch using a friendly young woman. Kite was bound to attend the service; they could set everything up in advance. But why the clumsy approach? It was possible that 'Emma' was private sector, working on behalf of a client who had taken an interest in him for reasons that were not yet clear.

'Are you OK to go now?' Fariba asked.

'Sure.'

'I hope you don't mind, but I took the liberty of booking us a table at Theo Randall's restaurant in the Intercontinental Hotel. You may know it. It's discreet and the food is very good.'

'I know it well.' The Intercontinental was on the north-eastern side of Hyde Park Corner, close to a safe house on Hertford Street that BOX 88 had been renting for the past two years. 'Took my wife there for her birthday,' he said. 'Shall we get a cab?'

'I have a driver,' Fariba replied with the nonchalance of the super-rich. 'He's waiting around the corner. I can meet you there if you want to walk? Otherwise he can take us whenever you're ready.'

Matt Tomkins had seen the whole thing: Cara's chat on the steps of the church; what looked like an exchange of business cards with the target; then BIRD walking off with his businessman friend towards a silver Jaguar XJ parked illegally on Egerton Place. There was a chauffeur at the wheel, working the hazard lights, but nobody had got close enough to take a picture of him. Tessa Swinburn had passed the number plate to Vosse, who was running it through the database at Thames House. Tessa had come on a moped with the intention of following the Jag while Kieran Dean tailed in the Astra.

'What happened?' Tomkins asked as Cara joined him outside

South Kensington station. She had covered the short distance from the Oratory on foot and looked flushed with success in a way that irritated him.

'I got his details,' she said, producing Kite's card from the pocket of her overcoat.

'We already have his details,' Tomkins replied tartly.

'Not these ones.' She made him look closer. 'The mobile is different. And the email. Cheltenham attacks those, we might get somewhere.'

Tomkins was forced to concede that Cara had made a breakthrough. He experienced a surge of resentment, sharp as bile. It was not enough that he should be regarded by Vosse as the most capable member of the team; others, particularly Cara, had to fail.

'So what are you going to do?' he said. 'Call him?'

'Dunno,' she replied. 'Need to talk it over with Robert.'

'Robert.' Not 'Mr Vosse' or 'the boss'. Tomkins wondered if they had a friendship outside of work. Maybe they went for drinks in the pub or tapas and talked about him behind his back. Maybe they were sleeping together. That kind of thing happened all the time at Thames House.

'He'll tell you to go for it,' he said.

'Might do. Might not.'

Tomkins's phone started to ring. Speak of the devil. It was Vosse.

'Cagney?'

'Cagney' was Tomkins's codename. Cara was 'Lacey'.

'Yes, sir.'

'Did you see the driver of the Jag?'

'No, sir.'

'You with Lacey?'

'Yes, sir.'

'Ask her if she got a look at him.'

Matt lowered the phone and asked Cara what she'd seen. A

BOX 88

woman was screaming at her infant son outside a branch of Five Guys and it was difficult to make himself heard.

'She didn't see him,' he told Vosse. 'Why? What's going on?'

'What about the bloke who walked off with our man? You said he was from the Middle East?'

'I didn't say that,' Tomkins replied. 'Lacey did.'

Cara scrunched up her face, trying to work out what the two men were discussing.

'Fine. Lacey said it.' Tomkins could hear the irritation in Vosse's voice. 'What did *you* think? Was he likely from that neck of the woods?'

'Yes, sir,' Tomkins replied.

'And it looked like they'd never met before but were getting along famously?'

That was an accurate characterisation of what Cara had told Tomkins, so he said: 'Yeah, that's right,' and waited to find out why Vosse was sounding so agitated.

'There's just something that doesn't ring true.'

'What's that, sir?'

'This guy's wearing a flash watch and walks around in thousand-pound shoes, right? According to Villanelle, there was a chauffeur in the driving seat of the Jaguar.'

'Yes, sir.'

'So explain this: why was the Jag rented from Europcar two days ago?'

4

The chauffeur was wearing a cheap black suit and a peaked cap. He opened the back door for Kite but did not acknowledge him. Kite took a last look up at the red-brick mansion blocks of Egerton Gardens and climbed inside, checking the windows and mirrors for moving vehicles. Sure enough, a dark blue Vauxhall Astra pulled out behind them as the driver moved away. Fariba had settled in beside him and was fastening his seat belt. Kite turned and reached for his own, taking the opportunity to look behind the Jaguar and commit the Astra's number plate to memory.

'Did you know that Edward Elgar was married at the Brompton Oratory?' Fariba asked.

'I didn't.'

'Also the racing driver James Hunt. And Alfred Hitchcock.'

'Wikipedia?' Kite asked.

Fariba laughed. 'Yes! How did you know?'

Kite assumed the question was rhetorical and sat back in his seat, wondering where the surveillance was coming from. It had been a feature of his long career that minor setbacks never troubled him very much; if anything, they got his blood moving a little quicker. But a tailing Astra and a clumsy approach from a charming, if inexperienced woman at the funeral still required

BOX 88

attention. If the heat was coming from MI5, Kite needed to tread carefully; if he was being looked at by amateurs in the private sector, he would put a surveillance team of BOX 88 'Falcons' onto them that afternoon and find out who was paying their bills.

'Do you have a favourite Hitchcock film, Lachlan?' Fariba asked.

Kite wasn't much of a movie buff but said *Vertigo* because it was the first title that came to mind. He thought of James Stewart falling from the top of a high building and pondered the change in Fariba's mood. On the steps of the church he had been polite to the point of deference; now, spread out in the back seat of his executive limo, he had relaxed into the role of international plutocrat, making empty chit-chat as his valeted Jag slipped through the Knightsbridge traffic.

'One of my favourites too,' he said. 'I'm glad we agree.'

Kite checked his mobile. He had sent a message on WhatsApp to Isobel but she had not yet seen it. He sent another—*Very sad service. Heading off for lunch with a friend of Xavier's. See you tonight. Love you*—and put the phone back in his jacket. One of the mourners was crossing the road opposite Harrods. Kite recognised him as Rupert Howell, a sports jock nicknamed 'Lazenby' at Alford on account of his saturnine good looks and jaw-dropping success with women. His hairline had since receded at such a rate that, from a distance, he looked like the elderly John Profumo.

'Something else I learned from Wikipedia,' said Fariba.

'What was that?' Kite asked, turning to face him. He looked briefly in the rear-view mirror but could no longer see the Astra.

'During the Cold War, the KGB used to leave dead drops in the entrance to the Brompton Oratory.'

Kite knew the story but played dumb. He wondered why a man like Fariba would use the term 'dead drop' without going to the trouble of explaining it.

'Really? I had no idea the Oratory was such an interesting place.'

'Neither did I. Neither did I.'

The mood wasn't right. Was it nerves or something more sinister? Perhaps Fariba was anxious about their imminent chat over lunch.

'Where are you from?' Kite asked the driver.

'He doesn't speak English,' Fariba replied quickly.

The chauffeur responded in a language Kite identified as Farsi, using a word—'*jakesh*'—which had been a favourite of an Iranian colleague who had done some work for BOX 88. It struck him as odd that a chauffeur would employ such a word—which translated roughly as 'pimp'—in a conversation with his boss and wondered at the context.

'Where's he from?' he asked.

'Isfahan,' Fariba replied.

'Just arrived?'

'No. He has lived in London for many years.'

Was it Kite's imagination, or did Fariba's answers seem strained? To work for BOX 88 was to live in a more or less permanent state of low-level paranoia; Kite had grown used to it in the way that a diabetic becomes accustomed to injecting himself with insulin four times a day. He was wary of Fariba just as he had been wary of the woman in the long black overcoat. Something was wrong.

The Jaguar passed through a canyon of construction work on the western approach to Hyde Park Corner. To the north, repairs were continuing to the Mandarin Oriental Hotel, gutted by fire and now rising again over Knightsbridge; to the south, the narrow facade of a nineteenth-century apartment block had been preserved behind thick steel scaffolding. The building behind it had been torn down. In its place, a steel-and-glass tower, doubtless financed by Chinese, Russian or Gulf money, was gradually being craned into the sky.

BOX 88

'What house were you in at Alford?' Kite asked.

'ACDP,' Fariba replied.

Housemasters at Alford were known by their initials, not surnames. Kite remembered ACDP and the location of the house, tucked away towards the back of the school close to a wooded area where boys would go to smoke Silk Cuts and look at copies of Penthouse and Razzle.

'Where was that? Close to my house?'

Fariba hesitated. 'Which one were you in?' he asked. 'Remind me.'

'Lionel Jones-Lewis.'

'The maths teacher?'

'Yes. The maths teacher.'

It was an odd, but not inaccurate way of describing Jones-Lewis—more commonly remembered by old Alfordians as 'Jumpy'—a bachelor housemaster who had somehow managed to avoid being fired despite three decades of predatory behaviour towards the boys in his care.

'Look at the arch. So beautiful at this time of year.'

The Jaguar was circling Hyde Park Corner. The Wellington Arch at the centre of the vast roundabout looked no more or less impressive than it usually did.

'Yes, it is very beautiful.' Kite knew that Fariba was trying to change the subject, so he pressed his point. 'We were almost side by side. LJL was down by the music schools, next to ACDP. We probably passed one another in the street every day.'

'I don't know,' Fariba replied. 'I think you and Xavier had left by the time I went to Alford.'

Neither of the two houses Kite had mentioned were situated anywhere near the music schools. Either Fariba wasn't concentrating on what Kite was saying or he was lying.

'Your tutor. Who were you up to?'

Kite had again employed arcane language specific to the school which only an old Alfordian would recognise. Fariba visibly faltered before answering, like a sudden and unexpected glitch in a well-oiled machine.

'Tutor?' he said. 'Are you one of those English public school-boys who likes to talk about Alford all the time, Lachlan?' He took out his mobile phone and waved Kite's questions away as he began to tap out a message. 'The truth is, I don't remember. It was all so long ago. Do you want to know my date of birth? My mother's maiden name?'

They were passing the Intercontinental, the driver indicating into the left lane as a motorbike overtook him on the opposite side. Like the itch at the back of the throat which foretells a period of sickness, Kite knew that he was in grave danger.

'Could you pull over for a second?' he said.

'But we're almost there.'

The driver turned off Piccadilly onto Old Park Lane, passing the Hard Rock Cafe. He spoke to Fariba in Farsi. Fariba gave a clipped, aggressive reply. Kite could feel their apprehension as the Jaguar passed the Playboy Casino and made an immediate right turn onto Cheshire Street. Rather than looping back towards the Intercontinental, they were heading east, deeper into Mayfair.

'You're going in the wrong direction,' Kite said as a car sounded its horn in the street behind him. 'The restaurant is the other way.'

'It's quite all right, Lachlan.' There was a forced nonchalance to Fariba's reply. 'We have a car park here that I prefer to use.'

Kite knew what was coming. It was an Iranian speciality. Fariba's team would have control of the car park and would likely switch him to a second vehicle as soon as they'd stripped him of his clothes and mobile. Kite was intensely angry with himself for letting his guard down at the funeral but had no time to mourn his mistake. The chauffeur had turned off Cheshire Street and was heading towards a barrier at the entrance to an under-ground car park. A man in a dark suit raised the barrier then lowered it as soon as the Jaguar had passed. The car nosed down

BOX 88

a steep ramp towards an ill-lit basement where two more men waited in the shadows. Kite knew that if he tried to open the back door it would be locked. So it proved.

He was cramped for space and had only seconds to make his move. Disconnecting his seat belt, Kite raised his hips so that his weight was pitched forward onto his legs. In the same movement he twisted quickly left, then right, using the momentum to slam his elbow into the side of Fariba's throat. Fariba gasped as Kite struck him a second time, but he had not made a clean connection with the carotid artery. Speed was critical. Grabbing a fistful of Fariba's hair, Kite now turned and drove his left knee up into the Iranian's face, but the chauffeur hit the brakes at the moment of impact and Kite was unbalanced, managing only to slam Fariba's head against the window as he fell backwards. With the Iranian momentarily dazed, Kite reached forward and grabbed a loose section of the driver's seat belt, twisting it tightly around his neck in an effort to choke him. He had to get into the passenger seat and leave the car by the front door, taking his chances with the men outside. But his grip on the belt was poor and the driver tipped back his chair to loosen the strain on his neck, pulling at the joints on Kite's hand so that he was forced to release the belt.

Fariba had now recovered. Calling out to the driver in Farsi he threw several punches into Kite's kidneys and snatched at his trailing foot in an effort to restrain him. Kite kicked back, striking Fariba in the face, then pushed forward into the front section of the car, pulled sideways by the driver as he tried to reach for the passenger door. Leaning forward, Fariba put his arms around Kite's waist and pulled him towards the back seat with astonishing strength. Kite freed his right hand and used it to gouge the driver's eyes. He could feel the softness of the eyeballs beneath his fingers and pushed harder, the driver yelping like a wounded animal. Fariba saw what was happening and chopped down on Kite's arm. The joint in his elbow screamed in pain. Then the door behind him opened and a third man entered the car. Fariba shouted at him as he slammed the door.

Kite was wedged between the two men and unable to move. The third man pinned his arms behind his back and seized Kite's neck in a headlock. The driver straightened his seat and moved the Jaguar down the ramp, rubbing one eye and swearing under his breath. Kite thought of Isobel, of their unborn child. Whatever ordeal was planned for him, he could now do nothing to stop it.

'What the fuck is going on?' he said, struggling to break free of the headlock.

Fariba smiled, shaking off the adrenaline of the fight.

'You did well,' he said, nodding towards the driver who was still muttering in Farsi. He was a large man, ponderous and cruel, and Kite knew that he had made an enemy of him. 'I thought everything was going so smoothly. Xavier said you were the best of the best.'

'Fuck you,' said Kite, fearing what his friend had told them.

Fariba exchanged a look with one of the men outside the car. He lowered the window and took a syringe from him, indicating to the man holding Kite that he should squeeze more tightly around his neck.

'It will be best if you don't kick out,' he said, and immediately stabbed the needle through Kite's suit trousers into the muscles of his right thigh.

Kite winced, feeling the needle almost at the bone, but the strength of the man's hold on him was so great that he could make no meaningful sound.

'I had such an interesting series of conversations with Xavier,' said Fariba. 'He told me all about the summer of 1989. All about Luc Bonnard and a woman named Martha Raine. Cast your mind back to that time, Lachlan. I need your memory. When you wake up, I want you to tell me everything you can about Ali Eskandarian.'

5

'Just because he rents a Jag from Europcar doesn't make him a terrorist. Doesn't make him BOX 88 either.'

Matt Tomkins and Cara Jannaway had jumped into a taxi outside South Kensington station and were trying to catch up with Dean in the Astra. Vosse was coordinating the pursuit from Acton.

'Maybe we should discuss this later,' Cara replied, nodding in the direction of the driver.

'Fair enough,' said Tomkins, and checked his mobile for Dean and Swinburn's positions.

Cara addressed the driver.

'Excuse me? Could you head to the Mandarin Oriental at the top of Knightsbridge?'

'What's that, luv?'

The driver had one ear tuned to the traffic, the other to James O'Brien on LBC. He turned down the volume on the radio.

'I said can we head towards the Mandarin Oriental Hotel just before Hyde Park Corner?'

'Sure thing. No problem.'

'See?' said Tomkins. 'He's not even listening to what we're saying.'

When the driver turned the volume back up, Cara indicated that it was secure to talk.

'Fine,' she said. 'His normal car could be in the garage. He might have rented the Jag to keep up appearances. Might be an operation they're working together. Who knows?'

'Who knows—'

'But who's the flash Arab? Looked like they'd never met before, then they go off together. BIRD sent a message to his wife saying he was heading to lunch with a friend of Xavier's—'

'I know that,' said Tomkins petulantly. 'I read the group chat. Could be he's bullshitting his wife.'

'Speaking of group chats . . .'

Vosse had sent a message to the team with an update on the Jaguar. The vehicle had been rented for only two days by a woman named 'Pegah Azizi' using a French driving licence which Thames House was checking with Paris. The vehicle was due back by six o'clock that evening.

'Azizi. What's that?' Tomkins asked. 'Iranian?'

'Sounds like it.'

Cara typed a reply: *No sign of a woman in the Jag.*

They could both see that Vosse was replying.

My thoughts exactly, he wrote. *BIRD almost at Hyde Park Corner. Stay on him.*

Cara switched lists, returning to the location feeds for Dean and Swinburn. Vosse was the only one with a fix on Kite's position.

'We're too far away,' she said, knowing that coverage of Kite's phone wouldn't be enough to pinpoint his position if he went into a high-rise or basement.

'Relax,' Tomkins replied. 'It's lunchtime. They're probably going for something to eat. We just wait outside whatever restaurant they choose, pick BIRD up on his way out.'

Cara looked into her lap.

'What if they're not going to lunch?'

BOX 88

Tomkins looked at her blankly. 'Where are they going then?' he asked.

'I dunno.' She stared out at the stalled London traffic, windscreens blinking in the lunchtime sun. 'I just have a weird feeling about this.'

Tessa Swinburn's moped became boxed in at a set of traffic lights near the Mandarin Oriental and she lost sight of the Jaguar as it pulled away towards Hyde Park Corner. Kieran Dean had managed to stay on Kite's tail a little longer, but his luck ran out on Old Park Lane when a double-parked Uber blocked his way while waiting for a pickup outside the Playboy Casino. Sounding the horn on the Astra, Dean watched in frustration as Kite's Jaguar made a right turn onto Cheshire Street, quickly disappearing from view. Less than a minute later, a Chinese man with a fat gut and an empty wallet wandered out of the casino and clambered into the cab. Moments later Swinburn was at last on Cheshire Street, passing a small, dimly lit underground car park. He assumed that the Jaguar had gone deeper into Mayfair and turned north in the direction of Shepherd Market. A lorry was unloading on a double yellow and Dean was again obliged to wait while the driver wheeled a trolley off the road. He then continued along the western edge of Shepherd Market, emerging within spitting distance of the Saudi embassy. There was no sign of BIRD in any direction.

Vosse called as Dean was waiting at a set of lights outside the Curzon cinema.

'Are you lot taking the piss?' he shouted. 'Villanelle's in outer space, Cagney and Lacey went the wrong way on Piccadilly. What the fuck are you doing on Curzon Street? Get your arse back to the Playboy Casino. BIRD's probably gone in there for a flutter with his pal from the Middle East.'

Dean reached for his second phone, loaded Waze and typed in 'Playboy Casino' as the lights turned green and a car behind him leaned on its horn. The journey time was estimated at less than five minutes, but he would have to go back out onto Park Lane and loop round via Hyde Park Corner.

'On my way,' he said.

Vosse had already hung up.

Cara had wanted the driver to turn north at the Hard Rock Cafe, but Tomkins had insisted that she'd seen the wrong car. As far as he was concerned, BIRD was still heading east towards Piccadilly Circus.

'Think about it,' he told her. 'They've got the Ritz up there, The Wolseley, White's and Boodle's. That's where men like that go for lunch. Not Shepherd's Market.'

Cara thought he was talking shit but knew that she didn't have the luxury of arguing with him: by the time Tomkins had realised his mistake, BIRD would be long gone. So, as the taxi waited in traffic, she thanked the driver, opened the door and stepped out onto the street.

'Where the fuck are you going?' Tomkins shouted.

'She's leaving you, mate,' said the driver as Cara slammed the door. 'Still want the West End, do we?'

The cab pulled away. Tomkins was left alone in the back, watching Cara hurrying along Half Moon Street in her black boots and long winter coat. He tried calling her phone but she wouldn't pick up. Instead he texted Vosse and told him what Cara had done, only to receive the reply: *At least somebody is using their initiative.*

By then, the taxi was outside Fortnum & Mason, BIRD's Jag was nowhere to be seen and Matt Tomkins was out of the hunt.

Cara understood from the group message that Vosse wanted the team to look for Kite in the area surrounding the Playboy Casino. There was a Four Seasons Hotel across the street, a branch of Nobu outside the Hilton on Park Lane, Theo Randall's restaurant

BOX 88

at the Intercontinental as well as a number of private members clubs—the Royal Air Force, the Cavalry & Guards—in the area. All of them would need searching.

Find BIRD, he had written. *Find the car. Villanelle's going to the Playboy. Divide up the rest. Let's get control of this situation.*

Cara could not shake off the sense that something was wrong. She looked at Kite's last known position on the corner of Old Park Lane and wondered why his phone had gone down. A basement? A signal black hole? Or something more sinister?

She entered Cheshire Street from the east. A van emerged from a side road ahead of her, turned right and almost knocked her off her feet as it sped downhill in the direction from which she had come. Two men were in the front, both of Middle Eastern origin, both wearing dark jackets and white shirts. The man in the passenger seat had a beard but no sideburns. Their appearance seemed at odds with the nature of their work; as the van turned left at the bottom of the street, she saw KIDSON ELECTRICAL SERVICES emblazoned on the side next to a London phone number and a website address. Memorising the number plate, she reached the corner and saw that the van had emerged not from a side street, as she had first thought, but from a small underground car park. There was an office block next door with a space outside for smokers. Two Chinese women in floor-length puffer jackets were vaping near the entrance. Cara spoke to the younger of the two women.

'Excuse me,' she said. 'Did two guys go in there? Both in grey suits and black ties, forty-ish? One of them British, the other from the Middle East?'

'Don't know anything,' the woman replied. It was obvious that she spoke only limited English.

'Didn't see anyone,' her companion added. She had bad teeth and a mangled London accent. 'Ask him.'

A security guard with a goatee beard and acne scars was coming through the door. Cara asked him the same question and received the same answer. No, he hadn't seen two men in grey suits and black ties. Perhaps they were around the corner in the casino? She gave him a brisk nod of thanks and turned her attention back to the car park. A sign on the wall said 'FULL', but the barrier was up and Cara could see movement inside a security hut at the base of the ramp. Her phone pulsed in her hand as she walked towards the hut, momentarily losing her footing on an uneven section of pavement. At the same time, a short, defeated-looking man in a brown woollen hat emerged from the hut. He was in his late fifties and wore a blue quilted jacket, torn at the shoulder, and scuffed black shoes. Like the security guard, he had a rough complexion but was very pale. Cara saw the stubborn, exhausted features of a man who had spent most of his life being pushed around.

'Can I help you?'

An Eastern European accent. Cara guessed from his features that he was from the former Yugoslavia. She reached the bottom of the ramp so that they were face to face. The car park was small with a low, breeze-block ceiling and space inside for no more than two dozen vehicles. A section of torn plastic pipe had been left along one wall next to a black mini-skip with 'Commercial Waste' written on it.

'Have two men been in here? Both wearing grey suits and black . . .'

There was no point in continuing. She had seen the Jaguar. Parked towards the rear of the car park beneath a faded poster of couples sitting around a roulette table in a packed casino. The man seemed to sense what she had seen and took a defensive step backwards.

'That car,' she said, pointing at it. 'Where's the owner?'

He shook his head. 'What is this? Can I help you?'

'Yeah. You can. That Jag.' Cara continued to point at the car. 'How long's it been here?'

BOX 88

'What do you want, please?' he asked, and Cara saw that he was afraid.

'I told you. The Jaguar.'

'You have car here? What is your name, please?'

On her second day at Thames House, an instructor had told Cara's intake that MI5 officers had the power to arrest members of the public and would be given identification cards made up by the Met so that they could pass for police officers. She had never had cause to take out her ID, but did so now, watching the attendant's already pallid features pale still further as he realised what was happening.

'Let's do this the other way round,' she said. 'What's *your* name, sir?'

'Zoltan,' he replied.

Cara suppressed a smile. It sounded like something he had made up on the spot, the sort of name you would give a robot dog in a Marvel movie.

'And you're the security guard here?'

'Yes, miss.'

'You've been here for the last hour?'

'Yes, miss.'

'So you saw that Jaguar coming in here less than ten minutes ago?'

The attendant shook his head. 'I was having cigarette.'

'Cigarette? Where?'

Zoltan pointed up the ramp onto Cheshire Street.

'So you didn't check the Jaguar in?'

'Excuse me?'

'You didn't see the driver? You didn't give him a ticket when he entered?'

'No, miss. Is there a problem?'

'Not yet, there isn't.' Cara could see that he was anxious. 'I'm just asking some questions.'

She walked towards the Jaguar, looking around for CCTV. There was a dusty, fixed position camera on the far wall, a dome lens in the ceiling closer to the hut. Standing in an empty parking space beside the Jaguar, Cara cupped her hand against the driver's window and looked inside. Nothing had been left on the seats.

'So you didn't see them?'

'Excuse me, miss?'

'You didn't see who got out of this car? Three men, ten minutes ago.'

'No. Like I tell you, I was having cup of coffee.'

'Oh, it's coffee now?' said Cara. 'A minute ago it was a cigarette. You should make your mind up, Zoltan.'

He took off the woollen hat and quickly flattened down his hair as if it would help him to organise his thoughts more carefully.

'Cigarette with coffee. Both. On my break.'

Cara walked back towards the hut. A sign bolted to the wall said: 'Petroleum Spirit. Highly Flammable. Switch Off Engine'. As she passed Zoltan, she said: 'So who was minding the car park while you were away?' and watched his eyes slip at the question.

'Sorry, miss?'

'I said who was minding the shop?'

'Nobody. They just came in.'

Guilt was coming off him like the smell of old oil and rats' piss in the car park. It annoyed Cara that Zoltan was so bad at lying, that he couldn't even summon the energy to deceive her with a basic degree of competence.

'They just came in,' she repeated. 'Who? The men in the Jaguar?'

'Yes. That is right. The men in the Jaguar.'

'They didn't need a ticket?'

BOX 88

'No. They come here all the time. That's their space.'

The guard pointed at the Jaguar. It was the first meaningful attempt he had made to deceive her, but the remark sealed his fate.

'So this is a branch of Europcar, is it?' Cara asked.

Zoltan looked bewildered.

'What, please?'

'Never mind.'

Without bothering to seek his permission, she walked into the security hut. Zoltan followed her. A digital radio was tuned to a station playing 'Tiny Dancer'. Zoltan turned it down as a Serbian-speaking disc jockey began speaking over the end of the track.

'Are those CCTV cameras in operation?' Cara asked.

'Not working.'

'Is that legal?'

Zoltan shrugged.

'Mind if I see for myself?'

He didn't have the courage to demand a warrant or to try to buy time by calling his boss. He managed to say only: 'OK, sure' before indicating the bank of television screens above his filthy, cluttered desk. Within minutes Zoltan had showed her how the security system worked, comprehensively contradicting his earlier claim that the CCTV in the car park was broken. The footage was blurred and indistinct, but as she moved through it, Cara was able to see images of every car and human being that had been on the ramp between midday and half-past twelve.

'Where's the rest of it?' she asked when the footage suddenly cut off.

'No more,' he replied. 'I go on coffee break, cameras they stopped working.'

'Because you switched them off?'

Zoltan smiled broadly and shook his head in apparent amusement as he said: 'No! Of course not.'

'No?' She watched him put the woollen hat back on his head. 'You sure about that, Zoltan?'

'One hundred percentage, yes. I am sure.'

Cara's patience was now running low. She fixed the guard with the look her father described as 'Medusa on crack' and waited for him to come clean. He was standing next to an old kettle and a newly opened box of Yorkshire teabags, rocking very slightly backwards and forwards as he ducked in and out of eye contact.

'Zoltan?'

'Yes?'

'Who switched off the cameras?'

'Nobody.'

Cara leaned towards the bank of screens and fast-forwarded from the point at which the images had blacked out. Sure enough, new footage appeared shortly after twelve fifty. Zoltan made a noise in the back of his throat as Cara clicked through several still images of the white van marked 'Kidson Electrical Services' as it moved up the ramp. There was no sign of Kite, nor of the two men from the Jaguar.

'Seemed to be working ten minutes ago,' she said and waited for what she hoped would be a suitably earnest and detailed apology. When it wasn't immediately forthcoming she said: 'How much did they pay you?'

At that point Zoltan broke. He collapsed onto a squeaking office chair with some of the foam leaking out of it. He put his head in his hands. The wheels on the chair kept dragging back and forth on a torn section of the *Daily Express* as he shuffled and begged and moaned. He started speaking in Serbian, doubtless cursing his wretched luck and his shabby, half-baked lies. It was probable that his whole life had been a series of failures,

BOX 88

each following relentlessly on the heels of the last, leading to this final humiliation.

'What's that, love?' Cara asked. 'You want to tell me something?'

'I cannot,' he said eventually. 'I promised.'

'Promised who?'

'The man.'

'What man?'

'The man who paid me.' Zoltan looked up with pleading eyes. 'He said if I tell anyone what he did, he kill me.'

Cara called Vosse and told him everything. While she waited for him to make the journey from Acton to Mayfair, she instructed Zoltan to close the car park then took a more detailed look at the CCTV. The white van had been parked in the space beside the Jaguar where she had stood and looked through the driver's window. A bollard had been placed beside it to reserve a slot which the Jaguar had later occupied. Cara knew that Kite had most likely been transferred into the back of the van which had driven past her on Cheshire Street. She passed the vehicle details by text to Vosse, wondering why Kite had so readily agreed to get into the Jaguar in the first place. Was it a deliberate switch? Had he been trying to throw off MI5 surveillance in a patch of dead ground? Surely not. If BOX 88 was all it was cracked up to be, they wouldn't employ a man as Olympically stupid as Zoltan to clean up after them.

Cara had made Zoltan a cup of tea and discovered that an unidentified Iranian man had paid him three grand in cash to shut the car park for twenty minutes and to turn a blind eye to whatever went on. She suspected that Zoltan had made similar arrangements with the same man in the past, but did not press for details. Instead she asked for a description of the Iranian's appearance and manner, neither of which matched her memory of the man with whom Kite had been talking outside the Oratory. Released from the torture of telling lies, and perhaps hopeful that his full cooperation might mitigate against the need for arrest, Zoltan described the Iranian's behaviour and movements immediately prior to Kite's arrival in the Jaguar. Three men had been left in the car park at half-past twelve—all Middle Eastern, all without names—while Zoltan had gone for a cigarette and a cup of coffee at a branch of Caffè Nero near Green Park station. By the time he got back, the Jaguar was parked underneath the poster and only two of the men remained.

'What were they wearing?' she asked.

'Smart,' said Zoltan. 'White shirts. Suit jackets.'

'Officer Hawtrey.' It was Vosse, using one of Cara's cover surnames as he came down the ramp. 'So this is him, is it?'

Zoltan stood up, unsteady on his feet. Vosse wasn't dressed in police uniform, but that didn't seem to concern the Serb, who nodded his head obsequiously as Vosse approached.

'Yes, sir,' said Cara. 'Zoltan Pavkov.'

Vosse addressed the suspect.

'My name is Galloway, Mr Pavkov. Chief Inspector Galloway of the Metropolitan Police.' Cara caught his eye and grinned while Zoltan was looking the other way. 'I'm here to ask you some subsidiary questions. I understand from Officer Hawtrey that you have a sum of money on the premises that you'd like to show us.'

'Yes, sir. Of course, sir.' Zoltan hurried into the security hut, emerging moments later with a Harrods carrier bag stuffed with twenty- and fifty-pound notes.

'And this was given to you by the Middle Eastern gentleman this afternoon?' said Vosse, taking the bag and inspecting its contents.

'Yes, sir.'

'Can I speak to you for a moment in private, Chief Inspector?' Cara asked.

BOX 88

'By all means.'

Leaving Zoltan alone at the base of the ramp, Cara and Vosse walked towards the Jaguar.

'Any sign of the van?' she asked.

'Kidson Electrical? Not yet.'

Vosse touched the roof of the Jaguar and peered inside. 'Looks spotless. They probably wiped it for DNA and fingerprints. Have you checked the boot?'

'Locked,' she replied. 'What about BIRD's phone?'

'Still down.' Vosse turned through three hundred and sixty degrees. 'Which means we could well be standing right on top of it.'

They looked around. Cara's eyes immediately settled on the black skip with 'Commercial Waste' written on it. Vosse followed the direction of her gaze and arrived at the same conclusion. The lid on the skip was closed and appeared to be locked.

'Mr Pavkov,' he called out. 'Do you have a way of opening that?'

Zoltan looked beyond the section of torn plastic pipe and said: 'Yes.'

'Could you do that, please?'

It was just as they had both feared. Inside the skip, thrown on top of a heap of old rags and plastic bottles which reeked of vomit and mould, was a dark suit jacket and a pair of black leather shoes. Vosse gasped at the stench as he leaned in to retrieve Kite's belongings, finding his wristwatch, house keys, wallet and mobile phone in the pockets of the jacket.

'Fuck,' said Cara.

'Fuck indeed,' Vosse concurred.

Cara didn't need telling that Kite's shoes, watch and wallet had been abandoned for the same reason that the kidnappers hadn't wanted his phone: any or all of them could contain a tracking device which would lead BOX 88 to their door. Wherever Kite had been driven, he had been taken there in a new set of clothes or his naked body dumped in a landfill, never to be seen again.

Vosse's phone sounded in his back pocket. He took it out and looked at the screen.

'Tell me something I didn't know,' he sighed.

'What's happened?' Cara asked.

'Pegah Azizi doesn't exist. Or should I say: *Pegah Azizi n'existe pas.*'

'Fake driving licence?'

'And credit card.'

A car came down the ramp. Zoltan waved it away shouting: 'We are full!' as Vosse put the phone back in his pocket and picked up Kite's wallet.

'Brian's trying to get the CCTV from Europcar, but I wouldn't hold your breath,' he said. 'Ten to one "Pegah" was wearing sunglasses and a hijab. We'd have an easier job finding Amelia Earhart.'

'So what do we do?' Cara asked. For the first time in her relatively short career, she had felt the blood rush of operational excitement, but was suddenly at a loss for ideas. She knew that formally arresting Zoltan risked exposing the secret investigation into BOX 88, but couldn't think how else to proceed. 'Do we call it in? Tell the police? Contact Six?'

Vosse took his time responding. He was flicking through Kite's wallet litter, pulling out Visa and Oyster cards, dry-cleaning receipts, a driving licence. A burglar alarm was going off somewhere in the neighbourhood and he looked up, grimacing at the noise.

'We do nothing,' he said.

'Excuse me?'

Cara was trying to remember her training. It frustrated her that she wasn't able to work out why Vosse was suggesting such a course of action. Was she going to be asked to cover up Kite's disappearance? Was Vosse going to stand down the investigation

BOX 88

into BOX 88? He saw the confused look on her face and put her out of her misery.

'We let him go,' he said, nodding in the direction of Zoltan Pavkov, who was pacing at the bottom of the ramp, rubbing his hand over his head and massaging the back of his neck. 'We keep his money, but we send him back to work. Tell him he's been a lucky boy. Tell him he has nothing to be afraid of. The world needs good car park attendants and he's one of them.'

Cara wondered out loud if it would work.

'Of course it won't work.' The beaming grin which accompanied Vosse's reply was the cheeriest thing Cara had seen all day. 'He'll panic. He'll call his paymaster. And because we'll be all over Zoltan's phones, because you and Cagney will be sitting outside his flat tonight, and because Eve and Villanelle are going to be following said Mr Pavkov home this afternoon and waiting for him when he comes into work tomorrow morning, we'll find out inside the next twenty-four hours who the fuck has kidnapped Lachlan Kite.'

6

When Kite regained consciousness he found himself lying on a hard bed in a small, windowless room fitted out with little more than a solitary bulb and a stained hessian rug. There were no pictures on the walls nor any other furnishings, save for a low plastic table close to the door on which someone had placed a bottle of water. As far as Kite could tell, there were no surveillance cameras. He was still wearing his shirt and suit trousers, but the jacket had been taken and his shoes were missing. There was no sign of his watch, wallet or mobile phone. Kite felt in his trouser pockets for his house keys, but they too had gone. All this was just as he had expected, just as he himself would have done in similar circumstances. The Iranians had been thorough. He was surprised that they had left the wedding band on his left hand; perhaps it had proved too difficult to remove.

The absence of a camera troubled him for two reasons. Firstly, it suggested that the security outside the room was watertight and that Kite's captors were not concerned about the possibility of escape. Secondly, it indicated that they wanted to leave no record on film of what was about to happen to him. Kite leaned on what he could remember from his SERE training but knew that survival would depend mostly on a mixture of intuition,

BOX 88

experience and blind good luck. He had been held captive once before, but in a different context and with no genuine risk to his life. He was brave, but he was also pragmatic. He understood the psychological demands of long-term confinement and accepted that few people can withstand the sustained sadism of a trained torturer, just as no person can survive indefinitely without food and water and rest.

As soon as he tried to move off the bed he felt a stabbing pain in his right thigh. He pressed his hand against the muscle, remembering the fight in the car. He was hungry and thirsty. Crossing the room, he broke the seal on the plastic bottle and drank from it. The top of his head was almost touching the bulb in the ceiling and there was no more than a few feet on either side of him in which to stretch and move. As he turned the metal handle of the door, finding it locked, Kite felt an ache in his kidneys but was otherwise free of pain. He recalled pressing his fingers into the driver's eyes. He hoped that he had done him lasting damage.

Kite sat back on the bed and closed his eyes. There was no discernible smell in the room except for his own stale sweat: no damp, no food, no cleaning products. It was possible that the Iranians had smuggled him into their London embassy, but more likely that he was in a safe house on UK soil. Moving Kite to an aeroplane and attempting to fly him back to Iran would have been too risky.

He listened for sounds that might give him some clue as to his whereabouts. It was extraordinarily quiet. All he could hear was the low hum of a ventilation system. Kite knocked against the wall with his knuckles and felt the dull, unyielding thud of what was probably brick or fibreglass. If the room had been soundproofed, that might indicate that it had previously been used for the purposes of torture, or simply that he was being held in a built-up area where any noise from the room might alert a passer-by. That Kite was not yet dead was an obvious sign that the Iranians intended to interrogate him. It was then that he recalled what Fariba had said in the car.

I need your memory. When you wake up, I want you to tell me everything you can about Ali Eskandarian.

Was it his imagination or had Fariba also mentioned Martha? Kite thought of Isobel and the morning they had spent at the house, Rambo kicking against her belly, the child he had craved for so long and might now never see nor touch. He remembered his conversation with Fariba outside the church and cursed himself for telling him that Isobel was pregnant. There was no precedent for hostile states harming the spouses of targeted MI6 and CIA officers, but in the age of Trump and Putin, of Xi and Assad, all bets were off. During periods when he was not overseas on an operation, Kite was usually in touch with Isobel several times a day. Without knowing the exact time, he knew that many hours had passed since he had last texted her. When he failed to return home, she would inevitably ring around their friends, eventually calling the emergency number he had given her which connected to the desk at BOX 88. By morning, there would be a team of Turings combing CCTV and signals intelligence for clues to his whereabouts. By then, however, it might be too late. Kite knew that Fariba's team would kill him as soon as they had extracted whatever information was required; you didn't grab a British intelligence officer on UK soil then spit him back once you were done. He needed to buy some time, to conjure a story about Eskandarian which would satisfy the Iranians while protecting the sanctity of BOX 88.

Why now? Why come for him thirty years after the events in France? The British had played no role in the assassination of Qasem Soleimani; it was implausible that the Quds Force were embarked on revenge. Kite could only assume that word of the ongoing backchannel negotiations between BOX 88 and the Iranian leadership had leaked to elements in MOIS, Iran's intelligence service. Personnel from the United States had been secretly

BOX 88

meeting senior government ministers from Tehran at a hotel in Dubai without the knowledge or approval of the White House. Perhaps Fariba assumed, incorrectly, that Kite was a member of the negotiating team? But why the specific interest in Eskandarian? Was there a mole inside BOX 88 with access to the file from 1989? Perhaps Fariba's interest was just a bluff, an opening move in a much longer game of interrogation. It was impossible to know.

Lying back against the flat, hard pillow, Kite remembered the woman outside the Brompton Oratory and the glimpse of the Vauxhall Astra tailing his Jaguar from Kensington. It was a slim ray of hope. If 'Emma' had been part of a larger surveillance team, it was possible that several vehicles had followed him onto Hyde Park Corner. If the Jaguar had been sighted on the ramp leading down to the car park, there was a chance that Kite's absence had been noted. Unless he could somehow fashion an escape, his odds of survival depended on who had been following him. If Emma was private sector, he was out of luck. She would go back to her office, write up a report on Kite's disappearance and head home for pizza and Netflix. If, on the other hand, she was MI5, Thames House had both the experience and the resources to probe more deeply into what had happened. Access to CCTV, number plate recognition cameras and cell phone activity might lead to a rescue attempt. Kite acknowledged the irony: BOX 88 had survived undetected for decades. That the Security Service might come to Kite's aid in his hour of need would be a welcome, if awkward slice of good fortune.

Yet he could not rely on outside intervention. The Iranian team that had grabbed him were thorough and professional, gaining control of the car park, likely making the switch in dead ground and transporting him, apparently without interference, to a safe house prison which was under their command. Kite considered his options for buying time. That he would deny he was a serving intelligence officer was a given: it was the golden rule Strawson had drummed into him at the age of eighteen. *Never confess, never break cover, never admit to being a spy.* Xavier may have told Fariba that Kite was MI6, but Kite would insist that he had stopped working for British intelligence many years earlier. They had the wrong man. They had made a mistake. I remember nothing about Ali Eskandarian. Let me go.

Kite rolled onto his side and stared out into the room. There were other tricks he could employ, though it would be risky to do so against trained MOIS personnel. He could complain of suffering from high blood pressure or diabetes and insist that medication be brought to him. He could feign psychological breakdown. Sticking to his cover as an oil executive, Kite could tell Fariba that he was insured against kidnapping and offer a release fee of several million dollars. But he doubted that such an approach would work. There had been something targeted and specific in Fariba's behaviour. It was obvious that he wanted information, not money.

The noise of a key turning in the lock. The door opened. Kite sat up to find the chauffeur pointing a gun at him. To his satisfaction, he saw that he had developed a black eye the colour of a ripe aubergine, the stain spreading across the bridge of his nose. In his left hand the driver was holding a clear plastic bag containing three aluminium boxes.

'Eat,' he said, placing the boxes on the table.

The chauffeur turned to leave. He had a look on his face of distilled contempt.

'Any chance of a knife and fork?' Kite asked with an edge of sarcasm.

'Fuck you,' he replied.

'I thought you didn't speak English?'

Kite smiled as the driver slammed the door. There was a portion of boiled rice in the first box, some moussaka and several cubes of grilled chicken. Kite ate the chicken, waited for the rice and moussaka to cool, then scooped them into his mouth using

BOX 88

his fingers. He wiped his hands on the tails of his shirt and lay back on the bed, wondering about Isobel. She was not a person prone to panic or anxiety, but he did not like the idea of her worrying about him while she was pregnant. He entertained the foolish idea that Fariba would listen to what he had to say, thank him for his time and let him go, but it was a forlorn hope.

The key turned again in the lock and the door opened. A well-built man in his thirties whom Kite did not recognise came into the room. He had a thick beard with no sideburns and addressed him in heavily accented English.

'Come with me.'

The man was dressed in a similar fashion to the goons Kite remembered from the ramp: dark trousers, white shirt, black shoes. As Kite stood up, he was sure that he saw a trace of cocaine in the base of the man's nostril: a tiny fleck of white powder caught in a damp nest of hairs. The man did not meet Kite's eye, nor try to bind his hands or prepare himself in any way for the possibility of an escape attempt. Instead he turned his back on the prisoner, leading him down a narrow, low-ceilinged passage lined with framed reproduction watercolours of European birds and flowers. Kite realised that he was on board a boat of some kind, almost certainly a large ship, likely not at sea because he had sensed no lateral movement in the water. The carpet was cheap and thin, and there was a very faint smell of diesel. The realisation gave him renewed hope. Ships have flares. Ships have hidden rooms and passages. Ships have radios.

'In here,' said the man, opening a door at the end of the passage.

Kite was shown into a room with blacked-out windows lit by two anglepoise lamps. Vinyl plastic sheets had been taped to the floor. For the first time he was afraid. There was a couch against the far wall covered in a white dust sheet with a wooden coffee table in front of it. Several cardboard boxes had been piled up in the corner of the room next to a television with a cracked screen. Two chairs were stacked on top of one another nearby. The guard lifted off the first of them, turned it in the air and set it down in the centre of the room, close to a metal toolbox.

'Sit,' he said.

Kite had no choice but to do as he was instructed. He waited for the guard to grab his hands and bind them, but he did not do so. Instead he left the room by a door in the facing wall and told Kite to wait. Kite looked around. Anything could happen in this place. Teeth. Toenails. Fingers. They had prepped the room. It would take all of his courage to withstand what was coming. He had to try to stop thinking about Isobel and to trust that she would be OK. He had to have sufficient faith in himself that he would not reveal the identities of BOX 88 agents and personnel under torture. If they were going to kill him, he hoped that his son would never find out what had happened here. And he prayed that it would be over quickly.

The door opened. Fariba walked in. He had changed out of the suit and was now wearing blue designer jeans and a white collared shirt. He smiled at Kite as if to reassure him. He still looked every inch the international playboy, fit and lean, as relaxed as if he had just walked off a yacht in Miami Beach and ordered a round of cocktails at the Delano. Kite wondered what had become of the real Jahan Fariba. It would have been simple enough for the Iranians to prevent him from attending the funeral and for the man standing in front of him to have assumed his identity.

'Lachlan,' he said breezily, as though Kite was an old friend whom he'd kept waiting for an unnecessary length of time. Fariba raised an apologetic hand and gestured at the vinyl sheets lining the floor. 'I'm sorry about all this. How are you feeling?'

'Just wonderful, thank you. Never been better.'

Fariba checked that the door behind Kite was locked and said: 'Sure.'

'What's going on?' Kite asked. 'Who are you?'

BOX 88

'Who *am* I?' Fariba seemed to find the question amusing. 'Well I'm not Jahan Fariba, that's for sure.'

'What's your real name?'

'My real name is Ramin Torabi. You may choose to believe that. You may choose not to believe that. I don't care either way.'

The Iranian's American-accented English was already beginning to grate. Torabi removed the dust sheet from the couch and sat down. The cushions were finished in cheap black leather. He made himself comfortable and stared at Kite with apparent fascination.

'Wow. It's quite something to have you here. Xavier told me so much about you.'

'Did you kill my friend?'

'Did I kill Xavier?' The Iranian tried to sound affronted by the accusation, but his reply was deliberately provocative. 'Maybe I did. Maybe I didn't. It's not particularly important.'

'It's particularly important to me.'

'I'm sure that's the case, buddy, but like I told you, I really don't give a shit.'

If there was one thing Kite hated being called, it was 'buddy'. He wanted to get up from the chair and finish what he had started in the car, but knew that as soon as he attacked Torabi, half a dozen armed Iranian goons would come rushing through the door to his rescue. This time there was a camera in the room, a dome lens in the ceiling. They were watching what was going on. Kite looked down at the metal toolbox. In one movement Kite could open it and use whatever was inside as a weapon. He knew that it had been placed there to tempt him.

'Seriously,' Torabi continued. 'I don't want to keep you here any longer than I have to. Truth is, we didn't think you'd react in the way you did. You were good! You sensed the danger. You kind of forced our hand when it came to getting you under control, you know?'

Kite saw that he was expected to reply, so he said nothing.

'I want to say something important before we start out. I understand how a situation like this works from your point of view. You're a professional. You've been brought here. You're trained for situations like this.' Torabi produced a glib, insincere smile, lit a cigarette and blew a lungful of smoke at the ceiling. 'You've been taught never to reveal anything about what you do. The first and the last rule of intelligence work—the same goes for Iranians as it does for Brits—is *never* confess. It's like Fight Club! The first rule of spying is you never talk about spying!' Torabi laughed explosively at his own joke, apparently under the impression that he was the first person to have made it. 'Men like you and I respect those rules. But I want us to take a time out and go past all that bullshit if we can. I know who you are, I know what you've done. So the sooner we dispense with the usual "I'm-innocent, you-have-the-wrong-guy" shit, the quicker we can get this thing over.'

'Can I speak?' said Kite.

'Not yet. I'm not finished.' Torabi swept a hand through his carefully combed hair, inhaling on the cigarette. 'You must have seen so many changes throughout your career.'

'Excuse me?'

'Starting out as a young intelligence officer in the last years of the Cold War, seeing the Berlin Wall come down, the collapse of the Soviet experiment. The West triumphant. You had won! Then suddenly nothing to do. No role to play any more.' Torabi waved the cigarette in the air and made a face of mock disappointment. 'What was the purpose of MI6 when you had nobody to spy on? You and men like your associate, Cosmo de Paul, you must have been so lost. I would love to speak to you about all this when we're done. Really I would.'

De Paul's name fell like an axe on Kite. What had Xavier said? Why did Torabi assume that de Paul was his 'associate'? Perhaps it was a deliberate tactic, the name casually planted to see how the prisoner would react. Kite maintained a poker face.

BOX 88

It was clear that Torabi had prepared his speech in advance, intending to unsettle or confuse Kite while simultaneously calming any nerves of his own that he might be feeling.

'Ramin,' he said. 'I think you've mistaken me for somebody else.' Kite knew that his denials would fall on deaf ears, but it was nevertheless essential to buy time by playing the innocent. 'My name is Lachlan Kite, I'm an oil—'

'Please!' Torabi raised a hand and stubbed out the cigarette. 'I already told you. This is what I don't want us getting into. So much bullshit, it insults the hard work and sacrifices we've both made during our careers. Let's not waste time denying who we are, huh? Tell me what it's been like, seeing everything change. One quiet day in the 1980s, no cell phones; the next, just a few years later, everybody is carrying one. Same thing with the Internet. No Facebook, no email, no apps; then suddenly everything is available online for the world to see. Spying has changed! I'm younger than you by—what?—ten years. I came into our profession long after the true Cold Warriors had left.' Torabi accompanied this remark with the same self-satisfied smirk with which he had reacted to his Fight Club joke. 'Your generation must have found it so difficult doing your job in the way that you'd been trained to do it. No more IRA to fight. No more ETA. No polite telephoned warnings to a newspaper from the latest Sunni group before they blow themselves up on the Central line. No more travelling under alias. No more false passports, no more dead drops and one-time pads. You've witnessed a generational change. It's like talking to someone who lived through the age of steam and found himself travelling on a fucking space ship! How have you survived all this time? You're a dinosaur, man. What a privilege to be sitting with you. Truly. What a privilege.'

Coke, thought Kite. He's high on something. These guys are all using. They need it for their nerves, to get through whatever it is they've been ordered to do. The guard who came to the room was on it. The chauffeur was probably jacked up on a couple of lines when he drove the Jaguar to Cheshire Street. That was the anxiety Kite could feel coming off them just before the fight. He thought of Xavier's troubles with drugs, of all the summer nights in his early twenties with Martha at raves outside London, Strawson berating Kite for 'wrecking his brain with Ecstasy'.

Torabi was still banging on:

'What fascinates me is, for all that time—thirty years of international diplomacy, Thatcher, Blair, Reagan, Clinton, Trump—you guys continued to hate my country. The British, the Americans, they *knew* the Saudis had bankrolled ISIS and 9/11. They watched as Sunni—*not* Shia—suicide bombers brought carnage to London and Paris and Madrid. You let the fucking Jews build a wall around Palestine and drive Arabs into the sea. But it was all still the fault of Iran.' Torabi gave a contemptuous laugh. '*We* were the bad guys! *We* were the ones you punished, the nation you tried to destroy. Not the Saudis. Not the Russians. Not the Chinese. Why little old Iran?'

Kite was as fascinated by Torabi's impassioned, sophomoric argument as he was perplexed by its purpose. Was his captor hoping to use Kite to broker a peace deal, unaware that BOX 88 was already doing just that with his own government's ministers in Dubai? Or was Torabi's heartfelt outpouring nothing more than an attempt to justify whatever violations lay in store for Kite in this chamber of horrors? Either way, he had no choice other than to continue to play the mystified innocent.

'As a matter of fact, I agree with almost everything you've just said,' he replied. 'I've never understood why the Americans have targeted Iran for so long, unless it's revenge for the humiliation of the embassy siege, which happened outside the living memory of more than three-quarters of the population. Maybe it's because you stoked the insurgency in Iraq or bankrolled Hizbollah for thirty years. How do I know? The Iranian govern-

BOX 88

ment hates Israel. A lot of Americans *don't* hate Israel. I'm not clairvoyant, but could that have something to do with it? There's no point in asking me these questions. I'm not a politician, Ramin. I'm just a guy who reads the *Economist* and the *New York Times*. There's no point in keeping me here if you think I'm some kind of spokesman for the British government. These are questions you should be asking in Downing Street or, better still, Washington.'

Torabi met Kite's denial with a slow, disappointed shake of the head. He looked down and scratched at a non-existent mark on his jeans. Kite stuck to his strategy.

'When you say that I'm a spy and I've somehow been trained for this eventuality, that I get kidnapped in broad daylight all the time and this is somehow a normal day for me, the only truthful thing I can tell you is that you really *do* have the wrong person.'

Torabi sighed heavily and looked along the couch, as though a third party in the otherwise empty room might have heard what Kite had said and been similarly disappointed.

'You see, buddy, this is what I didn't want us to go through. Next thing you'll be telling me you need urgent medication for Type 2 diabetes or high blood pressure or whatever they teach you to say to buy yourself time—'

'If I could just finish—'

'Sure. Go ahead.'

Kite moved towards a more detailed denial using what he knew about Xavier's personality.

'I genuinely don't know what you're talking about,' he said. 'I don't have diabetes. I don't have high blood pressure. You mentioned Martha in the car.' Torabi looked up expectantly. 'You mentioned Ali Eskandarian. You were with Xavier in Paris and clearly asked him what happened when we first left school a very long time ago in the summer of 1989. Is that right?'

'The summer in France. Yes.'

Kite knew that he was on the right track. He took a deep breath.

'Because I've spent so much time in the last thirty years travelling overseas, Xavier always believed that I worked for MI6. He wasn't alone. A lot of people have come to that conclusion. In fact there was even a guy I spoke to at the funeral who told me he thought I was a spook. I'm not, Ramin. Never have been. You're barking up the wrong tree.'

'So where did you learn to fight like that?'

It was the obvious flaw in Kite's strategy. He had reacted quickly and violently to the Iranians in a way that was highly unusual for an ordinary citizen. An instinctive lie jumped to his rescue.

'I didn't say I couldn't defend myself,' he said. 'I was mugged when I was thirty and I've been doing martial arts ever since. You obviously weren't who you said you were. I recognised the word "*jakesh*" and was pretty sure your driver was calling me a "pimp". You weren't familiar with Alford, despite claiming you'd been there as a boy. You were driving away from the restaurant and taking me into a car park with a bunch of heavies in black suits waiting on the road. I got scared. As you no doubt know, I'm a rich man. I travel in South America and the Middle East. My company takes out substantial kidnap and ransom insurance for its employees. I thought you were after my money.'

Torabi appeared to have stopped listening. He turned towards the door and shouted: 'Kamran!'

The chauffeur walked in. This time he was wearing sunglasses to cover the black eye. Kite would have found it funny had Torabi not stood up, walked behind his chair and put his hands on Kite's shoulders.

'Ask the prisoner if he works for MI6,' he said. 'If he denies it again, break one of the fingers on his right hand.'

7

Five hundred miles away, Xavier Bonnard's good friend Jahan Fariba woke up in a Frankfurt hotel room with no idea of the time and no memory of having gone to bed. He felt exceptionally well rested, but anxious and uncertain. Bright sunlight was visible around the edges of the curtains. There was a light on beside the television, another in the bathroom.

He looked towards the bedside table but could not see his phone, which he usually left charging overnight. It was only then that he discovered he was still partially dressed. Pressing his feet together under the duvet, Jahan realised that he was wearing a pair of socks. Pushing back the duvet, he saw that he was wearing the same shirt he had worn on the previous day for the meeting with the Iranians. He always took his watch off last thing at night, but it was still on his wrist.

He looked at the time. It was just after three o'clock. At first Jahan assumed that it was three o'clock in the morning, but the sunlight outside contradicted this. Perhaps his watch had stopped? But the second hand was moving as normal and the date had moved forward. It was the day of Xavier's funeral. Jahan had been due to catch a 7 a.m. flight to London. With a mixture of bewilderment and intense frustration, he realised that he had overslept.

How was it possible? He sat up in bed and looked around for something to drink. Padding into the bathroom, he drank several mouthfuls of lukewarm water, scooping it into his mouth from the tap. He looked at his reflection in the mirror, trying to remember what had happened the night before. He had met the Iranians in the lobby. Early evening drinks had turned into dinner, dinner had turned into . . . what? He had no recollection of anything that had taken place after they had sat down in the restaurant. There had been beers during the meeting, then probably some wine with the meal. Jahan was not a heavy drinker but he could usually hold his liquor. Certainly he had no memory of the night descending into cocktails and *digestifs*. Christ. Had he collapsed and been dragged to the room by the Iranians? Had they quietly called the front desk and arranged for Mr Fariba to be escorted back to his room? If that was the case, it was probably the end of the business deal.

Jahan found his suit jacket in a heap on the floor. He picked it up and went through the pockets, looking for his phone. There were four messages from his wife in Rome, half a dozen from various friends, as well as a text from the airline noting that he had failed to make his flight. A couple of old Alfordians who had been expecting to see him at the funeral had written to say that they had looked for him, without success, at the Brompton Oratory.

Jahan downloaded his emails. There were no messages from the Iranians. Should he write to them and try to find out what had happened? Maybe not just yet. It would only embarrass both parties. Better to wait and to contact them in a couple of days. Jahan realised that he had no memory of what they had discussed at the meeting, only that both men had seemed enthusiastic about the rebuilding project in Syria.

He was annoyed to have missed the funeral. Xavier's death

BOX 88

was a tragedy and Jahan had wanted to pay his respects to one of the most interesting and amusing men he had ever met. He tried to load Facebook on his phone, but the password on the account wasn't working and—to his confusion—there was only a blank space where his profile picture had been. Instead he wrote an email to the friend in London with whom he had been due to stay that night:

> Gav, I'm really sorry. I overslept and missed my flight. Missed the funeral too. Not like me to be so disorganised. I think I must have eaten or drunk something last night that didn't agree with me. I'm so sorry, but I'm not going to be coming to stay with you guys. Still stuck in Frankfurt and will just go straight home to Rome. Please accept sincere apologies for messing you around. Send my love to Kitty and the kids and hopefully see you soon. Jahan x

8

The chauffeur stood in front of Kite. With a blunt, joyless expression on his face, he said: 'Do you work for MI6?'

Kite leaned on years of tight scrapes and crises, slowing everything down, trying to breathe evenly, trying to think of a way to stop what was about to happen. He clenched his hand into a fist, wondering how Kamran would go about breaking the fingers. With pliers? With a hammer from the toolbox? Certainly with pleasure: it would be more than adequate revenge for the black eye.

'Kamran,' he said, trying to sound as calm as possible. 'I'm sorry about your eye. I was frightened. I was trying to defend myself. I apologise.' His words had no discernible impact on the driver, though Torabi looked interested. Kite kept going, determined to deny both men the satisfaction of knowing that he was afraid. 'It's difficult to answer your question. Yes, it's true, when I was a very young man, I worked for MI6.' Torabi's eyes flicked up. 'That's why your boss may be confused. Even by telling you this, I'm committing treason, but I don't want a broken finger.' He tried to laugh. 'I value my hands!'

Kamran looked at Torabi, who indicated that they should continue to listen.

BOX 88

'By the time I was twenty-five, I quit.' Kite prayed that what he was saying was going to work. 'In fact, if I'm completely honest, I was sacked. So the answer to your question is this: I do deny that I work for MI6 because I haven't worked for them since 1994. And I'll keep on denying it until I don't have any fingers left.'

'Why?' said Torabi.

'*Why?* Because it happens to be the truth.'

The partial, if inaccurate, confession had a miraculous effect. Torabi and Kamran exchanged a few words in Farsi and the chauffeur left the room.

'So it is true.' Torabi closed the door behind him. Kite felt a droplet of sweat fall onto the back of his arm. 'In the summer of 1989, while on holiday with the family of Xavier Bonnard and Iranian businessman Ali Eskandarian, you were working for British intelligence?'

Kite lied again.

'Not to my knowledge at the time, no. I was what you might call a useful idiot. The Americans took advantage of me. I was a friend of Xavier's who became embroiled in what happened. Mr Eskandarian was a businessman with links to the highest levels of the Iranian government, yes, and was therefore a person of enormous interest to the CIA. At the tender age of eighteen, I was hardly aware of this. I spent most of that summer drinking wine, smoking weed and chasing girls, including Martha Raine. Afterwards, the Americans questioned me, pretending to be consular officials, and obtained my side of the story. One thing led to another and I was later put forward for a job at MI6 during my first year at university. The CIA had recommended me. I went to Russia, I partied a little too much, MI6 found out—and they sacked me.'

'That's not what I heard.'

'And what did you hear, Ramin?'

Almost everything Kite had said, with the exception of his

youthful enthusiasm for red wine and Martha Raine, was an invention.

'I heard that you knew what you were doing. That Xavier later found out about it and was upset. He blamed you for a long time. Isn't that true?'

Kite remembered Xavier's rage and hurt, the lies he had been forced to tell as his friend's world came crashing down. Thirty years on, he was using those same lies again on Torabi.

'Xavier had the wrong end of the stick. His father got in his ear and blamed me for what happened. That wasn't true. It was the Americans. Christ, it was all so long ago! Why the hell do you need to know all this now?'

'All in due course,' Torabi replied, tapping out a cigarette and offering one to Kite. 'Forgive me,' he said. 'I should have asked before if you smoked?'

'Only when I want to.'

Torabi lit the cigarette and stood up. Kite also rose from his chair. The plastic floor rippled beneath his feet.

'Enough for now,' said the Iranian. 'I have business to attend to. You will be taken back to your cell until I am ready to deal with you. When I come back we'll start again. You'll tell me everything you remember.'

'About 1989?'

'Yes.'

Kite assumed that Torabi would allow enough time to pass for his prisoner to fall asleep, then order his goons to wake him up.

'Where am I?' he asked.

'That is not important.'

'Are we on a boat?'

Torabi looked surprised. 'What makes you say that?'

'The smell. The size of the rooms.'

'Maybe you are. Maybe you're not. Like I said, it's not important. Hossein will take you to your room.'

BOX 88

Kite could see that he would make no further progress.

'My wife is pregnant,' he said, hoping for a last-minute favour, but expecting nothing. 'She'll be worried. I'll be perfectly happy to answer your questions, but I'd appreciate it if you would somehow get a message to her explaining that I'm OK.'

Torabi opened the door, preparing to leave. Hossein, the man who had earlier escorted him to the interview, entered the room.

'You're OK for now, Mr Kite,' Torabi replied. 'Who's to say if you'll be OK later.'

9

Kite turned to Hossein and told him that he needed to use the bathroom. They were halfway along the corridor leading back to his cell.

'The what?'

'The bathroom. The toilet. The loo.' It was like a brief insight into the absurdities of the British class system: saying 'loo' meant you were posh; when Kite had used the word 'toilet' in his first term at Alford, the thirteen-year-old Cosmo de Paul had told him he was 'common'. 'Where can I find it?'

There was a door at the end of the passage. Hossein was holding a two-way radio and used it to call Kamran. The chauffeur duly appeared and the two men instructed Kite not to lock the door as they stood outside the bathroom, waiting for him to finish.

Kite used the time to assess what the room could offer. A small, blacked-out porthole confirmed that he was indeed on board a ship. He kept the tap running to provide a covering noise for a brief search of a cupboard beneath the sink. Inside he found two unused bars of soap, bottles of bleach and cleaning fluid, but not what he had hoped for: hydrogen peroxide hair dye or white spirit, something flammable and highly sensitive which

BOX 88

could later be either forcibly ingested by the guards or used as an improvised explosive. There was an out-of-date box of codeine, some diarrhoea medication and a few pills for seasickness. Kite put six of the codeine tablets in the pocket of his trousers, closed the cupboard and switched off the tap. At the last moment, he noticed a nail protruding from the wall beneath the sink. He grabbed the head and moved it back and forth, trying to disturb the plaster, but had succeeded only in shifting it a few millimetres from the wall when there was a knock on the door.

'Let's go,' said Hossein.

'Two minutes.'

Kite looked around for other loose screws or nails which he could prise from the walls and later use in a fight. There were none that he could see. The shower curtain was held up on plastic hooks. A metal towel rail might come away from the wall easily enough if Kite needed to use it as a weapon. There was a towel draped over it. He flushed the toilet and went out into the corridor.

'Everything OK, gentlemen?' he asked.

Neither man responded. Hossein waited until Kamran had closed the bathroom door, put a gun in the small of Kite's back and walked him to his windowless cell. As he reached for the door handle, Kite glanced down at Hossein's watch and saw the date and time. It was just after eleven o'clock at night on the day of the funeral. He wondered what Isobel was doing, how she was coping with his disappearance. Doubtless by now she had called the emergency number and whoever was on duty at BOX 88 had instigated a search.

'Do either of you have a phone?' he said, noting that neither Hossein nor Kamran had searched him as he came out of the bathroom. 'If you could get a message to my wife—'

'Forget it,' said Hossein. Kamran had already turned and was walking back down the corridor.

'I can pay you when I get out.'

Kite held out no hope that Hossein would oblige; he simply

wanted to find out what kind of man he was dealing with. A loyal colleague of Torabi—or a foot soldier? There was a momentary flicker of interest in his eyes, but his response was by the book.

'You couldn't afford me.'

'Hossein!'

Kamran had summoned him from the end of the corridor. Hossein pushed Kite through the open door, so that he almost tripped over the low plastic table, then slammed it shut behind him.

'Hey!' Kite cried out.

He heard the key turning in the lock, then the murmur of the two men as they spoke in Farsi outside. Kite walked over to the bed, put the codeine pills under the mattress and lay down. He was suddenly exhausted, yet knew that he would find it almost impossible to sleep. Torabi had organised everything so carefully: the car park, the ship, the switch of identity with Fariba. Kite knew what it was about Ali Eskandarian that the Iranians were so desperate to find out. What he could not understand was why it had taken MOIS thirty years to track him down.

10

The hours following the disappearance of Lachlan Kite gave Cara Jannaway her first opportunity to see the Security Service doing what it did best. For a woman who was not easily impressed, who had found her first year at MI5 to be peculiarly repetitive, even boring, it was quite an afternoon.

Within forty-five minutes of Vosse meeting Zoltan Pavkov, he had obtained a Home Office warrant to saturate the Serbian in round-the-clock surveillance. A technical team was dispatched to Zoltan's flat in Bethnal Green, rigging the kitchen, bathroom and living room with listening devices and adding a live feed from the camera in his laptop computer for good measure. Zoltan's shabby Fiat Punto was parked outside and received the same treatment: microphones were placed behind the dashboard and a tracking device in the recess between the boot and the back seat. Reaching an analyst at Thames House, Vosse instructed him to collate and analyse a file detailing Pavkov's landline and Internet usage, as well as his online banking records. Threatening arrest, Vosse had told Zoltan to hand over his phone, then invited Cara to take him for a ten-minute walk around the block while he cloned its contents via Bluetooth and downloaded an application which would transmit all of the phone's subsequent activity to a laptop in the Acton safe house. If Pavkov was dumb enough to call the Iranians, Cheltenham would catch every word.

Even then, Vosse wasn't done. Following a quick lunch in Mayfair, Kieran Dean and Tessa Swinburn were given instructions to follow Zoltan when he came off shift at four o'clock. Matt Tomkins was told to go home and get some rest, then to drive over to the Bethnal Green flat at 11 p.m. to take over the stakeout. Meanwhile number plate recognition cameras had spotted the white van in the City, moving east through Whitechapel. The last known sighting of 'Kidson Electrical Services' had occurred on East India Dock Road at 14.35, indicating that the vehicle was probably located within a one-mile radius of Limehouse.

'Needle in a haystack,' said Vosse, 'but at least it gives us an area to aim for. Once we see some activity from Zoltan's mobile, he'll get us to within fifty feet of BIRD.' Cara's boss held up the cloned device in his oversized hand. 'I'm going to look at his messages, check who he's been talking to. We'll call a few numbers, see who picks up. Unless the Iranians are being very, very careful with their comms, we'll have BIRD back home by the weekend.'

Cara didn't necessarily share Vosse's optimism but certainly admired his confidence and self-belief.

'What about BIRD's stuff?' she asked, pointing to Kite's belongings. Vosse had placed them on the boot of a nearby car.

'BIRD's shit?' he replied, with a knowing look. 'Good question. They left his wallet behind, his shoes, his phone, his watch. What does that tell you?'

Cara liked it when Vosse taught her on the job. She knew that she could learn from him, that he enjoyed the feeling of being the veteran taking an apprentice under his wing.

'Well, I suppose they're worried about being tracked,' she replied.

'More than that.'

BOX 88

Cara was stumped. She walked over to the car and picked up Kite's watch.

'Says Omega Constellation.' She held it up for Vosse. 'Looks genuine, looks expensive. Must be worth at least a grand. But they didn't nick it.'

'Quite,' Vosse replied, looking proud of his pupil. 'And the wallet?'

'Plenty of cash inside. Same deal. They were in a hurry, didn't have time to help themselves to a bit of easy money.'

'Go through it,' said Vosse. 'Might be useful later. Photograph the bank cards, there might be accounts we don't know about. Look at where he's been going on his Oyster, use the driving licence to check if he's hired any cars lately. There's a couple of business cards in there. Make a note of the names, they might cross-reference with someone in the BOX 88 research. I looked earlier. There are four photos. Keepsakes. One is Isobel, find out who the other people are. There's an old laminated picture of a cheerful-looking bloke standing behind a bar. Maybe Kite's father? Another one of a woman who looks a lot like him, taken more recently. Could be his mother, his sister. Are they still alive? If we can match the faces, we can start to piece together where BIRD is from, who he cares about, who might have information for us. Speaking of which, have a look at the activity on Isobel's profile for any sign of contact. Chances are she'll start to worry when she doesn't hear from him. Usually when he's away they text one another. She might know something we don't. Who these people are. Why they're interested in BIRD. What they plan to do with him.'

'What about the mobile?' Cara asked.

'Tricky.' Vosse ran his tongue around his teeth, like someone at dinner fretting over trapped food. 'Tried cloning it while you were walking the dog.' He nodded towards the ramp, where Zoltan was smoking his ninth cigarette of the afternoon. 'No dice. More firewalls than Xi Jinping's underpants. Without the access code or a fingerprint, it's a Cheltenham job. Could take days.'

'Shame,' said Cara. She was developing a sneaking regard for Kite's tradecraft.

'A phone is a thing of beauty, Cara, a joy forever. Its loveliness increases.'

'Keats used a mobile?' she said, wanting Vosse to know that she'd understood the reference.

'Clever you,' he said. 'Imagine what we could get from that thing.' Vosse looked down at the phone. 'All those names and numbers, all those places BIRD's visited, every message he's sent, every Uber he ever ordered . . .'

'A goldmine.'

'But the men who took it didn't want it.'

Cara saw that Vosse had realised something critical. She couldn't tell if the breakthrough had only just occurred to him or if he had been sitting on it for some time.

'Didn't even take the SIM card,' he said, pointing at the slot in the phone. 'Didn't take his watch or his money. No, they want something that couldn't be found in BIRD's phone calls, his emails, his text messages.'

'What's that?' Cara asked.

'They want his memory.'

11

Kite lay back on the bed. He closed his eyes, taking his mind back to 1989, a place which held the answers to each of Torabi's questions, a vault containing the operational secrets of BOX 88.

The memories were as clear to him as they had been for thirty years—every encounter, every thought, every conversation—as if he had written a detailed account of his experiences at Alford, in Scotland and later in France, and was reading from it in the dark, soundless cell.

* * *

It is early November, the events of the summer three months behind him. The eighteen-year-old Kite is in Martha's bedroom in Finchley, her parents away for the weekend, her older brother out at a birthday party. They have the house to themselves.

Most of Kite's friends had taken off on their gap years: picking fruit in Australia; taking *South-East Asia on a Shoestring* around Thailand and Indonesia; others burnishing CVs with teaching jobs at primary schools in Uganda and Tibet. Xavier was in Paris with his family, dealing with the aftermath of the summer. Strawson had asked Kite to stay put in London: BOX 88 wanted to put him through advanced training before he went to university the following year.

'Tell me about your dad,' said Martha. 'You've never said much about him.'

She was in bed rolling a joint, Kite sitting in a chair by the window watching people come and go in the winter street below. Ten days later, in that same house, he would be in the living room with Martha's parents watching the Berlin Wall being torn down on the *Nine O'Clock News*. Had anyone else asked the same question, Kite would have shut them down. He had been avoiding the subject of his father for half his life. But Martha was different. He wanted to tell her everything.

'Dad was called Paddy,' he said. 'Pierce Patrick Kite, but everyone knew him as Paddy. He wasn't born in Ireland. My grandparents lived in London during the war and only moved back to Dublin in the 1950s. Dad must have been fifteen or sixteen at the time. He had a sister who died in the Blitz as a baby—Aunt Catherine—so like me he was a kind of only child by default.'

'You had a sibling who died?' Martha asked. She looked concerned, as if Kite had suffered a terrible loss about which she had known nothing.

'No, no.' He poked her leg with his foot. 'I don't have any brothers or sisters. It was just me and Mum and Dad.'

Martha nodded, relieved, going back to rolling the joint. They had bought a packet of Rizlas and some cigarettes at a mini-supermarket on Regents Park Road. Martha had insisted on going to a place where her face wasn't known in case the man who ran the corner shop at the end of the street told her parents she was smoking pot.

'What did he look like?' she asked.

From his wallet Kite took out two colour photographs: the first showed his father proudly standing at the bar of the hotel in Scotland, arms folded, grinning from ear to ear; the second

BOX 88

was a picture of his parents sitting on a picnic rug at the Wigtown Show on a bright summer day in 1978.

'Wow, your mum is beautiful,' she said. 'They look happy.'

'They were.'

'Your dad's got such a glint in his eye. Looks very kind, but naughty. Bit like you.'

Kite turned from the window and watched as Martha lit a small lump of treacle-brown hash with her Zippo and crumbled it onto the Rizla.

'Whenever people talk about Dad they say he was a typical hard-drinking Irishman who seduced the girls and flew down the wing for the first XV and liked to quote Keats and Bob Dylan when he was pissed. I don't know how much of that is true. There are a lot of myths around Dad. I know he preferred Scottish whisky to Irish, Tennant's to Guinness. His Dublin friends would come over on the boat from Larne and tease him about that. I grew up around bottles of Laphroaig and Lagavulin, six-packs of Kestrel lager and McEwan's Export. There was alcohol everywhere. My father would hide half-bottles in the pockets of his suits and hang them in the cupboard. Whenever I smell booze on someone's breath, I instantly think of him and kind of hate them for it. Even at school on weekends when we were getting pissed, it was enough to make me stop drinking if I smelled it on someone. One time, Xav drank a bottle of sherry from an off-licence in Windsor in the space of fifteen minutes and threw up in his room. A friend and I had to clear up the mess, get him out of his clothes and into bed before Lionel, our housemaster, found him. Would have been expelled if he'd got caught—he was on final warning. It was like parenting him. I'd parented my dad when he was drunk, so what was the difference? He'd be out of his head at three in the afternoon and say: "Don't tell your mother, it'll only upset her." He'd pass out in different places. I remember Mum crying in their bedroom as she tried to wake him up for work. He was never violent or aggressive, but I can't think of a single moment when he wasn't drinking. At breakfast once, when I was about eight, I picked up his glass of orange juice by mistake, took a sip and it was full of vodka. He screamed at me to put it down, but it was too late. I spat it out and started crying.'

'Jesus.' Martha was holding the rolled joint, as if it would be disrespectful to light it while Kite was speaking so candidly. 'Was he drinking when your mum met him in Ireland?'

'Dunno. Maybe. Maybe not. Are you going to light that?' Martha clicked the lighter, the paper burning fast so that the end of the joint briefly flamed, sending up a plume of smoke. 'When he was a young man he was quite political apparently. Not IRA, but definitely on the side of the Catholic Irish, the Republicans. Then he married Mum, an English Protestant girl, which is basically why they decided to leave Dublin and come to Scotland. Dad had been running a pub in Temple Bar so he knew the hospitality business, how to change a keg, find waiters, chefs, that kind of thing. Somebody told me a pub is perfect cover for an alcoholic. Everything you need is right at your fingertips. So they bought a hotel together in the back of beyond, near Stranraer on that little peninsula that sticks out like a haemorrhoid from the south-west corner of Scotland.'

Martha laughed at that, giggling as she took a second hit on the joint. Kite asked if he should open a window, but Martha said no, it was too cold, and anyway she didn't want her neighbours smelling the hash.

'We'll have to go there one day, drive up,' said Kite, bending over and kissing the inside of her thigh as he took the joint. 'It's such a beautiful place. There's new owners now; apparently they're doing up all the rooms. The nearest village is Portpatrick— nothing but a harbour and a crazy golf course where I'd go a lot after Dad died just to be on my own or hang out with a friend who worked at the hotel.'

'Gary the waiter,' said Martha, remembering that Kite had

BOX 88

mentioned him in the summer. She seemed to be able to recall everything he told her: every name, every anecdote, every detail.

'Yeah, that's right. Gary.'

He took a long draw on the joint, held the smoke deep in his lungs and passed it back. Martha set it in a scallop shell ashtray by the bed and stared at him, huge eyes drawing in Kite's words.

'The hotel is called Killantringan. It's a beautiful old country house with a lawn in front running down to the sea. Surrounded on all sides by steep hills at the end of a long, isolated road. There's a cliff walk to the north which eventually takes you into Portpatrick. One night, in 1982, Mum and Dad had an argument about his drinking and Dad took off into the garden, ended up walking along the beach with a bottle and then somehow up over the rocks in the darkness and onto the path leading to the cliffs. He fell. Lost his footing at the top. Somebody found his body the next morning. And that was that.'

'I'm so sorry, Lockie.'

'Mum closed the hotel for three weeks, took me out of school and we went to stay with my granny in Sligo. When we got back, everything changed. I was expected to be the man of the house from then on, to work behind the scenes, helping out in the kitchen, turning down the beds at night, unloading deliveries with the other kitchen staff, chatting up the guests. I hadn't even turned twelve. I feel as though I went from being a child to a grown-up in the space of six months, you know? Then one day Mum announced that I was going to boarding school. No discussion. It wasn't anything either of us had ever talked about or mentioned—it would never have occurred to Dad. Not one of the big Scottish schools, either: Glenalmond or Fettes or Gordonstoun. No, she was sending me to Alford College, the most famous school in the world, five hundred miles away in the south of England. Turned out the head of admissions was an old boyfriend of hers. He arranged for a bursary, the rest of the fees would be paid by Dad's life insurance. I'd be starting in September

'84, which was less than a year away. She said I was too clever to go to one of the local schools and she didn't want me to feel trapped by the hotel, by how provincial things were up there. She said it would mean I'd have more of a life, more opportunities, play sport, meet interesting people . . .'

'Interesting people like Xav,' said Martha. Kite couldn't tell how serious she was being.

'Yeah,' he said. 'Like Xav.' He took another hit on the joint and passed it back.

'Were you upset?'

'Don't think so, no.' It hadn't occurred to Kite that he might have been. 'Actually, I remember being quite excited. Alford sounded a bit of an adventure. Being stuck in Scotland reminded me of Dad all the time and I was sick of feeling that way. If I was on the beach, just going for a walk, I'd think of him on the cliff or remember making dams with him in the stream that ran into the sea from the hills. We'd build these huge sand walls, massive blockades strengthened with rocks and driftwood and bottles. Great lakes of water would build up behind them. Dad would hum the *Dambusters* tune and say in his thick Irish accent: 'It's like the fockin' Aswan, Lockie!' Then we'd throw stones at the top until the dam started to break, bit by bit, until finally it gave out and a torrent of water would rush down to the sea carrying all the sand and seaweed and beach crap we'd used to build it up.'

Kite could feel the joint working through him. Martha took another hit and sat up against the headboard.

'It was the same if I was in Portpatrick or Stranraer or up in the hills behind the hotel. Dad was everywhere. He'd given me an air rifle for my birthday. We used to go shooting together, looking for rabbits. Just Dad and me, walking for hours. The first one I shot had myxomatosis. Usually the rabbits would run away as soon as they heard us coming, but this one was so ill it just sat there, stock-still, waiting for me to kill it. I was ten. Dad

BOX 88

lay beside me in the heather, showed me how to load the pellet into the rifle and line up the telescopic sight. When I hit it, he reacted like I was the Sundance Kid. He was so happy for me! For days afterwards he would refer to me in front of the guests as "the Red Baron". I didn't know what he was talking about. So that's what it was like once he was gone. Just this big absence, this hole where his gigantic personality used to be. I was so confused and angry with him for dying, you know? I felt like he'd let me down, let Mum down, made all of us so sad, the staff at the hotel, his friends. There were probably four hundred people at his funeral, mourners who came over on the ferry from Ireland, friends who drove up from England or flew into Glasgow and Prestwick. He touched a lot of lives.'

'What about your mum?'

Kite waited, weighing up the most diplomatic response. Martha had yet to meet his mother; he didn't want to tip the scales against her in advance.

'It hardened her, no question,' he replied. 'Here was this glamorous woman, married to a man she loved more than any wife had ever loved any husband as far as I could tell, but he'd loved alcohol more than he'd loved her. More than he loved me, come to think of it. Dad's true friends were Smirnoff and Gordon's and Famous Grouse. Those were the half-bottles I'd find in the pockets of his jackets in the cupboard where he hung his suits. Twice a week a van would come down from Whighams of Ayr carrying six dozen cases of wine and another of spirits for the hotel. Dad would be waiting to greet it like Joanne Whalley was going to jump out in a nurse's uniform.'

'She was the one in *The Singing Detective*?' Martha asked.

'Yeah. That's her.'

Martha climbed off the bed, came over to the window and hugged Kite. When they kissed he could smell the smoke on her breath and felt dizzy. The next thing he knew she had put *Kiss Me Kiss Me Kiss Me* on her record player and they were making stoned love to 'Catch'. Afterwards they went downstairs to the kitchen, made ham and cheese sandwiches in a Breville toaster and brought them back up to Martha's room with a bottle of Bulgarian white wine stolen from the fridge.

'So how did you do Common Entrance if you were going to a local school in Portpatrick?'

Kite was now in bed wearing a pair of boxer shorts, watching the naked Martha flicking through her record collection.

'Put the other side of the Cure on,' he said.

'It's a double album,' she replied, removing the record from the sleeve and putting it on the turntable. Lowering the needle, she hit the vinyl in the wrong place so that it scratched midway through the first song.

'What's this?' he asked as the song began again. He was looking at the bright red lips on the album cover.

'"Just Like Heaven",' Martha replied. 'You'll love it.'

'Mum hired a private tutor,' he said, answering Martha's question about Common Entrance, the exam every boy had to take if he wanted to get into Alford. 'Name was Roger Dunlop, as in Green Flash. He was a colleague of Billy Peele's from Alford with no wife, no family, made extra money in the holidays cramming boys for Oxbridge and A levels. He came up to Killantringan three times, stayed for free, taught me eight hours a day then arranged for me to sit all the exams at the hotel with a retired headmistress from Castle Douglas invigilating to make sure I didn't cheat.'

'Did you?' Martha asked, climbing into bed beside him.

Kite was drunk on his share of the Bulgarian wine and still slightly stoned.

'Cheat?' he said. *'Moi?* How could you even ask that question?'

In France, Xavier had told Martha that he and Kite had been less than model schoolboys, constantly in trouble with Lionel Jones-Lewis and permanently in the headmaster's office on one charge or another.

BOX 88

'You cheated,' she replied deadpan.

'Fine.' Kite raised his hands in mock surrender and looked around for more of the wine. 'I'd never studied Latin,' he continued when he had found and poured it. 'My dad was a working-class lad from Dublin. My mum was an ex-model who went to parties with Jean Shrimpton and left school at sixteen. They didn't exactly read *The Odyssey* to me as a bedtime story.'

'That's a good job,' said Martha. '*The Odyssey* is Greek.'

'Smart arse.' He pinched her shoulder. 'Anyway, Latin was what nice prep school boys from Sunningdale and Ludgrove were taught from the age of eight. They didn't go in for it at Portpatrick primary in 1982. Probably still don't. We had Miss Mowat, who was brilliant at maths and science, but not so good when it came to dead languages which hadn't been spoken in Scotland for two thousand years.'

'So poor Lachlan felt justified in cheating?'

Kite laughed at how much she was enjoying teasing him.

'Fully justified,' he said, and this time pushed her over so that she almost knocked the butts and ash out of the scallop shell. 'Alford insisted that all boys needed Latin, so I had to sit for hours and hours with Roger declining *amo, amas, amat* and translating endless paragraphs describing Hannibal crossing the Alps. I was actually all right at it, just couldn't remember a lot of the vocab. The night before the common entrance was a Sunday and the chef decided to walk out because Mum hadn't given him a pay rise. She'd stepped in and was cooking for a full dining room of thirty-odd people. I was chopping onions and carrots in the kitchen and fetching stuff for her from the fridge. Didn't get to bed until eleven and had no time to revise. Did you see *The Godfather* on TV the other day?'

Martha, who was straightening out the bedclothes, shook her head.

'OK, well Dad had rented it on video from a shop in Stranraer and never taken it back. The shop had given up on the fine, so we sort of owned it. I'd watched it at least six times without Mum knowing. There's a bit where Al Pacino tapes a gun behind a cistern in the bathroom of an Italian restaurant so that he can go in there, grab it and shoot the two people he's having dinner with. I just stole that idea. On the Monday morning I stuck a Latin dictionary behind the cistern in the staff toilet where the headmistress wouldn't see it if she went in after breakfast. Then, halfway through the exam, when I'd memorised all the words I didn't recognise, I asked if I could be excused. She said fine, no problem, I went into the staff toilet, stood up on the seat, pulled the dictionary down, quickly looked up all the words I didn't know, flushed the toilet and went back to the exam.'

'How did you do?' Martha asked.

'Got four points out of five,' Kite replied.

'Smart arse.'

The next day, Kite and Martha slept past one o'clock and went for lunch at Pizzaland. Back at the house, Martha's mother rang from Chicago, where she was giving a lecture at Northwestern University. Martha made no mention of Kite staying with her. Her parents knew she had fallen for a boy over the summer, but they had yet to meet him.

Returning to the bedroom, they put on *Kiss Me Kiss Me Kiss Me* for perhaps the fifth time in twenty-four hours, got back into bed, smoked another joint and opened another bottle of wine which Kite had bought in Swiss Cottage. Martha was seventeen and looked her age; Kite was eighteen but could pass for twenty-three or twenty-four. Telling her about his childhood, he had felt released from a straitjacket of secrets and shame. For years, Kite had kept the nature of his father's death hidden, even from Xavier, telling nobody that Paddy Kite had been an alcoholic. At Alford, to survive was to remain concealed; to thrive was to put on a mask, projecting nothing but confidence and strength to the outside world. It had occurred to Kite that, in

BOX 88

many ways, the school was the perfect breeding ground for a career in intelligence. During five years at boarding school, he had learned how to vanish into different versions of himself: how to survive on charm and intuition; when to fight and to take risks; when to impose himself on a situation and when to melt into the background.

Martha took out two Marlboro Reds, lit both of them and passed one to Kite. She asked how he had felt when he first arrived at Alford. Kite considered his answer for some time. Martha was at a crammer in North London after a brief stint at boarding school had ended in expulsion. He knew that, like most people, she thought of Alford as a nightmare fusion of *If . . .* and *Another Country*.

'You must have missed your mum,' she suggested.

Kite felt the bump of his mother's absent love and deflected the question. 'Yes and no,' he said. He tugged distractedly at one of the hairs on his chest. 'Every house at Alford has a matron in it who's supposed to be there to look after the boys. They call them "dames". A kind of surrogate mother.'

The cigarette hadn't lit properly. Kite took the lighter from her, trying again. One of the best things about leaving Alford was the realisation that he would never again have to set eyes on Joyce Blackburn, the ghoulish, humourless spinster who had been his 'dame' for five long years. A mean-spirited ally of Lionel Jones-Lewis, she had been widely loathed by every boy who had passed through Kite's house.

'So she looked after you?'

'In the way that Nurse Ratched looks after Jack Nicholson in *One Flew Over the Cuckoo's Nest*, yes.'

When he saw that Martha looked shocked, Kite reassured her. 'Don't worry,' he said. 'It was OK. Alford was fine.'

'That's it? *Fine?*'

Martha stubbed out her cigarette in the scallop shell and climbed out of bed. She suddenly seemed angry.

'I don't understand,' he said. 'What's the matter?'

'Your father dies, your mother decides to send you five hundred miles away to boarding school, you effectively leave home at the age of thirteen—and you're telling me it was "fine"?'

She wants to protect me, Kite thought. She wants to know everything about me so that she can be my secret sharer and confidante. If I tell Martha about my life, she will accept the decisions I have made, the insecurities I have felt, and she will love me. The realisation came to him in a euphoric moment, rushed through his mind by the joint and the wine and the constant, repeating pleasure of making love to her. Looking back, that was the moment when Kite knew that he wanted to be with Martha Raine for as long as she would take him.

'OK,' he said, with a degree of uncertainty. 'It wasn't always "fine".' He stubbed out the cigarette. 'I'll tell you the truth if you like. I'll tell you the whole story.'

12

If Lachlan Kite had been strapped to a rocket in the back garden of the Killantringan Hotel and fired into the night sky over Portpatrick, he could not have landed in a stranger place than Alford College in September 1984.

The thirteen-year-old Kite had never been further south than Hadrian's Wall. Edinburgh and Glasgow were the only large cities he had visited. He had met guests at the hotel from all over the world—Paris, Toronto, Melbourne, Chicago—but had never set foot in England.

His mother drove him there, across country via Castle Douglas to Carlisle, then seven hours of motorways all the way to London. They arrived in darkness. Kite peered out of the windows at the mass of people and cars, expecting to see Big Ben and Buckingham Palace, punks with needles of red and purple hair. Cheryl Kite had friends in town, but they took a room at the Penta Hotel on Cromwell Road where she sewed the final nametapes onto his socks and pants and took him for spare ribs at the Texas Lone Star.

'It's going to be so interesting, darling,' she said, lighting a Silk Cut. 'Are you looking forward to tomorrow?'

'Yes, I am,' Kite replied and felt his stomach turn inside out.

He was still a boy, his voice unbroken, his body pale and slim. He felt that he was on the verge of being cast into a land of vast hairy giants with chauffeurs to drive them around and butlers on call to ferry glasses of orange juice to their studies. That night Kite didn't sleep a wink. All he could think about were the photographs of Alford he had seen in a book Roger Dunlop had given him as a present for passing Common Entrance. Boys in tailcoats and top hats, lining the funeral route outside Windsor Castle following the death of King George VI; great men of yesteryear who had attended Alford in the Victorian era and gone on to run every corner of the British Empire; oil paintings of Alford's magnificent cathedral and cloisters, built by Henry VII to stand for a thousand years. To Kite's young eyes, the school promised to be a black-and-white time warp of ritual and convention so far removed from the life he knew in Scotland as to be almost incomprehensible. Kite's father had given him a small silver box as a Christening present, engraved inside the lid with the simple message: *To Lachlan, from Da* and the date of the service. Kite clutched it in his hand all night, whispering to his father as Cheryl snored in the next-door bed.

'Just give it a couple of weeks,' she said as she prepared to leave Alford the following afternoon, having spent most of the day walking around the school campus. 'Once you get used to it, I'm sure it'll be a great success.'

It took Kite a lot longer than a couple of weeks.

On his first morning, having woken at six o'clock in a tiny study on the top floor of a house on Common Lane, he had put on the tail suit his mother had ordered from Billings and Edmonds in Alford High Street and wrestled with a stiff collar for almost an hour until one of the boys with a room on his corridor offered to help. He showed Kite how to place the metal studs in the front and back collar of the starched white shirt, then to loop a narrow length of rectangular cotton over the top button so that it formed a tie.

BOX 88

'I look like a vicar,' said Kite when he glanced in the mirror. 'Get used to it,' the boy replied.

This was to be his uniform for the next five years. Kite became acutely conscious of the fact that he sounded Scottish; there seemed to be no other boy in his year, even the ones called 'Angus' and 'Ewan', who was like him. He was quickly nicknamed 'Jock' and set about flattening his accent, making the consonants more clipped, giving the vowels more air, so that he sounded less like a run-of-the-mill Scottish teenager and more like Little Lord Fauntleroy. A couple of years later, as his peers became increasingly self-conscious about their class and background, Kite adopted a faux-Cockney twang, an affectation which remained with him—as it did with dozens of old Alfordians—into his early twenties.

The thirteen-year-old Kite also had to adjust to the arcane language of his new school. Teachers were not 'teachers', as they had been in Portpatrick, but 'beaks'—and they were all men. A bad piece of homework wasn't just a bad piece of homework; it was known as a 'rip' because it was literally torn in half by a beak, who would then instruct the boy to show it to his housemaster. Break in the morning was 'chambers', terms were called 'halves' and each year's intake of boys was known as a 'block'. Stranger still—though they were never given a name—were the busloads of Japanese tourists who would park outside School Hall on weekdays and take photographs of the boys through the windows. Every time Kite walked past them in his tailcoat and stiff white collar, he felt like an exhibit in a human zoo.

Then there was Lionel Jones-Lewis. Kite's housemaster, a fifty-something old Alfordian, was the only grown man Kite had ever met who hadn't remarked on his mother's beauty. He had been a scholar at Alford just after the war, taken a First in Mathematics at Cambridge, completed his military service as a submariner and applied immediately for a job at his alma mater. 'LJL', as he was known, had been at Alford ever since. A formidable intellectual with a peculiar fondness for the traditions and idiosyncrasies of Alford life, 'Jumpy' Jones-Lewis was, on the surface, a camp figure of fun, shuffling back and forth from the playing fields of Alford in Wellington boots, custard-coloured cords and his favourite purple anorak. Yet those boys who were unfortunate enough to be in his house saw a different side of Jones-Lewis. Late in the evenings he would walk into a boy's room without knocking, hoping to catch him topless in a towel or in the process of removing his boxer shorts. Each study at Alford had its own desk where boys would do their homework in the evenings. In Kite's first term at the school, Jones-Lewis came into his study two or three times a week and crouched beside his desk, purportedly to help him with a maths problem or chunk of Ancient Greek. In reality, he was looking forward to feeling him up. As Kite talked, Jones-Lewis would run his hand up and down his spine, stroking his lower back in a way that made the young boy freeze with anxiety. At thirteen, Kite had been unsure if this was normal behaviour for a 'beak' or something that he should be concerned about. When he told his mother at Christmas, she laughed it off, saying: 'Don't worry, sweetheart. He's only being affectionate.' Eventually Kite asked Jones-Lewis to stop, forcibly removing his hand from his leg on a summer evening in 1985. From that day on, Kite was a marked man. Though Jones-Lewis never again laid a finger on him, he treated Kite with none of the charm and easy goodwill that he extended to other boys in the house. He made sure that Kite obeyed every rule and stricture the school could throw at him and came down hard on the frequent occasions when he stepped out of line.

Kite met Xavier Bonnard on his first day at Alford. Despite their contrasting backgrounds, they became the closest of friends. Both, in their separate ways, were dealing with problem fathers:

BOX 88

Kite's a dead alcoholic, Xavier's a philandering Parisian chancer living off his wife's vast wealth and seemingly limitless patience. While Xavier couldn't wait to be free of Alford, it was Kite's guilty secret that he often enjoyed himself. As it was for so many children from broken or otherwise unhappy homes, boarding school provided a respite from the permanent, stuck-record sadness of his existence in Scotland. Xavier seemed to understand this: indeed, he was proud of Kite when he made fifty for the cricket team or got to second base with a girl at a party. He knew that his friend was rootless and lost, but also fearless and clever in a way that was different from so many of the other boys in their house. Without Kite at his side to laugh at his jokes, smoke his cigarettes and accompany him on illegal trips to London, where they would hide out with girls at the Bonnard house in Onslow Square, Xavier might well have cashed in his chips and gone to school at the Lycée Charles de Gaulle in South Kensington. Nothing could alter his sincerely held view that boarding school was a moral and social scandal.

'Alford is basically an open prison,' Xavier had concluded by the end of his second year. 'Everyone gets their own cell. You're told when to wake up and when to go to sleep, your laundry is done for you and your meals are cooked three times a day. You're allowed out, but only when the warden says you can leave, and only if you're back by a certain time. There are exercise yards, escape attempts, people trading porn mags for cigarettes. Contact with the outside world is limited. We have one phone in the house and otherwise have to write letters which could be steamed open by Lionel if he thinks we're complaining about him to our parents. There are strict hierarchies among the inmates, homosexuals pursuing pretty boys, disgusting food and limited access to alcohol. You get released after serving your sentence but then have to adjust to life in the outside world. For the rest of your time on earth, you're known as an Old Alfordian. How is that different to being an ex-con from Wormwood Scrubs or Alcatraz?'

Xavier nevertheless did what he could to make his time at the school as enjoyable as possible. He was constantly in trouble with both Jones-Lewis and the headmaster, though the latter found it hard to disguise his affection for one of the school's natural iconoclasts. By the time he was seventeen, Xavier had been caught with a naked girl in his room, been suspended for scaling the roof of the school chapel (with Kite alongside him) and reprimanded for leaving a live chicken— purchased from a farmer in Maidenhead—in Joyce Blackburn's bathroom.

Xavier was also the unwitting key to Kite's future as an intelligence officer. A few months before the two friends were due to take their A levels, Kite was lounging around in Xavier's study at Alford, killing time on a cold February afternoon. Xavier's room had a permanent smell of Deep Heat and patchouli oil and was decorated in the typical Alford fashion: there were posters of Bob Marley and Nelson Mandela on the walls alongside snapshots of Christy Turlington, Linda Evangelista and Cindy Crawford culled from Rosamund Bonnard's back issues of *Tatler* and *Harpers & Queen*. Maghreb-style drapes hung from the ceiling, with copies of *Paris Match* and *The Face* magazine scattered on the ground in case any girls popped their heads round the door while visiting the house. The overall effect, Kite joked, was of sitting in a tent erected by a teenage Muammar Gaddafi. His own slightly larger study was down the hall and dominated by photographs of his sporting idols—Daley Thompson, Kenny Dalglish, Gavin Hastings—as well as a poster of Jimi Hendrix setting fire to an electric guitar.

It was snowing. Xavier had an illegal two-bar fire switched on against the cold and was trying on a vintage suede jacket he had recently bought in Kensington Market. Kite was lying on a beanbag in a moth-eaten Lou Reed T-shirt and 'Pop

BOX 88

trousers'—the Prince of Wales check trousers worn by the school's prefects. Xavier had put *Transformer* on in tribute to his attire. They were listening to 'New York Telephone Conversation'. Xavier, who had not long finished smoking a cigarette out of the window, sprayed himself with Eau Sauvage to smother the smell of tobacco.

'What were you saying about your dad?' Kite asked.

Xavier took the jacket off and threw it onto the bed.

'He's inherited a house in the South of France, near Mougins. Said I can invite a friend to stay in the summer. Wanna come?'

By then, Kite had been to Xavier's family homes in London, Gloucestershire and Switzerland. One more addition to the Bonnard real estate portfolio came as no surprise.

'Would love to.'

'You won't have to work at the hotel?'

Ordinarily, Kite spent at least three weeks of the school holidays helping his mother out at Killantringan, but she had put the hotel on the market and sold it to a couple from Glasgow. They were due to take over in July. Xavier remembered this and corrected himself.

'Oh, that's right. Your mum's moving out.'

'What are the dates?' Kite asked.

Xavier shrugged. He clearly planned to be there all summer, smoking pot, drinking vodka, chasing French girls.

'All I know is my godfather is coming to stay at some point. An old Iranian friend of my dad's. I call him the "ayatollah". They met in Paris when I was a kid. You'll like him. Come whenever you want. *Tu es ici comme chez toi.*'

Kite's French was good enough to understand the colloquialism: 'My house is your house.' At this stage, his only plans for the future involved passing his A levels and getting a summer job to make a bit of money before going to Edinburgh University in the autumn to read Russian and French. He said he would take the train down to Cannes sometime in July, reached for an almost-empty carton of orange juice lying on the floor beside him and finished it off.

'Cool,' Xavier replied. 'Stay for as long as you like.'

It was as simple as that. An invitation which would change the course of Lachlan Kite's life, accepted unthinkingly on a cold afternoon in February.

Without realising it, Xavier Bonnard had set his friend on the path to BOX 88.

13

Cara Jannaway opened her front door just in time to catch the start of *Channel 4 News*. She poured herself a glass of white wine and had drunk almost half of it before Krishnan Guru-Murthy had finished reading out the headlines.

She lived alone in a one-bedroom flat west of Hackney Marshes. Vosse had given her the night off as a gesture of appreciation for her work earlier in the afternoon. Cara's colleagues, Kieran Dean and Tessa Swinburn, had been tasked with following Zoltan Pavkov home; Matt was due to relieve them at eleven o'clock. Cara didn't envy him the night shift. It had been a long, eventful day and she was looking forward to running a bath, ordering a Deliveroo Thai and watching at least two episodes of *Succession*—three, if it wasn't getting too late and she felt like bingeing a third of the season. Before that, however, she had one more job to do. Vosse wanted her to call the number on the card Kite had given her at the funeral, 'just to see if there's any possibility someone picks up'. Vosse had suggested it was a way for 'Emma', her gallerist legend, to stay in character. If and when Kite got out of whatever situation he was in, he would hear the voicemail and perhaps respond to Emma's call. Cara had her doubts about the strategy, thinking it was an unnecessary risk, but Vosse had pulled rank.

She dialled the number. It rang out: seven, eight, nine times. Then:

'This is the Vodafone voicemail service for—*Lachlan Kite.*'

Kite had recorded his own name onto the automated message. It was startling to hear his voice, as if the events of the afternoon had never taken place and he was still at large, a free man giving MI5 the slip. Cara had rehearsed what she was going to say, trying to combine a tone of professionalism with a friendly rapport.

'Er, hi Lachlan. It's Emma from the Brompton Oratory. We met outside the funeral this morning and you kindly gave me your card. I was the woman who used to work at Karoo during Frieze. It was really nice to bump into you again. I'll try you another time.'

Cara hung up and took a long gulp of wine. She was struck by the thought that nobody would ever hear her message, that she might never see Lachlan Kite again. She went into the bathroom and switched on the hot tap, pouring a glug of bath oil into a stream of steaming water. The room quickly began to smell of lavender. Cara took out her mobile and tapped the Deliveroo app, repeating her regular order with a local Thai restaurant for stir-fried chicken and basil with a side of jasmine rice. The Tinder icon alongside showed thirty-four notifications. She opened it up and clicked through the profiles of the nine boys with whom she had recently matched, then spent the next fifteen minutes replying to their messages, playing it cool with short, gnomic answers and deleting anyone who called her 'babe' or 'darling'. Five minutes later her food had arrived. Cara tipped the driver, wolfed the stir-fry, sat in the bath reading a book for half an hour—and fell asleep in front of the television before she had even managed to locate the first episode of *Succession*.

•

BOX 88

Cara Jannaway's voicemail was recorded and filed on a server at BOX 88 headquarters and an alert sent to Kite's desk. In keeping with Service protocols, the number she had used to make the call was automatically investigated by a software programme known as INTIMATE KUBRICK and a report dispatched internally to B6, the Section within BOX 88 with responsibility for overseeing and maintaining agent cover. The report contained all open source information linked to Cara Jannaway's mobile number, including her home address, date of birth, banking and tax statements, education and employment history, medical records and a list of recent travel destinations. Hyperlinks within the report offered B6 access to her email, Instagram and Facebook accounts as well as to the list of apps downloaded to her iTunes account (which included Tinder). These could be investigated upon request.

It was Cara's position at MI5 that triggered a warning within INTIMATE KUBRICK so that the report was flagged for 'Immediate Attention'.

Officer with the Security Service (UK)
Ministry of Defence cover (joined October 2018)
Line Manager: Robert Vosse

Lachlan Kite's colleagues at 'The Cathedral'—the colloquial name for BOX 88 headquarters in London—now knew that their boss was under investigation by MI5.

Kieran Dean and Tessa Swinburn had followed Zoltan home from the Mayfair car park. It was arguably the easiest follow that either of them had ever been on, so oblivious was the target to any possibility that he might have picked up a tail.

Vosse had a fix on the Pavkov mobile but there was always a danger that the Serb might dump it on the Tube and try to throw them off. He had shown no obvious signs of intelligence—far less of training in anti-surveillance—but he might have watched the odd thriller or documentary on Channel 5 and learned a thing or two about being followed.

But no. Not Zoltan. Walking behind him on opposite sides of the street, sometimes at a distance of less than twenty metres, Dean and Swinburn were able to follow the Serb onto a packed Jubilee line train at Green Park underground station with extraordinary ease. Alighting one stop later at Bond Street, the unwily Serb travelled east towards Bethnal Green, picking up a six-pack of lager and some groceries at Tesco Metro on his way home. At no point did he use his phone, speak to any member of the public nor show any outward display of nervousness or concern about the day's events. When Swinburn called Vosse to tell him that Pavkov was safely housed, Vosse switched to the audio feeds from the Bethnal Green flat and was able to watch the target through the lens of the Serb's laptop computer, variously pulling the ring on a can of Stella Artois, opening a letter from Tower Hamlets Council and scratching his arse as he slumped into a deep brown couch.

'Doesn't seem all that bothered,' Vosse observed, wondering why, at the very least, Pavkov hadn't texted the Iranians to warn them that the police knew what had happened to Kite. 'Are you sure he didn't meet someone on the Tube? Pass a message in Tesco? Send a WhatsApp on a burner phone we know nothing about?'

'Hundred per cent, Bob,' said Tess, who was by then sitting on a bench in a park overlooked by the flat, waiting for Matt Tomkins to take over. 'Never left our sight. Didn't talk to anyone, not even a checkout girl.'

Another four hours went by before Zoltan Pavkov finally contacted the Iranians. In that time, Swinburn and Dean had gone home, Matt Tomkins had come on shift and the Serb had closed the lid on his laptop, bringing an end to any possi-

BOX 88

bility that Vosse would be able to continue to watch what he was doing.

'I think he's gone to bed, sir,' Tomkins observed just before one o'clock in the morning. 'Heard the toilet flushing five minutes ago, sound of someone brushing his teeth. Lights have been switched off in the kitchen and living room. Feels like he's called it a day.'

'Must have,' said Vosse wistfully. Tomkins wondered why he sounded disappointed. Surely this was the boss's chance to go home and get a few hours' sleep? 'All right then. Keep your eyes peeled. Call me if anything changes. I'm not going home, I'll sleep here in Acton. Eve and Villanelle will be there at seven to see what comes next.'

It was only when Vosse had hung up that Tomkins understood the nature of the boss's frustration: he had been hoping that Zoltan would slip up and lead him straight to the Iranians. That seemed naive. A MOIS team weren't going to allow a man like Pavkov to make such a basic mistake. No, if Five were going to find Lachlan Kite, they were going to have to do it the hard way. That meant Tomkins sitting on his arse in the driving seat of a banged-up Ford Mondeo for the next nine hours while everyone else on the team got some precious sleep. Tomkins felt the injustice of his predicament as a personal slight. What the hell had he done to merit working the night shift? Why was it always Cara who got the sweet gigs—dressing up and going to the funeral—while he was forced to sit around and wait and pick up the dregs of the operation? It wasn't even as if Zoltan was particularly useful to them. Tomkins was 99 per cent certain that the Iranians were going to kill Kite. On that basis, everything he did for the next nine hours—the next nine days, the next nine *months*—would likely be a complete waste of his time.

He sat back and looked down at the tablet on the passenger seat. If Pavkov made a call or sent a text, the screen would let him know. If he didn't, it wouldn't—and Tomkins didn't expect it to. He was wearing AirPods which picked up sound on the microphones inside the flat; they also allowed him to answer incoming calls from Vosse. The earpieces left a permanent low static hiss in Tomkins's ears, as well as occasional clicks and snaps of feedback, all of which intensified his annoyance and frustration. While Cara slept a soundless sleep less than two miles away in Hackney Marshes, Tomkins was getting cramp in a stakeout Mondeo with no music to listen to and a Serbian migrant across the street more likely to invite his neighbours round for an all-night barbecue than he was to get on the phone and contact the men who had kidnapped Lachlan Kite.

Tomkins looked up at Zoltan's one-bedroom flat on the second floor of the rundown, Brutalist residential block that the Serbian called home. In a way that he couldn't fully explain to himself, because he had read a lot of books and talked to a lot of intelligent, liberal people, Matt Tomkins didn't like Serbians. When he had first heard the name 'Zoltan Pavkov' from Vosse that afternoon, he had instantly felt a mixture of threat and resentment. It was the same with Bulgarians or Albanians or Romanians: Tomkins's guilty secret was that he didn't like any of them, male or female, young or old. In the same way that his father thought the country was full and there were too many foreigners clogging it up, Tomkins didn't think that anything good or constructive could come from allowing too many more Serbians or Albanians or Romanians to settle in the United Kingdom. He realised that it was wrong to think and feel this way—that it was actually *illegal* to think and feel this way—but he couldn't help himself. He would be fired from MI5 if anyone ever found out. Tomkins wasn't proud of the fact that he resented men like Zoltan Pavkov for taking the UK for a ride, but he secretly hoped to find someone discreet at work—perhaps even a small group of like-minded people—who shared his views.

Tomkins hadn't yet seen Zoltan in the flesh, but he already knew, just by the general tenor of his conversations with Cara

BOX 88

and Vosse, that he was lazy and corrupt and unreliable. Look at the facts. He lived in a shitty one-bedroom flat in Bethnal Green. He drove an illegal third-hand Fiat Punto which would probably blow a tyre and cause an accident if it went any faster than fifty miles per hour on a dual carriageway. He had taken money from MOIS to facilitate the capture of a suspected British intelligence officer and doubtless enjoyed dishing out £250 fines to customers in his car park who turned up five minutes late to retrieve their vehicles. What was the fucking *point* of someone like Zoltan Pavkov being allowed to remain in this country? He was just the right age to be a Balkan war criminal, an associate of Mladić or Karadžić, a soldier party to mass slaughter in Bosnia who had somehow tricked Britain into giving him political asylum, then Right to Remain, then a passport entitling him to exactly the same lifestyle as Londoners whose ancestors had lived in Bethnal Green for three hundred years.

'Chill out,' he whispered, aware that he was allowing himself to become agitated. 'Just chill.'

Tomkins took out his personal mobile and saw that he had received a couple of text messages, one from his mother, the other from a girl he had met on Tinder who didn't know how to read the signals and kept bugging him to meet up, even though she was much fatter than her profile photos and there had been zero chemistry on their one and only date. He was about to start flicking through Tinder, a few left and right swipes just to kill some time and put him back in control, when something caught his eye at the entrance to Zoltan's building.

A light had triggered. Somebody was coming out of the street door carrying a plastic bag and wearing what looked like a beanie. It was a man. He was short and stooped and—from a distance of sixty metres—seemed to match the description Tomkins had been given of Zoltan Pavkov.

'Fuck,' he whispered. His whole upper body tensed up. How

had he missed this? No lights had come on in the flat. There hadn't been a whisper through the AirPods. Then Vosse rang.

'Hello?' said Tomkins, aware that his voice sounded dry and nervous.

'Situation,' Vosse replied. No question mark in the numb inflection of the word, no 'Hi' or 'How are you doing?' Just 'Situation', as if Tomkins was a robot, a kind of MI5 version of Alexa, sitting in a car at one o'clock in the morning waiting to do the bidding of Robert fucking Vosse.

'Excuse me, sir?'

'I said *situation*, Cagney. What's it looking like? Where is our man? Still asleep? Watching *Belgrade Tonight* on the telly? Taking a much-needed shower? Any sign of him in the last ten minutes or can I go to sleep?'

'I think someone just came out, sir. I think it might be him, but I didn't hear anything on the micro—'

Vosse's response was explosive.

'*What?*' he said. 'You *think* someone just came out or you *know* the target is mobile?'

Tomkins looked again. The man in the beanie had stopped on the far side of the street. He was taking something out of his left trouser pocket. If a vehicle came towards him and Pavkov happened to look in Tomkins's direction, his face would light up in the front seat of the Ford like a Halloween pumpkin.

'I'm sure it's him,' he said, trusting his instinct. 'Woollen hat, like you said he was wearing in the car park. Same features, same height. It's a match.'

'Why didn't you tell me?'

'I'm telling you now. It only just happened when you rang.'

Tomkins worked out what was going on: either Zoltan was heading to a prearranged meeting or he had a burner phone inside the flat which he had used to contact the Iranians.

'Looks like he's going for his car,' he told Vosse, catching the glint of a streetlight on a set of keys in Pavkov's left hand. The

BOX 88

target walked away from the Mondeo in the direction of his own vehicle, parked thirty or so metres further away down the street.

'You need to follow him,' said Vosse. 'I'm blind here. All I've got is the microphone in the Fiat. The trace is dead.'

Tomkins was horrified. He lifted the tablet from the passenger seat and keyed through to the live feeds from Zoltan's Fiat Punto. He could see what Vosse could likely see on his own screen in Acton: a descriptor for the dashboard microphone implanted that afternoon, but no signal from the GPS.

'What happened to it?'

'Fuck should I know? Happens too often. These people have one job—give me a trace that works—and they can't do it.'

'Battery must have failed.'

'You *think*?' said Vosse with too much sarcasm for Tomkins's liking. 'What's his position?'

It was pitch-dark on the street and Zoltan had briefly vanished behind a line of parked cars. It occurred to Tomkins that carrying the keys might be a bluff for surveillance: the Iranians could be waiting for him in a second vehicle on an adjacent street. Should he follow on foot or remain in the Mondeo? Why the hell had Vosse left him on his own? Why wasn't Cara here in a backup car instead of fast asleep in Hackney Marshes?

'One zero zero metres down the street. Carrying a plastic bag. Interior lights in the Fiat just came on.'

Zoltan was getting into his car. Tomkins quickly checked the tablet to see if any messages had been sent or calls made from the Serb's mobile but the read-out was predictably blank.

'What's in the bag?' Vosse asked.

Tomkins tuned the AirPods to the mikes inside the Fiat and said: 'I don't know yet, sir.'

'Don't fucking lose him, Cagney. I don't have a fix on whatever phone he's using. There are no other eyes on this except yours. It's old school. No triangulation.'

'I understand that,' Tomkins replied.

He was determined to succeed—to follow Zoltan discreetly, to work out where he was going, to lead Vosse to the Iranians—but at the same time Tomkins was overcome by self-doubt. He knew that he didn't yet possess the skill to tail a moving car without giving himself away. Pavkov was acting in a clandestine manner. He was finally aware of a threat from surveillance. Why else go to the trouble of keeping the lights off inside his bedsit and slipping out in the dead of night with a carrier bag containing who knows what?

'Can you hear that, sir?'

The mikes in the Fiat had caught the sound of Pavkov rustling around in the bag. Tomkins lowered the volume on the AirPods to stop them deafening his eardrums. He frowned as he concentrated on the noises, trying to pick out what was happening.

'I can hear it,' said Vosse. More rustling of plastic, then the noise of something hard banging against a pane of glass. 'What can you see?'

It was against all protocol to sit inside a stationary surveillance vehicle and to train a set of binoculars on a target, but Tomkins did exactly that. He needed an advantage.

'He's doing something to the dashboard,' he told Vosse, adjusting the focus.

'Fuck. Taking out the microphone?'

'Don't know, sir. Unclear.'

The banging and the clattering and the general rustle of plastic continued. Tomkins saw the Serbian repeatedly reach forward towards the windscreen, as if he was trying to attach or remove a sticker from the glass.

'Wait. I've got it.'

He again adjusted the focus and Zoltan's head became crystal clear. The Serb had left the lights on inside the Fiat to help him carry out whatever task he was trying to complete. That was when Tomkins saw the pale blue glow on the screen of a TomTom. Pavkov was busily attaching it to the windscreen.

BOX 88

'I think it's a satnav, sir.'

'Say that again.'

'An old-fashioned TomTom. A GPS. He doesn't have a smart-phone so he's using it for directions.'

'Good for him,' said Vosse. 'But where the fuck is he going? Doesn't help us if he's navigating by the stars or being drawn in by smoke signal. We still don't know his destination.'

Tomkins started the engine on the Ford Mondeo. He had only passed his test eighteen months earlier and wasn't a particularly experienced driver. He had lived in London for the past four years and went everywhere on public transport. If Pavkov ran a red light or got away from him on a dual carriageway, Tomkins didn't trust himself to be able to keep up.

'He's pulling out, sir,' he told Vosse, leaving his headlights off for as long as possible so that Zoltan wouldn't see them flare in his rear-view mirror. 'Maybe Lacey could help? You could wake her up.'

'Fuck that for a game of soldiers,' said Vosse. 'This thing will be over in less than ten minutes. You just stay on his tail, son. You don't let that bastard out of your sight.'

14

Kite had fallen asleep in his blacked-out cell.

He was dreaming of Martha Raine when he heard the key turning in the lock. He woke in the darkness to Isobel's face staring at him from across the pillow, the mirage disrupted by a burst of light from an opened door.

'Time to get up,' Torabi shouted. He was standing next to Strawson. 'WHO WAS BILLY PEELE?'

'What?' said Kite, sitting up. He was sweating and the lights had gone out. He said: 'Torabi?' into the room but there was nobody there.

Kite had dreamed it all: Martha and Isobel, Strawson and Torabi, twisting through his unconscious mind like a helix. He reached down for the plastic bottle and drank some water. He had no idea of the time, no idea how long he had been asleep. He lay back on the bed and closed his eyes. He could still hear Torabi's voice in the fever dream:

Who was Billy Peele?

He was my teacher, but he was more than a teacher.

He was the brother I craved, yet he was not my brother.

He was a father when I had no father. He was my guide and instructor—and every young man needs a mentor.

BOX 88

Billy Peele was everything to me.

* * *

Three days have passed since Xavier has issued Kite with his seemingly innocuous invitation to spend part of the summer holidays at his father's house in Mougins.

The two friends are in a low-roofed, prefabricated Alford classroom at the edge of the school campus, close enough to the racquets building to hear the exhilarating metallic contact of the ball as it echoes and strikes against the stone walls of the court. It is a piercingly clear February morning, nine boys in tailcoats awaiting the start of Double History with William 'Billy' Peele. Cosmo de Paul, who has already taken the Oxbridge exam and requires only two E grades at A level to secure his place, is among them. De Paul is wearing Pop trousers and a Salvador Dalí waistcoat purchased for him by his mother in honour of the recently deceased Catalan surrealist. Leander Saltash, soon to be Kite's opening partner in the cricket first XI, is also in the room, as is Kite's friend, Desmond Elkins, who will be killed fighting for the SAS in Afghanistan fourteen years later.

Peele, as always, is late. The boys, all approaching or past their eighteenth birthdays, are too old to be flicking ink or throwing balls of paper around the classroom. Instead they pass the time boasting about the girls they have snogged at a recent Gatecrasher Ball and the quantities of 'snakebite' they consumed at the weekend in 'Tap', the school pub in which boys are permitted to drink alcohol. At ten to twelve, there is the familiar approaching squeak of Peele's under-oiled bicycle, then a clatter as it topples over outside the classroom. The boys mutter, 'He's here' and return to their desks, looking up in expectation of the great man's arrival.

Seconds later, Billy Peele bursts through the door.

'Gentlemen,' he proclaims. 'I am here to tell you that the most famous spy in the world has fallen off his perch.'

In one continuous movement, Peele slams the door behind

him with the heel of his boot, places a pile of books and essays on his desk, removes a black beak's cloak with the flourish of a matador wielding a cape at Las Ventas and spins it onto a nearby hook.

'The name is no longer Bond, James Bond, gentlemen. Double 0 Seven is dead.'

Peele's head snaps through ninety degrees, scanning the classroom of sleep-deprived students for a reaction to this astonishing newsflash. He is a physically fit, bearded thirty-eight-year-old with tortoiseshell glasses and his uneven, hastily assembled beak's bow-tie looks as though it could do with a wash.

'Is Timothy Dalton dead?' asks one boy.

'Good,' Xavier declares. 'He was shit in *Living Daylights*.'

'Language please, Monsieur Bonnard,' Peele grumbles. 'Language.'

'Not Dalton,' says another student, who will later go on to become MP for North Dorset and a vocal proponent of Brexit. 'Got to be Connery or Roger Moore. Is it one of them, sir?'

An exasperated sigh from Peele, Kite enjoying the show from the back row.

'Don't be so *literal*, Williams.' Peele cleans the whiteboard with an ink-stained Charles and Diana T-towel and clears what sounds like forty overnight Gauloises from his barrel chest. 'Think beyond the proverbial envelope. I said he has "fallen off his perch". An ornithological clue with an old Alfordian link. Any bright sparks out there with the faintest whiff of an idea what on the planet Pluto I'm talking about?'

A sustained silence. Lachlan Kite is as much in the dark as everyone else. To his right, Cosmo de Paul is arranging his books and stationery into neat piles, anxious for the class proper to begin. A levels are scheduled to kick off in less than three months and he wants straight A's for his CV. Peele, in common with every other A-level beak in the school, is supposed to be cramming the boys with every spare minute available.

BOX 88

'Bueller?' says Peele, mimicking the lifeless, energy-sapping teacher in the John Hughes movie and showing off a passable American accent in the process. 'Anyone . . . ? Bueller . . . ?'

At last a hand shoots up, two rows from the front. It is Leander Saltash, who has read every thriller of the last hundred years, from *The Riddle of the Sands* to *The Silence of the Lambs*, from *The Hunt for Red October* to *The Last Good Kiss*.

'I've got it, sir. Not the James Bond of the films but the James Bond of the books. The birdwatcher whose name Ian Fleming stole when he was writing *Casino Royale*. Is that right?'

'Mr Saltash!' Peele bangs a fist on the desk so that two marker pens jump and then roll onto the ground. 'An excellent answer! If you're not running the country by the time you're forty, consider your talents to have been wasted. You would look slightly less fetching with a blue rinse and a handbag than our dear Mrs Thatcher, but it seems a small price to pay.' Sudden eye contact with Kite, a knowing, private glance of the sort Peele bestows on him from time to time. 'Yes, James Bond, the *original* James Bond, American ornithologist and author of that page-turning classic, *Birds of the West Indies*—kites included, no doubt, Master Lachlan—whose seemingly mundane, commonplace name was indeed adopted by Ian Fleming—late of this parish—for the hero of his bewilderingly successful series of espionage capers. This is the man who has indeed gone to the great birdbath in the sky. May he rest in peace.'

Cosmo de Paul raises a hand, exposing a melting clock face on his customised Dalí waistcoat.

'Sir, will you be going over the Seven Years War today?'

'Just a moment, Monsieur du Paul.' It always pleases Kite when Peele deliberately mispronounces his surname. 'I have another announcement to make. Speaking of birdwatchers, it will no doubt please the assembled company to know that an American golden-winged warbler, never before seen on British shores, has been spotted in the car park of a Tesco supermarket in Kent.'

'That's great news, sir,' says Saltash.

'Yes it is, Mister Saltash! Yes it is!' Kite knows that Peele subscribes to the *Spectator* magazine and raids it for titbits that he can share with the boys at the start of each class. For this reason, among others, he always feels that Peele is playing the *role* of an eccentric schoolmaster, both for his own, and for the boys' amusement, rather than showing them any glimpse of his true character and personality. In private, Peele is far less theatrical and in every way more inscrutable.

'Speaking of distinguished novelists, what are the general feelings among you lot about Salman Rushdie and the lovely ayatollah's fatwa? Senor del Paul, before we reintegrate with the Seven Years War, would you deign to comment?'

Cosmo de Paul is a short, reed-thin late developer with a first-class brain and a third-class personality. He will later try to seduce Kite's girlfriend and, within a decade, expose him to the FSB as an intelligence officer. His views on the Rushdie affair are as impatient as they are predictable.

'I think he had it coming, sir.'

Peele looks suitably appalled.

'What do you mean by that?'

'If you walk into a field and poke a sleeping bull with a stick, don't be surprised if it wakes up and tries to kill you.'

'I'm not sure I follow the analogy. Isn't it sleeping *dogs* that we shouldn't be poking with sticks—'

De Paul talks over him.

'Rushdie has written a provocative book that deliberately set out to enrage one of the world's great religions. It's not surprising Muslims are upset.'

'Upset? That's how you would characterise the ayatollah's mood?'

De Paul hesitates. 'More than that, obviously.'

'Upset enough to encourage men to murder? Tell me, does anyone else share Comrade Cosmo's intolerant view? Does it

BOX 88

worry you that books are being burned in the streets of Bradford less than fifty years after the fall of the Third Reich? Does it concern you that a religious fanatic's refusal to tolerate Salman Rushdie's legal right to free speech led directly to the deaths of five men protesting against the *Satanic Verses* in Pakistan last week?'

Silence. Billy Peele is beginning to run out of steam. Unless somebody finds something interesting to say, he'll be forced to abandon Rushdie and return to the death of General James Wolfe at the Battle of Quebec.

'Tell me, Monsieur du Paul,' he says. 'Have you even read *The Satanic Verses*?'

'No, sir. I've been too busy revising.'

'I see.' It is evident from Peele's blank reaction to this excuse that he finds de Paul intolerably annoying. 'Anyone else?'

Peele looks to the back of the room, where Kite is simultaneously enjoying the sight of de Paul wriggling on Peele's hook, but aware that he could be asked at any moment to contribute to the discussion.

'Mr Kite! Give us the Scottish perspective. Your thoughts, please.'

Billy Peele is one of several beaks at Alford who regularly mention Kite's Scottish roots for purposes of comic relief. Kite is still known as 'Jock' and occasionally suffers someone making a joke about bagpipes or haggis or whether he wears boxer shorts under his kilt.

'I think the ayatollah wanted attention and got it, sir,' he replies. 'If the story hadn't been reported so widely, if the newspapers and television stations had just ignored Khomeini for what he is—a leader trying to look like a tough guy to whip up antiwestern feeling—then the whole thing would have gone away.'

'That doesn't seem realistic.' Peele's response is instant, though his expression betrays some interest in Kite's point of view. 'One can hardly ignore a call from the leader of the largest Shia country on earth for all Muslims to assassinate a Booker Prize-winning British writer. Isn't that censorship of a different kind?'

Kite sits forward in his seat and attempts to expand on his answer.

'What I mean is it's a great story, but everybody is overreacting. Nobody has actually read *The Satanic Verses*. Cosmo hasn't. Maybe even Ayatollah Khomeini hasn't. If Rushdie shaved his beard off, took a new surname and changed his address, I doubt if one in ten million Muslims around the world would be able to pick him out of a line-up.'

Peele is stopped in his conversational tracks. A broad smile breaks out on his face as he considers the ramifications of Kite's response.

'What about death squads?' he asks.

'What about them, sir?' Kite replies, not really knowing what 'death squads' constitute in this context.

'The Iranian intelligence service—the MOIS. They would be able to trace him, don't you think?'

'I don't know, sir. Maybe. Depends if the police gave away his new identity or leaked his new address. But it's not like all Muslims are trained assassins carrying around a rifle and a photo of Salman Rushdie hoping they suddenly run into him on the street so they can bump him off. Why should they even do as the ayatollah says? Rushdie's probably perfectly safe. He could still live with his family. He could still write under the same name. Plenty of writers have . . .' Kite loses his way. 'What's the word . . . ?'

'Pseudonyms,' says Cosmo de Paul, looking pleased with himself.

'That's right. Pseudonyms. So let's say Rushdie calls himself Rehan Raza, moves house, changes his kids' schools. Nobody's any the wiser. He could still go on holiday, just with a new passport. He could still meet his friends in the pub, as long as they remember not to call him "Salman".'

BOX 88

Peele looks as if he doesn't know whether to laugh, cry or applaud Kite's chutzpah.

'What about public appearances?' he says. 'What if Mr Rushdie wins an award and wants to go and collect it?'

'No way he could do that,' says Elkins. 'That would blow his cover.'

'Exactly,' says Kite. 'He just needs to be like J.D. Salinger. Nobody knows where he lives or what he looks like. But I bet he has friends and children and lives a pretty normal life wherever he is in America. If the ayatollah reads *Catcher in the Rye* and puts a fatwa on Salinger, apart from maybe changing his phone number and having his post sent to a new address, he can stay exactly where he is.'

Kite turned over on the hard bed, wanting to sleep but knowing that it would only be a matter of time before Torabi's men came into the cell to wake him.

He reached for two of the codeine tablets he had placed under the mattress, swallowing them with the last of the water. He was still troubled by the voice in the dream. He sat on the edge of the bed and placed his head in his hands.

Who was Billy Peele?

William 'Billy' Peele joined Alford as a schoolmaster in the winter of 1986, just in time to assume responsibility for Lachlan Kite's education in O-level history. Quick-witted, good-looking and seemingly a generation younger than the majority of his hidebound, fusty colleagues, Peele was soon worshipped by almost every boy with whom he came into contact. In a school which seemed to positively discriminate towards the recruitment of closeted middle-aged homosexuals, Peele was that rare thing: a bachelor beak who didn't want to fondle teenage boys. Physically fit and a crack shot—he ran the Alford Shooting VIII—he had reportedly served in the Royal Marines before moving into academia. As a straight single man, rumours inevitably circulated about his private life. 'Sex-A-Peele' (as he was nicknamed) had been spotted dining in Chelsea with the married daughter of a retired housemaster. An American student had caught a glimpse of him outside a nightclub in the meatpacking district of Manhattan talking to a woman who 'looked like Iman'. One boy, Christian Bathurst, claimed to have witnessed Billy Peele drinking 'several pints of Guinness' in the Fulham Road in the company of screen legend Richard Harris. Nobody—not even Lachlan Kite—knew what school Peele had been to nor why he had turned his back on a career in the military. It was believed that he had travelled widely in his youth, teaching English as a foreign language in Africa and the Middle East. Some said that he had a tattoo on his back, others that there was a lovechild in Paris. Depending who you spoke to, Peele's parents were either alive and living in Devon or dead and buried in South Africa, heroes of the anti-apartheid struggle murdered by agents of P.W. Botha. Peele was said to have a sister who lived in Australia and a brother who lived in Hong Kong. Sometimes he was an only child, sometimes he was adopted. In short, he was an enigma.

Billy Peele was arguably closer to Lachlan Kite than any other boy in the school. As much as it is possible for a student and his teacher to have such a relationship, Kite and Peele were friends. At least once a week, throughout the last two years of his time at Alford, Kite would visit Peele's flat on Alford High Street, either in the company of a handful of other boys attending a sixth-form tutorial, or in a private capacity. Peele became a confessor of sorts. Though Kite rarely discussed his father's death or spoke in any detail about his relationship with his mother, he nevertheless spent many hours in Peele's company, away from the lockdown rules and creepy inertia of Jones-Lewis's house. Recognising the vast gaps in his pupil's knowledge, Peele took it upon himself to educate Kite in the arts, urging him to read widely—beyond the narrow syllabus of English A level—and to

BOX 88

visit galleries in London, Glasgow and Edinburgh whenever he had the chance. Peele took boys to the cinema in Slough, arranged outings to the theatre in London's West End and accompanied them to football matches at his beloved Upton Park. In the summer of 1988, Peele took Kite and another boy to Lord's to watch the third day of the Test match between England and West Indies. Were it not for Billy Peele, Kite would not have read *Anna Karenina* and *The Naked Ape*, made a pilgrimage to see Rothko's Seagram Murals at the Tate Gallery nor watched *Paris, Texas, Some Like It Hot* and *Dr Strangelove*. Nor would he have witnessed Malcolm Marshall steaming in from the Nursery End and bowling Graham Gooch six runs short of his fifty. He was already the transformational figure in Kite's adolescence, even before he played the central role in orchestrating his recruitment to BOX 88.

Two days after the conversation about the *fatwa* against Salman Rushdie, Kite walked down Alford High Street to Peele's flat for his regular weekly tutorial. Four other boys were due to attend, but Kite was the first to arrive. He rang the doorbell and was invited inside. Peele, who was wearing jeans and what looked like a bottle green Royal Marines sweater, immediately offered him a beer.

'That was fun the other day,' he called out from the kitchen as he pulled a can of Budweiser from the fridge.

'What was?'

'*The Satanic Verses* debate,' Peele replied. 'I liked your take on it. Not a point of view I'd heard before.'

Kite wondered if he was being sarcastic but accepted the Budweiser with a nod of thanks.

'Gnat's piss, that stuff,' said Peele, indicating the can. 'You boys love it because you're all in thrall to American culture. One day you'll know the difference between beer and mineral water.'

'Mum refuses to stock it at the hotel.'

'Then your mother is a wise woman with impeccable taste.'

Kite took a first sip of the Budweiser and looked at all the books on Peele's shelves. He loved being in this room, with its Don McCullin photographs and military memorabilia, a tower of blank videotapes toppling over beside Peele's TV, the trace smell of Gauloises and aftershave. Women had been in this flat. One time Kite had found a scarf under the sofa left by one of Peele's girlfriends; it seemed to him impossibly exciting that a man could own a flat and shelves of books and take a girl to bed. He felt that he could be himself in this place, just as he could always be himself in Peele's company.

'How are your plans coming along for the summer?' Peele asked. He knew that Kite was looking for a job that would make him some fast money before he started university, but they hadn't spoken of it for a while.

'Think I might be going to the South of France,' he replied.

'Oh?'

'Xavier Bonnard's father has inherited a place near Cannes. He's going to be there in August. I might take a train down and hang out.'

Kite was struck by a sudden change in the expression on Peele's face. The moment passed in an instant, but it was as though the mention of Xavier's name had left a mark on him. The doorbell rang. More boys had arrived for the start of the tutorial.

'South of France, eh?' he said, heading for the door. 'August with the Bonnards?'

'Yes.'

'Well well well, Lockie. Sounds like you're going to have a lot of fun.'

15

The original hard copy of the letter Billy Peele wrote to Michael Strawson a day later can still be found in Lachlan Kite's file at The Cathedral. It is dated 27 February 1989. The envelope has no stamp nor postmark; it was delivered to Strawson's home address in Kensington by hand.

Dear Mike

It was very good to see you last week and to discuss things in more detail. Something has come up in connection with our Iranian project which I wanted to run past you. This is of course entirely separate to my work on CONSTELLATION.

As you know, I've been looking at various boys at Alford with an eye on the future. One, in particular, strikes me as someone potentially of enormous talent who could be a great asset to us in years to come.

I may have mentioned his name to you in passing, because I've been his Modern tutor for the last two years. Lachlan Kite. His father, Patrick (who may have been on MI5's radar in Ireland in the seventies) drank himself to death seven years ago. The mother, Cheryl, is a famous beauty who still runs the family hotel on the west coast of Scotland where Paddy met his demise.

(Vodka, cliff—to borrow from Nabokov.) By all accounts she's a rather chilly, if undoubtedly glamorous figure prone to mood explosions of Chernobyl-like intensity. Tends to leave a radio-active cloud of disapproval in her wake which sometimes brings her into conflict with her (only) son.

Lachlan is very bright, tough, charming, a hard worker, by all accounts successful with girls. In my many conversations with him, I sense what I often sense with too many boys at this place: the absence of structure, of the family hearth. In other words, he might respond very positively to the welcoming embrace of BOX.

Something else, which prompted this letter. A slice of pure chance which seems so unlikely, so serendipitous, that we'd be foolish to overlook the possibilities. LB's son, Xavier, is a close friend of Lockie's and has invited him to the South of France in August. In other words, his visit will coincide more or less exactly with the arrival of Eskandarian.

You can perhaps see where I'm heading. It's a risk, but we could have a man on the inside. An eighteen-year-old, yes, but we make a virtue of that. For who would suspect a public schoolboy at the start of his gap year—waiting for his A-level results, smoking, nightclubbing, sleeping till midday—of being anything other than what he appears to be? The potential is limitless. Eyes, ears, bins in the bedrooms, Eskandarian's move-ments, a sense of his mood and personality, the nature of his relationship with LB, possible intel on Lockerbie etc. For one so young, Lachlan is a very sound judge of character. Sees a lot. Feels a lot. Seems too good an opportunity to pass up, no?

The worry, of course, is that Lockie might be outraged and refuse to deceive his friend, but if my reading of his personality is correct, I believe to a high degree of certainty that this would not be the case. Indeed, I think he would leap at the chance, especially if he knew what was at stake in terms of our rela-

BOX 88

tionship with the Iranians and, of course, in preventing further terrorist attacks.

Lachlan is young, yes, but I've never known him to be feeble or crestfallen. This place is so buttoned-up and traditional even the cobwebs are Grade II listed, but he's made a huge success of Alford despite coming from 'the wrong sort of background'.

Let me know what you think. If you want to run your eye over him, he'll be working at his mother's hotel, Killantringan Lodge near Portpatrick, for the bulk of the Easter holidays (give or take one or two days in London at either end). Why not check yourself in and see how he responds to the Strawson treatment?

Speaking of holidays, I hope the General Secretary has packed his sun lotion and a good book. The way things are going—from Stettin in the Baltic to Trieste in the Adriatic—he'll soon be out of a job. Riots in Prague, Solidarity in excelsis, Hungary going multi-party, a pisspoor Russian grain harvest that would make Stalin blush—and full Soviet troop withdrawal from Afghanistan. The end is nigh, Michael!

Yours aye

W.P.

16

Term ended three weeks later. Kite followed his usual pattern of spending a few days in London with friends before reluctantly returning home to work at the hotel. His mother was expecting him back before the final weekend in March to help with the Easter rush. Killantringan was full, she had fired the head waiter for stealing money from the till and Kite was needed as an extra pair of hands both in the kitchen and behind the bar.

He boarded a train at Euston station just after ten o'clock on Good Friday morning, a day later than he had promised to be home, but there had been a party at Mud Club the previous night which he hadn't wanted to miss. Kite had taken Ecstasy for the first time, with Xavier and Des Elkins. An older woman who owned her own flat in Lambs Conduit Street had dragged him home but passed out in the living room just as Kite was taking off his clothes. He had no time to sleep. He knew that it would take him at least ten hours to reach Killantringan from London and that his mother would combust if he arrived home any later than Friday night. He checked his wallet, wondering if he could afford to catch a taxi back to Xavier's house, but realised he had spent every penny he possessed on beer, tequila,

BOX 88

two Ecstasy tablets and the price of entrance to the club. He searched the woman's flat unsuccessfully for loose change— finding a passport in the process which placed her age at twenty-seven—and decided to leave her a note. Still high, still hoping that one day he could come back here and go to bed with her, Kite found a sheet of paper in a kitchen drawer and scribbled: *Hi Alison. You fell asleep. Sorry I had to go but I live in Scotland and need to catch a train. Heading home today. It was really great to meet you. Lachlan x.* He wrote down the number of the hotel but began to worry that if Alison called during the Easter holidays, his mother would answer and let slip that her son was only eighteen years old. It was worth the risk. Kite left the note on the kitchen table and crept out into the street.

It took him an hour and a half to walk from Fitzrovia to Kensington, the last of the Ecstasy wearing off as he passed the Victoria & Albert Museum. He arrived at Xavier's house in Onslow Square just after seven o'clock. Xavier had made it home from Mud Club and was asleep in his clothes upstairs. His mother had bought him a black leather jacket almost identical to the one worn by George Michael on the cover of *Faith*. Xavier, who was sprawled on his bed in artfully-torn, stonewashed Levi 501s and a white T-shirt, had left it on the back of a chair. Kite went through the pockets, borrowed sixty pounds from Xavier's wallet, took a shower, ate a breakfast cooked by the Bonnards' Filipina maid and set off for Euston. As soon as the train had pulled out of the station he fell asleep in his seat, waking only once during the five-hour journey to Glasgow to buy a bacon roll and a much-needed bottle of water.

The first anomaly of that unusual Easter weekend occurred on the coastal train to Stranraer. Kite had boarded the service at Glasgow Central, having called his mother from a phone box to tell her that he would be home by nine.

'Where the hell have you been?' she asked, the sound of a second telephone ringing in the office beside her. Fifteen years in hospitality had softened her accent, but a trace of the East End was always detectable, especially when she lost her temper.

'It's OK, Mum,' Kite replied, feeling oddly numb as he cupped his hand over the receiver to smother the noise of the station. 'I had to go to a birthday—'

'It is *not* OK, Lachlan. You promised me you'd be back last night and I had no way of contacting you. I didn't even know where you were staying—'

'I always stay with Xav—'

'I've got thirty guests in the hotel, another twenty for dinner tonight. Mario turned out to be a bloody thief, so there's nobody here to take orders in the restaurant. I'm simultaneously trying to run the bar, ferry food from the kitchen to the restaurant, turn down the beds upstairs *and* keep a bloody smile on my face for the guests.'

'I'm sorry, I'll be back—'

'Just *get* here.'

Cheryl had hung up before her son had a chance to ask if someone might collect him from the station in Stranraer. Shortly afterwards, having sunk a hangover-busting can of Irn Bru and bought a copy of the *NME* at John Menzies, he boarded the service to Ayr.

It was a damp March evening on the west coast and the smell of the sea seeped through the train, telling Kite that he was home. He sat in an almost-empty carriage towards the back of the train, ticking off the towns through rain-streaked windows: Kilwinning, Irvine, Troon, Prestwick. These were the places of his childhood: grey, lifeless settlements a million miles from the dreaming spires of Alford and the wild child hedonism of Mud Club, Crazy Larry's and 151 on Kings Road. Kite didn't know much about ship-building on the Clyde or the coal industry in Ayrshire, but he knew that whole communities had been eviscerated by a decade of Thatcherism, two generations of men left without work or purpose. It may have been his hangover—too

BOX 88

little sleep and the after-slump of Ecstasy—but at that moment he felt a raw sense of separation from the country of his birth. It was as if he had left Scotland in 1984 as one sort of person and was returning, for the final time, as quite another. In London, surrounded by girls and Pimm's and parties, Kite and his friends tried to emulate the deracinated, coke-addled hipsters in *Bright Lights, Big City* and *Less Than Zero*; rolling towards Killantringan on an empty British Rail train defaced by litter and graffiti, he did not know who he was or what he was meant to be. The dutiful son to a demanding mother? The secret posh boy pretending to be a 'normal' Scottish teenager? He wondered if all of the privilege he had witnessed at Alford— the country houses, the Bentleys parked by chauffeurs on the fourth of June, the skiing holidays in Verbier and Val d'Isère— would become commonplace to him, a day-to-day feature of his adult life. Or perhaps Alford would prove to be just a blip and Kite would return to the world of catering and hospitality, graduating from Edinburgh University in four years' time to help his mother with whatever venture she took on after selling Killantringan.

The trouble started in Ayr where Kite had to change trains. He was obliged to wait on the platform for the service south to Stranraer. A group of three local youths in their early twenties were ragging around in the waiting room, smoking Embassy cigarettes and sharing a half-bottle of Smirnoff. They were wearing tracksuits and trainers and quickly clocked Kite—with his foppish public school haircut and collared shirt—for an outsider. The tallest of them, the ringleader, had a wraparound tattoo on his wrist which spread all the way up to his armpit. He flashed Kite a vicious stare and pointed at his bag.

'What's in there, big man?' he called out from the waiting room.

Kite wasn't afraid of him but knew that if it came to a fight, he was outnumbered.

'Kittens,' he said, immediately finding his old Scottish accent so that 'kittens' sounded like 'cuttens'.

'What's that? You making a joke, pal? You making fun of me and my boys?'

Kite shook his head slowly, felt his heart thump and said: 'Nah. Don't worry.'

'You're a funny man? Is that it? Telling me you got kittens in yer bag when you don't?'

Kite wondered why the hell he had said something so stupid.

'Relax,' he said. 'We're all waiting for the same train. I thought it would make you laugh.'

Kite was worried that his accent would slip, that he'd pronounce certain words in an English way and reveal his secret life in the south.

'I'm very relaxed,' said the leader, looking to his left, where the older of his two companions, a short, muscular skinhead, was rolling a cigarette. 'Pete, are you relaxed?'

'Aye, Danny.'

'Robbie, are you relaxed?'

'Aye, Dan. Very relaxed.'

There was nobody else on the platform. Just Kite standing outside a waiting room being sized up by three drunk Scots who would likely beat him up and steal his Walkman if they had the chance. Kite moved further along the platform, but Danny saw this and followed him, Robbie and Pete close behind. It was like being surrounded by a pack of hyenas on the scent of their prey. Kite knew that he couldn't run, that it was important to stand his ground, but he had heard stories of flick knives and muggings and wondered what it would take to make them walk away.

'Got a smoke, pal?' said the leader, coming right up into his face. He had a gold stud earring in his left ear and a Beastie Boys VW necklace. His breath stank of alcohol. Kite winced as he thought of his father.

'Maybe,' he replied.

BOX 88

At that moment, the Stranraer train came south through the sea mist hanging low over the tracks. Nobody spoke as it drew in beside them. There were four carriages, all seemingly empty. Kite had a packet of Marlboro Reds in his jacket pocket but reckoned Danny would grab the whole thing if he took it out and offered him one.

'Where you off to, big man?'

'Stranraer,' Kite replied, forgetting how to give the name a Scottish inflection. 'You?'

'None of yer' fuckin' business, ya' cunt.'

They were standing between two of the carriages. Kite felt his chest contract and walked to the left, expecting the youths to follow him, but either Robbie or Pete—Kite couldn't tell which—suddenly hissed and whispered: 'Hang on, Dan. Check this.' To his surprise they then boarded the carriage next door, laughing gleefully as they did so, leaving Kite alone. Something must have caught their eye: a new target, a new figure of fun. He felt a wave of relief, particularly when he saw that there was an elderly man a few seats away reading the *Glasgow Herald*. There surely wouldn't be any trouble while he was around. He wouldn't let an eighteen-year-old kid get beaten up in plain sight. Kite was safe. The train pulled away from the platform and he sat down.

Then the situation deteriorated.

Through the doors that separated Kite's carriage from the rear of the train, he could see the three young men gathered around a table. They were speaking to somebody. Pete was on his feet, laughing and swigging from the bottle of Smirnoff. Danny and Robbie had sat down. Kite saw that they were talking to a young black woman. A non-white face on the west coast of Scotland was as rare as a non-white face in the classrooms and playing fields of Alford. They had chosen their next target.

Kite stood up and looked more closely through the doors. The woman was trapped at the table with Robbie beside her and

Danny in the facing seat. She was about thirty and looked frightened. Kite checked the rest of her carriage. There was nobody else around. He was tired and hungover and dreading the long Easter shift ahead of him, but knew that he had to do something. His father would have expected it. It was the way Paddy Kite had raised his son.

'Excuse me,' he called out to the old man. His Alford accent had returned. He hadn't bothered to smother it. 'I think a woman might be getting hassled next door. Will you keep an eye on me?'

The old man, who was wearing a black anorak and a cloth cap, barely acknowledged what Kite had said. He didn't want any trouble, didn't want to get involved. Kite shouldered his bag and opened the first of two connecting doors. The train rocked through a set of points and he almost lost his balance as he opened the second door and entered the carriage. He heard Robbie saying: 'No, come on. Where are you from, darlin'?' as he was hit by a rancid smell of stale vomit and spilled beer. Pete had now sat down. The woman was surrounded.

'How's it going here?' Kite called out as casually as possible, finding his Scottish accent. 'Everything OK?'

Danny was startled to see Kite coming towards him. Kite put his bag on a nearby seat, removed the set of Walkman headphones from his neck and zipped them inside an outer pocket.

'You asked me for a cigarette,' he said, tapping his jacket. 'I found some more.'

He looked at the woman. It was impossible to tell from her expression if she was relieved that Kite had come to help her or if she believed that he was a friend of the men who had surrounded her and was coming to join in the fun.

'We're OK thanks, pal,' Danny replied.

'So what's going on?' Kite asked. 'Are you all friends?'

He was beside the table now, a sheen of sweat inside his shirt, his heart racing, but determined not to appear scared or weak.

BOX 88

'No. Are youse friends?' Danny asked.

'She your sister?' Robbie added, and the three hyenas erupted in laughter.

Kite decided to speak to the woman directly.

'Are you OK?' he said.

She was too frightened to reply.

'You still havenae told us where you're from, darlin',' said Pete, ignoring Kite as he finished the last of the vodka. Kite could feel Danny bristling and looked down at his tattoo. He wondered what it would feel like to be punched by an arm that size. There were three black students out of twelve hundred and fifty boys at Alford. One was the son of an African politician, another an American from New York, the last a scholarship boy from London. During a football match in 1987, Cosmo de Paul, whose grandfather and great-grandfather had been at the school, had called him a 'fucking nigger' but had not been expelled. Kite thought of that now as he tried to defuse the situation as best he could.

'If you don't know her,' he said, 'why are you hassling her?'

'Hassling her?' said Danny, making a mockery of the word. 'How come it's your business anyway, you posh cunt?'

'I don't like bullies,' Kite replied, suddenly very frightened. He was amazed, and oddly humiliated, that he had been identified as posh. If any of these men was carrying a knife they surely now would not hesitate to use it.

'I don't give a ratsy fuck what you do and do not like, pal, ken?'

'Leave him alone,' said the woman. She had a pronounced West African accent and a desperate look in her eyes.

There was a collective sarcastic sigh, then a long romantic 'ooooh' as the three men mocked what she had said. Pete made a kissing sound with pursed lips. A wild, joker's grin spread out across Danny's face. Robbie gleefully shouted: 'They're in love, Dan. He fancies a fuckin' black bird.'

Kite was breathing the vodka, the same nauseating chemical stench he remembered smelling a hundred times on his father's breath. He knew that he only had to survive for another three or four minutes before the train reached the next stop at Maybole and he could get help. There might be more passengers on the platform, perhaps a stationmaster who could get the situation under control.

'It's sad what's going on here,' he said, trying to reassure the woman with his eyes.

Again Danny pounced on his choice of words.

'Sad, is it? Are you gonna cry? Is that what's gonna happen, ya' fuck?'

If Kite had been less hungover, if there had been two of them, not three, if he had been sure that they weren't carrying knives, he would have thrown a punch at this moment, just as he had decked Richard Duff-Surtees three years earlier with a sweet right hook at fly-half. But his physical courage deserted him. He knew that he was going to have to stand his ground and try to win the fight with patience and words.

'I'm not going to cry,' he said. 'I'm not frightened by you. I think you're the ones who are weak. What's a woman on her own supposed to do when—'

'A black woman, mind,' Robbie interjected, but his response sounded oddly feeble.

Pete began to sing the refrain from an advert Kite had seen on the TV for fruit juice: '*Um Bongo, Um Bongo, they drink it in Um Congo.*' Robbie laughed wildly at this and joined in, saying: 'Aye, she probably wants a banana.'

'It doesn't matter where she's from or what colour her skin is,' Kite answered, watching Danny very carefully because he was waiting for him to stand up and strike. 'There's three of you. One of her. She's not causing trouble. Pick on someone else.'

As if Kite had pressed a button, Robbie and Pete immediately

BOX 88

stood up out of their seats and turned to him, Danny doing the same and saying: 'OK, big man. We'll pick on you then.'

'No!' the woman shouted, but she did not move from her seat. Kite backed away, praying that the train, which seemed to be slowing down, was coming into Maybole. The three men had formed a sort of column and were following him towards the back of the train, closing down the space. Kite couldn't go left. He couldn't go right. He was trapped. Danny hawked up a ball of phlegm from his lungs and spat it at his feet.

'Tickets please, gentlemen!'

All of them looked towards the front of the carriage. A ticket inspector had entered at the far end. He was at least fifty and recognised immediately that there was a problem.

'What's goin' on here?' he shouted.

'Fuckin' nothing, man,' Pete muttered.

'Just havin' a wee chat with our pal here,' said Danny.

They scuttled back like boys caught smoking cigarettes in the woods at Alford, all blank faces and innocence, leaving Kite with a decision either to grass them up or hope that they left the train at Maybole.

'Are you all right?' said the inspector. The woman had come out from behind the table and was standing near the central door of the carriage.

'I'm fine,' she said. 'Everything's fine.'

Kite saw the lights of Maybole up ahead. He had never been more relieved in his life.

'You getting off here?' the inspector asked. He had directed the question at the woman, but Danny said: 'Aye, we're getting off. Nay bother.'

'My husband is meeting me,' the woman answered, loud enough for the youths to hear.

Kite realised he was in the clear. Everyone was leaving. The woman would be safe in Maybole. Her husband was probably waiting for her on the platform.

'OK,' said the inspector. 'So let's get going, gentlemen, please, before I find out any more about what was happening here. Gather your belongings and be on your away.'

Laughing and jostling one another, without a further word either to Kite or the woman, the men opened the door onto the platform and stepped off the train. The woman waited until they were several metres away then spoke to Kite.

'Thank you,' she said. 'You were very brave.'

'No problem,' Kite replied. He felt a wave of satisfaction as euphoric as the first surges of Ecstasy on the dance floor at Mud Club. 'Take care of yourself.'

A white man in a business suit was waiting on the platform, looking up expectantly. Very slowly, the woman stepped down from the train and walked towards him. As he hugged her, Kite saw the woman begin to sob as she slumped in his arms. The ticket inspector turned to Kite.

'She's a long way from home,' he said.

Kite had neither the will nor the presence of mind to find an adequate reply. He merely showed the man his ticket, went back to his bag, and sat down.

An hour later he was in a taxi passing through the outskirts of Stranraer, heading out towards the ocean on dark, empty Wigtownshire roads. Kite had phoned the hotel from the station to let his mother know that he had arrived, but nobody had answered.

'You look bloody awful,' she said when he walked through the staff entrance just after eight o'clock. 'Have you had *any* sleep at all?'

Cheryl gave her son a perfunctory hug but work was on her mind and she quickly returned to the restaurant. Kite was past the age at which he consciously longed for his mother's embrace, yet would have welcomed even the slightest display of tenderness or excitement at his arrival. Instead she said: 'As soon as you've

BOX 88

got changed you can turn down the beds in Adam, Bay and Churchill, then take over from Paolo in the bar.' There was no opportunity to tell her what had happened on the train, no questions about his journey or an offer of something to eat. It was left to the other members of staff to greet him more warmly. The chef, John, and his number two, Kenny, looked up from their work and grinned, Kenny saying: 'There he is, the man from Atlantis. Welcome home, Lockie,' as Moira, a roly-poly waitress who had worked at the hotel since the mid-seventies, came into the kitchen and nearly dropped a tray of dirty plates in surprise.

'Lockie! We didnae know you was coming tonight. How's my favourite boy?'

Kite briefly disappeared into Moira's vast bosom and felt the scrape of facial hair against his cheek as she kissed him. There was little time to loiter and chat. John called out 'Service!' and Moira was soon ferrying two bowls of seafood stew back to the restaurant. Kite withdrew to the staff area, found a clean white shirt and a pair of black trousers, shaved with a Bic razor and applied some deodorant to his armpits. The remains of staff dinner were congealing at room temperature on a Formica table: a foil tray of lasagne, a few dehydrated kernels of sweetcorn and a Tupperware box of salad, comprised mostly of red onions and damp chunks of iceberg lettuce. Kite was famished and wolfed the remains of the lasagne, washed down with a hair-of-the-dog can of Heineken discovered at the back of the fridge. By eight-thirty he was on the back stairs, heading up towards Adam, the smallest of the hotel's twelve rooms, located directly above the vast walk-in fridge used by the chefs to store fresh fish, cuts of meat, dairy products and puddings.

Turning down the beds during dinner had been Kite's first job at the hotel as a child. When his father was still alive, he had dutifully gone from room to room, straightening out bedspreads and plumping up pillows, tipping out ashtrays and wiping them clean with a tissue. For each bed he was paid a flat fee of twenty pence, which he normally spent on sweets in Portpatrick. When Kite was thirteen, his mother had told him: 'Always watch out for the way people talk to waiters in restaurants. If they're rude or surly, don't have anything to do with them.' This observation had resonated with him and, as he grew older, Kite realised that he could learn a lot about people simply by studying how they behaved. Each bedroom on his nightly errands, for example, told Kite a different story about its occupants: sheets crumpled and discoloured by sex; letters and business papers left out on desks for prying eyes; money and jewellery scattered on the tops of dressing tables and spilling out of suitcases. An individual's interests could be gauged by the books they were reading, their standard of living by the quality of their clothes and the value of their belongings. American guests were the easiest to spot: they came in droves during the summer months, armed with golfing magazines and books about their Scottish ancestors, and always tipped fabulous amounts of money if Kite found them in their room during his nightly rounds. In time, however, without ever hearing them open their mouths, the young Kite reckoned he could tell if a guest at Killantringan was French or British, American or Italian, married or single, happy or depressed. Even now, as an experienced old hand armed with a duster and a hangover, he secretly looked forward to snooping in the various rooms to which his mother had sent him. He cleaned Adam in under five minutes, concluding that its occupant was a single, possibly lonely woman from Dusseldorf with interests in fishing and Communist Eastern Europe: there was a spinning rod propped up against the wall and her West German passport bore stamps from Poland, Yugoslavia and Romania. She was reading a romance novel (in English) and was midway through a bottle of medium sweet sherry which she had left on the windowsill to chill.

Having locked up, Kite walked the short distance to Churchill. The room was so named because it was alleged that the British prime minister had stayed at Killantringan during the Second

BOX 88

World War, meeting General Eisenhower for secret talks about the D-Day landings. When Kite knocked on the door, he heard a deep, full-throated American calling out 'just a moment please' and was preparing to say: 'I'll come back later' when a huge bear of a man, Churchillian in girth and stature, opened the door. The man was at least fifty and held a tumbler of whisky in his left hand. He looked surprised to see Kite standing in front of him and was momentarily lost for words.

'I beg your pardon, sir,' said Kite. 'I just wondered if you needed your bed turning down?'

'Ah!' the American replied instantly. 'You must be young Lachlan.' With his steady blue eyes and the flicker of a smile, he appeared to be sizing him up. There was a list of residents on a clipboard downstairs with the names of the guests staying at Killantringan. Kite hadn't had time to check it and consequently had no idea who he was speaking to. He assumed the American was a WASP golfer from New England or Florida with plans to play rounds at Troon and Turnberry: there was a set of clubs in the hall behind him. 'Your mother has told me so much about you,' he said. 'You were expected last night, is that right?'

'Er, that's right, sir. I was held up in London.'

'Party?' the man asked with a grin.

Kite wondered why he was being so familiar. Was he one of his mother's lovers?

'A party, yes. A friend of mine's eighteenth.'

'Not to be missed, then, huh?'

The American set his tumbler of whisky down on a low table and, to Kite's surprise, reached out to shake his hand.

'My first time staying at Killantringan,' he said. 'Love what your mother has created here.' His grip was dry and enveloping, the lines on his face partially hidden beneath a scattering of salt-and-pepper stubble. 'Very good to meet the son and heir to all this. My name's Strawson. Michael Strawson. You can call me Mike.'

17

'You just stay on his tail, son. You don't let that bastard out of your sight.'

Vosse's words rang in Matt Tomkins's AirPods as he followed Zoltan Pavkov through the back streets of Bethnal Green. He was convinced Vosse would never have spoken to Cara or Tess like that; he wouldn't want to risk accusations of misogyny or—worse—a ticking off from Personnel for using aggressive language around female colleagues. Yet apparently it was OK to patronise Matt Tomkins and call him 'son', just as it was fine to stick him on the night watch while everyone else on the team got a prized night's sleep. The rules were different for white men. Tomkins was in the minority now.

He had been driving without lights for more than half a mile, keeping at least fifty metres back from the Punto to reduce the risk of Pavkov spotting him in his mirrors. At last, turning east onto Whitechapel Road, Tomkins switched on the headlights as he joined a group of four vehicles bunched behind the target.

'How are you doing?' Vosse asked. His voice was like a kettle-drum in Tomkins's ears. He wished he could cut him off and just get on with the follow. It was hard enough trying to antic-

BOX 88

ipate where Pavkov was going without the boss bugging him every thirty seconds.

'Heading east on Whitechapel Road, sir. I'm concealed behind a black cab. I don't think he's spotted me yet. I think I'm cool.'

'I'll be the judge of that,' said Vosse. It didn't sound like one of his jokes. 'I can see your position. The Iranians have obviously given him a meeting point. Hence the satnav. You've got to stay on his tail, Cagney. Don't do anything stupid.'

At that precise moment, Tomkins stalled. He couldn't believe it. His foot came off the clutch too quickly and the Mondeo's engine just seemed to give out from beneath him. There was nobody on the street to witness his humiliation, yet Tomkins felt that all of London was looking in and laughing at him. As he turned the key in the ignition, Vosse said: 'What was that?' and Tomkins lied, saying that the car alongside had stalled in traffic. He pulled away moments later, thankfully with no distance lost, still three cars back from Pavkov.

'He could be heading for Limehouse,' Vosse suggested. Tomkins remembered that 'Kidson Electrical Services' had last been sighted on East India Dock Road, which was a mile to the south-east.

'It's a maze down there,' he replied, trying to build in an excuse if he lost Pavkov in the high-rise labyrinth of Canary Wharf. 'Nowhere to hide if he's going into one of the car parks.'

'Just concentrate and do your job. The whole city is a fucking maze, Cagney.'

Again Tomkins told himself that Vosse wouldn't have spoken to Cara that way: wouldn't have sworn, wouldn't have lost his temper. That was because Cara was special. Cara was a woman. Vosse tiptoed around her, just like he tiptoed around Tess.

'Shit.'

'What's happened?' Vosse asked.

The Serb had made a right-hand turn up ahead, through a set of lights which had moved swiftly from green to amber.

Tomkins accelerated to the junction and ran the red light, keeping Pavkov in his line of sight as he explained what had happened.

'OK, good,' said Vosse. 'You're passing Stepney Green. That means Limehouse is still on. That means Canary Wharf could be his ultimate destination.' There was a gasp of pleasure in Tomkins's AirPods. 'He's taking us to the nerve centre, Cagney. He's leading us all the way to BIRD. These people are fucking idiots. Don't lose sight of him and we'll have all of them in custody by the time the sun comes up.'

The Punto suddenly lurched into a lay-by fifty metres ahead, hazard lights morsing. Pavkov had not indicated. There had been no warning at all that he was going to pull over.

'Fuck!' said Tomkins.

'What's happened?'

'Target stopped. I had to drive past him. If I'd braked, he'd have seen me.'

'OK, OK,' Vosse replied. Tomkins was simultaneously trying to negotiate the traffic in front of him and looking back in his mirrors at Zoltan's position. 'I'm searching routes for you. Don't do anything stupid.'

Being told that for what must have been the fourth time riled Tomkins so much that he decided to take matters into his own hands. Rather than wait at the next set of lights, in the hope that Pavkov would follow, he turned left onto a quiet residential street perpendicular to Stepney Green. He intended to circle back in an anti-clockwise loop which would surely bring him up behind the Punto in less than ninety seconds.

'Where are you going?' Vosse asked. There was a distinct note of worry in his voice.

Tomkins looked at the map on the dashboard of the Ford Mondeo and realised that he had done something very foolish. There was no way of getting onto Stepney Green without going all the way back up to Whitechapel Road. He would have to stop and do a three-point turn. Meanwhile Pavkov was out of

BOX 88

his line of sight, at least two hundred metres behind him and ready to drive off at any moment.

Vosse was going apoplectic in his ear.

'You can't get back round! Fucking hell, Cagney. I told you I was looking at routes. I told you not to do anything stupid. You're going to lose him.'

Tomkins felt as though a small bird had flown in through the back window and been let loose inside the car. He could not seem to clear his head to make a decision of any kind. He wanted to ask Vosse to stop shouting at him, to stop telling him not to do anything stupid. Should he execute a U-turn? Should he drive all the way back up to Whitechapel Road and just hope that Pavkov was still parked in the lay-by? The whole thing was so shameful and embarrassing. Tomkins momentarily went into a blank white panic, a kind of system shut-down from which there was no escape. He could not function. He had been trained to deal with pressure, but his training had let him down. Why the hell had he turned off the road? *I'm good at exams*, he told himself, slipping into self-pity. *I sailed through all the tests and interviews to get into MI5.* The moment he had been put under any sort of operational pressure, he had cracked. Tomkins wished he could be out of the car and back at home, sitting on the edge of his bed or on a stool, lifting dumbbells in the mirror. That was his happiest, purest state. He always felt good about himself when he could see his body reflected back at him, the firmness of his abs, remembering the voices of the women who had complimented him on the way he kept himself in shape. But he wasn't back at home. He was messing up a surveillance operation in a shitty Ford Mondeo with Robert Vosse raging in his ear.

'What do you think I should do?' he asked.

'Wait,' Vosse replied in a firm, optimistic tone of voice. Something in his manner had changed. Tomkins was given sudden renewed hope that the operation had not been entirely ruined. 'Listen,' Vosse added.

Tomkins heard a tertiary noise in his AirPods, the sound of movement inside the Fiat Punto picked up by the MI5 mikes. Pavkov was scrabbling around, the same banging and clattering and rustle of plastic as before.

'Did you hear that?' Vosse asked.

'Yes, sir,' Tomkins replied but, to his horror, heard the note change of the Serb switching on the engine. Pavkov was preparing to drive off. Tomkins finally came to his senses and executed a rapid U-turn, but as he reached the set of lights at the junction with Stepney Green, there was no sign of the Punto either to the left or the right. Pavkov had disappeared.

'I can't see him, sir.'

'Fuck!' said Vosse. 'Fucking fuck. You've lost him.'

Where had he gone? How had Zoltan vanished into thin air?

It was like the bird had been set loose inside the car again. Tomkins had visions of the Iranians laughing at him as Pavkov pulled up at his secret destination, mocking the incompetence of MI5 and gloating over the imminent death of the hostage, Lachlan Kite.

Then—a miracle.

A voice on the microphone inside the Fiat. Not the Serb's, not a passenger he had picked up. Another sort of third party altogether.

Directions for number 19 Spindrift Avenue, London E14 9US

It was the voice of the satnav. Pavkov, the stone-cold idiot, had typed in the address given to him by the Iranians. The Tom-Tom had dictated that address to the Punto microphones.

'Bingo,' said Vosse. 'High noon on Spindrift Avenue. That's where they're holding BIRD. Get as close as you can, Cagney. I'll meet you there ASAP.'

18

Cheryl Kite may have believed that you could tell a lot about a person by the way they treated staff in restaurants, but Michael Strawson had a rather more developed and exhaustive philosophy of human nature. He reckoned everything you needed to know about an individual's character and temperament would be revealed by round-the-clock surveillance.

For this reason he had put the eighteen-year-old Lachlan Kite under light, Grade III observation for a forty-eight-hour period prior to his arrival at Killantringan. Rita Ayinde, one of the surveillance Falcons at BOX 88 in London, had telephoned Strawson from Maybole station with the second of her two reports into the target's movements and behaviour. The first had given Strawson little to chew on. Rita told her boss that Kite had spent the better part of Wednesday inside Xavier Bonnard's house, venturing out only for lunch with friends at the Stockpot restaurant and to watch *Dangerous Liaisons* at a cinema on Fulham Road. The following morning, having apparently stayed up most of the night playing computer games, Kite and Xavier had slept past midday, gone for a smoke and a walk in Hyde Park, then attended an eighteenth birthday party at Borscht & Tears, a Russian restaurant on Beauchamp Place. From there Kite's friends

159

had moved on to Mud Club on Charing Cross Road. Drugs were available on the premises but the surveillance officer on duty had not observed Kite in the act of buying or consuming narcotics. The target had gone home with a woman identified as Alison Hackford, a twenty-seven-year-old estate agent with Knight, Frank & Rutley, leaving her apartment on Lamb's Conduit Street shortly before dawn and proceeding on foot to the Bonnard residence. It was not known why Kite had not taken a taxi or public transport. Strawson, who had lost a son to heroin, hated drugs and wondered if Kite might have been high; Rita suggested that he may simply have run out of money to pay for a bus fare.

'Then he should have been smart enough to talk his way into a free ride,' Strawson replied.

From day one, he had been sceptical about Lachlan Kite. It wasn't just the risk of using an untested teenager on an operation of such importance; it was making a private citizen conscious of BOX 88's interest in Ali Eskandarian. What if Kite said no? What if he refused to betray Xavier's trust and consequently put the operation in danger? Yet Billy Peele's recommendation had been so effusive, and the opportunity to observe Eskandarian at close quarters so tempting, that Strawson had decided to take the chance. He would look at Kite over the Easter weekend, test him in his home environment, assess his suitability for the job and let Peele know of his decision.

It was the second telephone call from Maybole which persuaded Strawson that Kite was possessed of huge potential. With Rita role-playing a lone Nigerian woman on the Stranraer train, and three local assets hired to scare her, Kite had displayed calmness and courage in defusing a possibly dangerous and violent situation.

'He was scared,' she told Strawson, 'but he didn't back down. He could have stayed in the next carriage and ignored what was happening. He didn't do that. I like him. He's a brave boy.'

Bravery only gets you so far in this business, Strawson

BOX 88

reflected, sitting in his room at Killantringan. If politeness or sentimentality had provoked Kite's reaction, then he likely wasn't the right fit for BOX 88. Nor was Strawson interested in a gung-ho, crusading macho man. If France was going to work, he needed Kite to be calm and level-headed; to be possessed of a sense of right and wrong, yes, but also to be able to stand down without losing face whenever the odds were stacked against him. He was impressed that Kite had come to the aid of a seemingly defence-less black woman sitting alone on a train, but wondered what might have happened had three genuine Scottish racists, armed with acid or knives, responded differently to Kite's approach.

There was a knock at the door. Strawson called out 'Just a moment, please' and went to open it. To his great surprise, Lachlan Kite was standing in front of him.

'I beg your pardon, sir. I just wondered if you needed your bed turning down?'

Strawson could read a lot into a face and quickly assessed the young man about whom he had heard and read so much.

'Ah! You must be young Lachlan,' he said, struck by the fact that Kite looked older than the photographs Strawson had seen. He looked tired, but alert and physically fit. Perhaps that partly explained why he had been able to seduce a woman almost ten years his senior the night before.

'Your mother has told me so much about you,' he said. 'You were expected last night, is that right?'

'Er, that's right, sir. I was held up in London.'

You sure were, thought Strawson, and wondered if the lines around Kite's eyes, the erratically shaved five o'clock shadow, were a consequence of taking drugs at Mud Club or an indi-cation that Kite was developing his father's fondness for the bottle. If either was the case, BOX 88 would have nothing to do with him.

'Party?' he asked, wondering what sort of answer Kite would give.

'Yes. A friend of mine's eighteenth.'

Kite's manner was efficient and polite, to the point of obse-quiousness, which Strawson assumed was either a by-product of his education—Alford College prided itself on churning out charming, Establishment-ready smooth-talkers—or merely a role Kite played whenever he found himself addressing guests at the hotel. There was something hidden in his expression, a sadness at the back of the eyes.

'Not to be missed, then, huh?'

Kite didn't appear to feel ashamed or remorseful about what-ever it was he had done the night before. A different sort of adolescent might have lied or tried to boast about it. Strawson shook his hand. Eye contact, a friendly smile, a decent grip: all the things that Alford taught its fee-paying boys, but welcome nonetheless. Strawson had the sense of a young man of strong character possessed of what people liked to call 'an old soul'. He instinctively liked him.

'My first time staying at Killantringan,' he said. 'Love what your mother has created here. Very good to meet the son and heir to all this. My name's Strawson. Michael Strawson. You can call me Mike.'

'Lachlan,' said Kite. 'Or Lockie. Whatever you prefer.'

Kite was not to know it, but with the Stranraer train behind him, and no slip-ups under surveillance, he had passed the first phase of the BOX 88 assessment. Now Strawson needed to test his basic observational skills and, more importantly, his honesty. Was Lachlan Kite tuned in to his surroundings or—in common with most teens of his age—zoned out in an off-world adolescent orbit, daydreaming of girls and drink and parties? Was he the kind of young man who would lie and steal if he thought he could get away with it; or was there an internal code of honour, a basic sense of right and wrong?

Preparing the room was simple enough. He told Kite that he

BOX 88

did not need his bed to be turned down and sent him on his way. Strawson then closed the door, scrambled the tuning on his television, pulled the aerial cable out of the wall and left a £20 note visible under the bed.

Next, he put his glasses behind a vase of flowers on the windowsill, dragged a side table into the bathroom and set a lamp on top of it, making sure to plug in the extension lead at the wall. He left a half-finished cup of black coffee balanced precariously on the sink and a money clip containing exactly two hundred pounds in low denomination notes on a nearby shelf. If Kite later came back to the room when Strawson wasn't there to pocket a couple of twenties, he would know that Billy Peele's boy was nothing but a common thief, abandon any possibility of recruiting Kite for France, play a round of golf at Turnberry and treat the rest of the Easter weekend as a well-deserved vacation.

19

Kite had finished tidying the last of the three rooms and was walking back towards the rear staircase when the American in Churchill popped his head out of the door and said:

'Hey. Seeing as you're here, could you help me with something? I got a problem with my TV, Lachlan.'

'Of course,' Kite replied.

The American held the door open so that Kite could enter the room then closed it behind him with a gentle click. Kite had a flash memory of 'Jumpy' Jones-Lewis entering his bedroom at Alford without knocking, hoping for a snatched glimpse of thigh or stomach, but didn't get a creepy vibe from Strawson, who seemed harmless and hearty. Besides, there was a framed photograph of a woman Kite assumed to be his wife balanced on the bedside table next to a *Good News Bible* and a hardback copy of *The Satanic Verses*. Kite had never seen one before and wanted to pick it up.

'Have you just arrived, sir?' he asked, because his mother had long ago taught him that it was important to make small talk with guests.

'Just got in yesterday,' Strawson replied. 'Flew into Prestwick.'

'And you're on your own?'

BOX 88

The bed had only been disturbed on one side. Kite had also clocked the absence of women's clothing in the room. Sometimes his love of detection, his fascination with the minutiae of strangers' lives, got the better of him.

'That's right. My wife is back in London. We live over here actually.'

Kite had work to do in the bar and didn't want to get caught in a lengthy conversation, so he said, 'Ah, right', and asked what was wrong with the television.

'Can't seem to find any channels,' Strawson replied. 'Doesn't help that I can't find my glasses anyplace.'

Within three minutes Kite had worked out the problem: not only had somebody scrambled the tuning on the television, they had also removed the aerial from its socket in the wall. He fixed both, spotted Strawson's glasses behind a vase of flowers on the windowsill, and asked if the American needed help with anything else.

'Just something in the bathroom,' he replied, indicating that there was a problem with one of the taps.

Kite followed Strawson into the bathroom, noticing a stray £20 note under the bed. He bent down to pick it up.

'Don't lose this,' he said, setting it on the bed.

There was more money in the bathroom, a roll of notes in a clip on the shelf beside the window. Kite could have used the cash to pay back Xavier but would never have countenanced stealing from a guest. He didn't trust some of the other staff in the hotel to be so honourable and told Strawson about the hotel safe.

'So is it true?' the American asked, having pocketed the money.

'Is what true, sir?'

'That the great man stayed here?'

They were standing in front of the large, free-standing bath in which Sir Winston had allegedly immersed himself in 1943.

'As far as I know,' Kite replied. He had never been sure if

Churchill's visit to Killantringan was bona fide, or if it had been invented by his father as a PR stunt to drum up custom. 'Further up the coast there's Culzean Castle,' he said, 'where your President Eisenhower stayed several times.'

'Is that right?' Strawson replied.

Yanks always loved hearing that.

Strawson indicated that the hot tap on the bath was stuck. Kite released it easily and also moved a coffee cup which was at risk of falling into the sink and smashing. To his consternation he saw that a side table had been dragged into the bathroom with a free-standing lamp balanced on top of it. If the lamp fell into the water while Strawson was taking a bath, he would find himself travelling back to Prestwick airport in a coffin.

'Sir, can I suggest that you don't leave that lamp there?' He explained the danger of electrocution if the socket came into contact with the bathwater, trying not to sound too condescending. The American cursed his stupidity, thanked Kite for his 'presence of mind' and showed him to the door.

'Will there be anything else, sir?' Kite asked. He could feel his mother growing impatient downstairs.

'Not for the moment, thank you,' Strawson replied. 'This has been very instructive.'

20

All the way to Spindrift Avenue, Matt Tomkins had felt a serene sense of achievement and inner peace. Zoltan's satnav had saved the day, every road, every turn and instruction dictated to his AirPods courtesy of the microphones in the Fiat Punto.

Turn left onto Upper Bank Street

As a pleasing coincidence, Tomkins's route had taken him past a bar in Mile End where, almost a year earlier, he had attended a birthday party with some old school friends. The men had been competing about what car they drove, where they went on holiday, how much money they were making in start-ups or the City. They'd asked Tomkins what he was doing, and he'd given them his usual civil service cover, working at the Ministry of Defence, downsizing regiments, the usual lies and bullshit. There had been sneers from the men about his salary, a woman he liked asking how he could work for 'Tory scum' that started wars and armed the Saudis. He had wanted to tell her he was MI5, but had to stick to his cover, arguing that Saudi Arabia was a vital regional ally and that the situation in Yemen wasn't just a simple case of right and wrong. She had laughed at him contemptuously and walked off, high on coke and moral rectitude, leaving Tomkins to wonder if life in the Security Service was all it was cracked up to be. He had only applied to MI5 for the challenge, to see if he could make it past the selection board. He had never intended to make intelligence work his career. But MI5 had seen something in him—he'd never known precisely what—which had made Tomkins feel valued and admired. For a long time after that party he felt he'd made the wrong choice: he would have had a lot more peace of mind, not to mention money, if he'd followed his brother's advice and gone into sales or the City. But now look at him! Whistling past that same bar in the small hours of the morning, participating in work of immeasurable importance to the secret state, work which might save a man's life, might even lead to the arrest and incarceration of enemy intelligence officers bent on bringing Britain to her knees. You couldn't buy that sort of power and excitement. If the woman who had rejected him could see him now, she'd know what a mistake she'd made. She'd understand why Matt Tomkins wasn't just a run-of-the-mill banker or corporate lawyer, why he had chosen a life dedicated to public service, lived in secret, making a difference from the shadows.

Tomkins had driven past Limehouse while Robert Vosse was doing eighty-five on the Westway in an unmarked BMW. Pavkov had taken a wrong turn in Canary Wharf, the satnav sending him east, then north, then south, a delay which bought Tomkins and Vosse precious time. Tomkins arrived ahead of both of them, parking in a residential street adjacent to Spindrift Avenue.

'I'm here,' he told Vosse. 'Have you called for backup?'

'Now why would I want to do a thing like that?' the boss replied, the roar of the traffic lending his voice a dreamlike quality. There was a conspiratorial tone to Vosse's response which made Tomkins feel as though they were uniquely bound together, like cops in a buddy film closing in on the bad guys. 'The whole point of the operation is that it's sealed off. I can't have colleagues knowing about BIRD and BOX. We call for backup, everyone's

BOX 88

going to want to know why you and me are running around Canary Wharf at two in the morning chasing Iranians. No. We have to do this thing together, Cagney.'

You and me, thought Tomkins. *We have to do this thing together.* Meanwhile Cara is fast asleep and Tessa Swinburn is miles away. You snooze, you lose. The operation is reaching a climax and I'm at the centre of things, where I deserve to be. Making decisions, doing my job, impressing the man who needs to be impressed.

'What do we do when the meeting takes place?' he asked.

'We follow whoever comes to talk to our friend from Belgrade,' Vosse replied. Tomkins heard a sudden burst of acceleration from the BMW. 'With any luck they'll talk in the Fiat and we'll get everything down on tape. Then either a foot-follow or it's back in the vehicles. If the Iranians show up in a car, I've brought some kit and can tag them. That should lead us to BIRD.'

It sounded easy enough, though Tomkins began to wonder if Vosse was being over-confident. As he sat in the Mondeo, the tablet on the seat beside him, he tried to work out the variables. What if Zoltan was going to a private address? What if he met the Iranians on the street or one of them got nervous about surveillance? They were a team of at least four, which meant three of them could be staking out the meeting point in advance, looking for signs of trouble. Surely Vosse had thought of all this? An officer with his experience wouldn't want to get too close to the prize for fear of scaring them off.

'Where are you?' Vosse asked.

'Parked adjacent to number nineteen, sir. Out of sight down a side street.'

'I can see that,' he said. 'Barnfield Place? OK. Anybody taps on the window, you're a cab driver waiting for a fare. Keep your engine running and your hazard lights on so it looks like you're not trying to hide.'

That was smart. Vosse was aware that the Iranians could be running counter-surveillance, looking out for cars that shouldn't be there, sudden arrivals or movements on the street. Tomkins put the hazard lights on and listened as the satnav gave the last of its instructions to Pavkov, telling him to make a left turn onto Spindrift Avenue. He had finally arrived. Tomkins tried to imagine where the Serb would park, what the section of street looked like, who might emerge from the shadows to greet him. He could only sit and wait in the cramped Mondeo, listening out for approaching cars, approaching men, waiting for the boss to arrive, waiting for the Iranians.

'Target is in position,' he told Vosse. 'Just pulled into Spindrift. Sounds like he's parked and switched off the engine.'

'Copy that, Cagney. I'm coming into Limehouse. Ten minutes away.'

Tomkins pressed the AirPods deeper into his ears, focusing on the sounds picked up by the microphones. He heard a cough, the click of a lighter, then a sudden nervous inhalation on a cigarette.

'What have you got?' Vosse asked.

'Stay off comms,' Tomkins whispered.

He shouldn't have spoken to the boss like that, but he could tell that something was happening inside the Punto. There was the sound of a window going down then another cough as Pavkov cleared his throat.

'You are Zoltan?' said a voice. The accent was unmistakably foreign. It had to be one of the Iranians.

'Who are you?'

'They sent me. Tell me to ask you questions. I get in.'

Tomkins tried to control his breathing, listening as closely as possible to the take from the Punto. He looked down at the tablet and saw that Vosse was already in Canary Wharf, the BMW perhaps three or four minutes away.

'Wait.'

This from Pavkov. Tomkins heard the noise of a door being opened, then a rustle on the microphones as somebody climbed into the Fiat.

BOX 88

'I never saw you before,' said Pavkov.

'Good,' the man replied. 'That's the way I like it.'

'I don't understand.'

'Who came to the car park?' he asked.

Tomkins wondered if he should be writing things down, short-noting the conversation in case something went wrong with the tech.

'A man and a woman,' Pavkov replied.

'They were police?'

'Police, yes.'

'You are certain of this?'

'They showed me identification,' said Pavkov. 'Yes, I am certain.'

'How did they know what happened?'

'How should I know the answer to this?'

'What did you tell them?'

'I told them I didn't know what they were talking about.'

'You are sure of this?'

'Of course I am sure.'

Pavkov was lying. Cara had debriefed him on her encounter with the Serb. He was trying to pretend to the Iranians that there wasn't a problem.

'Try again,' said the man. 'What did you tell them?'

'I'm telling you the truth,' Pavkov replied. 'The lady come, she ask if anything happened in the car park maybe half hour earlier, I tell her I don't know what she's talking about. She say someone complained because of the noise . . .'

'Noise?'

'Yes, maybe a neighbour or something? Then her boss shows up, another police, asks the same questions.'

'Was he in uniform?'

'What please?'

'The boss. Was he dressed like cop? Like police officer?'

'No.'

'And you say he asks you same thing?'

'Yes.'

'Why are you lying, Zoltan?'

Tomkins thought it was obvious: if he told the Iranians the truth, he was a dead man.

'I am not lying,' the Serb replied. 'I am not a liar, my friend.'

Tomkins heard a long, nervous exhalation of cigarette smoke, then the growl of a motorbike in the distance. Taking out one of the AirPods he realised he could hear the bike both in real time and on the Punto microphones. That meant it was close, moving east to west past Barnfield Place, doing no more than fifteen or twenty miles per hour.

'Bike,' said Vosse on comms. 'Visual?'

'Negative,' Tomkins replied.

'I'm here. I have line of sight to the Fiat.'

Tomkins hadn't heard the BMW's approach, hadn't looked down at the tablet for ages. Sure enough, he could see the small pulsating icon of Vosse's vehicle parked on the corner of Spindrift Avenue. Surely he was too close to Pavkov and the Iranian? Surely he would spook them?

'What else?' the Iranian asked.

Tomkins realised that he could no longer hear the motorbike. Either the rider had parked nearby or driven north towards the City.

'Nothing else,' Pavkov replied.

'They follow you here?'

Tomkins felt his stomach somersault. The Iranians suspected that Zoltan had a tail. Maybe somebody in a first-floor window had seen the BMW pulling up outside. Maybe there was a stakeout position on Barnfield Place.

'Nobody follow me,' the Serb replied. 'Why would they do this? They suspect nothing.'

'Nothing.'

Tomkins couldn't tell if the Iranian was making a statement

BOX 88

or asking a question. The take quality on the microphones was extraordinarily clear, but trying to picture the faces of the two men in the Fiat, their moods and gestures, was like trying to move stars around in the night sky. Tomkins felt isolated and near-hopeless. If anything happened, he did not know what he was supposed to do. Stay where he was? Follow the Iranian bagman? He was waiting for somebody to tell him how to act. It didn't make sense that Vosse hadn't called for backup. Surely arresting the two men in the car was now the surest way of locating Kite?

'They ask if something happened,' Pavkov continued. 'I tell them nothing happened. They don't know you were there, in car park. They don't know you pay me. I don't tell them nothing.'

'It's OK, Zoltan. We believe you.'

'What are you doing?' Pavkov asked. He sounded unsettled. 'You making a call?'

Just then, the burst of the motorbike roaring into life, much closer to the Fiat than before. The noise of the engine smothering the sound of movement inside the car, the microphones picking up the breathlessness of a short struggle, a stifled cry and a gulp for air. Tomkins knew that something was badly wrong. He heard the slamming of a car door then the deafening scream of the bike as it accelerated away from the Punto. Vosse was instantly on comms.

'Jesus Christ . . .'

'What happened?' Tomkins asked.

The next thing he knew he was out of the Mondeo, sprinting. He saw Vosse ahead of him, holding his head in his hands as he stumbled back from the Fiat. Tomkins reached the passenger side and looked down into the car. Zoltan Pavkov was slumped in the driver's seat, his head tipped back, his throat cut from ear to ear. Blood had sprayed onto the windscreen, black as tar in the darkness.

'We get out of here,' Vosse told him. 'We disappear.'

21

'Who's the Yank in Churchill?' Kite asked his mother in the hotel office five minutes after finishing his chores upstairs.

'Mr Strawson?' she replied. 'Isn't he gorgeous?'

Kite didn't know how to respond: he never liked hearing his mother describing other men as 'handsome' or 'good-looking'— or 'gorgeous'. When he was fourteen she had brought a boyfriend on holiday. They had stayed in a cheap hotel on Skye, just the three of them. Night after night, Kite had had to listen to them screwing in the next-door room.

'Is he religious?' he asked.

'What makes you say that?'

'Got a Bible beside his bed. Unless you've started handing them out to guests?'

Cheryl shook her head. As always, she was doing several things at once: flicking through the reservations book while searching for a pen, grabbing a Consulate cigarette from a packet on the desk, adjusting her hair by tucking it behind her ears.

'Not doing the Gideon Bible just yet,' she said. 'Is Paolo waiting for you in the bar?'

It was her way of saying that Kite should go back to work. He had given up waiting for his mother to ask him how the

BOX 88

Easter term had gone or to enquire about his journey from Euston. Perhaps she would get around to it in the morning.

'I'll see if he's there,' Kite replied.

Killantringan was an eighteenth-century shooting lodge which had been converted into a hotel shortly after the end of the Second World War. The bar was located in one of two former drawing rooms and decorated in a style his grand-mother had described as 'shortbread tin chic': the sofas and armchairs were upholstered in red and green tartans, the walls covered in reproduction oil paintings of stags and men in kilts, the shelves stocked with antique hardback books and dog-eared, long-ago copies of *Country Life*. The carpet was an occasionally stained Royal blue with frayed edges and black spots indicating where guests had accidentally dropped lit matches and cigarettes. With a log fire burning nine months out of twelve, the intended effect was of a cosy, wood-panelled country house that had been in the same family since the Highland Clearances.

The bar itself had two taps serving draught SKOL and Bass Special, a collection box for the RNLI and a till that regularly became stuck and had to be prised open with a screwdriver. Kite had served behind it for at least two years, retreating into the back office on the rare occasions that a police officer or employee of Customs and Excise visited the hotel. Otherwise his mother confidently told any guests who enquired about Lachlan's age that he was twenty years old and looking forward to a career in hospitality.

'How are you doing there, young man?' said Michael Strawson. He had managed to get to the bar and order another tumbler of Laphroaig in the time it had taken Kite to walk down the back stairs, throw out the rubbish, talk to his mother in the office and switch shifts with Paolo.

'Mr Strawson,' he said. 'Everything OK upstairs?'

'Everything is A-OK.'

There were seven other guests in the bar: an elderly couple sitting silently together looking out over the moonlit lawn and the silvery sea; two laughing pals in their fifties who looked and sounded as though they were probably Irishmen over on the ferry from Larne; a Frenchman and his elegantly coiffured wife, both in their late thirties and wearing tweed; and Strawson himself, looking for all the world like a famous American country and western singer whose name Kite could not for the life of him remember.

'Are you staying here for the Easter weekend?' he asked.

Kenny Rogers. That was it. Strawson looked like a slightly larger, more dishevelled version of Kenny Rogers. Kite immediately starting hearing 'Islands in the Stream' in his head and turned up the volume on the Richard Clayderman album playing in the bar to clear the earworm.

'That's right. Leaving Monday. You're here for the spring break, am I correct? Your mother told me you go to Alford College. That's quite a school. How do you enjoy it?'

Kite picked the second of the two questions and told Strawson that he was coming to the end of his time at Alford, revising for A levels over the Easter holidays, and hoping to go to Edinburgh University in September to study Russian and French.

'*A ty govorish' po Russki?*'

Kite's knowledge of Russian extended to 'yes' and 'no', to '*glasnost*' and '*perestroika*', but he knew that Strawson had asked him if he spoke the language and replied: '*Nyet.* But they start from scratch, and students get a year studying in the Soviet Union, so hopefully I'll pick it up quite quickly.'

'*Mais votre français est courant?*'

Kite was knackered from the long journey and had been hoping for a quiet shift in the bar. He assumed that Strawson was trying to show off his knowledge of both languages, so he humoured the American by saying that his French was not fluent, but good enough to understand most conversations:

BOX 88

'*Mon français n'est pas couramment, mais je peux comprendre la plupart des conversations.*'

'Very good, very impressive,' the American replied. 'So you get a good education down there at Alford? I heard it was all strange customs and ancient traditions. Secret handshakes, that kind of thing.'

'There's a bit of that.' One of the Irishmen came to the bar and ordered two pints of SKOL. Kite poured them as he continued his conversation with Strawson. 'There are definitely some strange customs.'

'Such as?'

He put the first of the two pints on the bar. He was thirsty and would have given a lung for a cold, hair-of-the-dog pint of lager, a Marlboro Red and a night in front of the television. When backs were turned at the hotel, Kite sometimes poured himself a heart-starting shot of vodka or knocked back a quick glass of wine. Strawson was standing in the way of that. It felt as though he was going to sit on his bar stool until two in the morning firing questions at him.

'So there's a thing called "capping",' he replied, on the assumption that Strawson would get a kick out of the story.

'And what's that?'

'If you're walking down the street and a beak—that what's we call a teacher—is coming towards you, you're meant to raise your right hand and kind of salute him by touching the brim of a non-existent hat on your head.'

'Say *what*?'

Kite handed the Irishman the second of the two pints and gave him change from a five-pound note.

'It dates back to the old days when Alfordians wore top hats. Some teachers don't care, but others are a little power-crazed and insist on it.' Kite wiped spilled lager from the counter and threw the wet cloth into the sink beneath the bar. 'It's funny, when I first went there five years ago and came back here to the hotel, I started capping the guests. My mum kept asking me if I was pretending to be a soldier.'

Strawson reacted delightedly to the story and asked Kite to pour him another inch of Laphroaig. Kite did so, added the whisky to Strawson's bill, then walked around the bar, returning shortly afterwards with a tray of empty glasses and dirty ashtrays which he set down in the passage leading to the back office. It occurred to him that exactly twenty-four hours earlier he had been doing shots of vodka in Borscht & Tears with Des and Xavier, who were doubtless spending the night at home watching videos and eating pizzas cooked for them by their mothers or private maids. Xavier was due to fly to Geneva the next day for a fortnight's skiing in Verbier; Des's parents had booked a family safari in Kenya through Abercrombie and Kent. Meanwhile Kite would be stuck at the hotel for three weeks working ten-hour days and fielding questions from the likes of Michael Strawson about the idiosyncrasies of life at Alford. He wished he could drive to Prestwick, catch a flight to Heathrow and spend the rest of the holidays in bed with Alison Hackford.

'Say, Lachlan, I gotta question for you.'

It was Strawson again, calling to him from the bar. Kite heard a seagull clack in the sky above Killantringan. He called out: 'Just a moment, sir,' tipped the ash and butts from an evening of cigarettes into the bin, put the dirty glasses in the dishwasher and returned to the bar.

'Yes, Mr Strawson. What can I do for you?'

'You like a riddle, young man?'

'A what, sir?'

'A puzzle. A brain-teaser.'

About as much as I like eating cigarette butts or talking to strange Americans about school, Kite thought, but he put a professional smile on his face and said: 'Sure.'

'I was looking at your light switches there.' Strawson indicated a panel of four switches beneath a reproduction oil painting of

BOX 88

The Monarch of the Glen. 'Reminded me of a riddle I was taught in the army back in the sixties.'

On Peele's recommendation, Kite had seen *The Deer Hunter* and *Full Metal Jacket* and wondered with a buzz if he was talking to a real-life Vietnam vet.

'What was the riddle, sir?'

Strawson twisted on the bar stool so that he was facing out into the room. The elderly couple had gone upstairs to bed. The Irishmen were laughing and drinking their pints. The wife of the French guest had momentarily left the room, leaving her husband alone with a copy of *The Scotsman.* Strawson had no other audience but Kite.

'OK. There's a room with nothing inside it except a single bulb hanging from the ceiling. There's a door into the room. You are on the outside and you can't see in. Next to the door are three light switches: call them A, B and C. One of them turns the light on and off. The other two are dummies. You have to work out which switch operates the light, but here's the catch: you're only allowed to go into the room one time.'

Kite barely understood what Strawson had told him and asked him to repeat what he had said. He was tired and not in the mood to think deeply about anything very much; he sensed that Strawson was trying to make a point about the limits of an Alford education. This irritated Kite, who was possessed of a strong streak of stubborn, competitive pride. He wanted to solve the riddle and prove the American wrong.

'So the switches are all set to "off"?' he asked.

Strawson smiled and nodded. 'There are no tricks. It's a regular room and it's a regular lightbulb. A chair won't help you. You don't need a desk. You can't see inside and you can't open the door, look at the bulb and try the switches one by one. Somehow you have to work out which switch is connected to the lightbulb. A, B or C?'

Kite was not aware of the process by which he arrived at the answer, but it came to him within less than a minute. All it took was a quick walk down the passage, a few moments to clear his head in the hotel office, a glance up at the lightbulb blazing in the ceiling and he had it.

'Heat,' he said, walking back into the bar.

Strawson's eyes glowed with admiration. 'Go on,' he said. Kite could tell from his expression that he had solved it.

'You turn on switch A. You leave it on for five or ten seconds. You turn it off. Then you flick B, open the door and walk into the room. If the bulb is on, you know it's operated by B. If it's off but the bulb is hot when you touch it, you know that it's operated by A.' Strawson nodded appreciatively. Kite didn't even need to finish but wanted to do so for his own satisfaction. 'If it's off and the bulb is cold, you'll know the switch is C.'

Strawson slid off the stool, turned to face Kite and applauded quietly.

'Very impressive, young man,' he said. 'Very impressive.'

All weekend the tests continued.

Just before six o'clock the following evening, Cheryl Kite was driving back from the Cash & Carry in Stranraer with a boot full of supplies for the hotel when she was flagged down by a middle-aged man whose car appeared to have a puncture. She was not far along the narrow, single-track road which ran down-hill towards Killantringan past fields of heather and grazing sheep. Service was due to begin in the restaurant at half-past six (Mr Strawson, in common with many of his compatriots, preferred to eat early) and the last thing she needed was to be delayed by a motorist with a flat tyre.

Cheryl pulled up in front of the stranded Ford Cortina and immediately recognised the driver as one of two Irishmen who had been drinking in the bar the night before.

'Are you all right?' she asked, walking towards him. 'Flat tyre?'

BOX 88

'Oh thank goodness you're here,' the man replied. He was in his early fifties and looked very distressed. 'We were down at Killantringan last night, d'you remember? We're staying over at the Portpatrick Hotel. I'm Seamus. My friend here is in a bad way. He needs the hospital. Can you help us?'

Cheryl peered inside the car. Sure enough, the second of the two Irishmen was curled up on the back seat nursing what appeared to be an appalling stomach cramp. He was moaning and gasping. Cheryl wondered why the hell his friend hadn't driven him straight to Stranraer.

'You should take him to a doctor,' she said. 'Is there a puncture? Have you run out of petrol?'

'I can't drive,' Seamus replied, looking utterly shamefaced. 'Billy has a licence. Only he started feeling terrible twenty minutes ago and can't get himself behind the wheel. You're the first person to come past, God bless you.'

And so it was that Cheryl Kite had no choice other than to abandon her own vehicle at the side of the road and to drive the two men and their Ford Cortina all the way back to Stranraer, with Billy in the back seat calling out to God and chastising Him for a 'terrible appendicitis' and Seamus saying over and over again that Mrs Kite was 'the kindest woman in all the world' and apologising repeatedly 'for inconveniencing you in this way'. As soon as she reached the medical centre, Cheryl took Billy inside then rang the hotel from a callbox in the waiting room. It was already half-past six. Paolo had taken off for Easter celebrations with his family in Glasgow and Lockie was the only person left at Killantringan with the wherewithal to run the hotel.

'Lachlan?' she said, when Kite picked up in the office.

'Mum? Where are you?'

'I'm in bloody Stranraer with a bloody Irishman who probably drank too much of our whisky last night and developed cirrhosis of the liver.'

Given what had happened to her husband, Cheryl had a predictably short fuse when it came to men overindulging an appetite for alcohol.

'*What?*' Kite replied. 'How did you end up with—'

'Never mind.' He could tell that she was annoyed and just wanted Kite to listen to what she had to say. 'I'm not going to be able to get back for at least another hour. You'll have to take orders for dinner, make sure people in the bar get served, ask Wilma to turn down the beds upstairs if she's not needed in the restaurant. And tell John he'll have to take pasta off tonight's menu. It's sitting in the boot of my fucking car two miles up the road.'

'I could drive up with someone and fetch it.'

Cheryl cursed. 'It's locked and I've got the only key.'

There was no night manager at Killantringan. Shortly before dawn on Good Friday morning, Michael Strawson had sneaked downstairs and placed microphones in both of the office telephones. Listening to the call in Churchill, he was impressed by Kite's apparent sangfroid.

'Mum, it's fine. I'll handle it. Don't worry.'

'I'm not *worried*,' she replied tersely. 'I just need you to take care of things. Do you think you can do that? Do you know what needs to be done?'

'Like I said, I'll handle it. How long do you think you're going to be?'

'How should I know? They're both a pair of wet blankets. If I don't at least make sure they see a doctor, God knows what will happen to them.'

'Maybe check them in, then get a taxi back to your car?' Kite suggested.

'Yes, that's a good idea. Could you ring one for me?'

She gave him the address of the medical centre. Kite immediately rang the local taxi service in Stranraer, wondering why his mother couldn't have done it herself. Inevitably, there was no

BOX 88

answer. He tried again three minutes later and was told that all of the firm's drivers would be busy until at least half-past eight. Listening in, Strawson considered this to be a slice of good fortune: it would give him an extra hour to observe how Kite coped in his mother's absence. He needed to see how the young man reacted to adverse circumstances, to setbacks and confrontations. If he could run the hotel solo, and deal with whatever variables Strawson and his team chose to throw at him, BOX 88 would be given a good indication of his ability to cope with the inevitable operational pressures of France.

Strawson threw everything at him. The dining room was full so he sent his lemon sole back (twice) and claimed that a bottle of Puligny-Montrachet 1982 was corked when it wasn't. He complained about the volume at which the Richard Clayderman album was playing in the bar, saying that he had already heard it three times over the night before and couldn't Kite find something else which was less 'predictable'. Before dinner he had asked Kite, who was trying to make a brace of gin and tonics in the bar, to write down the addresses and phone numbers of the best five golf courses on the Stranraer peninsula. Could Kite call each of them in turn and ask if it was necessary to reserve a tee-off time for the following afternoon? With Cheryl Kite still fifteen miles away in a Stranraer hospital, detained by two role-playing Irishmen, Strawson then demanded to have cheese and biscuits and a glass of red wine sent to Churchill after dinner, despite knowing that the hotel did not offer room service. Kite took the tray up himself, only to be told that Strawson was 'allergic to Stilton' and that there was not enough hot water to fill the room's enormous, free-standing bath. Kite apologised for the numerous inconveniences Strawson had suffered and promised to knock the price of dinner off his bill. He then rushed to the attic to turn on the thermostat, switched the Stilton for a slice of Caboc, told Wilma to take orders in the restaurant and quickly took a round of orders in the bar. The crowning moment came when Rita

Ayinde organised a power cut which left the hotel in almost complete darkness for fifteen minutes. With the guests grumbling that they were unable to see the food on their plates, Kite found a torch and a box of candles in the office and had almost illuminated every room on the ground floor when the lights suddenly came back on, to widespread relief and applause. Throughout all this, at no point did Kite display any signs of panic or irritation. When his mother returned, and failed to acknowledge the extraordinary lengths to which her son had gone to keep the show on the road, he did not lose his temper nor storm out into the night. Only once, when the elderly couple—to Strawson's delight—whispered something about 'Fawlty Towers' within Kite's earshot, did the young man look as though he might be on the verge of losing his cool. But he maintained his composure, pushed through the swing doors connecting the restaurant to the staff area, and doubtless vented his spleen on whichever unfortunate member of staff happened to get in his way.

The following day, having attended a chilly Easter Sunday service at Portpatrick parish church, eaten a decent lunch at the Crown Hotel and played nine holes of links golf at Dunskey, Michael Strawson took out a sheet of writing paper in Churchill and composed a letter to Billy Peele while gazing out at the misty cliffs of Killantringan.

Dear Billy

You were right. He's worth pursuing. Smart, charming, quick on his feet, doesn't panic when the shit hits the fan, which it surely will because it always does.

We tested him as best we could. He got the light-switch riddle inside two minutes—which is more than you ever did. A lot of these privately educated types are good in front of a book or at a cocktail party but have as much practical common

BOX 88

sense as a rooster wandering around in a swamp full of alliga-
tors. He'll be an asset to us. Let's take the chance.
Two things:

1. Keep an eye on his social life. If there's alcohol in the
pipeline, or drugs, I need to know. And sooner rather
than later. I don't want a guy who starts out as Bobby
Ewing ending up as Hunter S. Thompson.
2. Is there a soft underbelly? Is he sentimental? I need
more on that. The way he interacts with his mother
makes me think he's burying a lot, keeping some kind of
rage (or is it compassion?) below the surface. None of us
got a chance to talk to him much about his father. Again,
I don't want a bleeding heart as an Achilles heel. God
knows this world needs upstanding men of unwavering
ethical principle, but not on my team.

Speaking of the mother, you're right. Attractive—but chilly.
A man might want to be her lover but I don't envy young
Lachlan being her son. To be added to the list of famous beau-
ties, which already included Fawn Hall and Pamela Bordes at
the last count. No doubt you obtained Miss Hall's televised
testimony. You always had an eye for a pretty girl, Billy. Iran-
Contra. What a shitshow.
Have you made it through Satanic Verses? At one point
Salman refers to your prime minister as 'Mrs Torture' and later
as 'Maggie the Bitch'. Charming from a guy enjoying round-
the-clock protection from Special Branch at the expense of the
British taxpayer.
Yours aye
M.S.

22

Kite was woken by the sound of pounding on the door of his cabin. The rattle of a key in the lock, a holler of 'Get up!' then someone shaking him in the darkness.

'What's going on?' he mumbled.

As soon as Kite had sat up in bed, a light snapped on. Hossein slapped him hard across the face.

Kite swore, disorientated, and clutched his jaw. He climbed to his feet so that he could defend himself against any further attack. Hossein allowed him space in which to stand and Kite took advantage of it, dropping a punch into the Iranian's stomach which doubled him over. Kamran, the driver, burst into the room behind them and the two men put Kite under control, Kamran seizing his arms from behind, Hossein putting him into a headlock.

'You come with us,' Hossein ordered.

'Fuck you,' Kite told them. He was enraged by what they had done. He managed to stop the men dragging him from the room by slamming the heel of his right foot into Hossein's shin. The Iranian yelped in pain. Kamran bent down and gathered Kite's legs like sections of pipe and together they carried him, raised in the air, to the room at the end of the passage.

BOX 88

Torabi was waiting. He seemed amused that Kite was being carried like a rolled carpet into the room and mumbled an order at his men. They allowed the prisoner to get to his feet.

'Your goon punched me in the face,' Kite complained as he was forced into the chair. He was back in the role of the beleaguered oil executive. His hands were pulled behind his back and the wrists bound with wire. 'What the hell's going on?'

Kamran and Hossein left the room. Kite realised that the wires around his wrists might be loose enough to work free.

'What's going on is they don't like you,' Torabi replied. 'I don't much like you either. What were you expecting? A cup of coffee and a hot shower?'

Kite shook his head, suppressing his anger. He didn't know how long he had been in the cell but reckoned it couldn't have been for more than a few hours.

'Did you send a message to my wife?' he asked.

There was a gun on the table beside Torabi. The Iranian picked it up and placed it behind his back in the band of his trousers.

'Oh sure,' he said. 'I did exactly what you asked.'

'What's that supposed to mean?'

'It means I'm not here to send comforting messages to your friends and family. I'm here to get the truth.'

'So you keep saying,' Kite replied. 'What time is it?'

'Time to talk.' Torabi pushed down the sleeve of his shirt so that it covered his wristwatch. As if noticing the toolbox for the first time, he picked it up and set it down on a section of plastic flooring in the corner of the room. 'Who was with you at the funeral?' he asked.

'Nobody,' Kite replied, watching Torabi sit down. 'I went alone. My wife was at—'

'I know where your wife is. Who followed you from the church?'

Kite was unsettled by the reference to Isobel but encouraged by the news that he had been followed. Had 'Emma' tailed the

Jaguar to Cheshire Street and alerted the authorities? Perhaps MOIS had got wind of the manhunt. That Kite was alive, and still on board the boat, indicated that Torabi was for the moment content that their location was secure.

'What do you mean, you know where my wife is?'

Torabi produced a supercilious grin. It had become his way of avoiding questions he didn't want to answer.

'Tell me who could have followed us from Knightsbridge? Do you have private security? Are you currently involved in an operation?'

'Don't be ridiculous.' Torabi's questions confirmed that 'Emma' had indeed been part of a broader surveillance effort targeted against him. He was certain she was MI5. 'I told you. I haven't been operational as an intelligence officer for over twenty years. I don't have private security. I wish I did. I wouldn't be in this situation. What is it that you expect me to tell you beyond what I've already confirmed?'

Kite knew that it was vital to continue to stick to his cover, to play the innocent oil executive for as long as possible, however much it angered and frustrated Torabi. The longer he could spin out his tale, inventing and improvising memories of Eskandarian, the longer he could keep the Iranians on the boat. All MI5 likely needed was a number plate fix on the vehicle they'd used to transport him from the car park. CCTV might give images of the individuals involved in the kidnapping. Those photographs could be cross-checked against known members of MOIS operating in the United Kingdom and beyond. Phone attacks and satellite recognition would do the rest.

'When we spoke before, you said that you would be prepared to talk about your experiences in France as a teenager,' said Torabi. 'Is that still the case?'

'Of course it's still the case,' Kite replied. 'I'll tell you whatever I can remember. All I want to do is get this thing over with and

BOX 88

go home. It would help if I could have a cigarette. Also some coffee to clear my mind.'

Torabi laughed. 'You can have a cigarette if you want one. Coffee's not on the menu.'

'Fine,' Kite replied. 'It'll just take me longer digging up the memories. You're asking me to think back to stuff that happened thirty years ago. I can barely remember what I ate for breakfast yesterday, far less what I was doing in 1989.'

'Is that right?'

Torabi eyed him with suspicion.

'Yeah, that's right.'

The Iranian was still wearing the same crisp white shirt and designer jeans that he had changed into earlier. His hair was now less carefully tended and he had removed his shoes. He might have been a man relaxing at home in front of the television.

'I believe I mentioned during our last talk the importance of not wasting my time.'

'You did,' Kite replied. 'What of it?'

'I told you that it was critical not to lie to me about who you are, about what took place in France.'

'I haven't lied to you.'

'No? I'm not so sure that's true.'

'Can we just get on with it? What did you mean when you said you know where my wife is? Have you been in contact with her?'

Torabi nodded his head. 'How convenient that you should ask these questions.'

Something turned over inside Kite, the dread of what the Iranians might have done to Isobel.

'What are you talking about?' he said.

'Kamran.'

Torabi shouted the name. The chauffeur came through the

door like an obedient dog, glancing at Kite as he came to a halt beside his master.

'Lachlan, it's a shame that I'm going to have to play this card, but time is precious. I need a guarantee that you won't lie, that you won't waste my time. We may have to move from this place and that could mean the possibility that you don't come with us. Does that make sense? Do you understand what I'm telling you?'

'Not really.'

'It means that I need to know what I need to know as soon as possible. If I don't get what I came for—if you don't give me the information I want—there will be consequences.'

'What have I denied you?' Kite replied. 'What information do you need? Tell me and I'll try to help.'

Torabi spoke quietly in Farsi. Kamran handed him a mobile phone. Kite heard the drum beats of a FaceTime call ringing out and the Iranian turned the screen towards him.

'Speak to her.'

It took Kite a moment to understand what was happening. He tried to make sense of what was on the screen because at first he thought that he was looking at a blank image onto which someone had somehow projected his own reflection. Then Isobel's confused, anxious face came into focus. Kite lurched forward, stunned.

'Sweetheart?' she said to him.

She was seated in a chair, looking down into the lens, flanked by two men whose faces Kite could not see.

'What happened?' he said. Kite pulled at the bonds on his wrists, wanting to attack Torabi, but he was unable to move. 'Are you OK?'

'Lockie? What's going on? Where are you?'

She did not sound as frightened as she looked. There was a calmness in her voice which almost reassured him. He knew that, no matter what was done to her, she would not panic. She had been through a lot in her life and she would survive it.

BOX 88

'Have they hurt you?' he said. He was trying to identify where she was being held. 'Where are you? Is the baby OK?'

'Enough,' said Torabi, reaching for the phone.

'No, wait!'

The Iranian leaned closer towards him and whispered into his ear.

'Tell her she'll be fine. Tell her your precious baby won't be harmed. Why? Because you're going to cooperate. You're going to tell the truth.'

'Sweetheart, don't worry,' Kite said, shutting him out, defying him. 'I'm fine. There's been a misunderstanding. Are you feeling OK? Is the baby all right?'

'I'm fine,' Isobel replied. 'Why are they holding you? You haven't done anything. They think you're a spy—'

Thank God for you, he thought. It was obvious that what was happening to them was linked to Kite's work. Isobel was unaware of the existence of BOX 88, but knew enough about Kite's work to protect him.

'I know they do,' he said. 'They're confused—'

Torabi snatched the phone back, breaking the connection.

'I see your wife is well trained,' he said, passing the mobile to the chauffeur. 'We're not confused. Perhaps she's like you and Mr de Paul. Perhaps your wife also works for MI6?'

'You piece of shit.' Kite twisted from side to side, pulling at his bonds, but they would not slacken any further. 'You're insane. Let her go.'

Even as he confronted Torabi, Kite was working through the implications of the exchange. Why was Torabi again bringing up Cosmo de Paul? Around the edges of the screen he had seen a section of carpet which matched the living-room floor of the Sussex cottage. Why hadn't the Iranians moved her from the one place where she might be found? And why was Torabi risking a FaceTime call that could be swept by Cheltenham?'

'We will let her go as soon as you cooperate.'

Kite shouted at him. 'I have told you I will cooperate! She's a pregnant woman, for Christ's sake.'

He ached for his unborn child. Kamran stepped behind him and pulled down on his arms, the wire cutting into Kite's wrists. He hissed in pain. His impotence in the face of these men was like the powerlessness he had felt as a child when his father had been drinking. Kite detested the loss of control, the impossibility of fighting back.

'Lockie,' said Torabi. 'Can I call you that?' He sat back in the sofa with a smug smile and indicated to Kamran that he should leave the room. 'You can now see, in case you doubted it before, that I am a serious person who means to find out what I need to find out. Before this exchange with your wife, you may have believed that it was more important—more *noble*—to protect your employers than to save your own skin. The British can be sentimental like that. Maybe you put a low value on your own life. Who knows? But undoubtedly you value the life of Isobel and her unborn child. So perhaps their unfortunate situation will be enough to persuade you to stop wasting any more of my fucking time.'

23

'Listen, Matt. You could have gone through your whole career without seeing something like that. We're not dealing with normal people here. I'm sorry you were exposed to it. Not surprised you're in a mess, not surprised at all. If it's any consolation, Zoltan wasn't a family man. No contact with his kids, no wife to leave behind as a widow, not many friends. The sort of person who would sell his soul to MOIS for a few grand and knowingly send a man to his death. I'm not saying he had it coming, but Zoltan Pavkov got in with the wrong crowd and paid the ultimate price.'

Tomkins and Vosse were sitting in the BMW somewhere in Whitechapel. Tomkins wasn't sure where they had ended up or why Vosse had chosen this place to stop and debrief. He was barely listening to what the boss was saying. All he could think of was Zoltan's jackknifed head, the bloodied neck slung back and opened up like intestines on a butcher's slab. He kept picturing the frozen, terrified stare in Zoltan's eyes, the horror of what had been done to him.

'You need to concentrate on what I'm about to tell you, son,' said Vosse. They were side by side in the car. Tomkins was in the passenger seat, staring ahead at a grey concrete wall. It occurred to him that the man who had murdered Pavkov must have been sitting in the same seat in the Punto, must have reached across with his knife to cut him from ear to ear. Or had he been behind him all that time, positioning himself so that the blood which had burst from Zoltan's neck onto the wheel and dashboard didn't spray all over him? No doubt that was the sort of thing they took into consideration before murdering a person in cold blood. 'There'll be questions from the team. We tell them the truth. Whatever anybody asks, we don't hide anything. We tell them what went on tonight.'

'What about everyone else?' Tomkins asked. He dreaded the answer because he already knew what it would be. 'What if the police come asking questions?'

Vosse tried to put a comforting hand on his shoulder, but Tomkins shrugged it off.

'Look. This is the business we're in. We operate in the shadows. Nobody is to see us, nobody is to know we were there.'

'*Operate in the shadows*? What the fuck?' Ordinarily Tomkins wouldn't have lost his temper with Vosse, but this wasn't an ordinary morning. 'We're not in a comic book. This isn't the fucking *Avengers*. A man got murdered and I heard it all playing out on the mikes, every word. I heard the sound of a man dying. What happens when the police find the microphones in the car? What happens then?'

'They wonder who put them there. They never get a plausible answer.'

'What if one of the neighbours saw me running up the road? What if CCTV has the number plate of this car, the number plate of the Mondeo, pictures of you parked two hundred metres away, then running towards the scene of the crime?'

'Unsolved murder, Matt. Unsolved crime. Happens all the time in every town and city in the world. There won't be a trace on the vehicles. They're Service cars. Understand? Police run the plates, they get sweet fuck all.'

'And video? Someone with a phone?'

BOX 88

'What are the chances?' Vosse was sounding increasingly irritated by Tomkins's questions. 'It was two o'clock in the morning. You saw how dead the place was. You telling me some hedge fund master of the universe was sitting up in his silk pyjamas doing an Abraham Zapruder?' Tomkins shook his head and frowned, not understanding the reference. 'Fine. If the film comes out, we deal with it. If your face or mine, by some miracle of coincidence and modern technology, appears on Twitter or the *Six O'Clock News*, we turn ourselves in, most likely on the instructions of the DG. Even if that happens, we'll be protected.'

Tomkins asked what he was supposed to say if he was pulled in for questioning.

'The DG's away. Soon as she gets back next week, I'll tell her what's happened. She's the only one apart from the people on our team who knows about BOX 88. I'll tell her that BIRD went missing, that the Iranians were cleaning house. Believe me, she won't want this getting out. If the Met come asking questions, she'll shut them down. There are precedents, many of them.'

Tomkins was momentarily reassured that Vosse already had it all worked out, was capable of processing ideas and making rational decisions outside of normal procedure, normal morality. Yet he couldn't help thinking about Zoltan's death, the fear of being collared as a witness to murder who had failed to come forward. He knew that MI5 officers were part of a special breed, that the usual rules didn't apply, but it felt unethical not to go to the police and tell them everything they needed to know.

'Am I making myself clear?' Vosse asked. 'Am I getting through to you?'

Tomkins nodded. He wasn't sure what the question referred to. He said: 'Sure.'

'Go home, Matt. Get a few hours' sleep. Take a couple of days off. Don't talk to anyone about what happened. Don't google the incident, don't have a crisis of conscience and drive to your nearest police station. The last thing we need is integrity encroaching on all this—'

'All right!' Tomkins snapped. He felt that he was going to cry. It astonished him how badly he had reacted to what had happened. 'I promise I'll go home. I'll lie low. I won't talk to anyone. I won't do anything.' He knew that he sounded petulant and noticed a look of irritation flash across Vosse's face. 'Sorry,' he added desperately. 'I'm just tired. I'm in shock. This is the first time anything like this has ever happened to me.'

'Sure, Matt. Sure. We all have to go through it some time.'

'What about Cara?' he asked.

'I'll call a meeting,' Vosse replied. 'You don't need to be there.'

Tomkins could sense that he was being sidelined, but he lacked the energy and the desire to fight for his place at the table.

'What will happen next?' he asked.

'Leave that to me. Don't worry about it, son. Just take the rest of the week off, get your head straight. Call me in a day or two. OK?'

Cara woke up to a message telling her to get to the Acton safe house as soon as possible. When she arrived, she found Tess and Kieran nursing Starbucks lattes, Vosse looking like he hadn't slept and no sign whatsoever of Matt.

Vosse explained what had happened. Kieran turned the air blue, Tess almost spat out her coffee and Cara suggested that one of them go back to Zoltan's flat and try to find the burner phone he had used to contact the Iranians. Vosse was impressed that she had thought of this but he'd already been to the flat and discovered that somebody had got there ahead of him, removing both the laptop and any trace of the phone. Cara poured herself a glass of water and listened as Vosse stressed the need for absolute secrecy until he had the chance to tell the DG. Amid the general chaos, Kieran was instructed to watch the car park in case the Iranians came back for the CCTV, Tessa was told to

BOX 88

go to the Brighton hospital where Isobel Kite was due on shift and Cara was given the address for Kite's cottage in Sussex. Both were to try to approach Isobel and find out what she knew.

'If she's in a state, chances are she's hit the panic button and BOX 88 personnel will be on the scene,' he told them. 'There might be activity at the house or near the hospital. Get me photos if you can. I want faces of these people. If we can't follow Kite any more, we can follow one of them.'

An hour later Cara was on the train to Lewes looking at an old-fashioned Ordnance Survey map of the hills surrounding Kite's cottage, working out which route to take and preparing what she might say if Isobel was at home and answered the door. There was a man in his early twenties on the train sitting across the aisle from her who did that thing that boys on trains always did, which was to stare at her repeatedly, then to shyly look away whenever Cara looked up and tried to make eye contact. They never found the courage to smile, far less to come over and make conversation, and always got off the train without a nod or a gesture of farewell.

She was surprised that she didn't feel more shocked about what had happened to Pavkov. In a way, Zoltan had been her agent. He would likely still be alive if Cara hadn't worked out the scheme he was running with the Iranians. As a result of her interference, a man was dead: he'd made contact with the people who had kidnapped Kite and they had cut his throat. It was brutal and shocking. Why, then, did she feel so little? Was it delayed shock? She was more concerned about Matt, who had apparently been all over the place after seeing Zoltan's body. Poor bloke. He lived at such a pitch, kept himself coiled so tight and anxious, he was bound to unravel when things got nasty. Cara knew that she was made of sterner stuff. If she was the type of woman who was going to mourn for a corrupt Serb who'd sold out Lachlan Kite for three grand, she was in the wrong job.

The train was on time. Cara caught a cab from Lewes station

and was soon gliding through the English countryside, passing signs for Brighton and Glyndebourne and Firle, the gentle, well-tended hills of the South Downs dotted with sheep and compressed by a low grey sky. She kept thinking of *The Holiday*, the romcom with Jude Law and Cameron Diaz, wondering if it had been filmed in Sussex. She paid the driver at Jevington and set out on the short walk towards Kite's house, dressed in sturdy hiking boots and a dark weatherproof jacket so that she looked like a common-or-garden rambler. She had a long lens camera in her backpack as well as books about trees and birdwatching in case anybody got suspicious and stopped to ask what she was doing. On a training exercise in Wales, she had role-played the part of a camping enthusiast, sleeping rough, pitching a tent, eating food cooked on a gas stove. This job was a breeze by comparison: she got to stroll around in the fresh air in some of the prettiest countryside in England. It was like taking a day off.

As Cara was emerging from a copse of beech trees a couple of miles from Jevington, it began to rain. She pulled up her hood, continuing along a straight, uneven path strewn with leaves and shards of flint. She saw that the cottage was nestled in a forested bowl with sloping hills on all sides; perhaps Kite had chosen it so that he could see who was approaching from every point on the compass. The most direct route to the front door lay across a fallow field running down to a stream at the northern edge of the property. Cara did not want to be exposed in the open field so instead walked in a slow corkscrew loop towards the narrow road on the far side of the house.

After five minutes she stopped and took out the camera. In the shelter of a large oak tree, Cara trained the lens on the cottage, pulling focus from a distance of four hundred metres. The curtains were closed on the ground floor. Blinds were also down and curtains closed in the upstairs rooms. The property had been photographed only once, by Vosse and Tessa. Cara knew from those images that Kite and Isobel did not keep the

BOX 88

curtains closed during the day. It was possible the house was locked up and Kite's wife had gone to London to look for him.

Cara had bought a cheese sandwich at the station in Lewes and now took it out. It was dry and tasteless but she was grateful to have had something to eat. The rain showed no sign of easing up as she put the camera back in the rucksack and made her way down to the road. She tried to text Vosse to give him an update but there was no signal in the valley. Ordinarily Kite and Isobel were able to send and receive messages at the house on 4G; maybe the network was down. Vosse had asked her to try to make contact with Isobel, so she walked towards the cottage with the intention of seeing if she was home.

There was a vehicle parked in the drive. A car fizzed past on the short stretch of road running in front of the cottage, spraying Cara with droplets of puddled rainwater. She rang the doorbell. No response. The blinds and curtains were also closed on this side of the house. She waited for almost a minute then rang the bell a second time. A bird was singing in the trees on the far side of the cottage. There were no other sounds. The sky was grey and lifeless. It was obvious that nobody was inside.

As she was turning away, Cara thought that she heard a noise inside the cottage, but concluded that it was just her ears playing tricks on her. She waited a few more seconds longer then went back to the road. Still no signal on her mobile. She decided to walk back to Jevington and to call a cab from a phone box.

Four hundred metres from the cottage, she heard the sound of an approaching car and stepped up onto a grass verge to allow it to pass. To Cara's surprise she saw that it was the same vehicle—a burgundy Skoda Octavia—which had driven past her only moments earlier. The vehicle slowed as it came towards her. There was a middle-aged black woman at the wheel, a male passenger in the back seat. Perhaps it was an Uber and the driver was lost. She stopped beside Cara, but it was the man in the back seat who wound down the window.

'Excuse me,' he said. He was good-looking and had an American accent. 'Are you Miss Jannaway?'

Cara was astonished. Had something happened in London? Had Vosse sent a car for her?

'I am,' she said. 'Who are you?'

The American opened the back door. Cara leaned down and saw that the driver was pointing a gun at her.

'Get in,' he said. 'Move.'

24

Michael Strawson checked out of Killantringan Lodge early on the morning of Monday, 27 March 1989. He caught a flight from Prestwick to London, couriered his letter to Billy Peele and went back to work at The Cathedral.

Kite spent the rest of the Easter holidays hidden away in his bedroom revising for A levels. Mornings and afternoons were the best times for this: Cheryl and Wilma could cope with any guests who turned up for lunch or tea and Kite was only required to leave his desk if a delivery van turned up and needed unloading. The evenings were different. Cheryl wanted Kite to work in the hotel and he would often not get to bed until after midnight. Waking early each morning, he would make his way through *Mansfield Park* or a booklet on the Tudor monarchs, distractedly thinking of Des tracking leopards in the Serengeti or Xavier skiing powder in the Swiss Alps, a glass of glühwein in one hand, a chalet girl in the other. Not for the first time, Kite began to feel trapped in the wrong kind of life.

After almost three weeks of this he told his mother that he needed a break and caught the train back to Euston. He checked in to 'Hotel Bonnard', his nickname for the house in Onslow Square, and spent three days partying with Xavier, getting drunk at The Fridge and buying more Ecstasy in Mud Club. Kite could find no trace of Alison Hackford in either venue and decided to turn up unannounced at her flat on the final night of the holidays. When a man answered the door, Kite pretended to be a Jehovah's Witness and scarpered.

The next day he was back in his house at Alford, a schoolboy of eighteen pulling on his tailcoat for the final time. As the term progressed, Kite played cricket for the second XI, saw plenty of Billy Peele, spent a long weekend packing up his belongings at Killantringan and sat nine A-level papers in the space of three weeks. By the middle of June, his five-year encounter with Alford College was over.

As if he had been waiting for the whistle to sound on his pupil's final exam, Peele left a note in Kite's pigeonhole congratulating him on finishing his A levels and inviting him to a celebratory dinner at Colenso's, an upmarket Italian restaurant in Windsor. Kite was surprised to discover that no other boy had been invited; perhaps Peele intended to organise a series of farewell meals of which Kite's was the first. He duly obtained permission to attend the dinner, put on a sports jacket and a pair of jeans and walked the short distance down Alford High Street into Windsor.

He had passed Colenso's many times in five years but had never eaten there. A pretty, glass-fronted building with views over the Thames, the restaurant was typically frequented by day trippers and elderly couples taking their Alford grandsons out for lunch. A lone oarsman was piloting a single scull towards Queen's Eyot, a family of swans moving lazily in his slipstream. Kite had been told to arrive at seven but was five minutes late. Unable to spot Peele at any of the tables, he checked the reservation with a waitress and was surprised to be told that Peele had booked a private room for four guests. Removing his jacket, Kite followed the waitress up a short

BOX 88

flight of stairs and was shown to the door of a small dining room overlooked by Windsor Castle.

'Just in here, sir,' she said.

Sitting on the far side of a circular wooden table covered in a white cloth and a vase of flowers, was Billy Peele. Beside him, to Kite's astonishment, was the young black woman he had helped on the Stranraer train. Next to her, slimmer and clean-shaven and rising to his feet as Kite walked in, was Michael Strawson.

'Lachlan,' he said, dropping a napkin onto the table. 'Congratulations on completing your exams. May I formally introduce you to my associate, Rita Ayinde. I believe you two know one another from Scotland. Billy and I are old friends. I hope this isn't too much of a surprise. We've invited you here today because we wanted to talk to you about something.'

25

'It was so much easier with your friend,' said Torabi, taking the gun from his waistband and laying it on top of the pile of boxes. The weight caused the boxes to topple slightly and they came to rest against the wall. 'Xavier was an addict. He was weak. He wanted to talk, he wanted to tell the truth about what happened. All I had to do was take him to lunch, buy him a bottle of wine, some coke. Next thing you know, he's back at my apartment opening up like a canary.'

'It's singing,' said Kite.

'What's that, buddy?'

'It's "singing" like a canary. Not "opening up".'

'You think I give a shit?'

Kite felt the wire around his wrists. He looked at the gun resting on top of the boxes, no more than six feet away. Since the call with Isobel he had been struggling to fight a mood of fatalism which had settled on him.

'He obviously didn't tell you what you needed to know or I wouldn't be here.' Xavier was dead. Kite had nothing left with which to mourn him. The only thing of importance now was saving Isobel. He had to get off the ship. He was convinced that he had been followed by MI5 and that a full-scale manhunt was

BOX 88

underway. Torabi's decision to keep him on the boat suggested that he was not aware of the threat. Either that or he was certain that Kite's location could never be discovered.

'It's not a great look for a guy of forty-eight, is it?' the Iranian continued. 'To be addicted to cocaine, to alcohol, to a life of what you can only describe as self-indulgence. To be incapable of saying no to yourself. To have so little control of your own mind, your own appetites. A man should have conquered his demons by the time he is middle-aged. He should have come to terms with himself.'

'I didn't realise you were such a philosopher.'

Kamran was standing behind Kite, occasionally applying pressure to his forearms so that the wire dug deeper into his wrists.

'My wife is pregnant.'

'I know! When is the child due, Lockie?'

'Fuck you.'

'Then tell me about Eskandarian.'

'I've already said. I don't have the special information you need. Xavier knew more about what happened that summer than I do. It was his house, his catastrophe. I was just a guest.'

'A guest who was a spy for MI6.'

'You're being ridiculous.'

At least they appeared to have no knowledge of BOX 88. That was one small consolation. Torabi picked up a sheet of paper from behind the television. His physical movements were still eerily smooth and precise. Standing with his legs slightly apart, his back straight, he proceeded to read from the document in a manner that reminded Kite of the priest at the Brompton Oratory.

'Does the name Abolghasem Mesbahi mean anything to you?'

Kite was possessed of an extraordinary facility for deceit, honed over three decades in the secret world. If something was black, he could persuade a person that it was white; if it was round, he could convince them it was flat. He lied with every instrument at his disposal: his movements and gestures, his words and actions. It was therefore very easy for him to deny ever having heard the name Abolghasem Mesbahi when he knew very well that he had been a senior Iranian intelligence officer who had defected to the West in 1996.

'I've never heard of him. It means nothing to me.'

'And Ahmed Jibril?' Torabi asked. 'Do you know this person?'

Again, Kite knew the name very well. Jibril was a former Syrian army captain and erstwhile leader of the PFLP-GC, the Popular Front for the Liberation of Palestine. He had led one of the many terrorist groups blamed for the bombing of Pan Am 103 over Lockerbie in December 1988. His name had also been linked to Ali Eskandarian.

'Do I *know* him?' Kite replied. 'No, I don't know him. Friend of yours?'

'I take it you have heard of Abdelbaset al-Megrahi?'

That one was too obvious to lie about. Anyone with a passing knowledge of current affairs in the last thirty years knew the identity of the Libyan intelligence officer who had been convicted by a Scottish court of planting the Lockerbie bomb.

'Yes, of course I've heard of al-Megrahi. Why are you asking me about Lockerbie? Surely that's ancient history?'

It hadn't been ancient history in 1989. Eskandarian had been suspected of being a key player in the plot to bring down Pan Am 103, an American airliner which had blown up over the Scottish town of Lockerbie, killing 11 people on the ground and all 259 passengers and crew. But why was Torabi digging it up now, more than thirty years later?

'Tell me this. When Ali Eskandarian arrived at the house in France, had you been told by MI6 of his links to the PFLP?'

Torabi was reading names and dates from the sheet of paper, asking Kite questions around which he could duck and weave with the ease of a boxer evading telegraphed punches.

'That's one of the strangest questions I've ever been asked. I

BOX 88

feel like it's almost a waste of time denying it. You obviously don't believe that I wasn't working for MI6.' Hossein was standing beside Kite and stepped into his eyeline. 'Of *course* I didn't know Ali Eskandarian was in the PLO—or whatever it is you just referred to. Do you think my mother would have let me go on holiday with a Palestinian terrorist?'

Torabi nodded at Hossein, who immediately struck Kite hard across the jaw, catching him a second time on the opposite side of his face as he recovered from the first blow. Too disorientated to speak, Kite instinctively tried to raise his hands to protect himself but felt the wire biting deep towards the bones of his wrists.

'Enough lies,' Torabi snapped. 'What did William Peele tell you about Eskandarian's relationship with the CIA? Did you know that he became friends with Luc Bonnard in Paris in the 1970s?'

Kite was appalled that Xavier had given up Billy Peele. Somehow he had to stick to his story, but could no longer be sure of how much, or how little, Xavier had told him.

'You think Billy Peele was involved? My fucking history teacher who was on holiday in France? Are you *serious*? That's Xavier's cocaine-induced conspiracy theory. He blamed him for everything, just like his dad blamed the Yanks. Peele was on holiday in the same town as us. Xavier took so much coke in the next fifteen years he convinced himself that one of his old teachers from Alford was watching the house for MI6! Pure paranoia. Now he's thrown me into the mix as well, from the silence of the grave. It's total horseshit.' Torabi glanced quickly at Hossein, as if he was in danger of losing face in front of the prisoner. 'Yes, it's true that Luc and Eskandarian became friends in Paris when they were both living there in the seventies. So what? If you want to know what the CIA knew about Eskandarian's links to the PLO, ask the fucking CIA! How should I know? I was eighteen years old. When I wasn't stoned,

I was drunk. When I wasn't drunk, I was trying to sleep with girls.'

Christ, he thought suddenly. Martha. Had they gone for her as well?

'Not the PLO,' said Torabi, catching Kite's deliberate mistake. 'The PLFP. You know very well that in 1988, an Iranian civilian airliner was shot down by the USS *Vincennes*, an American aircraft carrier operational in the Gulf. All two hundred and ninety people on board, including sixty-six children, were killed. You know very well that according to the confession of Abolghasem Mesbahi, in retaliation for this act of terror the Iranian government of the late Ayatollah Khomeini engaged Ahmed Jibril, a Syrian terrorist, to target an American airliner carrying at least the same number of innocent civilians. You know that with the assistance of his comrades in the PFLP, including Abdelbaset al-Megrahi, Jibril successfully brought down Pan Am 103 by smuggling onboard a barometric pressure device, hidden inside a cassette recorder, which exploded over Lockerbie.'

'Do I know that, Ramin? *Do* I? You make a habit of assuming a hell of a lot about what I know and don't know, about who I am and who I used to be. I was working at my mother's hotel in Scotland when the plane exploded over Lockerbie. If the bomb had gone off ten minutes later, it would likely have come down over my home town. That's the extent of my memory of what happened. I had no idea Eskandarian was suspected of involvement in the plot until you just brought it up. The last time I thought about Megrahi was when the British government agreed to send him back to Libya to die. I thought that was disgusting. I still do.'

Torabi was briefly silenced. Kite felt the heat in his swollen jaw from Hossein's blows. He could not tell if his performance was working or if his lies would lead to yet further misery for Isobel, but he decided to ramp up his denials.

'What is the purpose of this? My wife is pregnant. You are

BOX 88

holding both of us against our will. I can't help you when what you seem to be interested in finding out is so far outside my area of expertise. I will tell you whatever I can remember from France. Perhaps there will be a detail which you can add to something Xavier said which will help you to piece together whatever it is you seem so desperate to know. But, please, release my wife. Let her see a doctor. I'm begging you. This can't go on much longer.'

Torabi remained unmoved. He muttered something in Farsi to Hossein, who left the room. Kamran hawked a ball of phlegm into the back of his throat. Kite wondered if he was going to spit it on his neck. He looked around, trying to think of ways of freeing his wrists. There was so little he could do. He remembered the metal bar in the bathroom, the nail protruding from the wall. They were all he had.

'Listen to me,' said Torabi. He lit a cigarette then suddenly pulled Kite forward, dragging him by the collar so that the chair came with him, scraping across the floor. 'An hour ago I sent one of my men to kill someone. A weak man who risked my entire operation. His mistake was to be stupid. *Your* mistake is to treat me as if *I* am stupid. Here's what I'm going to do.' Torabi grabbed Kite's head and held the lit cigarette against the back of his neck. The ember seared his skin. 'I am sending that same person to the place where we are holding your wife. If in less than two hours you have not told me everything you and the British government know about the life and career of Ali Eskandarian—his links to the PFLP, his relationship with the CIA and with Iranian exile groups in France—he has orders to cut open your wife and to kill the child inside her. For all I care she can watch it die as her own life ebbs away. Do you understand what I am telling you?'

Torabi released Kite's head and stepped backwards, throwing the cigarette on the ground. The back of Kite's neck felt as though it had erupted. Tears formed in his eyes, not from fear but from pain. There was a stench of burned hair.

'I understand,' he gasped.

He closed his eyes. He was not a man to pray, to believe in divine intervention or the possibility of miracles, but if his hands were somehow to have been untied in that moment, he would not have hesitated to kill Torabi. Kite tried to forget what had happened, to ignore the burning sensation on his skin, to believe that he could save Isobel.

'What is your decision?' Torabi asked.

It was the first rule that Strawson and Peele had drummed into him all those years ago. *Never confess. Never break cover.* Somehow he had to keep talking long enough to give MI5 time to find him without giving away the truth about Eskandarian.

'My decision is the same as it has always been,' he said. 'I'll tell you everything I know. Everything I heard about what happened in France when I discussed it with MI6 later.'

Torabi studied Kite's face very closely, weighing up whether or not his offer was sufficient to meet his needs.

'In return, I'll need several things,' Kite continued. 'I want the pressure on my wrists to be reduced because I can no longer feel my hands. I want the wires cut and no more torture.'

'*Torture?*' Torabi replied, as if he had no idea what Kite was referring to.

'You know what I mean,' he said, twisting his head to expose the flesh that Torabi had burned.

'What else?'

Kite involuntarily shook his head from side to side in an attempt to ease his pain. 'I need water. I need something to eat. And a chance, when I'm finished, to speak to my wife, to be reassured that she is safe.'

'Bring him some water,' Torabi replied flatly, speaking to Kamran in English. 'Find him something to eat.' He leaned over, picked up the lit cigarette and extinguished it in an ashtray. 'As for your wife, you've already spoken to her. You don't speak to her again.'

26

The young Lachlan Kite was rarely lost for words, but as he stood in the doorway of the private room at Colenso's, he could think of nothing to say which might adequately express his surprise and confusion. Billy Peele was grinning at him. Michael Strawson, last seen climbing into a taxi at Killantringan, was suddenly a friend of Peele's who had materialised at what was supposed to be a private dinner arranged to celebrate the successful completion of Kite's A levels. Most baffling of all, the timid black woman from the Glasgow train was now a strikingly well-dressed associate of both men, striding towards Kite with a glint in her eye, a glass in her hand and a beaming smile.

'I owe you an explanation, Lockie,' she said. There was no longer any trace of a West African accent. 'Blame my colleagues. They wanted me to see what kind of man you are. They wanted me to test you.' She stuck out her hand. Kite shook it as if in a trance. 'Rita,' she said. 'Thank you for looking after me. Plenty of others would have turned the other cheek.'

'I don't understand,' Kite replied, looking up at Peele for answers.

'Of course you don't,' he said. 'Why would you? Hall of

mirrors. Come and sit down and have a drink. We'll explain everything.'

There was a fourth place laid at the circular table. Kite moved gingerly into his chair, like someone suffering with a bad back. He thought about the TV show *Game for a Laugh* and looked around the room, searching for hidden microphones and cameras. Perhaps Peele had arranged a surprise party and Xavier and Des were about to appear from a concealed room somewhere in the restaurant. He remembered his mother's affection for Strawson and briefly speculated that she was going to show up to congratulate him on finishing his exams.

'Wine?' Peele asked.

'Definitely.'

Strawson boomed a hearty laugh. Peele could see that Kite was struggling and had the good grace to look slightly ashamed of himself. As he poured the glass of wine, he endeavoured to explain what was going on.

'I haven't been entirely honest with the boys about my life pre-Alford,' he said. Rita sat down and flapped a napkin into her lap. She was wearing perfume, a smell as rare and as coveted by Alford boys as bottles of vodka and packets of cigarettes. 'For Royal Marine, read soldier turned spy. Sixteen years ago I was recruited into—'

'You're a *spy*?' Kite replied. He did not fully understand what this meant—he had an image in his mind of Ian Ogilvy in *The Saint*—but understood enough to know that what Peele had once been was rare and extraordinarily exciting.

'Of a sort,' Peele replied.

'Are you all spies?' Kite asked, looking at them in turn.

Strawson remained impassive. Kite remembered the money on the floor in Churchill, the riddle of the light switches, the lamp teetering over the edge of the bath. The whole thing must have been some sort of test. But how was it possible for these

BOX 88

people to have arranged for three skinheads to scare the shit out of him on the evening train to Ayr?

'We'll get to that,' said Strawson, appearing to enjoy his own reply.

'We work for a special alliance of British and American intelligence,' said Rita. 'We work for BOX 88.'

'BOX 88,' Kite repeated quietly. He thought of phone booths, of Post Office deposit boxes, of the year 1988. He was utterly confused. 'What is that? I've heard of MI5, of MI6, the CIA—'

'We are all those things,' said Strawson. 'And more.'

Peele smiled over the rim of his glass. 'From time to time the Metropolitan Police have referred to MI5 as BOX 500, to MI6 as BOX 850. We're something rather different. Nothing to do with 1988, nothing to do with neo-Nazis.'

'Neo-Nazis?' Kite asked.

'The number eighty-eight has been co-opted by certain elements in the far right. Something to do with Heil Hitler, where the number eight stands in for the letter "H". Never mind.' He put the glass down. 'Before we go any further, Lockie, we need to ask you an important question.'

Strawson nodded solidly, prompting Peele to continue.

'We're considering the possibility of involving you in an operational capacity. This will require of you a great sacrifice as well as an absolute guarantee that, when you leave this room, you never speak to anyone—not your mother, not Xavier, not anybody—about what has been said here today.'

Why was he bringing up Xavier? Kite gulped his wine and almost lost control of the glass as he put it down on the table.

'What kind of sacrifice?' he asked, wondering if they were going to ask him to break the law. He wouldn't have minded doing so—in fact, the idea of being involved in something illegal was oddly thrilling—but he needed more detail.

Strawson leaned forward. 'Do we have your guarantee that

you will never speak of this, or any subsequent meeting that might take place, ever again?'

Kite felt that he had no choice other than to agree. He looked at Peele, as if his tutor might offer him some much-needed words of advice or encouragement, but realised that nothing was going to happen until he promised to keep his mouth shut.

'Sure,' Kite said. 'Yeah. I won't tell anyone.'

He meant it. He had the evolving sense that these people were capable of anything. Whatever they were about to tell him, he knew that it was something extraordinary from the world, beyond Alford, a secret much larger than school or Killantringan or drunken parties in London. Kite recalled the feeling of being a small child overhearing the whispered conversations of grown-ups in adjoining rooms.

'You want to serve your country? You want to protect your fellow citizens, keep them safe in their beds?'

Strawson's questions unbalanced Kite still further. He could scarcely understand how he could serve his country or protect people from harm in the way that the American had suggested. But again his instinctive response was to agree.

'Of course. Who wouldn't?'

'Excellent!' Peele exclaimed. 'So let's get on with it, shall we?'

Kite saw that he had misjudged him; or, more accurately, had failed to detect the secret Peele was hiding even from those closest to him. He was a teacher and a friend, yes, but he was also plainly a man of violence and lies. Kite understood Strawson to be potentially even more devious, packed with American charm and bonhomie but possessed of an iron will and ruthlessness as plain to see as the squalid perversions which lurked inside Lionel Jones-Lewis. As for Rita, what did he know? That she was a convincing actress. That she smelled of the promise of release from Alford, of future summers with girls. It occurred to Kite that she was the only black woman he had ever spent any length of time with in his eighteen and a half years on the planet.

BOX 88

'What kind of things would you need me to do?'

'Good question,' Strawson replied. But then they had to pause, because two waitresses walked into the room and served the food—a starter of smoked salmon arranged inside neatly cut triangles of crustless brown bread. Only when they had left the room and closed the door behind them did Strawson continue. Even then he showed little interest in answering Kite's question directly.

'BOX 88 is unknown to both the Metropolitan Police, MI5 and all but a select few government officials and civil servants on both sides of what Billy here likes to refer to as The Pond. We straddle the Atlantic.'

Kite looked at Rita, remembering that she had described BOX 88 as a 'special alliance' between British and American intelligence. He glugged a mouthful of wine.

'The intelligence community in the United States hit a brick wall some time ago,' Strawson continued. 'I don't know how much you know about the CIA, but let's just say that the Agency hasn't exactly covered itself in glory since the Second World War. Something had to change. We were operating ideologically, obsessed with the spread of Communism, obsessed with the Soviet threat, neglecting to take a long-term view. As a consequence, we failed to anticipate significant global shifts and political earthquakes. You could cite the 1979 Iranian Revolution as a prime example.'

Peele coughed and picked up his fork, as if he sensed that a lot of what Strawson was saying would be going over Kite's head. Rita also made a start on her smoked salmon. Kite put a look on his face which he hoped would convey the appearance of someone absorbing and understanding every word that Strawson uttered.

'At the same time, British secret intelligence—that is to say its foreign manifestation, MI6, not MI5—saw their future being curtailed, their wings clipped, by creeping bureaucracy. You won't be aware of this, but both MI5 and MI6 have been undergoing a process in recent years of emerging into the sunlight after decades in darkness. Government oversight is the new order of the day, just as CIA is answerable to Congress in Washington.' Strawson took a sip of water. 'In short, the Brits couldn't do what they used to do. They couldn't do what they *wanted* to do. Intelligence was being left in the hands of the politicians—and let me tell you, if you let those guys enjoy too much operational control, to push you this way and that because of their own narrow electoral outlook, it's bound to lead to setbacks.'

It was a natural point at which Kite might have been expected to say something, but he did not want to seem foolish by asking the wrong question. Peele saw that he was hesitating and came to his rescue.

'What Mike is trying to tell you, Lockie, is that five years ago a small group of officers inside MI6 created a new unit within the Service which would not be bound by the same rules and regulations that applied to colleagues. They called this unit BOX 88. Allow me to explain how normal, run-of-the-mill intelligence-gathering works. It's commonplace for the prime minister of the day to issue what are called "requirements". Mrs Thatcher, for example, can come to MI6 and say: "Get me everything you have on Mikhail Gorbachev." So off they go and get her everything they have on Mikhail Gorbachev. But what if she wants too much of the same thing? What if she can't be persuaded to look at Syria, at France, at Iran with the same kind of vigour, despite our belief that individuals in those nations present either an existential threat to the security of the British people or, more often, an opportunity to—for want of a better term—make the world a better place?'

'You mean you go behind the prime minister's back?'

Strawson coughed behind his napkin.

'To all intents and purposes, yes,' Peele replied. 'That's exactly what we do. We go behind the backs of presidents and prime

BOX 88

ministers, of secretaries of state, heads of the Foreign Office and so forth. BOX 88 does the things they don't want us to do, that they don't *ask* us to do, which they don't realise *need* to be done.'

'But, Mr Strawson—' Kite checked himself. He was still at Killantringan, bringing cheese and biscuits to the guest staying in Churchill. 'Mr Strawson is an American. You said you were in the CIA? How does that work? Have the two agencies always been tied like this?'

Strawson scratched a point behind his ear. In the time it had taken Peele to explain the origins of BOX 88, he had consumed his smoked salmon, leaving the bread triangles untouched in a neat pile at the edge of his plate.

'I never said I was CIA, but—yes—I was CIA for a long time.' He reached out and touched Kite's forearm in a way Kite hadn't expected and which he didn't particularly appreciate. 'Let's say I saw the rot set in. The British came to me in '83 and I learned about BOX 88. We discussed creating a partnership. I spoke to select colleagues who arranged for a certain percentage of the overall intelligence budget to be diverted to BOX as a complement to the minimal UK spending available. We now have a network of contacts within NSA and GCHQ Cheltenham, referred to as "Turings", who provide us with what's known as "signals intelligence"—satellite imagery, computer attacks and so forth—under the guise of supporting frontline services at Five, Six and CIA.'

'If we discover things,' Peele continued, 'and we think the prime minister or the president of the day should know, we send that intel up the food chain, via the normal channels, so that the frontline services get a pat on the back. At any one time there have never been more than six individuals in MI6 and a dozen more at Langley who know about BOX 88. We're a rumour, probably not even that, and we intend to keep it that way. We tend to recruit young—usually graduates in their early twenties—but there are personnel of all ages, from all walks of life, working for us here and in New York. The current head of M16 is what we call "conscious"—that is to say, he knows about BOX. The serving director general of MI5 is not, ditto Sessions at the FBI. They'd likely be appalled if they found out.'

Kite was baffled. If what Peele was telling him was true, he was one of only a handful of people on the planet who knew about this organisation. Why the hell were they letting him in on a secret of that magnitude? What had he done to land himself in this predicament? It occurred to him that Peele must have been preparing him for this moment for months.

'I have a lot of questions,' he said.

Everyone laughed. 'I'm sure you do, young man!' Strawson replied.

'Do you all have normal jobs? Like Mr Peele is a teacher?' He looked at Rita. 'What do you do?'

Kite realised that he had not touched his food and wolfed the salmon in four quick mouthfuls as Rita explained that she worked at 'The Cathedral', the London headquarters of BOX 88, telling her friends that she was a secretary when in fact she worked in intelligence.

'And you, sir?'

'Call me Mike,' Strawson replied, encouraging Kite with a brisk nod. 'To my friends in the United States, I work for an American policy unit based here in the UK. To my friends in the UK, I'm advising an investment bank in the City on growth in the North American sector.'

Kite didn't know what a 'policy unit' was but understood that this probably wasn't the time to ask. Instead he fired more questions at his hosts, receiving what he considered to be logical, comprehensive answers. He learned that, contrary to popular belief, mainstream MI6 and CIA officers were not 'licensed to kill', but that the ranks of BOX 88 were filled with former Navy SEALS and ex-SAS who carried out targeted kidnappings and assassinations to order. He was told that approximately 230 staff

BOX 88

worked at BOX 88 headquarters in the World Trade Center in lower Manhattan and a further 135 at The Cathedral. The bulk of the work carried out by BOX 88 was conducted overseas by a network of undercover agents operating under what Peele described as 'non-official cover'.

'In other words,' he said, by now tucking into a hearty-looking fish pie, 'these individuals present themselves as bankers, businessmen, journalists and so forth, but their deeper purpose is to conduct operations on our behalf.'

Those operations, Rita explained, had included plots to destabilise Communist dictatorships behind the Iron Curtain; to foment opposition to the Politburo among the Chinese student population in Beijing, leading directly to the protests in Tiananmen Square; helping to overthrow Haitian president Jean-Claude Duvalier and preventing numerous terrorist attacks around the globe.

'But we can't stop everything,' said Strawson. 'We don't have the range. We didn't stop Lockerbie.'

By this point they had finished eating their main courses. Peele had asked the restaurant staff to leave them undisturbed. Kite remembered the night of the Lockerbie bombing. He had been working at the hotel. His mother had switched on the news, seen a graphic of the flight path and commented that it would have blown up over Killantringan just a few minutes later. To his surprise, Strawson revealed that he had discussed the tragedy with Cheryl while staying at the hotel.

'We lost someone on the flight,' he said. 'A colleague from the New York office. Buddy of mine in London, banker named Tom Martin, also knew three of the victims personally. A mother and a father in their thirties and their little girl, Gaby. She was only eight. Used to come by their house and play with his daughter.'

The American leaned over. He picked up an envelope from the ground. Kite sensed that he had arrived at a critical juncture in the long meeting. From inside the envelope Strawson produced several colour photographs which he passed across the table.

'I gotta warn you, son. You'll need a strong stomach.'

Kite looked at the top photograph. It was the now-famous image of the nose cone of Pan Am 103 resting on the ground near Lockerbie. What followed was a sequence of images as horrifying and distressing as any Kite had ever seen: a body hanging from the rafters of a house; another ensnared in a tree. He saw men and women still strapped into their aeroplane seats sitting in a row on the ground. Kite knew that this was another test—they wanted to see if he was tough enough to absorb such horror and to emerge from it unscarred—so he moved painstakingly through to the last of the photographs—a ghastly image of a man standing almost upright in a field, having plunged from the sky and become embedded in the Scottish soil—and put the pictures down on the table. He could not help himself letting out a heavy sigh and felt their eyes on him, judging him, as he leaned back in his seat.

'Those are awful,' he said. 'Those poor people.' His skin was fizzing with revulsion but he managed to compose himself enough to ask: 'Why did you show them to me?'

'We think there's a chance it might happen again,' said Rita. 'Investigators have been looking at a link with Iran. Specifically, an individual who may have helped to finance the Lockerbie bombing by funnelling money from Tehran to Gaddafi.'

Kite touched the pile of photographs. *Tehran.* A sixth sense made a link in his mind between Xavier and the Iranian man who was coming to stay at the villa in France. He remembered Xavier mentioning him back in February. *My godfather is coming to stay . . . I call him the "ayatollah".* Why else had Peele brought up Xavier's name at the start of lunch?

'Another Lockerbie?' he said. 'They're going to blow up a plane?'

'Worse than that.' Strawson looked up at Windsor Castle. 'A

BOX 88

chemical weapon released onto the New York subway. Sarin. That's the chatter from Tripoli. That's what we've been trying to understand.'

Kite knew nothing about chemical weapons, only what he had seen in movies and read in comic books.

'Forgive me,' he said, 'but what does all this have to do with me? You said you wanted to involve me in an operational capacity?'

'We do,' Peele replied. 'Very much. Strange as it may seem, you're in the perfect position to be able to help us.'

Kite looked at him. He recalled a dozen different moments from their relationship: the Test match at Lord's; conversations at Peele's flat on Alford High Street; history lessons in the class-room beside the racquets courts. All that time, his tutor had been watching him, weighing him up, preparing to throw him into this secret sect. The realisation confirmed something that Kite had believed about himself for as long as he could remember: that he was somehow different to other people, not superior, but separate from the mainstream. He had often felt as though he was standing at the edge of a fast-flowing river watching all of life rushing past. Peele was encouraging him to jump in.

'It involves your friend Xavier,' said Rita. 'It involves your holiday in France.'

Xavier's name clicked into place like the last few turns of a Rubik's cube. Kite had known that it was coming. The Iranian. 'The ayatollah.' He was the key.

'The businessman who will be staying with the Bonnard family,' Rita continued, 'is a man named Ali Eskandarian. All of our intelligence suggests that he is a prominent individual at the centre of the terrorist network. Either he has the power to facilitate this attack or he has the wherewithal to put a stop to it. We mean to find out. And we need you to help us do that.'

27

The driver continued to point the gun at Cara as she climbed into the back seat of the Skoda. The American reached across and closed the back door.

'What's going on?' Cara asked.

The American did not respond. He smelled of stale tobacco and cheap aftershave. The black woman, who was at least fifty, passed him the gun and drove off along the lane. She did not drive fast. She did not seem anxious or in any way concerned about what had just taken place. It was as if grabbing lone female ramblers on quiet country lanes was something that she did all the time.

'How did you know my name?'

The American was about thirty-five, obviously military. Lean, tanned, scarred. Strong hands, hair cropped close, pale blue eyes as clear as topaz. Even in her frightened state, Cara was conscious that he was attractive. The car turned onto a muddy track, passed over a cattle grid and came to a halt behind an abandoned farmhouse.

'We get out here,' he said.

She knew, without being told, that he was BOX 88. It was the only plausible explanation.

BOX 88

'Not until you tell me what's going on.'

The American took a beat before seizing her by the arm. The force of his grip was so overwhelming that Cara cried out as she was dragged across the back seat. He pulled her from the car until she said, 'OK, OK, I'm coming, let me go.' After that she walked in front of him towards a barn where two men were hunched over laptops. They did not look up. There was a smell of spilled oil and manure. The woman drove off in the Skoda without a word. The American told Cara to sit down on a hay bale and put the gun on a rusted tank onto which someone had graffitied a smiley face and the words 'Tanks for the memories'.

'My name is Jason,' he said.

'Good for you.'

'Your name is Cara Jannaway. You were born in Norwich in 1994. You had a Thai meal delivered to your apartment last night. Stir-fry chicken. You have a brother called Jude, a sister who died when you were six. You're on Tinder and had a date last week with an actor called Nick. Swipe for long enough and you'll probably match up with your colleague, Matthew Tomkins. You've worked for the Security Service for almost a year. Your boss is Robert Vosse. Yesterday you went to a funeral pretending to be "Emma" and gave your card to a man named Lachlan Kite. Any of this sounding familiar?'

Cara tried not to look as shaken as she felt. Unwittingly a smile appeared on her face as she realised that her hunch had been right: Kite had known she was phoney. He had handed her the card so that BOX 88 could investigate 'Emma' as soon as she was dumb enough to ring the number. The rest would have been easy: Tinder, Deliveroo—it was all on her phone. The DG's whistle-blower had said that BOX had personnel working for them in all the services, on both sides of the Atlantic. Finding out how long she'd been operational would have been as easy as frogmarching her into the barn.

'Sounds familiar,' she replied. 'But leave my sister out of it.'

'Drink?' said Jason.

'What are you offering? Champagne? Lucozade Sport?'

Cara saw the edge of a smile on one of the laptop boys, but Jason remained stony faced.

'I meant water,' he said.

'I know you did, handsome.'

Jason took a step towards her, a warning not to get too smart. Cara felt herself tense up. She knew what sort of man he was. She had met his sort before. Back home in Norwich there had been boys who had left school at sixteen, dealt drugs and broken hearts for a few years, gone to prison for a stretch, joined the army as a last resort. Iraq and Afghanistan had given their lives meaning, handed them a chance to channel their rage. She reckoned Jason was their American doppelganger, signing up after 9/11, tours of duty in Baghdad and Fallujah, now ex-Special Forces on call to solve whatever problems BOX 88 needed solving, violently or otherwise. He dragged a hay bale in front of Cara and kicked it into position. His legs were so strong it was as though the bale was filled with air.

'Keep joking around and this goes badly for you,' he said.

'Easy, Jase,' muttered one of the laptoppers. He was in his late twenties and had a northern English accent. 'All friends here.' Cara looked up and saw what looked like a sequence of messages scrolling on the screen of his laptop.

'What was MI5 doing at the funeral?' Jason asked. Cara had opened her mouth to respond when he added: 'Don't lie. We have a clock ticking.'

'Tell me who you are and I'll tell you what you want to know.'

'We're on your side. The same side. I work with Mr Kite. I look after him.'

Cara was about to say: 'You're not doing a very good job,' but thought better of it. Instead she said: 'You're BOX 88?'

BOX 88

Jason flinched. One of the laptop boys stopped typing for a split second, then resumed.

'We're British intelligence.'

'And American intelligence all at the same time?'

'There's a clock ticking,' Jason replied.

The answer was in their silence and evasions. Cara felt her stomach flip over.

'Fair enough,' she said.

'So—again, Cara—what was the Security Service doing at Xavier Bonnard's funeral?'

'I'm not permitted to tell you that,' she said. It amused her that he had pronounced 'Xavier' in the American way, as if Bonnard was a character on *X-Men*. 'You need to ask Robert Vosse.'

'I don't have time to ask Robert Vosse. I'm asking you. The people who have Lachlan took his wife as well. Isobel is inside that house, pregnant, with a gun to her head. She's a friend of mine, they both are, so I kind of want to get her out in one piece. Understood? Help me join the dots. Forget due process. Forget what you think is the correct thing to do.'

Cara was shocked that the Iranians had grabbed Isobel, but not surprised. It was the right move in terms of getting Kite under control.

'I'm part of a very small team looking at Kite's links to BOX 88,' she said. Giving up her cover was like confessing to a lie as a child. 'It's an internal MI5 investigation prompted by a whistle-blower in SIS. If you guys are as good as everyone says you are, then you probably already know this.'

Nothing from Jason. Nothing from the two men staring into their laptops. Cara filled the silence.

'I spoke to Kite,' she said. 'Like you said, I was running an alias. Emma. Said I'd met him at the Frieze art fair. We know Kite collects paintings, it seemed like a good route in.'

Again, no response from Jason. Just an expressionless stare that demanded: *Keep going.*

'He obviously saw through the legend. Didn't trust me. Gave me the card, hoping I'd use it. I did just that. The rest is history.'

Jason appeared to be making an assessment of whether or not Cara was telling him the truth.

'That was your only interaction?'

'Face to face, yes. But a lot has happened since then.'

She asked for some water. He gave her a litre-bottle labelled Highland Spring which tasted as though it had come out of a tap on the farm. Cara told Jason about the Middle Eastern man at the funeral, the rented Jaguar, the switch at the car park, the kidnapping of Kite and the murder of Zoltan Pavkov. After fifteen minutes the older woman came back in the Skoda and introduced herself as Rita. Rita started listening to the story as well. Cara had the sense that one of the two men using the laptops was taking down everything she said. By the time she had finished, she was hungry. She asked for some food and was given a stale sausage roll. There was still no signal on her mobile phone. She asked if BOX 88 had put an electronic bubble around the house so that the people holding Isobel would have no way of contacting their team.

'Exactly,' said Rita. She seemed impressed that Cara had correctly deduced this. Either that or she just had one of those faces which was friendly in all weathers.

'Fred is across their comms,' Jason explained, scratching the back of his neck. Fred was the man with the northern accent who had come to Cara's aid. He briefly looked up and smiled. 'London is translating what they send in, translating what they send out. Whoever's inside wants to speak to his boss, wants to know what to do with Isobel. We're going to clone the incoming messages, assume the identity of whoever is giving them their orders, tell them to move the prisoner to a new location. When they do that, we go in.'

BOX 88

Go in, thought Cara, knowing what that meant but not wanting to look troubled by the prospect. She had realised that neither Rita nor Jason had any idea who had kidnapped Kite. Nor did they know where he was being held.

'Stick to Canary Wharf,' she told them. Rita shot Jason a glance. One of the laptoppers leaned over and scratched an itch on his ankle. On the furthest of the two screens Cara could now see infra-red images from the cottage. 'That's where the van was last seen,' she said. 'That's where they killed Zoltan.'

'Canary Wharf?' Jason asked, as if Cara might have made a mistake.

'Yeah,' she told him. 'Why?'

'Nothing.'

Cara had been around spies long enough to know when someone was keeping something from her.

'What's in Canary Wharf that's so important?' she asked.

'Mind your own business.'

28

Before the meeting in the Windsor restaurant, Lachlan Kite had thought of himself as a reasonably settled, confident person. He was not beset by many of the commonplace, day-to-day insecurities of the young and felt that he had adjusted well to the death of his father. He knew that he was slightly vain and self-aware, but these were hardly sins of great magnitude for a young man of his age. For example: Kite consciously tried to model his appearance on River Phoenix, growing out his hair as much as the Alford rules had allowed (nothing below the collar, no dyes, no buzz cuts) and letting it fall moodily across his eyes whenever a girl hoved into view. In this respect he was no different to many of his friends, who variously copied Morrissey or Ben Volpeliere-Pierrot in their attempts to look cool. Kite was hard-working, ambitious and looking forward to the future. He was fun to be around, loyal to his friends and a dutiful, if occasion-ally exasperated, son. Unlike many of his fellow students at Alford, he felt equally comfortable in the presence of men and women. He could look at himself in the mirror and feel sure that he was more or less on the right path and that he had every chance of living a long, happy life.

After the meeting in Windsor, Kite felt completely unmoored.

BOX 88

It was as if everything he had imagined might happen to him in the future, his sense of himself, even his attitudes towards his friends and family, had been turned on its head. Saying yes in the restaurant had been easy: after all, who could turn down such an opportunity? Within a few days, however, the prospect of going to France and carrying out what he had agreed to do struck Kite as being morally reprehensible. He was being asked to spy, to deceive his oldest and closest friend. He was being invited to lie and to betray, to appear to be one sort of person when in fact he was quite another. Worse, he would be spying in a house belonging to a family who had nurtured and cared for him for five years. It was duplicity of the worst kind. Kite could not tell his mother what he was intending to do nor confide in any of his friends. Had his father still been alive, he too would have been ignorant of the choice his son had made. Would Paddy Kite have approved of what he was about to do—or been appalled that his son had so easily agreed to slip into a double life?

In the days that followed the meal in Colenso's, there had been another stone in Kite's shoe. Whenever he cast his mind back to the Easter weekend, he understood the purpose of Strawson's visit to Killantringan and accepted that it had been necessary to test him: to organise the power cut, for example, and to ensure that his mother was delayed in Stranraer so that BOX 88 could analyse how he reacted under pressure. Yet at a distance of several weeks from these events he felt oddly humiliated, not to mention angry that Strawson had so carelessly jeopardised his mother's business. A group of adults of vastly wider life experience had set him up. The feeling was not dissimilar to Kite's memories of his first weeks at Alford when, as a guileless thirteen-year-old, Cheryl had thrust him into an ecosystem of mindboggling social and historical complexity, expecting him to come to terms with traditions and rules about which Kite had known next to nothing. Lionel Jones-Lewis had presented himself to Kite as a warm, friendly father figure, only to be revealed within a matter of weeks as the sort of man who had become a schoolmaster solely so that he could live his life surrounded by attractive teenage boys. Why should Kite do the bidding of people who had consciously manipulated him in such a way? He had believed in Rita's predicament on the train and felt foolish for saving her from thugs whom Strawson confessed had been working for BOX 88. Kite was stubborn and determined and proud. He was intrigued by the nature of the French operation, flattered to have been singled out for such a prestigious job and drawn to these unusual characters from the secret world. Certainly he did not think that Strawson was in any way as seedy nor as deceitful as his former housemaster. Nevertheless, on several occasions he thought about knocking on Billy Peele's door and calling the whole thing off.

What stopped him was the potential threat from Eskandarian. The idea that he might be able to play a role—however small—in preventing a terrorist atrocity in the United States convinced Kite that he should set his ethical concerns to one side and commit himself to BOX 88. At his second meeting with Strawson and Rita Ayinde in London's Ravenscourt Park a few weeks later, Kite confirmed that he was happy to go ahead.

'I'm relieved,' said Rita. 'We wondered if you might have been having second thoughts.'

'It wasn't an easy decision,' Kite told her. 'I don't feel great about Xav.'

'Of course you don't.' They were walking along a broad promenade in bright sunshine, Rita on one side of Kite, Strawson on the other. 'Think of it as doing him a favour. If his family are giving shelter to a terrorist financier, the sooner they find out, the better.'

Kite was still unclear what was so important about Xavier's 'godfather'. As they made half a dozen circuits of the park, Strawson told him everything he needed to know.

'Short of recruiting someone at the highest levels of the Iranian

BOX 88

government, we couldn't be looking at a more influential figure in Iran than Ali Eskandarian. Son of a wealthy *bazaari* who allowed him to run around Paris in the 1970s, he was a rich kid on the side of the Revolution. Worked in the oil ministry from '79 onwards, moved to Health in '83, starts spending more and more time in Russia, which is when he first appears on CIA radar. Langley didn't think he was important enough to keep tabs on. The less said about that, the better. Maybe they were too busy on Iran-Contra. We have Eskandarian attending conferences all over the world. Gets himself a reputation as a westernised liberal even when MI6 see him making contact with the PFLP—that's the Popular Front for the Liberation of Palestine. Even then the Brits don't think he's worth watching.'

'More fool them,' said Rita.

'Eskandarian moved into the private sector in '85, made a ton of money, but all the while he was maintaining links with senior people in the regime apparatus. Right now, we have him as the ten-million-dollar bagman for Lockerbie. We think he's taking orders from the very top in Tehran.'

'Why do you think that?' Kite asked, not wanting to sound naive.

'Eskandarian advises the new guy in charge, Rafsanjani, behind the backs of the senior clerics,' Strawson replied. 'Back in January he arranges a trip to France, wants to see his old friend from Paris days, Luc Bonnard. Khomeini apparently says no problem, go to Luc, go to France. Then Khomeini dies. They have an election coming up in Iran at the end of July. Rafsanjani is expected to win and be confirmed as the new president. Does Eskandarian cancel his trip? No, he does not.'

'I don't really get it,' said Kite. So much information had been thrown at him that he was beginning to feel swamped.

'The question is straightforward,' the American replied. 'What's so important that Rafsanjani is prepared to let one of his closest friends and advisers, potentially the financier for

Lockerbie, roam around France for two weeks in August, right after he might become president? What did Khomeini set in train that we don't know about? The world has been looking at Tiananmen since the spring. Nobody is paying any attention to a highly influential Iranian go-between who arranged a so-called vacation in France six months ago and is sticking to it, regardless of the fact that the ayatollah is now dead and his country in turmoil. What is Eskandarian planning? Who is he meeting? And how does Luc Bonnard fit into all this?'

Kite had an almost photographic memory and could file away names and dates and events with relative ease. Nevertheless, he wished that he had been permitted to write notes on what he was being told.

'Luc?' he replied. 'He's involved in this?'

Ayinde caught Strawson's eye, but neither responded directly to Kite's question. Instead, Rita said:

'Think of yourself as someone who is helping to fill in a corner of a very large canvas. There may be something you discover in France—something you're completely unaware of but which nevertheless makes sense to us—which could later become crucial to our understanding of who exactly we're dealing with and what their precise intentions are.'

'So how do I go about doing that?' Kite asked. 'How do I fill in this canvas?'

They were standing in a tunnel beneath a railway line at the south-eastern entrance to the park. Strawson came to a halt as a train thundered overhead.

'It's easy,' he said, obliged to step to one side as a child ran past them. He raised his voice so that he could be heard above the noise of the train, his words echoing in the dark tunnel. 'We spend the next three weeks teaching you.'

29

How well can you ever know a person?

In the six years that Isobel Paulsen had been involved with Lachlan Kite—falling in love, getting married in Stockholm, becoming pregnant with their child—she had always known that a day like this would finally come. Eighteen months into their relationship he had told her that he wasn't in fact an oil trader, that when he went to work in Canary Wharf he wasn't going to the headquarters of Grechis Petroleum, he was instead going to a suite of offices occupied by individuals working in secret on behalf of British intelligence. The revelation in itself hadn't particularly surprised her; Isobel had always suspected that Kite was hiding something from her. He was clever, physically fit, charming and unsentimental: it made sense that he was a spy. What troubled her was the realisation that his past would now remain hidden from her forever. There were vast tracts of his life about which she would know nothing: operations, successes, failures, lovers. He had spoken several times of a former girl-friend, Martha Raine, the woman who had telephoned him from New York with the news of Xavier's death. Isobel came to under-stand that Martha had been inextricably linked with Kite's early years as an intelligence officer; a woman she had never met had access to a greater intimacy with her husband than she did. Isobel was envious of this, no question. She tried to tell herself that Kite's past was no different to anyone else's. We all have secrets, she thought. We all have shame. We have all had relationships which have shaped us. Yet somehow what had passed between Martha and Kite was richer in Isobel's imagination, more complex and meaningful, than any of her own entanglements.

When she saw her husband's face on the screen of the cell phone, Isobel did not panic. She did not worry that Kite looked tired and shaken, that his life was at risk or that she might never hold him again. She had seen Kite at his most vulnerable—in illness, in grief, in personal tragedy—and knew that he was strong enough to withstand whatever was happening to him. She did not doubt him.

'I'm fine,' she had told him, trying not to worry him or make him fear for the baby. 'Why are they holding you? You haven't done anything. They think you're a spy—'

He would have understood that she was trying to protect him. They were talking to one another without talking to one another, speaking intimately without the scum who were holding them understanding. Isobel was confused and worried, yes. She did not know why these men had taken her hostage, nor why Kite was being held captive by their associates. She did not know where he was or what they wanted from him. Yet she had never felt so extraordinarily close to him. This was *their* shared fate, *their* crisis, *their* test. It had nothing to do with the past, with Kite's secrets, with Martha Raine. They would survive it together and emerge stronger and happier than they already were. They would have their baby.

Isobel made a conscious decision to think like this. Doing so was the one way she could help Kite and preserve her own peace of mind. Taking this approach was the best protection for her child.

It was a version of prayer.

30

By the middle of July, Killantringan had been packed up and sold off, leaving Kite effectively homeless. Rather than go to Sligo to stay with his extended family, he moved into a BOX 88 safe flat in Hampstead, telling his mother that he was staying with friends, telling friends that he was staying with his mother. Over the course of the next three weeks, Peele taught Kite how to clear a dead letterbox, how to discern if he was under surveillance and how to carry out a brush contact in a crowded place. All these were elements of tradecraft which, Kite was assured, would likely serve no useful purpose in France. Nevertheless, it was important for him to familiarise himself with the basic principles of espionage so that they became second nature to him, 'like throwing a rugby ball or riding a bike' as Peele put it. In his former teacher's assessment, there was a 'negligible chance' that Kite would be placed under surveillance during the operation. After all, he was Xavier's best friend, not a stranger to the family who had wandered in off the street. If the French or the Iranians were on the lookout for trouble, their lenses would be trained on Ali Eskandarian, not on Lachlan Kite. That was the beauty of it: Kite was going to be hiding in plain sight, reporting on everything going on at the villa, and all the while keeping up the pretence of being a diffident eighteen-year-old school leaver with nothing on his mind but lying by the pool with a Milan Kundera, drinking beer and working on his suntan.

So much of what Peele taught him was, initially at least, confusing to the eighteen-year-old Kite. He had known that France, like the UK and a great many other countries, had highly sophisticated intelligence services capable of everything from surveillance to state-sponsored assassinations. Yet prior to his training, his knowledge of the secret world had extended to a handful of Ian Fleming novels and a rental of *Defence of the Realm* from the video shop in Stranraer. Kite had never seen the television adaptations of *Smiley's People* and *Tinker, Tailor, Soldier, Spy*. He was too young to remember the public unmasking and subsequent reputational disgrace of Sir Anthony Blunt. He had seen spy movies in which people unscrewed the handsets of telephones and dropped bugs into the mouthpiece, watched Bond films in which Roger Moore or Timothy Dalton were strapped to chairs and interrogated under bright white lights. Such incidents belonged to a different world, a dimension of fantasy bearing little resemblance to the experience of learning at Peele's knee and accumulating knowledge on the workings of BOX 88.

On the first day at the Hampstead flat, for example, Kite was instructed to memorise the names of every metro station on the New York subway in case they appeared as targets for attacks on a document at the villa or were mentioned during conversation. A memo from Strawson suggested that Kite should also familiarise himself with the city's history and culture, on the basis that a codename for the alleged plot might make reference to some aspect of New York life of which Kite was unaware. Peele duly drew up a list of names and places—from DAKOTA to LIBERTY, from IDLEWILD to ROCKEFELLER—covering four sheets of A4 paper, front and back. He did the same for chemical and biological weapons, telling Kite to listen out and

BOX 88

look for certain keywords—among them BIOPREPARAT, FERMENT, EKOLOGY—as well as scientific terms—ATROPINE, PRALIDOXIME, SARIN—which reminded Kite of sitting his chemistry O level.

Peele spent many hours explaining to Kite precisely how he was going to help once he reached Mougins. BOX 88 needed as much information on Eskandarian as possible. That meant Kite reporting on any visitors to the house and providing detailed accounts of the Iranian's conversations and general behaviour. He was to befriend Eskandarian and earn his trust. Prior to Kite's arrival, a team of Falcons would arrange for the villa to be bugged, but he would be taking equipment of his own and would be required to assist the Falcons if anything went wrong with their technology. BOX 88 had rented a property several hundred metres from the Bonnard villa which was to be used as a listening post; that is to say, as a location from which agency personnel could run the operation against Eskandarian. Every morning—or whenever he felt it necessary to file a report—Kite would put on his running gear, jog round to the safe house and knock on the door. A member of the BOX 88 team would be there to receive him.

'Xav doesn't really think of me as a jogger,' Kite had pointed out when the plan was first mooted. 'Isn't he going to find it a bit weird?'

They were sitting in the Hampstead safe flat playing back-gammon. Peele brushed his concerns away.

'You used to go for runs at Alford, yes?'

'Yes, sir.' Kite still occasionally referred to his former school-master as 'Sir', a habit which he would quickly grow out of as the summer progressed. 'I mean, yes. But only in the rugby season. In the winter.'

'So start going for runs again. Let Xavier know you've been keeping yourself fit over the summer. You want to play rugby at university, you enjoy the feeling of being in good shape.'

'Why don't you just bug the Bonnards' house and record everything Eskandarian says? Why do you even need me?'

'Because it's not just what Eskandarian says that's of interest to us. It's how he behaves, how he treats people, who he meets, what he conceals. Besides, the property will likely be swept in advance of his arrival. The MOIS will want to know that the house is clean and that no interested parties have planted naughty microphones in naughty places.'

'The MOIS?'

'Iranian intelligence.' Peele lit a cigarette and rolled a double-five. 'They know people like us are going to be keeping an eye on people like Eskandarian, sniffing his bottom, going through his underwear drawer. They know that their top business people are vulnerable to approaches from foreign intelligence services. They'll want to know that Ali's letters aren't going to be steamed open, that the only bugs in his bedroom are spiders and flies, not microphones that record every sweet sentence of his pillow talk.'

'So he'll be coming to the villa with other people? With bodyguards? His wife?'

'No wife—not married. Bodyguard possibly. He might send someone in advance. He might travel with a security detail. He may even have these things forced on him by Rafsanjani. At this stage we simply don't know. My guess is that a few hours before Eskandarian reaches Cannes, various Iranian gentlemen of limited charm will spend several hours checking every orifice of Luc's villa for things that shouldn't be there.'

'What about staff? The Bonnards are bound to have a cook, a maid, all that kind of thing.'

'Good question.' Peele took one of Kite's checkers and placed it on the spine of the board. Kite swore and wondered aloud how the hell Peele kept getting such lucky dice. 'The same Iranian gentlemen of limited charm will likely want names and dates of birth of everyone who comes regularly to the house, as well as

BOX 88

a reassurance that the chef hasn't been slipped a hundred thousand francs by the DST to put mercury in Ali's *oeufs en cocotte*.'

'What's the DST?' During classes at Alford, Kite had loved Peele's way with words, but there were times now when he wished he would speak more plainly. Sometimes it was hard extracting a coherent meaning from his former tutor's flights of rhetorical fancy.

'I occasionally allow myself to forget how inexperienced you are, Lockie.' Peele took another checker and laid it alongside the first. 'The DST is Frog liaison. Domestic intelligence. The French equivalent of MI5, of the FBI in America.'

'So the French government know that Eskandarian is coming to France?'

'We must assume so, yes.' Kite groaned as he rolled a one and a two, unable to release his checkers back onto the board. 'It's not unusual for wealthy Iranians to holiday in the South of France, but Eskandarian certainly won't have wanted to advertise the fact in advance. We have reason to believe he'll be travelling on a French passport because there's been no visa requirement at the Iranian end. In any event, it hardly matters. Saturation surveillance from the Frogs might work in our favour. Likewise, if the MOIS become concerned that their man is being watched, they'll think it's on the orders of Paris or Washington. The last person they'll suspect of going through Ali's dustbins is little old you.'

Kite soon lost the game of backgammon, just as he lost four in every five matches they played. Sometimes they would take the board to a pub in the neighbourhood, other times they might set up in an outdoor café on the Heath. It was all part of his training: Eskandarian was known to be a keen backgammon player and being able to challenge him to a decent game would put Kite at a slight social advantage. Every detail had been worked out by BOX 88, right down to the system of signals with which Kite and the team would communicate once he arrived at the villa. In the absence of a pager—the possession of which Kite would never have convincingly been able to explain to Xavier—they were going to have to rely on what Strawson described as 'Moscow Rules'.

'We're going to want to talk to you and you're going to want to talk to us,' the American explained over a fillet steak at Wolfe's, the hamburger restaurant behind Harrods which was his home away from home. 'There needs to be a way of doing that which doesn't involve one of us coming to the villa and knocking on your door, or you going outside and using Luc's car phone to ring the safe house.'

'Sure,' Kite replied. 'So what do I do?'

'If you need to tell us something, and you can't find a legitimate reason to go for a run, put an item of red clothing in the window of your bedroom. We'll be watching the house. We'll see it. Then write us a note, fold it up, stick it inside a packet of cigarettes. Billy can teach you how to do all this.' Peele, who was sitting beside Kite working his way through a cheeseburger and a glass of Côtes du Rhône, nodded. 'Then you have a choice. If you're stuck at the house and can't get into Mougins, use the dead-drop site. There's a small orchard at the bottom of the garden, at least a hundred yards from the terrace, where you can go for a smoke. Leave the cigarette packet on the wall. It forms a boundary with the access road. We can grab it from the other side. Again, you can rehearse all this with Billy.'

'What if I can get into Mougins to see one of you in person?'

'Well that would make life slightly easier,' Peele interjected through a mouthful of chips. 'We'll see you leave, someone will follow you into town—or wherever it is you happen to be going—and will make it very obvious to you that they're one of us.'

'How will they do that?'

'You know the *FT*? Pink, easily spotted. They'll be carrying one. Depending on who's around and who may or may not be

BOX 88

watching, you can either pass them the packet in broad daylight or do it in brush contact.'

Kite had long since finished his lunch. He found that he rarely ate as much as his two older companions, preferring to ask questions and digest their answers whenever he found himself sharing a meal with them.

'What about in an emergency?' he asked.

'What kind of emergency?' Peele looked as if he was finding it difficult to imagine what could possibly go wrong.

'I dunno. I get rumbled. Eskandarian suddenly leaves.'

As with most things, Strawson had a solution at his fingertips.

'If the shit has well and truly hit the fan, fly the signal. Use the phone in the house and telephone your mother. If you ask her if there have been any letters sent to you by Edinburgh University, we'll know that's a code, that you're in trouble and we'll find a way of getting you out. How's that?'

'What if she's not there? What if she doesn't answer?'

'Makes no odds. Leave what sounds like a message with the same question. Have there been any letters sent to you by Edinburgh University? That's a last resort though, Lockie. We don't envisage circumstances in which you would find it necessary to do such a thing. Fallback only.'

Kite took that as a tacit warning not to compromise the mission unless it was absolutely critical. The American had a way of oscillating between moments of avuncular tenderness and strict, almost dictatorial control; this was certainly an instance of the latter. Kite felt locked in a master-servant relationship with Strawson and saw that Peele was also somewhat in his shadow.

'And if you need to get hold of me?'

'Same principle,' Peele replied. An attractive waitress drifted past the table and smiled at him in a way that made Kite slightly envious. 'If you see a man or woman lurking with an *FT*, follow them to a secure place and hear them out. They may want to speak to you directly, they may want to pass you a message.

Again, that message will most probably be inside a packet of cigarettes. Read it, absorb it, flush it down the toilet. Try not to go mad and think that every passing stockbroker at Heathrow airport carrying a rolled-up copy of the *Financial Times* is BOX. You'll recognise them when you see them. They'll have a way of making themselves known.'

'And what if I'm not able to go out? What if it's raining or we've all decided to spend the day at the villa?'

Strawson sounded a sudden, booming 'Ha!' and said: 'You've thought it all through, haven't you, Lockie?'

'I just want to be thorough.'

'Quite right too.'

Peele honoured Kite with a proud smile and explained the correct procedure.

'If you're stuck at the villa, wander down the drive. Look at the wall on either side of the gates. If it's marked in chalk, that's a signal that we need to talk to you. Find an excuse to go for a run or, better still, walk into Mougins to buy a coffee or some aspirin. We'll find a way of letting you know what we need to let you know.'

As the days passed, such responses became commonplace, both from Peele, whom Kite saw all the time, and from Strawson, whose appearances were more infrequent. After the meal at Wolfe's, for example, Peele role-played a number of different scenarios so that Kite became comfortable with the writing of secret messages, brush contacts and clandestine meetings. He found the work intensely interesting and rarely felt out of his depth. It was only when Strawson turned up at the Hampstead flat to talk about bugs that Kite began to feel he was at risk of getting in over his head.

'They're not like the movies,' the American explained, 'however much we'd like them to be.' He was wearing chinos and a pressed shirt and was gregariously combative in a way Kite hadn't seen since Killantringan. 'I can't just leave a wristwatch on a bookshelf

BOX 88

and hope it'll pick up three weeks' worth of conversations. At BOX we like to call these things "tentacles". For a tentacle to work, it needs to be connected to a power source. That's why so many of them are found in light fixtures and televisions.'

This had all been news to Kite, who quickly realised that Strawson was preparing him for what would undoubtedly be the most risky part of his assignment.

'You have a Nintendo Gameboy you use all the time, right?'

'I do,' Kite replied.

'Something like that the Falcons can refit as a voice-activated microphone. It'll maybe last two days on modified battery power. Same applies to your Walkman. Anything that can be left lying around in plain sight, hidden in a cupboard or drawer, which won't seem out of place to passers-by if they happen upon it. These are the kinds of things we'll be looking at when we put you in place. Another idea we had for the Bonnard villa was a ghetto blaster.'

'You can't call it that!' Peele exclaimed. Kite started laughing. 'Nobody calls it a "ghetto blaster", Mike. You mean a tape deck. A stereo.'

'I'm the boss here and I prefer ghetto blaster.' Strawson tacitly acknowledged that the term sounded ridiculous. 'We can leave one at the villa, make it look like something the great-uncle used to own. It'll be converted to relay conversations when connected to a power source.'

'Won't the MOIS find it if they sweep the house?' Kite asked.

He had remembered what Peele had said about Iranian officials coming to the villa prior to the Bonnards' arrival.

'They will if we leave it there for them to find it. Trick is to take advantage of the window of time between the MOIS giving the place the all-clear and the Falcons arriving at the house with whatever tentacles they've cooked up. That might be a two-day window, might be two hours, we don't exactly know yet. We have a number of devices we like to use in these situations—

lamps, hi-fis, anything with a power cable—that we'll hope to have in place by the time you get there.'

'And if they're not in place?' Kite asked.

'Then we work out what to do next. You turn up with a Gameboy and a Walkman, no way anybody's going to ask to take them apart. We fail to fulfil our side of the bargain—let's say there's not enough time or opportunity to rig the house before the Bonnards arrive—then maybe yes, we ask you to get inventive and move some items into place.' Kite was not at all sure precisely what Strawson was asking him to do. It sounded vague but perilous. 'The most important thing is this. You don't take any unnecessary risks.' The American's eyes widened in expectation that Kite would understand the importance of what he was being told. Kite, still wary, produced an encouraging nod. 'You never do anything until you're a hundred per cent convinced the coast is clear. You don't get up, creep around in the middle of the night. You don't sneak out during dinner and hope that nobody notices you're gone. You're not Bruce Willis. You're sure as shit not James Bond. We're not putting sedatives in the iced tea so that Special Agent Kite can go about his business undisturbed. You have something to do for the Falcons, you wait until everyone is out of the house. And I mean *everyone*. This doesn't work any other way.'

Kite tried to imagine circumstances in which he was left alone in the villa while Xavier and the rest of the Bonnard family took off for the day with Eskandarian. He couldn't think of one, but didn't envisage that it would be too difficult to plant a bug without being seen by a third party. He could fake an illness, pretend to be suffering from sunstroke or a bad back. The possibilities were limitless.

'What about photographing stuff?' he asked. From day one he had hoped that he would be given a miniature camera, like something dreamed up by 'Q' Branch. 'A couple of days ago

BOX 88

Billy suggested you might need me to copy documents, that kind of thing.'

Strawson responded with another strong caveat against taking unnecessary chances.

'Look, Lockie: again, only if the place is empty and you can guarantee being left undisturbed. Even then, is it likely Eskandarian is going to be leaving sensitive documents lying around the house? Maybe, maybe not. You own a camera?'

'I do,' Kite replied. 'Olympus Trip.'

'That's a 35 mm, right?' Strawson looked quickly at Peele. 'We've had a lot of success with those in the past. Modified lens for close-up work. Trips are good because they're small enough to fit into your pocket. If you do get the chance and the coast is clear, we'd be interested in Iranian and Libyan ministerial papers, documents in Arabic, Russian or Farsi, anything and everything that relates to subways, airlines, technological components, blueprints, diagrams of any kind. Mail is likely to be sent to the house, there may be government communiqués, bank statements and so forth. You see anything from Malta, you holler.'

'Malta? Why Malta?'

'Just holler.' Strawson again caught Peele's eye but, as ever, it was impossible to decrypt the secret that passed between them. 'It's an outside chance Eskandarian will leave anything out, but it's worth at least giving ourselves that possibility. I'll make a note to talk to the Falcons, and Billy can give you more detail once the camera is ready.'

By the time July drew to an end, Kite had been given a complete picture of what his work in France would entail. He was under no illusions that his friendship with Xavier, not to mention his reputation as a decent and trustworthy human being, would never recover should he be exposed. Everyone at Alford would know what he had done; the scandal would affect him for the rest of his life. This realisation in itself did not leave Kite feeling particularly anxious; if anything, he was exhilarated by the challenge BOX 88 were setting him and convinced that he could meet it. What concerned him was that Strawson and Peele weren't being completely candid about the risks he was facing.

It was perhaps for this reason that Kite's subconscious began to get the better of him. On at least four separate nights in Hampstead he was beset by dreams of inadequacy. In one textbook scenario, he marched out to bat for Alford in a cricket match at Lord's only to discover that he had failed to put on his pads and gloves; in another, he was trapped in a spotlight on stage in front of an expectant audience of his peers with no clue as to what role he was playing nor what lines he was supposed to have learned. Needless to say, he said nothing about these dreams to Peele, instead consoling himself with Strawson's views on the chances of being caught.

'They're never going to catch you because you're never going to do anything suspicious. They find a microphone, you didn't put it there. They search your room, somebody planted whatever they found. Carrying something incriminating? Same deal, you have no idea how it got there. You left your bag unattended, your room unlocked, bad people took advantage of that and tried to frame you. You're just nice guy Lachlan Kite, son of Cheryl, old Alfordian, friend of Xavier Bonnard. Nobody knows your real mission is preventing the deaths of tens of thousands of people on the New York subway. There are no circumstances in which you can admit to working for BOX 88. Understand? Never confess, never break cover, never admit to being a spy.'

31

Kamran cut the wires behind Kite's back. Kite had suffered a deep cut on top of the left wrist and had lost all feeling in his right hand. He made a fist with it, clenching and releasing the fingers while massaging the wrist. Torabi handed him a used tissue with which to mop up the blood.

'I need to use the toilet,' Kite told him as he was passed a bottle of water.

Torabi said something in Farsi and ordered Kite to stand up. Kite drained the water, put the bottle on the floor and was escorted from the room. Kamran put a gun in the small of his back. Hossein went ahead to open the bathroom door.

'Leave it open,' he ordered.

'I want some privacy.'

The two guards looked at one another and laughed.

'We're not coming in unless we have to,' Hossein replied.

'What am I going to do? Dig a tunnel? There's nothing in there except a bar of soap and a shower curtain. At least let me close the door.'

Kamran indicated that it would be acceptable for Kite to do that.

'No lock,' he said.

'Fine,' Kite replied.

As soon as he was inside the bathroom, he closed the door and lifted the seat on the toilet. He noisily unclipped his belt, pulled it free of his trousers, and sat down. The two guards were talking in the passage and did not appear to be taking much notice of what was going on. Quietly, Kite opened the cupboard under the sink, ducked down and started pulling at the loosened nail, shaking it from side to side, trying to turn it. It moved slightly. Reaching back, he flushed the toilet and used the covering noise to scratch away at the plaster with the belt buckle until an inch of the nail was visible. He could feel it very gradually moving away from the wall. Kite reached for the bottle of bleach and squirted some into the space around the head, hoping that it would loosen the plaster. For another thirty seconds or so he chipped away. The bleach was running down the paintwork, making no discernible difference, but Kite knew that the nail was coming. Pinching the metal head so it dug deep into the skin of his thumb and index finger, he at last yanked it free of the wall.

He stood up, almost striking the back of his head on the cupboard, and turned on the tap. The nail was about four inches long. If he could get one of the men alone, he could use it to disable them. More than one and he doubted that he would be fast enough to disarm them before they used their weapons. He slipped the nail into his hip pocket and looked up at the metal towel rail.

'Hey!'

It was Hossein. There was a loud succession of knocks. He said: 'Let's go. Taking too long.' The attachments at either end of the rail shifted when Kite moved it up and down. It was stuck to the wall only by adhesive. He could pull it free from the wall or, if that proved impossible, kick it down by standing on the rim of the bath. Kite looped the belt around his trousers and called back: 'Yeah, just a minute. I'm washing.'

BOX 88

He urinated in the sink, switched off the tap and went outside, resuming the role of the hapless oil trader.

'No luck,' he said.

'What's that?' Hossein looked confused.

'I can't go to the bathroom properly. I'm too tense.'

'You think I care? Don't be fucking disgusting, man. Move!'

Kamran stuck the gun in Kite's back and pushed him forward. Kite continued with the act, re-entering the room in a forlorn state.

'Ready?' Torabi demanded.

'I don't feel well,' he told him.

'I don't have time for you not to feel well. Sit down. We made an arrangement. Eskandarian in exchange for the life of your wife and child. A simple trade.'

Kite slumped into the chair. As soon as Kamran and Hossein left them alone, he could use the nail, setting the head in the ball of his hand, pushing back Torabi's neck and driving it up through the throat. To Kite's despair, Kamran suddenly grabbed his arms, pulled them behind his back and tied his hands with a set of plasticuffs.

'Hey! We agreed no wires, no handcuffs.'

'I don't trust you.' Torabi was looking at him, pursing his lips. 'I don't care what we agreed.'

'I can't think straight if my hands are tied.' He could feel the nail against his hip. 'My wrist is already bleeding. I lose the feeling in my arms.'

'Poor little Lockie,' Torabi mocked him in a childish voice. 'Just talk, you piece of shit. Just tell me what happened in France.'

32

And so Kite began.

He told Torabi nothing about what happened at the motorway service station en route to the villa, nothing about the lamp, nothing about the Mougins safe house or the plot to attack the New York subway. The story he told was a story of innocence to experience, the tale of a naive eighteen-year-old who went on holiday with the Bonnard family, found himself embroiled in a tragedy and came home a changed man.

There was no Carl or Strawson in Kite's recollection of the summer, no dead drops or modified Olympus Trip. He told the truth about Bijan and Abbas, just as he told the truth about Luc and Rosamund. Kite did not conceal what had happened with Martha. He told Torabi what Xavier had likely told him in Paris before he died. One version of events, seen only from one point of view.

The rest was lies.

This is what happened.

On the morning of Wednesday, 2 August 1989, Lachlan Kite arrived at the Bonnards' house in Onslow Square. His suitcases were packed, his training complete. The family were waiting for

BOX 88

him on the ground floor: Xavier, sporting a patchy beard; his younger sister, Jacqueline, who looked permanently tired and moody; Rosamund, smelling of expensive perfume and wearing a bright yellow jacket with broad shoulder pads; and Maria, the Filipina maid, who greeted Kite with a delighted smile and a moist kiss. He remembered a similar encounter, two years earlier, when the Bonnards had invited him to Switzerland on a skiing trip. That time he had just been a normal teenager, innocent of the ways of men. Xavier's parents had always been so kind to him, taking him under their wing and treating him like a surrogate son. Now he was set to betray them.

He looked down at his luggage. Zipped inside were the commonplace belongings of a typical young man—a Walkman, a Gameboy—but his own had been refitted into devices with the power to strip the Bonnard family of every inch of their privacy. In that moment, standing in the hall of the house, his mind full of tradecraft and protocols, he felt wretched for deceiving them.

The plan was to fly to Charles de Gaulle, to meet up with Luc in Paris, spend a night at the Bonnard apartment in St Germain and then to make the eight-hour journey by car to the villa in Mougins.

'Everybody remembered their passports?' Rosamund asked, zipping an Eximious washbag into her suitcase.

'Passport, passage, pesetas,' said Jacqueline.

'You say that *every* time we go abroad,' Xavier groaned.

The relationship between Xavier and his more conservative, less reckless younger sister had always been fraught. They bickered and griped, steering clear of one another's friends, going to separate parties, favouring different parents. Xavier was close to his mother but fought constantly with his father. By the same token, Luc favoured Jacqueline, whom Rosamund treated no differently to Maria or the family dog; that is to say, politely and patiently, but without evident warmth. Kite put her indifference down to the steely, compassionless DNA of the English aristocracy. Rosamund was beautiful, well-educated and extremely rich. She wanted for nothing except two healthy children and a dutiful, faithful husband. On the latter count, Luc had most definitely let her down. Brought up to believe that emotions should be suppressed at all costs, Rosamund rarely complained but seldom seemed unequivocally happy. What was important to her was to present an ordered, graceful face to the world, to acknowledge her boundless natural gifts and privileges without feeling guilty about them and certainly without showing them off in a way that might be interpreted as vulgar.

'Maria's going to come with us to Paris then stay behind while we're at the house. You're going to have a little bit of a holiday, aren't you, Maria?'

'Yes, Lady Rosamund.'

'Shall we go then?' Xavier's mother glanced at the ormolu clock on the mantelpiece. 'Golly, our plane leaves in three hours.'

There were no problems at either airport. A chauffeur met the Bonnards at Charles de Gaulle and they were driven at speed into the heart of Paris, a city Kite knew only from books and films and which he found spellbinding at first glance. The distant Eiffel Tower, the grandeur of Notre-Dame, the café crowds gathered at outdoor tables seemingly on every street, were like glimpses of a dream world. It felt as though he was passing into a different realm, a new phase of his life comprised of great luxury, of secrets and glamour. He had grown accustomed to the privileges enjoyed by Xavier's family, staying regularly at Rosamund's country pile in Gloucestershire and twice at Luc's chalet in Verbier. Even so, Kite was astonished by the splendour of the Bonnard apartment, a vast penthouse in Saint-Germain-des-Prés with views of the Seine, Invalides and the Jardins de Luxembourg. Rosamund explained that Luc's family had bought the property shortly after the war. Most of the time it lay empty, though Luc travelled to Paris for work at least once every two months. Kite knew that Xavier suspected his father of running

BOX 88

a French mistress—indeed he claimed to have found a bra jammed down the back of a Louis Quinze day bed in the drawing room. Luc had denied the accusation, insisting that the bra must have been left by a guest but urging Xavier not to say anything to his mother in case she got the wrong impression.

Luc himself was a man whom Kite respected but had always struggled to like. Tall and immensely good-looking, he had inherited a fortune and tripled it through various opaque business activities which Xavier feigned not to understand. Strawson and Peele had said that there were 'question marks' surrounding Luc, though they had not elaborated on this and Kite had been too busy concentrating on his training to pursue the point. Besides, the source of Luc's wealth was of less consequence to him than the manner in which he treated his son. Xavier fought with his father not because he was a confrontational, moody teenager— quite the opposite, in fact—but because Luc always seemed to be in a permanent state of competitive disappointment with him. Self-confident to the point of arrogance, he would accuse Xavier of laziness, even of lacking strength of character, rarely showing him any genuine affection. To make matters worse, Luc had always been friendly towards Kite, generous as much with his time as he was with his money. On more than one occasion, Xavier had said: 'Dad would much prefer you as his son', a remark to which Kite had no reasonable answer other than to say that his friend was talking nonsense.

They arrived in Paris in time for a late lunch at Brasserie Lipp. Afterwards they walked across the Seine, passing the Pompidou Centre en route to the Louvre where I.M. Pei's pyramid, built to celebrate the 200th anniversary of the Republic, had finally been opened to the public. Rosamund declared it a 'monstrosity' but, to Kite, it was one of the most extraordinary buildings he had ever seen. He took photographs of the Louvre complex with his doctored Olympus Trip 35, not just to famil-iarise the Bonnard family with his new-found passion for photography, but for the more honest and prosaic reason that he wanted to preserve his memories of such a beautiful place.

While the others went to Café de Flore for tea, Xavier and Kite holed up in the Marais, self-consciously smoking Gitanes Blondes and staring moodily at passing girls.

'You OK?' Xavier asked.

'Me?'

'Yeah. You seem a bit distracted.'

Kite's heart skipped a beat. Was his excitement and anxiety about what lay ahead already so obvious? The entire day he had felt as though he was inhabiting two bodies: his old cheery self, the trusted family friend; and a new person, the cunning, artful spy playing a dangerous game.

'It's just all this'—Kite gestured at the shops and the girls, the street life of the Marais—'my first time in Paris. Taking it all in.'

Peele had taught him never to embellish a lie. To make it short and sweet and get out fast. If a person rambled on without cease, giving answers to questions that had never been asked, it was a sure sign of guilt.

'You were weird this morning, too.'

Kite shrugged and apologised, wondering what to say.

'Maybe it's Mum. Killantringan. She's basically bankrupt after paying off her loans. I don't have anywhere to live when I get home, not sure if I've done OK in my A levels. It's just been a weird summer.'

'Well, you can relax now.' Xavier patted him on the back. 'You can take it easy.' A breathtakingly pretty girl with a Godard bob walked past their table and smiled. '*Mon Dieu,*' he whispered. 'Do you think that will ever stop?'

'Girls?' Kite replied.

Xavier nodded.

'Probably not.'

BOX 88

'We'll go out in the south,' Xavier said. 'Antibes. Cannes. You're bound to get lucky.'

'You, not me,' Kite replied. Xavier had the advantage of his father's saturnine looks, expensive clothes and a certain enigmatic magnetism, at once feral and poetic, which too many girls—as far as Kite was concerned—found irresistible.

'We should get back,' Xavier announced, throwing a few francs on the table. 'Mum wants to take Maria out to dinner at La Coupole. It's her fortieth.'

Kite was embarrassed not to have had the opportunity to buy Maria a present. Xavier took him to Shakespeare & Co on the way home, finding the owner closing up but happy to let two young students browse quickly inside. Xavier knew the history of the bookshop and encouraged Kite to buy something by Hemingway or F. Scott Fitzgerald. The owner recommended *The Beautiful and Damned* ('much better than *Gatsby*') and Kite asked that it be wrapped up. Later, as the family were presenting Maria with presents at dinner, she cried when she saw that he had bought her a book, as if nobody had ever thought to credit her with greater intelligence than the ability to make scrambled eggs or to turn perfect hospital corners on a king-size bed.

'Gracias, Master Lockie,' she said, pulling him in for a kiss. She had put on a dress for the occasion and did not look out of place among the glamorous denizens of La Coupole. 'I will treasure this. I will read it *slowly*.'

Kite had never experienced a restaurant quite like it. The ripple of Left Bank conversation, the music of cutlery and cut-glass, waiters in black tie gliding from table to table as though they had been on the same shift since the liberation of Paris. It was a world away from the chaos of the Killantringan dining room where prawn cocktails and defrosted lasagne had been the order of the day. Kite had been practising his French with Peele almost every day for three weeks but still didn't recognise half the dishes on the menu. Luc announced that he had been coming to La Coupole with his family since childhood and always reserved the same table, nestled between pillars within touching distance of an extraordinary stained-glass dome in the centre of the room. Compelled by Luc to experiment, Kite willingly played the wide-eyed tourist and asked for snails as a starter. Xavier tried to make him order *Andouillette* as a main course until his mother interjected and told Kite that it was a 'revolting' sausage made primarily from offal which 'tastes like a loo brush'. Xavier cursed her affectionately for spoiling the joke and went to the bathroom.

While he was gone, Luc turned to Kite.

'Lockie, there's something I need to talk to you about.'

His eyes had a way of going dead in moments of seriousness. Kite's stomach caved in on itself.

'Of course,' he said.

'My friend Ali is arriving tomorrow. Xav's told you that he's an Iranian businessman. Is that correct?'

Kite leaned on his training. *Don't talk unless you have to. Keep your answers short. Nobody expects you to be anything but a dozy teenager.*

'Yeah.' He nodded. 'Said he was some kind of godfather?'

Luc smiled. 'A Muslim godfather, yes. Ali and I were good friends in Paris when Xavier was living here as a child. He has close links to the new president. We've been trying to have a holiday together for years and we're finally making it happen— despite all the changes going on in Iran at the moment.'

'What changes?' Kite asked. He wondered why Luc was bothering to tell him so much about his relationship with Eskandarian. It was almost as if he was trying to conceal some-thing.

'Oh, you know.' He gestured towards the street. 'The death of the ayatollah. And there was an election last week. We thought

BOX 88

maybe that would prevent Ali from coming, but thankfully he is flying out tomorrow.'

Again, Kite wondered why Luc felt obliged to explain the situation to him. It was more than just politeness. Was Xavier's father trying to persuade him into thinking about Eskandarian in a particular way?

'That's great,' he replied. 'You'll be happy to see him.'

'I will.' Luc took a sip of wine. 'I don't want you to worry, but there is a certain threat to Iranian public figures when they travel overseas. Ali will be coming with a bodyguard. The chances of anything happening are zero. It's only for show.'

'OK,' Kite replied.

Strawson had suggested that Eskandarian would travel with protection; this merely confirmed it.

'I just thought I would say something in case you were surprised when he turns up. Various people may come to the house this week to meet him, but more likely he will go off and do whatever he has to do during the days. My hope is that we can all have a nice holiday together.'

'Mine too,' Kite replied.

He thought about MOIS sweeping the house and considered the scale and complexity of BOX 88's interest in Eskandarian. Kite wondered if Luc had any idea about his friend's alleged links to Lockerbie and the PLFP; did he know that he was spending his summer holiday with a man who could be aiding and abetting terrorism? Xavier came back to the table. Kite shuffled to one side to make room for him and returned to his food. Jacqui was talking to her mother.

'So we're meeting Martha in Cannes?' she said. 'You've spoken to her parents?'

Both Xavier and Kite looked up, dogs on a scent.

'Martha's coming?' said Xavier, gulping wine to cover his surprise.

'Martha Raine?' said Kite, a chunk of *choucroute* briefly lodging in his throat. 'She's a friend of yours?'

To dozens of pining boys at Alford, Martha Raine was a mythical beauty, a goddess as unattainable as Katherine Ross or Emmanuelle Béart. Kite had glimpsed her only once, at a party the previous summer, tried to engage her in conversation over a bowl of rum punch—and failed miserably. Later, smoking on the balcony as the party was winding down, he had watched her slipping into the passenger seat of an Alfa Romeo Spider driven by an old Alfordian who had once bowled him out for a golden duck in a house cricket match. The image of her driving off in the car, soft-top down, the man's hand caressing the back of her neck, had remained with Kite as a glimpse of another world as rarefied and as dazzling as the dining room at La Coupole. He could not believe that she was coming to the villa and that her visit would coincide with the surveillance attack on Eskandarian. Had Strawson and Peele known this and yet said nothing?

'Yeah, we were at school together when we were younger,' Jacqui replied. 'Do you know her?'

Xavier played it cool. 'She's all right,' he said.

'I was talking to Lockie.'

Kite swallowed the chunk of *choucroute* with a glug of Sancerre.

'Me? No. Don't know her. Met her once briefly. At a party. We talked for ten minutes. She was with a boyfriend. It was last summer, I think. Yeah, last summer.'

Rosamund hid a grin behind her hand, aware of Martha's beauty and immediately intuiting the impact she had made on Xavier's friend.

'She had a *boyfriend*?' Jacqui asked, screwing up her face.

'Yeah, some guy with an Alfa Romeo. Older than us. Left Alford three years ago.'

'He wasn't her boyfriend, Lockie. He was just a twat from your school.'

'You seem to know a lot about her,' Xavier added.

BOX 88

'Not really.' Kite felt his face flush with embarrassment. Christ, if he couldn't conceal a schoolboy crush on Martha Raine, how the hell was he going to keep his activities for BOX 88 a secret from the Bonnards? 'We just had a good chat. About books.'

'What books?' Rosamund joined in the fun.

'I don't remember.'

Xavier began to hum the theme to 'Our Tune', a popular slot on Radio 1 in which the DJ, Simon Bates, related a saccharine romantic story sent in by a listener. Kite would have told him to fuck off but because he was wearing a jacket and tie and eating dinner in La Coupole courtesy of the Bonnards, he remembered his manners.

'Very funny,' he said. 'How long is she coming for?'

'Long enough, I would imagine,' Rosamund replied, catching her husband's eye. 'Long enough.'

33

Cara had sat on the hay bale for an hour watching the light fade and the boys on the laptops working their magic. Rita had told her that they were transmitting text messages into the cottage purporting to come from whoever was in charge of the Iranian operation.

'There are three men in the house holding Isobel,' she said. Cara had the impression that Rita had known Kite and Isobel for years and was deeply concerned about them. 'They're all Farsi-speakers, taking it in shifts to watch her. The house isn't rigged with explosives, these aren't martyrdom, virgin-waiting-for-me-in-paradise bozos. It's personal, using Isobel as leverage. They want something from Lockie. Their boss is interrogating him, says he's getting somewhere, getting what he wants.'

'Do they know that?' Cara asked. She was uncharacteristically nervous talking to Rita, didn't want to sound ignorant or out of her depth. 'Do the people guarding Isobel know that Kite is talking?'

'Who said he's talking?' Rita replied sharply. 'He'll be telling them what they want to hear. No way he gives up operational secrets. No way.'

'Of course . . .'

BOX 88

'To answer your question. No, they don't know what we know. They've been blind for the past two hours waiting for a message from London. We've given them no signal at the cottage, killed the wi-fi. They still think it's a local problem, not a bubble. We put together a sequence of texts in Farsi matching the style and character of what they're used to. Released them fifteen minutes ago, along with some genuine texts from the boss. They got them in bursts, like the weather cleared up and the signal suddenly found an extra bar, then lost it, then found it again. Understand?'

'I understand,' Cara replied. 'Mix'n'match. They won't know what's genuine, what's not.'

'We've told them everything's fine in London. All going according to plan. That way they start to relax. Could be one of them's allowed to go to sleep, someone else fancies a wash. Either way they start to let their guard down. Jason wants them dozy before he goes in.'

'Shock and awe,' said Cara.

'Shock and awe,' Rita repeated. She looked out towards the road.

'Why don't you just tell them to release her?' Cara suggested. 'Send in a text ordering them to abort?'

Rita's eyes wrinkled in satisfaction. 'I like your thinking,' she said. 'But what if they kill Isobel before they go? She's heard their voices, maybe even seen their faces. They'd be leaving a living witness.'

Cara felt chastened. 'Fair enough.' she said. 'So when's Jason going in?'

Rita looked at her watch. 'Waiting for sunset.'

'Do you have a clearer idea of where they're holding Kite?' Earlier Cara had seen Rita talking to Jason, looking at a map of East London.

'Only to within half a mile,' she replied. 'They've been careful. The genuine texts are always coming from different places. They're leaving wherever it is they're holding Lockie, messaging the cottage from random locations, then putting a Faraday around the phone so we can't trace the signal. Trouble is, this half a mile has a hundred thousand people inside it. You were right, by the way. The metadata is all coming out of Canary Wharf.'

Cara had a mental image of Kite somewhere in the bowels of a high-rise, his hands tied, his mouth gagged.

'Can they find him?' she asked, gesturing towards the laptoppers.

Rita shrugged and said: 'Eventually.' She looked up at the sky. It looked as though it was going to rain. 'Ideally, Jase goes into the cottage and talks to one of them, gets an address, narrows things down.' Cara glanced up at Jason, who was putting on full Special Forces battle rig at the edge of the barn. She wondered how he would go about 'talking to one of them'. She didn't imagine it would involve a handshake and a cup of tea. Another soldier had arrived on foot in the previous twenty minutes, also American. He was standing behind Jason carrying a set of night-vision goggles. Cara had the absurd thought that they both looked overdressed.

'Who *are* these guys?' she asked, not expecting an honest answer. 'SO15? 22?'

'Our guys,' Rita replied and looked away. '22' was the colloquial term for the SAS. SO15 was Counter Terrorism Command. As far as Cara knew, Americans were not permitted to serve in either unit.

'Do they have jurisdiction to do this on UK soil?'

'Can do it on any soil they like.'

'There's no police to make arrests,' Cara observed. 'Or are they coming later?'

Rita looked at her as though she was being naive.

'No police,' she said. 'Not that kind of job.'

Robert Vosse had called Cara an hour earlier, asking for an update. Rita had ordered her to tell him that there was nobody

BOX 88

at the cottage, nothing to report, that she was coming back to London on the next train. It was the first time Cara had ever lied to him. Since then, she had felt like a child observing the grown-ups going about their mysterious business, watching and waiting, powerless to help.

'Status?' Jason asked.

'Isobel's in the lounge, two alongside,' said Fred, the laptopper from the north of England. On one of his screens Cara could see a live, infra-red, worm's-eye view of the eastern side of the cottage. Jason had told her the images were coming from the cam net of a Special Forces soldier, codenamed STONES, concealed in a tree line a hundred metres from the back door of the property.

'Third enemy?' Jason asked. Behind him, the American soldier put on a battle helmet. The identification tag CARPENTER was sewn into his uniform.

'Upstairs,' Fred replied. 'Movement on the first floor. Could be resting.'

'Sweet dreams,' Jason replied. 'Send the seventh.'

Everybody looked towards Wal, the younger of the two technicians. He was wearing a beanie and looked no more than twenty or twenty-one. Cara hadn't known what Jason meant by 'the seventh' but assumed it was another dummy text message. She was suddenly sick with worry. She had never been involved in an operation of this kind nor been so close to the possibility of success or failure, life and death.

'Confirm?' said Wal.

Cara looked at the infra-red images moving back and forth on the screens. A radio in the barn crackled.

'Vehicle.'

'Wait!' Jason snapped, raising his hand. Wal took his hands off the keyboard, like a pianist pausing mid-phrase. Cara had recognised the voice on the radio as a fourth SF soldier, codenamed KAISER, positioned behind a hedgerow further along the road. No cars or vans had driven past the farm since she had been intercepted more than two hours earlier.

'Description, KAISER,' Jason whispered on comms.

'Skoda saloon, blue. Driver alone. Unknown if enemy or local.'

'Hold the seventh,' Jason replied. 'I say again, do not send the seventh message.'

He knew what Cara knew. That whoever was in the car could be an Iranian who would immediately tell the men inside the cottage that the communications coming in and out of the property had been compromised.

'We stop him?' CARPENTER asked, just as the car swept past the farmhouse.

'Too late,' Jason replied. They all waited in silence, staring at the laptop screens, at the worm's eye view of the cottage. The headlights burned the infra-red as the vehicle turned into the drive in front of the house. 'That's not a delivery guy from Amazon,' he said. 'That's enemy.'

34

'You're wasting my time,' said Torabi. 'I don't need to know about your journey to Paris, where you ate, where you smoked cigarettes with Xavier. I need to know about Eskandarian.'

Hossein had left the room, taking Kamran's gun. It was obvious that he wasn't coming back. Kite was sure that he was the man Torabi had dispatched to the cottage to kill Isobel.

'You said you wanted to hear everything about France,' he said. He had no choice but to keep drawing out the story for as long as possible, giving MI5 time to find him. 'I'm telling you everything that's important.'

'You are taking too long.'

'Let me speak to my wife. I want to know that she's safe.'

To Kite's surprise, Torabi looked at his cell phone and said: 'That is no longer possible.'

'Why?'

He did not need an answer to the question: it was written in Torabi's face. They had lost contact with the house.

'Luc was with you all the time?' Torabi asked. The change of subject was further confirmation that something had gone wrong. Kite assumed that BOX had put an electronic bubble around the cottage. 'What was he doing in Paris before you arrived?'

'I have no idea.'

'You drove with him to the house?'

'Yes,' Kite replied. 'We had two cars. If I remember correctly, Luc was driving a Mercedes, Rosamund had a Citroën or a Peugeot. Both rented. She and Jacqui collected Martha from the airport in Cannes.'

Torabi's phone vibrated. He checked the screen and shook his head, irritated by what he had seen. As he tapped out a reply, he said: 'Why is that important?'

'Why is what important?'

'Collecting Martha from the airport?'

Kite sensed an opportunity to kill more time.

'It's important because when I look back to that summer, the first person I think about is her. Not Xavier, not Eskandarian, not Luc. I think about Martha Raine. You should know that, if you're interested in understanding what I was thinking.' Torabi set the phone to one side. 'In spite of everything that happened, Martha became the most important person in my life for the next fifteen years. Xavier and I remained friends. What happened to the others was a tragedy, yes, but it just became a sad story, something I only thought about from time to time.'

'I don't believe you,' Torabi replied.

Kite decided to lay it on thick.

'Surely you remember that feeling you'd get when you were a young man? That crazy, dizzying sensation of longing? I can still picture the first time I saw Martha at the house, as if it was yesterday. What she looked like, what she was wearing. And I recall how embarrassed I felt telling her that we'd met before at a party. She didn't remember me. At the time I thought: "I'm just another chump. I'm going to be spending a week with this girl in the South of France and it's going to be torture." But it didn't turn out that way. In fact thanks to the encouragement of—'

Torabi stopped him.

BOX 88

'I get it,' he said. 'You fell in love. You're trying to tell me that it would have been impossible for you—maybe even forbidden—to have an affair with this woman while you were working for MI6.'

'Exactly!' Kite replied, pleased that Torabi had understood what he was trying to do. 'Xavier was deluded. Whatever he told you was bullshit. It would have been impossible for me to spy on Eskandarian. I was just an innocent bystander.'

The Iranian lit a cigarette. For a moment Kite was concerned that he was going to burn him again; he could still feel the sting of the wound on his blistered neck. Instead Torabi remained in his seat, smoking impassively. He was once again the man of the boardroom, as relaxed as he might have been sitting in the lounge of an Abu Dhabi sports club or enjoying an after-dinner cigar with clients in Milan. Kite shifted the position of his leg and felt the weight of the nail against his thigh. If he moved too much there was a risk it would fall out of his pocket onto the floor.

'If you lie to me, I will know,' Torabi told him, drawing on the cigarette. 'Keep talking.'

35

Rosamund and Jacqui drove south in the Citroën. Luc took Xavier and Kite in the Mercedes. They left Paris just after nine o'clock on Thursday, 3 August.

Kite sat in the back seat listening to his Walkman, which still continued to function in the normal way, allowing him to listen to the music—Eurythmics, Supertramp, Tears for Fears—for which he had been ridiculed by his friends at Alford for years. Only if Kite inserted a specially tailored blank cassette, provided by the Falcons, would it also record up to twelve hours of conversation on a set of fresh batteries.

A few miles beyond Clermont-Ferrand, Luc stopped for petrol at an *aire* on the autoroute. Kite looked around to see if Rosamund had followed them off the motorway, but the Citroën was nowhere to be seen. There was a queue for petrol. As Luc waited to fill up, Kite and Xavier walked towards a makeshift picnic area on a stretch of grass outside the service building. It was a humid afternoon. Clouds were blocking the fierce heat of the sun as they sat at a wooden table smoking. Kite could hear the low roar of the motorway, the crying of a small child nearby. He looked back at the petrol pumps, but there was no sign of Luc. He was probably still in the queue. Parents were dragging tired, squab-

BOX 88

bling toddlers back and forth from the service building. At the next table a family of Germans were eating slices of pizza from paper plates.

'What were you listening to?' Xavier asked.

'Dylan,' Kite replied, remembering that *Blood on the Tracks* was the last tape he had inserted in the Walkman. 'You?'

'Was just chatting to Dad. Long way. Keeping him company.'

'Sure.'

A man wearing a black baseball hat was standing directly in Kite's eyeline at a distance of about twenty feet. He slowly turned around until he was facing the table at which Kite and Xavier were seated. Kite clocked him but looked away without studying his face. An elderly woman was preparing a bowl of water for a panting dog. The man took a step forward. Kite saw that he was carrying a copy of the *Financial Times*. He was electrified.

'Need a slash,' he said, stubbing out the cigarette only two-thirds through. 'Meet you back at the car?'

'Sure,' Xavier replied.

Kite walked towards the entrance to the service building, passing within touching distance of the man. His heart was galloping with the adrenaline surge of making contact with a member of the team. He was trying not to move too fast, too conspicuously. Had BOX been following the Mercedes all the way from Paris? Had something already gone wrong?

Kite moved through a set of sliding doors, remembering what Peele had taught him about meetings in the open. There was a large shop to his left stocked with puzzle books and magazines, bottles of wine and sunhats. Immediately ahead, crowds of people were queuing in a long line for hot food. Above their heads, illuminated signs advertised pizzas and burgers and *plats du jour*. A buxom woman had set out bowls of olives and cubes of local cheese at a wooden stall in the centre of the hall. There was a smell of burned bread. Kite kept walking, passing an amusement arcade where a man in a white singlet was furiously thumping a fruit machine. Where to go? If he went into the toilets, he might be spotted by Luc or Xavier. If he went into the shop, he could be seen from the picnic area. Kite came to a halt, allowing the man to pass him. Surely there was somewhere in this vast, crowded place where two men could talk and not be disturbed?

The man walked down a narrow passage towards the rear of the building. He appeared to have a plan. Kite waited for a count of three, checked that Xavier and Luc were not behind him, then followed him along the passage.

He came to a Fire Door and pushed it open. The man was waiting for him on a patch of concrete to the left of the door. He was wearing jeans and a *Goats Head Soup* T-shirt. He gestured Kite into a sectioned-off area where three industrial bins were giving off a stench of rotting food. The clouds had moved away. It was searingly hot.

'We don't have much time, so I'll make this quick. The name's Carl. You OK?'

'I'm fine,' Kite replied.

He was a lean, undernourished man of around thirty-five. He didn't look like the sort of Englishman who would ordinarily be reading the *Financial Times* on holiday in France. Kite guessed that was the point.

'Eskandarian is arriving late this afternoon. Landing in Paris at five, catching a flight to Cannes at seven.' Kite made a mental note of the flight times. 'The villa was swept by MOIS early this morning. They were thorough. They didn't find anything. Looks like the French aren't interested in our man. Team went in straight afterwards, tried to rig some tentacles. They didn't succeed in the way they wanted to succeed. Were disturbed by the house-keeper coming back and had to get out. Understand?'

Kite nodded although he wasn't sure precisely what Carl was telling him. Was the operation being called off?

'Take a look at this.'

The man produced a colour photograph from his pocket which

BOX 88

looked as though it had been torn out of a brochure or Sunday supplement. It was a picture of a table lamp with a broad wooden base and wide burgundy shade. Kite noticed three warts on the back of Carl's right hand.

'All they managed to do was get the stereo into the poolhouse and this lamp into the first bedroom you come to on the first floor of the villa. It's a small room, unlikely to be where Rosamund puts Eskandarian. If you get the chance, before the target shows up, find out where he's going to be sleeping and try to switch the lamps. Only do this if it's a hundred per cent safe. Make sure everyone else in the villa is downstairs, maybe outside taking a swim after the long drive. You are under strict orders not to attempt the switch after Eskandarian arrives. Is that understood?'

'I understand,' Kite replied. He wanted to ask if Carl had been following him all the way from London, via Lipp and Coupole and the Marais.

'They're sorry they didn't get the job done. Couldn't be helped, time window was squeezed to less than four minutes. You're the fallback. That's why you're there. Just plug the lamp in and get out. Somebody catches you, you say your own light fused and you went to switch it with another one from a different room. *Capeesh?*'

Kite nodded. 'Capeesh.' He had not anticipated that there would be this much pressure so early in the operation.

'Here.' Carl passed him a packet of cigarettes and some Hollywood chewing gum. 'In case anyone asks what took you so long, you were buying these.'

'OK. Thanks.'

'Luc make any calls on his car phone?'

Kite shook his head. He knew that BOX could access the phone line when the car was stationary, not when it was moving.

'OK. Remember what I told you. Good luck. Go.'

Kite did as he was told, walking away from the stench of the bins, back down the passage, committing the colours and design of the lamp to memory, his heart racing in a way that no amount of training in Hampstead had prepared him for. The entire conversation with Carl had taken less than two minutes. Why had he asked about Luc using the phone?

Kite went into the gents. Xavier was coming out of one of the cubicles. He looked up and was surprised to see Kite, but they did not say anything to one another, merely grunting as they passed. Moments later Kite was back at the car, Xavier already in the passenger seat, Luc sitting impatiently at the wheel.

'Why did you take so long?' he snapped. Luc Bonnard was not a man who liked to be left waiting around.

'Sorry.' Kite put the cigarettes on the seat. 'Bought some gum. Want any?'

'*Ollywood?*' Xavier replied in a cod French accent.

'Oui,' Kite replied, relief flooding through him like the first blissful rush of Ecstasy. 'Hollywood. Tuck in. There's plenty. How far are we from the house?'

36

They reached the villa before the others. Kite had memorised the layout of the roads surrounding the house and was confident he would have been able to guide Luc to the property even without the aid of the Michelin map Xavier passed to him on the last stretch of motorway beyond Grasse. He had seen aerial photographs of the villa, pictures of the rooms, architectural drawings of every floor, surveillance shots of the swimming pool and gardens. As Luc turned through the iron gates and proceeded along the gravelled drive, Kite had the sense of a place he already knew intimately springing into vibrant, three-dimensional life. He stepped out of the car and looked up at the house for the first time. He was surprised by the size and complexity of the building; it was even larger than he had imagined. The vast lime tree at the entrance concealed much of the southern facade and there were little iron tables, ceramic pots and plants in the nooks and crannies of the forecourt.

'It's beautiful, Papa,' said Xavier, his voice sounding humbled and raw. Kite picked out the kitchen window to the west, the pool hut to the east through an opening in the garden wall. The paint on the wooden shutters of the master bedroom had faded and was slightly chipped. Cicadas were thrumming in the hills.

Kite had heard this colossal, tropical sound in movies and songs, read about it in books by Wilbur Smith and Graham Greene, but was experiencing it in the real world for the first time.

'It really is,' Luc replied, putting his arm around his son in a rare moment of physical affection between them. 'I think we'll have fun here. Lockie, what do you think of it?'

'Amazing,' said Kite, seeing the ancient wooden front door for the first time, the giant oil jars flanking the entrance, the ravishing bougainvillea wilting in the August sun. 'You say this belonged to your uncle?'

'Great-uncle. He had no children. I guess I am the lucky one.'

'You're definitely that,' Xavier muttered, and the intimacy between them vanished as quickly as it had come.

Luc opened the boot, releasing a blast of stuffy heat. Kite set the bags on the drive, carefully taking out his Gameboy so that both Luc and Xavier would see it. When switched on—the screen had been broken to make it look permanently damaged—the device would send a signal to a receiver in the grounds of the property allowing BOX 88 to listen in on any conversations taking place within a fifteen-metre radius of the microphone. Kite showed Xavier the damaged screen.

'When did that happen?' he asked.

'Dropped it last night,' he replied.

It was the latest of what he knew would become a thousand lies. Kite suddenly resented the cynical ingenuity of the Falcons and cursed the men who had come to the villa the day before and failed properly to rig the house for sight and sound. A stereo in the poolhouse. A lamp in the wrong bedroom. That was all they had managed, after months of preparation. It was mystifying. Surely they could have delayed the housekeeper coming back to the villa and not left Kite to pick up the pieces? Or had Carl lied and the lamp was yet another way of testing him?

'Swim?' Xavier asked.

Kite thought of the cool prospect of the water, of Martha

BOX 88

arriving soon and diving in to join them. Carl's words of advice were in his head: *Make sure everyone else in the villa is downstairs, maybe outside taking a swim after the long drive.* He recalled the rancid smell of the bins and was grateful when Xavier offered him a cigarette, breathing in the rich smell of the tobacco.

'Don't swim yet,' Luc ordered. 'Come inside first, put your bags in your rooms. See the place. Why do you have to smoke all the time? Put it out.'

Kite dutifully extinguished his cigarette after only a couple of puffs though Xavier defied his father and kept smoking as they followed him into the house. There was a large wooden table in the centre of the hall on which somebody had placed a vase of fresh flowers. The floor was a mosaic of faded brown tiles. On top of a baby grand piano in the southern corner were various framed photographs, including a black-and-white shot of Luc as a handsome teenager standing next to a man whom Kite assumed to be his great-uncle. Both of them looked cold-eyed and rather pleased with themselves. The walls of the hall were two-tone: below eye level, they had been painted a now-fading blue; above this was a broad band of pale cream plaster. The walls were adorned with several paintings that Kite did not remember seeing in the photographs shown to him by Peele. One was of a beautiful woman in a silk dress, done in the style of Renoir, another a watercolour of an orchard being worked by a farmer and his wife, seemingly in the early part of the century.

'I remember this smell so well,' said Luc, sounding uncharacteristically sensitive. 'It is the smell of my childhood.'

They left the bags by the entrance and walked in a slow clockwise loop around the ground floor, beginning in the kitchen, where baguettes and bowls of tapenade had already been left out for supper and covered with net frames to ward off flies and wasps. A smell of cooked onions reminded Kite of the kitchen at Killantringan. The dining-room table next door was laid for eight, which made him wonder who else, apart from Eskandarian, would be joining them for dinner. Luc then led them outside via the large sitting room onto the terrace where Kite was supposed to leave the ghetto blaster. He immediately identified a socket behind one of the sofas which could provide a power source. A large backgammon board had been left out in the shade of the veranda. Kite looked back into the living room. He knew from memory that the next room was Luc's office, then a connecting corridor leading to a smaller room identified as the place where the family would most likely relax and watch television. He was beginning to plot how he might go about moving the lamp.

'The garden is spectacular, no?' Luc announced. Kite wasn't green-fingered, and Xavier didn't appear to be listening, but his father carried on regardless. 'Plumbago, oleander, wisteria, agapanthus.' Each plant was identified in his thick French accent. 'There is very little flowering at this time of year, perhaps only the hibiscus.' It sounded as though he had memorised the names in order to impress them. 'But what do you care? I didn't care about gardens either, when I was your age.' In French, he added: 'One day you will understand and appreciate all this, Xavier. I hope anyway. At the moment you don't consider it important.' He switched back to English. 'All you boys think about is wine and girls and cigarettes.'

'Sounds a bit like you,' Xavier replied. 'I must be a chip off the old block, Papa. We have a lot in common.'

Luc's mood darkened; he did not like to lose face in front of his son. He stepped back inside without responding. Xavier remained in the garden smoking the last of his cigarette, making knowing eye contact with Kite. It occurred to him that Luc was in some way jealous of his son, resentful of his quick wit and essential good nature. How else to explain the thinness of his skin whenever Xavier dared to tease or defy him?

'Lockie!'

Luc was summoning Kite back into the house. Xavier nodded at him, indicating that he should go inside.

BOX 88

'I'll be two minutes,' he said. 'Really need to fart.'

Kite was still smiling at this as he made his way into the office. Luc was seated behind a vast teak desk, looking every inch the cat who got the cream.

'Not bad, huh?'

'Not bad,' Kite replied. 'What a great place to work.' He clocked a fax machine in the corner, a record player by the window. He knew from his conversations with Peele and Strawson that they had been keen to rig the study: the bookcases and light fixtures, the skirting boards and fax machine, would all have made ideal locations for hidden microphones.

'Perhaps,' Luc replied flatly. 'I prefer not to work on vacation though it is not always possible. I want to enjoy myself, but there is always something to do. I haven't seen Ali in a long time.'

Right on cue, Hélène, the housekeeper who had disturbed the Falcons, walked into the room. A sharp-eyed, diminutive woman of at least sixty-five, she embraced Luc like a long-lost son, remarked on his good health and asked if Kite was Xavier. Luc laughed and quickly cleared up the confusion, summoning Xavier into the study. Kite had the strange, disconcerting sense that Luc had been embarrassed by Hélène's mistake, as though Kite were too low-born, too poorly turned-out ever to be considered the son of Luc Bonnard. Xavier duly shook Hélène's hand, then left his father talking to her as he joined Kite in the last of the rooms on the ground floor, the sitting room in the south-east corner. He was bemoaning the 'ancient' TV and the 'shitty' video recorder when Kite heard the low rumble of an approaching car and the crunch of gravel under tyres. The shutters in the room were closed against the heat. Xavier opened them with a flourish just as Rosamund switched off the engine on the Citroën.

'Friends, Romans, countrywomen!' he shouted through the window. Kite was behind him, nonchalantly staring out at the Citroën and waiting for his first glimpse of Martha. She eventually emerged from the back seat wearing tight denim jeans and a crop top that showed off her stomach. She was as striking as he remembered. She gazed up in awe at the house, immediately taking out a camera and firing off several shots of the entrance, dappled light cutting through the branches of the lime tree and falling on her face. Kite was mesmerised by the way she moved, such confidence and grace it was as if she was deliberately taunting the world with her self-assurance.

'You're not watching *television*, are you, darling?' said Rosamund peering through the open window.

'Course not, Mum. We're doing drugs.'

It wasn't a taunt that Lady Rosamund found particularly funny. Kite and Xavier lingered in the room as she and Luc unloaded the luggage from the Citroën, carrying it into the house. Kite could hear Martha talking to them, her voice already having a hypnotic effect on him. There was a turntable beside the television. He flicked through a stack of vinyl records, mostly jazz and classical, covers showing Herbert von Karajan conducting the Berlin Philharmonic and Dizzy Gillespie with his cheeks blown out. Xavier went through the drawers of an old armoire, finding a pack of cards, a bottle of white spirit, a rusted tin full of old centimes.

'This guy just died, right?' he asked, holding up the Karajan. With this many people in the house, he was wondering when he would ever get a clear opportunity to move the lamp.

'No idea. Want to see upstairs?'

'Sure.'

They bumped into Luc in the hall, Jacqui's voice audible on the terrace at the back of the house. Kite didn't want to seem to be rushing to the first bedroom. He waited for Luc and Xavier to pass him, then followed them upstairs.

'Where are we all sleeping?' Xavier asked.

'I'll show you,' Luc replied abruptly. He was clearly still smarting from Xavier's remark on the terrace. 'There's a cabin at the bottom of the garden but it has no roof yet, so we will all

BOX 88

have to be in the house. There's plenty of room. Lockie, do you want to be in here?'

He indicated the closed door of the first bedroom at the top of the stairs. Xavier opened it and coughed at a small eruption of dust. Kite immediately spotted a lamp on a low wooden table beside the bed identical to the picture Carl had shown him. It wasn't as big as he had imagined, and noticeably newer than some of the other furniture in the room. The Falcons had either bought it recently or reconstituted an existing lamp from the house.

'This looks great,' he replied, slinging his bag on the ground. He assumed that Luc and Rosamund would be in the master bedroom across the corridor on the southern side of the house.

'Xavier, you will be in here.' Luc indicated a large bedroom at the end of the passage overlooking the terrace. Kite knew that three empty bedrooms remained on the first floor and that there were two more above them in the attic. Would the girls be upstairs or would Eskandarian take that suite of rooms? If the Iranian was just across the corridor it would make switching the lamps much easier. Kite could walk across the passage in two strides and be back in his room within moments.

'Nice,' said Xavier, stretching out his arms in appreciation of the width and scale of his room. There was a huge double bed, a sofa beneath a large bay window, a door connecting to a sizeable en-suite bathroom. 'Where's Jacqui going?'

'There are two bedrooms on the other side, above the nursery,' Luc replied. 'What my uncle used to call the nursery, anyway. The girls can go in there and share a bathroom.' Kite's heart sank. 'Ali will need his privacy. I have put him in the attic. In the future, Jacqui can sleep there. Or you two can argue over this room and switch.'

'No way,' said Xavier. 'Shotgun.'

'You haven't even seen the other rooms,' his father replied. 'How can you be so certain?'

Even this simple question was loaded with unnecessary malice. Xavier again caught Kite's eye and shrugged, as if to say: 'What did I do?' They climbed the stairs to the attic, which was just as Kite had visualised: a cramped landing, with bedrooms on either side divided by a bathroom. He noticed that the smaller of the two rooms had been converted into a makeshift office with a modern desk and swivel chair. There was a single bed in the corner, but the sheets had not been made up. Eskandarian would presumably be sleeping in the other room. Kite looked around for a lamp and found one on top of a chest of drawers behind the door. It was small enough to switch with the light from his bedroom but not as modern in design as the one created by the Falcons. Kite walked across the landing and immediately spotted a button telephone beside Eskandarian's bed. It hadn't been in any of the photographs. Luc had probably had it wired in on the Iranian's instructions. BOX 88 had been monitoring his phones and fax messages for several months, but neither Peele nor Strawson had mentioned anything to Kite about a phone line in the bedroom. So where to put the lamp? Near the phone, so that the Falcons could eavesdrop on any calls, or across the landing in the makeshift office, where perhaps Eskandarian would hold private meetings with visitors to the house? Kite wished that he could seek out Peele's advice, but it was too late to walk over to the safe house. Besides, the switch had to be made before Eskandarian's arrival.

'Has he got married?' Xavier asked.

'Who, Ali?' The windows were not particularly clean and Luc was checking for dust on the sills. 'No. He likes women too much. He was engaged to a girl in Paris eleven years ago, but when he went home to Iran, she didn't go with him.'

This was new information. BOX 88 knew that Eskandarian was a ladies' man who preferred to remain single. On trips to Europe and Asia in the previous six years, surveillance reports had mentioned women in Eskandarian's entourage with whom

BOX 88

he was casually involved. As far as Kite was aware, there was no record on file of a fiancée.

'Is she still around?' Xavier asked. He was checking out the bathroom, picking up bottles of bath salts, turning the ancient taps at the sink.

'Non,' Luc replied, continuing in French: 'She moved to Barcelona. Married a Catalan nationalist and had a baby. She likes politicians.'

Kite didn't know what a Catalan was but resolved to elicit the woman's name for his morning report. He would need to ask the question without it sounding nosey and unnatural. With luck, she would come up in conversation at a later point.

'OK, now we swim,' Xavier announced and immediately called out Jacqui's name. His voice boomed around the attic. 'We're going to the pool!' he shouted. 'Mum! You coming?'

'There's no need to shout, darling.' Rosamund had appeared at the bottom of the stairs, looking as serene and composed as ever. 'Yes, we're all going.'

Martha was beside her, a towel looped around her neck. She had already changed into a pale cream summer dress. A dark blue swimsuit was visible in silhouette underneath. She stared directly at Kite as she looked up the stairs.

'Hi. I'm Lockie.'

'I know. I'm Martha.'

'We've actually met before,' he said.

'Really?'

'Yeah. At a party in London last year.'

'Oh? I don't remember.'

Xavier was standing beside him. Kite felt his cheeks flush. He was slightly crushed that Martha had no recollection of their meeting, although she seemed embarrassed by her failure to remember, rather than indifferent.

'Hi, Xav,' she said, adjusting her hair as she looked up the stairs.

'Hey.' Xavier walked down towards her and they hugged in a way that made Kite edgy. 'Good flight?'

'Fine, thanks. So lovely to be here. The house is amazing.'

Kite wanted to play it cool but found himself following Xavier downstairs and nodding at Martha, aware that he probably looked like a lovesick puppy. She smiled at him, as if apologising for the effect she was having, and walked off. Luc emerged from the master bedroom.

'You coming, Papa?' Xavier asked.

'Maybe,' Luc replied. 'I have a lot to do. I have to find my trunks.'

'Come,' said Kite. He was impatient to clear the house. 'You've driven for eight hours. It'll be good to swim it off.'

To his relief, Luc agreed and assured both of them that he would appear at the pool 'before too long'.

'Great,' Xavier told him. 'So let's go.'

Kite took his time, changing into swimming trunks, putting sun cream on his pale Scottish skin, listening out to see if Luc was on his way to the pool. Xavier appeared wearing a pair of canary yellow Bermuda shorts, a towel clutched in his right hand, a packet of cigarettes in the other.

'Ready?'

'Sure.'

Kite had no alternative but to go with him. Walking the narrow paths of the garden, bordered by rosemary bushes and olive trees, he could hear the splashes and laughter of Jacqui and Martha up ahead in the pool. Luc and Rosamund were still in the house. They would probably spend at least half an hour unpacking and talking to the staff, then go for a swim. Kite looked at his watch. It was past five-thirty. Eskandarian would be landing in Paris in less than an hour. That left a three-hour window in which to switch the lamps, but no clear opportunity in which to do so. Kite wanted to prove himself to Peele and

BOX 88

Strawson. He thought of Carl on the motorway and didn't want to let him down. The cicadas were still humming in the hills. He ducked beneath the fallen branches of a palm tree and emerged into a clearing in front of the pool. The door to the swimming hut was already open.

'Look what I found,' said Jacqui, triumphantly carrying the ghetto blaster. Kite hoped she didn't trip and fall in the water or accidentally drop the stereo and smash it on the concrete paving.

'At least we'll have music down here,' Xavier said. 'How's the temperature?'

Martha was nowhere to be seen. Kite assumed she was taking photographs in the garden. He took off his T-shirt and walked to the edge of the pool, bending down to stick his hand in the water. The next thing he knew Xavier had pushed him and Kite was surfacing to uproarious laughter.

'Right!' he shouted and sprung out of the water, chasing the cackling Xavier around the edge of the deep end, only to collide with Martha as she emerged from the hut.

'Shit, sorry,' he said, grabbing her shoulders to halt his momentum yet covering her in droplets of cold water.

'That's OK,' she replied nonchalantly and dived into the pool with the ease and grace of a kingfisher. Kite had a nose full of her perfume, the astonishing sensation of her skin on the tips of his fingers. He caught up with Xavier only to see brother and sister jump into the water simultaneously. Kite bombed in to join them. For the next twenty minutes he showed off in front of Martha, beating Xavier in a swimming race, holding his breath underwater for two minutes, ducking him from behind whenever his friend wasn't looking. His exploits seemed to have no effect on her. Martha mostly chatted to Jacqui and appeared to ignore him. Eventually Rosamund emerged from the garden, keeping her Paris salon haircut bone-dry as she swam an elegant, upright breaststroke. Kite sat on the steps of the pool listening to a Neil

Young cassette which Xavier had grabbed from the house. Waiting for Luc to come to the pool was like waiting for a train that would never come. Kite had to stop himself looking up at the house every time he heard movement in the garden.

Finally, at around six-fifteen, Xavier's father emerged in a pair of dark red Speedos and dived in with an almighty patriarchal splash. Kite instantly stood up, announced that he was going to the house, and prayed that nobody would follow him. To his relief, both Xavier and Jacqui seemed keen to join their father in the pool. Rosamund was happily talking to Martha about photography.

'Can you bring more cigarettes?' Xavier called out.

'Sure,' Kite replied.

As soon as he was past the palm tree, he ran along the narrow paths of the garden towards the rear of the house. At the veranda, he took off his espadrilles and wiped his feet on the mat. The house was still and silent. Kite walked quickly through the sitting room to the hall, bounded up the stairs two at a time, checked that each of the bedrooms on the first floor was empty. Then he went into his room and unplugged the lamp. Still wearing his damp swimming shorts, he carried it up the narrow staircase to the smaller of the two attic bedrooms and placed it on the floor. He unplugged the lamp behind the door in Eskandarian's makeshift office and carried it out onto the landing. Having plugged in the modified lamp, he left the room as he had otherwise found it.

A noise below. Kite stopped moving. As noiselessly as possible, he picked up the lamp from the landing and darted into the bathroom. Somebody was walking up the stairs. He could lock the door and pretend to be using the toilet, hoping that whoever was coming up wouldn't hear him. The person had reached the landing. Kite had no choice other than to close the door and slide the lock as deliberately as possible. He couldn't hide. It would be disastrous to be caught sneaking around.

BOX 88

'*Bonjour?*'

A woman's voice, tentative and confused. Hélène. There was a low glass table beside the bathroom window with a small plastic tray on it. Kite put the lamp on the tray and allowed the flex to fall behind the table so that if the housekeeper came in she might not notice that the lamp was out of place. He thought of Strawson testing him in the Churchill bathroom. This was a different order of anxiety.

'*Oui?*' he said.

'Monsieur Bonnard?'

'No, it's Lachlan. Xavier's friend,' Kite replied in French. 'I'm just using the bathroom.'

Hélène said something in response that Kite could not understand. He heard her moving around in the office. He prayed that she would not notice the switched lamp. A woman like that, who had worked in the house for so long, would surely know every piece of furniture in every room. If the Bonnard family now came back to find Kite trapped in the bathroom, with a lamp missing from his bedroom and another mysteriously moved to the attic, it would take a miracle of quick thinking to dig himself out of trouble.

Relax, he told himself. *Be cool.* He remembered conversations with Peele about controlling his breathing and took a deep breath through his nose. He continued to listen as Hélène moved around the office. Was she putting sheets on the unmade bed? That would take at least five minutes. Christ, maybe she was going to sweep the floors and clean the windows? Kite knew that he should make some noise and lifted the toilet seat. What was she doing that was taking so long?

Footsteps on the stairs. Was somebody else coming up or was Hélène finally going down? He waited, listening at the door. Kite's whole future seemed to depend on the next few moments. He was sure that she had gone, yet he needed to be certain. He kept listening out but there was no further sound.

At last he made his decision. He flushed the toilet and ran the tap at the sink to make it sound as though he was washing his hands. Kite then opened the door. There was laughter in the garden. Xavier was coming back. Kite remembered what Peele had told him. *We think you won't panic if you find yourself under pressure.* Time to prove him right.

Kite went out onto the landing and down to the first floor, leaving the lamp behind. He could neither see nor hear Hélène, but was sure that at least two people were now entering the house.

He had to take the risk. He sprinted back up the stairs, grabbed the lamp, pulled the flex free from the table and waited on the landing, listening out for Hélène. He could hear Xavier laughing somewhere downstairs. Luc was with him. They were making so much noise it was impossible to hear anything else. Kite had no choice. Moving as quickly as he could, he carried the lamp down to the first floor. At the bottom of the stairs he waited again, saw that the coast was clear and hurried across the corridor to his room, closing the door behind him. He dropped the lamp on the bed and sat beside it, breathing hard. He felt as though he had walked through deep mud across a vast open field, exposed and vulnerable. Xavier was bounding up the stairs.

'Lockie?'

Kite picked up the lamp, put it behind the door and said: 'Yeah?' with as much nonchalance as he could summon.

'You OK? You didn't come back.'

'Sorry. Thought I'd lost my headphones.'

'Ah, OK. We're going into town. Want to come?'

'Sure.'

If only he had waited, he could have stayed behind while everyone went to Mougins. Kite put his head in his hands. He again controlled his breathing in the way Peele had taught him: a deep breath in through the nose, holding it for a count of seven, then slowly out through the mouth. 'Buddhist mumbo-jumbo but it works,' he had said, turning the doubling dice to sixty-four

BOX 88

in yet another backgammon triumph. Kite looked up at the ceiling. He had done it. He had successfully switched the lamps. The sense of achievement, after so many weeks of study and preparation, was exhilarating.

He changed into a pair of trousers and put on a clean T-shirt. Hélène was placing fresh flowers in a vase outside Luc and Rosamund's bedroom. She had a quick, bustling manner and seemed to have been waiting for him to emerge from his room.

'There is a toilet just here, sir,' she said in French, indicating the bathroom door beside them. To Kite's relief, it was evident that she thought he had simply lost his bearings and wandered into the wrong area of the house.

'I realise that now,' he replied. 'Thank you.'

Seconds later, Xavier emerged from his room.

'What was that about?' he asked. Hélène had gone into the empty spare room to close the shutters.

'Nothing,' he replied. 'I was just introducing myself. Let's go into town.'

37

Isobel heard the car pulling up outside the cottage. For a short, sweet instant she imagined that it was Kite coming home to save her, but then the youngest of the three men, the one with the acne and the narrow chin, stood up and walked towards the door.

'Who is it?' Isobel asked him.

The man pressed a finger to his lips and looked at her accusingly, urging her to keep quiet. It had been easy to unsettle and annoy them in this way. From the moment the men had surrounded her outside the house and dragged her back inside, she had known that she would have to resort to manipulations. She had grown up with two older brothers and knew how to deal with men. She was a pregnant woman who had worked in paediatrics for almost six years. She knew that she could feign illness and hysteria, play on their sentimental weakness for their mothers and sisters, make them think that she would lose the baby if they did anything to hurt her.

The baby. Right from the start, Rambo had kept kicking, almost as if he knew that his mother needed support and encouragement. When the oldest of the three thugs had grabbed her and pushed her up against the car, Isobel's belly had compressed against the metal. Initially, she had feared an abruption, but once

BOX 88

she was back inside the house—screaming at them to let her go, calling them every name under the sun, making out that she would die if she didn't immediately lie down—Rambo had given her a sequence of kicks, almost like an acknowledgement of the brilliance of her performance, and Isobel had felt a wave of relief.

As the day proceeded, she kept up the act. She groaned in pain whenever she moved. She went into the bathroom and came out complaining that she was bleeding and needed to go to hospital. The leader didn't fall for that, but it didn't matter. What was important was to keep up the show, to make them feel guilty for what they were doing to her, to make them imagine what it would be like to live the rest of their lives knowing that they had been responsible for the death of a woman and her unborn child. One of the guards, Karim was his name, was kinder and less volatile than the others. She made him fetch pillows, water and food. She sobbed and told him she was in constant pain. He liked football. He had told her that he supported Arsenal. She had promised him that she would make sure her son supported the club for life if only they would let her go.

Soon their patience wore out and, before Isobel could do anything to stop him, the leader had jabbed a needle into her thigh. She quickly lost consciousness. Yet even this played into her hands. When she woke up, she was groggy and worried about the child. Almost immediately, she felt Rambo kick, but continued to act as though the baby had been dangerously sedated, that she needed sugar and water and proper medical care. At one point, two out of the three goons watching her—'goons' was a favourite word of Lockie's—were rushing around the kitchen like waiters in a bad farce variously searching for non-existent glucose tablets, biscuits, bags of decaffeinated green tea.

'What did you put into me?' she demanded of them. 'My leg aches. I can hardly move. What kind of man puts a needle into a pregnant woman? You could have killed both of us!'

They spoke to one another in Farsi, telling her nothing about why they had seized her husband or where he was being held. Isobel knew that it was connected to Lockie's work. 'I've made enemies,' he had once told her. 'I've made mistakes. I've enjoyed successes. One day people might try to come after me. The rules have changed. In the old days, people like us were off limits. Not any more.' When he didn't respond to their emails and messages, they would wonder what had happened to him and send someone to the cottage to investigate. Isobel had to believe that. The alternative was too awful to contemplate.

Eventually the effort of keeping up the act began to wear her out. Even Rambo grew tired. Isobel could tell that the baby had gone to sleep. One of the guards had gone upstairs to rest. Karim was beside her, flicking through the sports pages of *The Times*. That was when the car pulled up outside, bright lights against the closed curtains.

'Stay where you are,' Karim told her. 'A friend has come to help us.'

38

Luc stayed behind at the villa and Rosamund drove Kite, Xavier, Martha and Jacqui into town. While she bought English newspapers at a shop on the outskirts of Mougins, Xavier stocked up on vodka and absinthe at the local supermarket. Jacqui pointed out that he and Kite had already bought bottles of duty-free Smirnoff and Jim Beam at the airport; why did they need even more alcohol when there was plenty in the house? Xavier told his sister that she was 'boring' and should mind her own business. They had a brief, bickering argument beside a chicken *rotisserie* while Kite and Martha looked on. Kite realised that Xavier was still thinking like a schoolboy, hoarding alcohol in secret rather than realising that he could go out and buy it whenever and wherever he pleased. He watched him put the bottles into Jacqui's tote bag, pleading with her to keep it quiet. Jacqui complained that they were too heavy, so Martha hid the absinthe in her bag. Her friendship with Jacqui was a mystery to Kite. Xavier's sister was conservative and short-tempered, an academic goody two shoes with straight A's from birth. Martha, on the other hand, seemed to possess the loose, easy nonchalance of the free spirit. Xavier had told him that the two had met at Roedean when they were eleven. Martha had been expelled a few years later for reasons which remained shrouded in mystery. Kite concluded that it was probably one of the lasting effects of boarding school; lifelong friendships were forged regardless of temperament or circumstances.

They walked into the village. Kite and Martha had their first proper conversation, discussing *Dangerous Liaisons*, which she had seen at a cinema in St John's Wood. He had the sense that she was assessing him, biding her time and working out if Lachlan Kite was worthy of her attention or just another drooling old Alfordian who couldn't keep his eyes off her. At a café in the main square, Xavier bought a round of drinks and began to flirt with her, making jokes which Martha found funny and mentioning the various clubs and parties he had been to in London where they might have crossed paths. Kite remained mostly silent. Xavier finished his first vodka and tonic within five minutes and ordered a second while the others nursed glasses of beer and wine in the fading sun. Kite was half-expecting to catch sight of Rita or Strawson in the village, but there was no sign of them. He assumed that they were settling into the safe house, finding out if Eskandarian had landed safely in Paris, checking the sound feed from the lamp. He was worried about the stereo. He had to find a way of moving it up to the house so that it would relay conversations from the terrace, but it seemed likely that Xavier and the girls would insist on keeping it down by the pool so that there was music to listen to during the days. Kite could hardly move it back to the terrace every night after dark. That would look suspicious.

By the time Rosamund found them at the café and said it was time to go home, Xavier had knocked back three vodka and tonics and taken a surreptitious swig of the absinthe from Martha's bag. Kite looked at his watch. It was almost eight o'clock. If Eskandarian's flights were on time, he would be landing in Cannes at any moment. Climbing into the front seat of the Mercedes and exchanging pleasantries with Rosamund,

BOX 88

he felt as though he was going back to work at the hotel: there was the same sense of impending pressure and responsibility. Yet he was surprised to discover that he relished this feeling. He was looking forward to meeting Eskandarian, just as he was keen to see Peele and Strawson in the morning and to receive his next set of instructions.

'Someone's breath absolutely stinks of alcohol,' said Rosamund, driving down the hill from Mougins.

'Sorry, might be mine,' said Kite, covering his mouth. He wanted to look good in front of Martha by taking the hit for Xavier. 'I should stick to Coke.'

A snigger in the back seat, a stagey sigh from Jacqui. The rest of the journey passed in silence and they were back at the villa within five minutes. Turning through the gates of the house, Kite looked to the west and tried to work out which of the several houses along the road was 'Cassava', the property rented by BOX 88. In the morning he would set off on his run and find out. He needed to prioritise what Peele and Strawson would want to hear so soon after Eskandarian's arrival. He had to identify something that these men of age and experience did not already know.

Back in the house, everybody went to their respective rooms to wash and change for dinner. Somebody, presumably Hélène, had opened the window and closed the shutters in Kite's room. Peele had not anticipated this. If Kite at any point left a red T-shirt on the windowsill as a signal, only for Hélène to move it and close the window, the signal would not be seen. He had brought two T-shirts which were now effectively useless for the purpose of communicating with BOX 88. He trusted that Peele would come up with an alternative system in the morning.

Kite showered and returned to his room. He could tell by the atmosphere in the house—the smells emanating from the kitchen, the sense of people hurrying back and forth, the sound of ice cubes being dropped into a bucket in the hall—that Eskandarian was expected at any moment; it was only a short journey from the airport to Mougins.

'Smoke?' Xavier asked, sticking his head round Kite's door.

He was wearing a pale blue button-down shirt and smelled of shower gel. They went outside and walked down to the pool. Mosquitoes were swimming in the lights, but Xavier had brought a spray repellent which he told Kite to apply to his arms and neck.

'They get the munchies,' he said. 'Vicious bastards.'

He took out a lump of hash and proceeded to crumble it into a joint.

'You smuggle that over on the plane?' Kite asked.

Xavier shook his head. 'Paris.'

When they had been sitting in the Marais, a young African man had approached their table with a whispered offer of cannabis. Xavier had disappeared to the bathroom moments later; that was when they had done the deal.

'Might be shit shit,' he said, pronouncing the second 'shit' like 'sheet'. 'Only one way to find out.'

It was perfectly good, though not particularly strong. They shared the joint, then Xavier rolled another. With Eskandarian's arrival imminent, Kite was wary of getting too stoned and left Xavier to smoke the bulk of it. Soon his friend was looking out at the silhouetted hills from a deckchair by the pool, quietly singing chunks of 'Mr Tambourine Man' in a mood of disconnected sadness which unnerved Kite.

'You OK?' he asked.

He suspected that Xavier was troubled by something but unable or unwilling to articulate what it might be.

'Fine, fine,' he said, mumbling the words of Bob Dylan as he drew on a cigarette. 'Do you ever hear from Billy Peele?'

Kite's senses had been slightly slowed by the joint. The question jolted him back to full sobriety.

'Not since we left,' he replied, wondering why Xavier had

BOX 88

chosen this, of all moments, to confront him. He tried to sound relaxed as he said: 'Why do you ask?'

'I was just thinking about him. He was one of the good ones. You'll still be friends, no?'

'As much as you can be friends with a beak.' He needed to ascertain where was this coming from. Why was Xavier suddenly so interested in Peele? Had he seen them together in Hampstead? Kite said: 'I doubt we'll stay in touch.'

'Shame.'

Kite studied his friend's face in the darkness but found no trace of irony or hidden meaning. It was perfectly possible that Peele's name had surfaced in Xavier's consciousness for innocent reasons. They stood up and walked towards the pool. Hélène's elderly husband, Alain, had switched on the underwater lights. The surface looked eerily white and cloudy.

'We should try and have a pint with Billy when we get back,' Kite offered, remembering Peele's entreaty never to embellish a lie. He should have let the subject drop. Xavier gave a long sigh, seemingly having already lost all interest in the subject and said 'Nah, fuck it' before losing his footing and stumbling on a paving stone near the water's edge.

'Easy.'

'I'm fine. No problem.'

He began to sing again—'My senses are stripped, hands can't feel or grip . . .'—chopping up the words and misquoting lines from the song with the same detached air of melancholy as before. Kite wondered if he had had an argument with his mother or father, both of whom kept a sharp eye on Xavier's drinking. He was about to ask him when a set of headlights appeared in the distance. Kite followed their progress along the road. After three hundred metres the vehicle turned into the Bonnards' drive. This was surely Eskandarian.

'Looks like the ayatollah's here,' Xavier confirmed. A car door slammed. Kite couldn't see what was going on at the house—it was almost dark and there were trees and hedgerows blocking the view—but Luc's voice was audible on the drive. Kite heard the booming, joyous laughter of the Iranian as he greeted his friend, then Rosamund saying 'Ali! Welcome!'

'What's he like?' Kite asked.

'Can't remember.' Xavier looked back at the pool as if he had forgotten something. 'Haven't seen him for years.' There was a moment's hesitation, then: 'Actually, that's not true. I saw him in London about two years ago. My father does business with him.'

'What kind of business?'

Kite was working, mining his friend for answers. Strawson and Peele hadn't mentioned a business relationship between Luc and Eskandarian. Xavier's response was oddly aggressive, as if he disapproved of whatever was going on between them.

'I dunno. Why don't you ask him?'

'Why would I do that?'

'Ask him about sanctions. Ask him: "Aren't there supposed to be sanctions with Iran?"'

'What are you talking about?'

Kite had stumbled on something potentially of interest to BOX. Xavier put his arm across his back and let his weight fall on him.

'Forget it,' he said. 'It's all good. All kosher. Luc Bonnard is a fine man, not a bad man.' He switched to French and said: 'Daddy never puts a foot wrong.'

Eskandarian was not quite what Kite had expected. Courtesy of Strawson and Peele, he had seen several photographs of his quarry: corporate mugshots, as well as a video of a speech Eskandarian had given at a conference in Munich. In all these, he was modest in appearance and conservatively dressed. Kite was half-expecting to come face to face with a kind of Persian Obi-Wan Kenobi, a pious holy man dressed in long robes similar

BOX 88

to the Muslim elders he had seen emerging from mosques in Ealing and Uxbridge Road. Instead he was confronted by a tanned, jovial Middle Eastern man wearing designer jeans and brown suede loafers. An enormous Rolex glinted on his wrist and there was a Ralph Lauren logo on the chest of Eskandarian's spotlessly pressed Polo shirt.

'Ali, this is Xavier's friend, Lockie.'

Eskandarian scrunched his face up at the name, as thousands of others had done throughout the course of Kite's life.

'*Lockie*? OK. What is that short for?'

There was a slight American intonation to Eskandarian's accent. They were shaking hands, the grip firm, the eye contact warm. Was this a man capable of coordinating mass murder?

'It's from Lachlan,' he said. 'Spelled with an "a". I'm Scottish. North of the border it's Lack, everywhere else people call me Locklan or Lockie.'

Eskandarian mimed a baffled confusion.

'Then I think I will stick to Lockie!' he said. 'Very good to meet you, young man. And where is Master Xavier?'

Right on cue, Xavier stumbled into the hall behind Kite, his eyes slightly bloodshot, his grin at once wary and provocative, as if he knew that it was impolite to be drunk and stoned in front of his father's distinguished guest, but that he didn't much care. Eskandarian was evidently a man of the world and instantly understood that Luc's son had enjoyed one too many. He made short shrift of the introduction, avoiding commonplace adult remarks about how much Xavier had grown, embraced him briefly, said that he was grateful to have been invited to spend time with the Bonnard family, and invited Rosamund to show him to his room.

It worried Kite that he warmed to Eskandarian on first impression. Without a father of his own, he knew that he had a tendency to lionise older men; he was supposed to be maintaining focus, reporting back to BOX everything he saw and heard about

Eskandarian, not what he felt or wanted to believe about him. Kite could feel the after-effects of the hashish, a slow, mellow cloud pillowing his senses as he walked outside to clear his head.

A man in a black suit was pulling suitcases out of an Audi Quattro. Kite assumed that he was a taxi driver, but as the man turned around, he spotted a handgun holstered inside his jacket. Eskandarian had brought a bodyguard. Kite raised a hand in greeting but was ignored. A second vehicle with a taxi light on its roof was coming down the drive. The Bonnards hadn't mentioned any other guests coming for dinner, but Luc instantly appeared from inside the house to greet the new arrival. Kite was conscious that he was standing around to no real purpose. He lit a cigarette to give himself something to do, keeping his eyes on the taxi. The driver opened the back door. An astonishingly beautiful Asian woman in her late twenties stepped out in high heels and a figure-clinging black dress.

'You must be Hana,' said Luc, addressing her warmly in French. 'Welcome. Ali is upstairs.'

Strawson and Peele had said nothing about a girlfriend turning up, but she was too provocatively dressed to be a secretary. The woman, who appeared to be of Thai or Vietnamese origin, handed the taxi driver a clutch of francs as he unloaded her suitcase from the boot. When Luc introduced her to Kite, Hana offered him a soft, warm hand and a slightly patronising smile before going inside. She was obviously keen to be reunited with Eskandarian.

'Who's that?' Kite asked.

Luc gave him a seedy man-to-man wink. 'Special friend of Ali's from Nice. She'll be staying with us for a few days.'

Kite was not naive. He assumed Hana had been paid for. He had seen adverts for prostitutes at the back of the *International Herald Tribune* but couldn't conceive that Lady Rosamund Penley would countenance having a high-class hooker in the house. Luc mistook his silence for young lust and commented on her beauty.

'Incredible-looking woman.'

BOX 88

'Yeah,' said Kite, preferring Martha in every way. 'She's . . . exotic.'

Luc went back inside, leaving Kite alone with the bodyguard. They did not acknowledge one another. It was as though Kite were standing on one side of a wall and the man in the black suit on the other. To his surprise, the bodyguard opened Hana's suitcase and quickly searched it, like a security guard at an airport. Kite caught sight of a black lace bra and felt a pang of lust. He turned and looked up towards the first-floor windows. Martha was billeted in the furthest of the two bedrooms with a view over the swimming pool. The light in her window was visible as a narrow glow seeping through closed shutters. He extinguished the cigarette in an old oil jar by the door and introduced himself to the bodyguard.

'I'm Lockie,' he said, indicating Hana's suitcase. 'Can I help you with that?'

He might as well have been addressing the brick wall which moments earlier had been separating them in Kite's imagination. The bodyguard said nothing. He did not offer a name, a hand to shake nor any sense of gratitude for Kite's offer. For reasons which he couldn't properly explain to himself, Kite had expected somebody friendly and easy-going, a retired policeman from Isfahan with a pot belly and a few funny stories. He hadn't anticipated that the guard would be at least a decade younger than Eskandarian, fit and strong and pitiless. He was unshaven and looked so tired that the bags under his eyes were slightly yellow in appearance. The underlying menace in his face was unsettling. He grunted as he picked up the case and carried it into the house. Out of some dark recess in his memory, Kite thought of the cassette recorder smuggled onto Pan Am 103.

'How's it going down there?'

Martha was leaning out of the window. She had put her hair up and was wearing a necklace of pale stones that showed off her tanned neck.

'Hello!' he said. 'You two ready for dinner?'

'Looks like you are,' she said, and Kite didn't know how to take the remark. It was almost as if she knew how important the meal was going to be in terms of his first engagement with Eskandarian.

'Ali just got here,' he said. 'And his special friend.'

'Special friend?' Martha asked, lowering her voice to a stage whisper.

'You'll see,' he said. 'Come down and have a drink. I'll explain everything.'

39

Kite did not get to sleep until four o'clock the following morning. The dinner finished by midnight, but Xavier kept him up by the pool, smoking the rest of the hash, working his way through half the duty-free Jim Beam, smoking cigarettes whenever he wasn't drawing on a joint and singing Leonard Cohen songs to the quiet, shuttered neighbourhood. Martha and Jacqui had followed Eskandarian and Hana to bed, pleading tiredness after the long drive from Paris. The bodyguard—whose name turned out to be Abbas—had taken the room across the hall from Kite. Luc attended to what he called 'some business' in his office, then joined Rosamund upstairs. Kite had craved sleep, not solely so that he could avoid waking up with a hangover, but because he was genuinely tired. Yet he felt that he could not abandon Xavier, both out of a sense of friendship but also to avoid arousing his suspicion.

He had set an alarm for seven-thirty, having agreed with Strawson and Peele that he would appear at the house at eight o'clock on the first morning. He woke with an ice-pick headache and stumbled downstairs in search of food and water. He found Hélène in the kitchen with a basket of fresh pastries and several baguettes. She gave him a pain au chocolat and a bottle of Badoit.

The pastry was still warm. Kite took them back to his room and changed into his running gear. Heading back downstairs, he passed Rosamund coming in the opposite direction.

'You're up early,' she said.

Kite was aware that he looked bleary-eyed and probably stank of booze and cigarettes.

'Yeah. Couldn't get back to sleep,' he said.

'Really? But you were both so late to bed.' She allowed Kite to absorb the fact that she had heard them coming in from the pool in the dead of night. 'I thought I heard an alarm clock.'

Kite was hyped up and keen to reach the safe house but needed to find an adequate excuse to explain the alarm.

'I stupidly forgot to switch it off,' he said. 'Woke me up ten minutes ago. I'm off for a run.'

'Very *American* of you to go jogging, Lockie. But I suppose if it helps clear your head . . .'

Kite had never been able to work out whether or not Rosamund liked him. She had the habit he had noticed in posh English women of treating everyone she met with the same bland courtesy and studied warmth, as though people were best held at arm's length and inspected carefully for traps and flaws.

'I'm an elite athlete, Ros,' he grinned. 'Keep myself in prime condition.'

'Lucky us,' she replied. Kite trotted out of the door before the conversation could go any further.

It was hot, even at this hour. Kite stretched beneath the lime tree, casually looking up at Martha's bedroom window. The shutters were open but her room was dark. He jogged down the drive, discovering the Audi Quattro parked in a lay-by on the far side of the gates. Abbas was already awake and seated in the driver's seat. Kite proffered a friendly wave, but the bodyguard remained impassive as Kite ran past. He hoped that he would not get out of the car and watch where he was going. The map Kite had seen of the safe house put it six hundred metres down

BOX 88

the long stretch of road beyond the Bonnard house. If Kite ducked in through the gates, Abbas might see him.

To Kite's relief, the ground fell away more than he had antic-ipated. There were several houses jigsawed into the hillside and by the time he had arrived at the sign saying 'Cassava', Kite was well out of sight of the Audi. There was nobody else on the road, no engine noise to indicate an approaching vehicle. He stopped running, as if working out whether or not to continue downhill or to go back in the direction from which he had come, took one last glance behind him to make sure that he was not being followed, then hurried through the open gate.

The house was much smaller and more modern than the Bonnard villa. Olive trees and rosemary bushes lined a white-washed wall separating the property from the road. A pale blue Peugeot was parked on the drive. Kite knocked on the door and stood in a shaded porch for no more than a few seconds before it was opened by Carl, who nodded him inside. He had a tea towel in his hand. The house smelled of fried bacon. Kite had no appetite.

'How are you this morning?' Carl asked. It didn't sound as though he cared much about the answer.

'Fine thanks,' Kite replied. 'I managed to move the lamp.'

'We know.' Carl did not congratulate him for this nor remark on the take quality from the attic. Perhaps Strawson or Peele wanted to get there first. Instead he showed Kite into a living room where both men were waiting for him in rattan chairs, mugs of coffee in front of them. There was something startling about seeing them together in this new environment. Peele was wearing dark blue trousers, espadrilles and a Lacoste shirt. He looked tanned and slightly unkempt, younger than he had seemed in Hampstead just a few days earlier. His hair was already turning blond in the summer sun. Strawson was more formally dressed in a pale linen suit, like a character in a Graham Greene novel behaving disreputably in the tropics.

'There he is!' said Peele, standing up and greeting Kite with a beaming smile. 'The prodigal son. How are we this morning?'

'Fine, thanks.' Kite felt suddenly ill-at-ease. 'Good to be here.'

Strawson did not move. Kite had the impression he was in a sour mood. There had been moments during his training in London when the American had snapped at Kite and been impatient with his progress. At the time Peele had told him not to worry: Strawson was just overworked, concerned that the operation might not go ahead because of the death of the ayatollah. Kite mustn't take it personally. It was just the way things were.

'Late night?' Strawson asked pointedly.

Kite cursed himself for not taking a shower or at least brushing his teeth before coming to the meeting.

'Yeah. Unfortunately. Xavier kept me up and I couldn't—'

'Save it. You sure you're up to this, Lachlan?'

Kite was stung by the question.

'Why wouldn't I be?' Strawson must have seen him smoking the joints with Xavier. Stupidly he added: 'Look, I'm not into drugs.'

'Who said anything about drugs?'

'I just assumed—'

'Smell coming from your poolhouse last night, you could have been at Woodstock.'

'Mike, he's fine,' Peele interjected.

'What have I done wrong?' Kite was tired and lost his cool. It was pathetic of Strawson to be so uptight over a late night and a bit of mild Moroccan black. 'I'm here on time, aren't I?'

'You look like shit. You smell like shit.'

'I'm not being paid. I'm doing this as a volunteer. For my country.'

'Don't pull that one. We offered you money, you turned it down.'

Peele stepped between them.

'Gentlemen,' he said, adopting a jovial, conciliatory tone. 'Let's

BOX 88

try this again. We're all off on the wrong foot. Mike, it was the first night of Lockie's holiday. Our boy has to behave in character in front of Xavier. If that means smoking the odd joint and drinking a beer or six, so be it. He could hardly go to bed on the first night of his holiday with a mug of Horlicks.'

'Fine,' Strawson conceded. 'But I'm telling you, kid. Stay off the hashish or whatever it was your friend was smoking last night. You need to keep your wits about you. That stuff fries your brain. This isn't schoolboy fun we're engaged on here. The stakes are very real for us, for thousands of people who might die because of this man's activities. You need to stay *sharp*.'

'Some interesting information emerged in the poolhouse last night,' Kite replied. He didn't need Strawson to emphasise the importance of the operation; it had been drummed into him a thousand times. 'You want to hear it?'

The American looked surprised that Kite wasn't backing down. 'Sure. Tell us then,' he said. 'We'll decide whether it's interesting or not.'

Carl went into the kitchen to fetch a pot of coffee. Kite was thirsty. He reminded Strawson that he had done exactly what was expected of him and had moved the lamp almost as soon as he had reached the villa.

'Is it working?' he asked, when Strawson didn't respond.

'Oh, it's working all right,' Peele smirked. He leaned back on the sofa as Carl returned with a full cafetière. 'Kept poor Hana up all night—'

'Enough,' said Strawson, who was nevertheless struggling to suppress a smile of his own. Kite was relieved by the change in atmosphere. Perhaps the whole thing had been a good-cop-bad-cop routine designed to keep him on his toes. 'You don't have a lot of time, kid. Give us your first impressions.'

'Can I have a cup of coffee first?' Kite asked.

Carl duly poured one.

'My first impression is that Luc is doing some kind of business with Eskandarian that may be illegal. Xavier was hinting that sanctions were being breached. Do you know anything about that?'

Peele and Strawson looked at one another as if they did indeed know all about it, but weren't going to share that knowledge with Kite or Carl.

'Keep going,' said Strawson.

'That's all I know. Just something Xav said down by the pool. Like he knew but didn't approve of it. It might just be my imagination, but he's been acting weirdly ever since we arrived. Drinking more than normal, stockpiling booze.'

'OK,' said Peele in a vague, non-committal way that suggested he was neither surprised by this nor particularly interested in Xavier's behaviour.

'What about the girlfriend?' Strawson asked.

For a moment Kite thought Strawson was referring to Martha, then realised his mistake.

'Hana? She's his mistress. Told me they met last year in Paris.'

'When she was—what? Twelve?' Peele asked with a grin.

'Her family are originally from Vietnam.' Kite was suddenly hungry again and asked for bacon with the coffee. Strawson told him there wasn't time. 'She's lived in France since the late seventies. I sat next to her at dinner, but she was mostly talking to Xavier.'

'Who were you talking to?'

'Martha and Jacqui.'

Kite was wary of questions about Martha. He didn't want BOX picking up on the strength of his feelings for her.

'Age?'

'Who, Hana? No idea. Sorry.'

'Surname?'

Kite shook his head.

'Can you get it from her passport?' Peele asked.

Kite looked at Strawson to assess the level of risk. Strawson

BOX 88

looked back in such a way as to persuade Kite to make up his own mind whether or not he could pull it off.

'I can try,' he said, trying to sound confident. 'If they're out of the house, I can search their bedroom.'

'Might be easier than that,' said Peele. 'There's a safe where Luc and Rosamund keep the family jewels. Ask them. Maybe you can get the combination or the key, take a look when you're putting your own passport inside.'

'Too complicated,' said Strawson. 'Not important. What else?'

'There's a bodyguard. Abbas.'

'We know.'

'Not exactly friendly.' Kite remembered the black look Abbas had given him as he jogged past moments earlier. 'I've tried saying hello a couple of times, but he acts like I'm not there.'

'Don't engage with him,' Peele replied. 'It's his job to protect his boss from Iranian exile groups, not to make pals with eighteen-year-old public schoolboys on their gap year.'

'What about the ghetto blaster?' Strawson asked. 'Or what are we calling it? The *stereo*.'

'Stuck by the pool,' Kite told him. 'I'll try bringing it up tonight so that we can listen to music on the terrace. Hopefully it'll get left there. But I know Xavier likes having it down by the sun loungers. He had it on last night.'

'Yeah, we heard.' Peele rolled his eyes. 'How many times can two teenage boys listen to *Appetite for Destruction* without losing the will to live?'

'It was *G N'R Lies*,' said Kite. 'Same band. Different album.'

All three men ignored him. Kite took a sip of the coffee. It was still boiling hot. Carl hadn't offered him sugar or milk. He was wary of asking for either.

'And the girl?' Strawson asked.

Kite knew that he meant Martha but played dumb.

'Which girl?'

'Brigitte Bardot via Raquel Welch. The one with the curves. Martha, is it?'

'Martha, yeah.' Kite thought it was a bit of a stretch to compare her to Brigitte Bardot and Raquel Welch, but felt oddly reassured by the remark, as if Strawson were complimenting him on his good taste. 'She's great. Old school friend of Jacqui's. Very relaxed, very clever. Seems fun.'

'Yeah? You falling for her? Because we sure as shit don't need you with your head up your ass the next two weeks. Leave her to Xavier.'

Kite, irritated, said: 'I think that's going to happen anyway', even though at dinner he had detected what he was sure was Martha's gathering interest in him. She had told him about her childhood in America, where she had lived until the age of ten, and seemed impressed by Kite's knowledge of books and paintings. It made sense for them to be together. Martha was hardly likely to risk annoying Jacqui by hooking up with her errant older brother. Besides, Xavier had been astonishingly flirtatious with Hana, who had seemed to enjoy his company whenever Eskandarian's back was turned. She was only seven or eight years older than both of them, which probably made her the same age as Alison from Mud Club. Kite understood Xavier well enough to know that he wouldn't think twice about stealing Eskandarian's girlfriend from under his nose. In fact, he would see it as a challenge.

'She likes taking photos.' Kite had stumbled on something harmless to say.

'What kind of photos?' Carl asked.

Peele looked up, as if Carl had been under orders not to say anything. 'The ones you take with a camera?'

Kite rescued him, saying: 'All sorts. She's always snapping away. In Mougins, at dinner, down by the pool . . .'

'Encourage that,' said Peele with a firmness that slightly concerned Kite.

BOX 88

'What do you mean?'

'I mean encourage it! Make sure she keeps taking lots of photographs. Especially of anybody who comes to see our man. There haven't been any visitors to the house so far. Am I correct?'

Kite could feel BOX 88 creeping into Martha's privacy. He didn't like it, yet there was nothing he could do to prevent it. He was hardly in a position to tell Peele and Strawson to ignore her.

'Time?' Strawson asked.

'I should go soon,' Kite replied, without looking at his watch. 'What else do you need apart from Hana's surname?'

'You haven't told us anything about the reason we're all here,' said Peele. 'Eskandarian. What do you make of him? First impressions. The famous Kite intuition.'

Kite took another sip of the coffee, flattered by the description. He spotted a small jug of milk by the window. He walked over, picked it up, poured some into his coffee and sat back down.

'He's a lot more westernised than I was expecting. Smokes Winston Lights, drank a Kir before we all sat down for dinner, then lots of wine, cognac afterwards. Didn't seem to affect him. I've seen guests at Killantringan put away what he drank last night and pass out in the residents' lounge.' Strawson was listening intently. 'He seemed to be well versed in French culture. There was a conversation going on that I couldn't really hear about Jean-Paul Sartre and Paris in the sixties. He's very hands-off with Hana, no touching, no kissing. She said he only invited her to Mougins two weeks ago. Rosamund was keeping an eye on her at dinner, but it's hard to work out if she approves or disapproves—'

'Eskandarian,' said Peele, pointedly looking at his watch. 'Stay with your thoughts on him, not Lady Muck. What kind of things was he talking about at dinner?'

Kite was embarrassed to admit that he had barely spoken to the Iranian all night. He painted a picture of his friendship with

Luc as something deep and lasting; the two men had obviously been very happy to see one another. Strawson and Peele seemed particularly interested by this, though the depth of the relationship came as no surprise to them.

'There was no mention of Malta or New York or anything to do with Lockerbie. He's very charismatic. Speaks fluent English and French.' Kite began to feel that he was telling Strawson and Peele things they already knew.

'It's OK,' said Peele, seeing that Kite was struggling. 'Early days, isn't it? You'll have a chance to chat to him, listen in to what he's saying. It's the people who come to meet him we're interested in. Also the chat on the mikes. We've got the phone line covered, but they'll be cautious saying anything much on that.'

Kite noticed the use of 'they', not 'he'. BOX were clearly more interested in Luc than they had let on.

'There was one thing,' he said. 'Maybe you knew, maybe you didn't. Luc told me Ali had a fiancée in Paris before he left for Iran.'

The three men looked at one another.

'We did not know that,' said Strawson.

Kite was elated. He was proving his worth. 'They split up,' he said. 'She married a politician in Catalonia, Catalunya, some country I'd never heard of—'

'Jesus Christ!' Peele jumped to his feet. 'Didn't we teach you *anything* at Alford? Catalunya is a province in north-eastern Spain. You'll find Barcelona there if you look hard enough. Did you get a name?'

'No, sir,' said Kite, unwittingly imitating their classroom relationship.

'All these women with no surnames,' Strawson declared. He stood up and walked over to the window. 'What are we doing about the Gameboy?'

'I've got it in my room,' Kite replied.

BOX 88

'Any chance of leaving it in Luc's office? Wandering in for a chat when he's not there, accidentally on purpose sliding it under the bookcase?'

'Battery will only last two days,' said Carl.

'Then our boy gets it out and puts new ones in,' Strawson replied, as if Kite wasn't there.

'You comfortable doing that?' Peele asked.

'Sure.' Kite was determined to say yes to all but the most brazenly dangerous or illegal requests. 'And there's the Walkman too. Might as well use that if I have it.'

'Just keep an eye on the bodyguard.' Strawson was staring outside at the olive trees and the whitewashed wall. 'Don't do anything while he's around. He's the one guy could fuck this up for you.'

For you, thought Kite. Not 'us'. He knew that BOX would pack up and go home, leave him to swing if he was exposed.

'I understand,' he said. 'I won't do anything reckless.'

Peele again looked at his watch.

'You'd better go,' he said. 'Remember what I told you. Make sure you're sweating and out of breath by the time you get back.'

'Sure.' Kite suddenly remembered the wall. 'Christ,' he said. 'Something else that's important.'

'What?' said Strawson.

Kite explained that Abbas had been parked close to the wall where BOX were intending to leave a chalk mark if they wanted to contact him. Strawson told him not to worry. Abbas wouldn't be spending more than a few hours at a time with line of sight to the wall. The signalling procedure could still go ahead.

'What about the windows?' Kite asked.

'What about them?'

'Hélène had closed my shutters when I came back from Mougins last night. If I leave a T-shirt there during the day, she might move it. You may not see it.'

Kite could tell from their reaction that this was regarded as a slightly more taxing problem. Peele nevertheless solved it almost immediately.

'Just use the cigarettes,' he said.

'What do you mean?'

'If you want to talk to us, just leave a packet of cigarettes on the wall at the bottom of the garden. If there's a note, we'll read and respond. We'll check the site every hour or so. But leave the shirt as a signal anyway. Hélène may not always close the shutters.'

Strawson turned from the window. He had his hands behind his back, the left arm slightly crooked so that he was holding the wrist at an awkward angle. Kite was reminded of a painting he had seen of Napoleon surveying a battlefield. Strawson explained that another operation meant he had to leave France, but that he would be back within three days to check on progress. Kite was oddly relieved by the news, even as Carl and Peele offered him reassuring smiles. He venerated Strawson, but his presence in the safe house felt like an extra layer of pressure.

'I'll be fine,' he told him. 'Good luck with whatever it is you're doing.'

They shook Kite's hand and wished him well. Carl went out onto the road, gave the all-clear and Kite jogged away from the house. Within five minutes he had made a steep uphill climb and was soaked in sweat. It was time to go back to the villa. The Audi was no longer parked in the lay-by. Abbas had moved it back to the lime tree and was eating breakfast alone at a small table in the area outside the kitchen which Hélène used for hanging out the washing. To Kite's relief, but not to his surprise, the bodyguard did not look up as he went into the house.

The dining room was laid out for breakfast. Luc was at the head of the table reading *Le Monde*, hair slicked back in the style of Gordon Gecko, Rosamund beside him engrossed in a paperback of *Oscar and Lucinda*. There were plates of ham and cheese in front of them, baskets of pain au chocolat and croissants. On

BOX 88

a side table Hélène had left out bottles of Evian and Badoit and a jug of freshly squeezed orange juice. It needed a stir. There was a large red coffee jug on a mat in front of Luc, little bowls of jam and yoghurt and honey.

'Good run?' Rosamund asked, spotting Kite at the door. She was sipping her customary cup of Twining's English Breakfast tea. 'Feeling better?'

'The next one will be easier,' Kite replied. 'Going to try to go every day.'

'Well don't have a heart attack, for goodness' sake.' She turned to Luc. 'Darling, did you know Lockie was an elite athlete?'

'Maybe he has someone he's trying to impress.'

Luc's reply was not as jovial nor as teasing as it might have been; there was a sting to it. His face was hidden behind a photograph of Francois Mitterrand on the cover of *Le Monde*. Kite picked up a plum and pretended to throw it at him. Rosamund apologised with her eyes.

'Enjoy your breakfast,' he told them. 'I'm going for a shower.'

40

The next forty-eight hours passed without serious incident. On the first day, Eskandarian, Hana, Luc and Rosamund went to lunch in Menton with friends, leaving the others behind. Abbas went with them. When Alain and Hélène drove into Mougins to buy food, Kite was able to take advantage of their absence to look, without success, for Hana's passport and to leave the Gameboy wedged behind a chest of drawers in Luc's office. He contrived to make it appear as though it been left among a pile of books and magazines on top of the chest and had fallen down the back. Eskandarian had also left a pile of papers on a stool in the living room. With Xavier, Martha and Jacqui by the pool, Kite flicked through them, seeing documents in Farsi, Russian and English, but without his camera to hand he had no opportunity to photograph them. Instead he looked for the keywords he had memorised from his training—BIOPREPARAT, PRALIDOXIME, IDLEWILD—and made a mental note of the senders' names, scribbling them down on a sheet of paper in his bedroom. He would have risked going up to the attic to search Eskandarian's rooms had Luc not come back astride a brand-new bottle green Vespa which he told Xavier and Kite

BOX 88

they could use to 'buzz into Mougins'. Kite asked if Martha and Jacqui were insured to drive it. Luc shook his head.

'Just you two,' he replied. 'I don't want the girls riding it.'

That night they ate supper outside. Alain, who had a cigarette permanently clamped to his lips and was always busy about the house hanging pictures and making repairs, lit mosquito coils at the southern end of the terrace. A smell of cardamom and citronella drifted across the table as they ate chilled pea soup and *poule au pot* in the moonlight. Kite was again seated next to Hana and therefore prevented from speaking at any length to Eskandarian. By eleven he was tired and retired to bed, leaving Xavier, Jacqui and Martha watching *Betty Blue* on VHS.

The next day Kite woke up at eight, jogged over to the safe house, gave Peele the list of names from Eskandarian's correspondence and returned to discover that Eskandarian, Luc and Hana had already gone into Vence to look at the Matisse chapel. He knew that BOX 88 would be covering their every move outside the villa, photographing anyone of interest with whom Eskandarian came into contact. Meanwhile Rosamund busily made changes to the house, twice driving into Antibes and returning with the Citroën full of crockery, glassware and ornaments to replace many of those bequeathed to Luc by his great-uncle. On the second trip, Martha and Jacqui went with her, leaving Kite and Xavier by the pool. They returned to the house only to grab a snack, take a shower or vegetate in what Luc still insisted on calling 'the playroom'. Kite again looked for Hana's passport without success, concluding that she was probably carrying it around in her handbag. Peele was keen to join the dots between Xavier's father and Eskandarian and had instructed Kite to take a look at the documents on Luc's desk and to leave his Walkman under a sofa in the living room. Yet there was never a moment when Alain wasn't lurking around, changing a plug or hanging a picture and generally making Kite feel that it would be discovered almost as soon as he had planted it. The last thing he wanted was Alain catching him in the act of rifling through Luc's personal effects or approaching him in front of Eskandarian and saying that he had found his Walkman in an unusual place.

Everything changed on the third day. After a late breakfast, the family and their guests drove in three cars to Cannes with the idea of spending the day at the beach. Kite brought a hacky sack which he promptly lost in the sea, having thrown it too far beyond Xavier, who allowed it to sink to the bottom of the Mediterranean rather than swim out to fetch it. They then bought a Frisbee, teaching Eskandarian how to throw and catch it on the flat sands, doubtless to the consternation of surveillance teams of any persuasion photographing the Iranian from stakeout positions overlooking the beach. It was Kite's first proper interaction with the Iranian and as the disc skimmed low over the beach he again found it impossible to imagine that the easy-going, laughing man running this way and that was the brains behind the Lockerbie atrocity, the mastermind of a follow-up attack in New York of even greater malignancy. Hana and Jacqui lay on towels chatting in the sun, having forged a somewhat unlikely bond. Martha had gone into town with Rosamund to buy more film for her camera. At all times Abbas sat on a fold-up chair a few metres from Eskandarian, his manner composed, his expression utterly inscrutable. He continued to wear a black suit, even in the heat of the midday sun, and, with the exception of Luc, rarely made any effort to speak to other members of the party.

They went for lunch at an upmarket brasserie in the centre of Cannes, Abbas eating a bowl of spaghetti at a separate table. Afterwards Eskandarian, Luc and Hana returned to the villa with Abbas, Rosamund drove into Antibes to buy more furniture for the house and Martha and Jacqui went shopping for clothes. Xavier had drunk more than a bottle of rosé with his swordfish and promptly fell asleep as soon as he lay down on the beach.

BOX 88

Kite was left alone with *Papillon,* the book he had been reading for the previous three days. He decided to walk up to the main road and finish it in a café.

The August crowds were scattered along the promenade in shorts and bikinis and flip-flops. Waiters criss-crossed the pavements carrying trays of drinks and food to customers at the cafés and restaurants lining the beach. A bi-plane was trailing an advertisement for a local nightclub high over the glistening sea as Kite looked around for somewhere to sit. As he gazed up at the sky he was almost run over by an accelerating Renault 5. The driver leaned on his horn, swore at him and drove off. Kite picked a café a block behind the beach. He wanted to read *Papillon* without the distraction of the cars and crowds on the promenade.

He had only been seated for a few minutes when a man of Middle Eastern appearance walked up to his table and asked, in good English, what Kite was reading. He had short, curly black hair and was clean-shaven. A slight hare lip gave his face an undertow of menace, but he was not physically imposing. He was wearing stonewashed denim jeans, Reebok trainers and a pale green shirt from Benetton.

'*Papillon,*' Kite replied quietly. He did not want to get into a long conversation with a stranger who was probably interested only in selling him counterfeit tapes or sunglasses.

'You are English?'

'Scottish.'

'Ah! Scottish!' Kite sensed that it would be some time before the man left him in peace. 'Sean Connery! Robert Burns! You wear kilts, yes?'

'Every day.'

The man laughed uproariously, repeating the words 'Every day' several times until he had calmed down.

'And you are on holiday here in Cannes? You have come to France before?'

Kite's antennae twitched. Who was this guy? What did he

want? On closer inspection, he didn't look like a salesman. He wasn't carrying a suitcase full of shades or videos. His eyes were sharp and intelligent, his hands and clothes clean. There was about him a kind of fanatical intensity which Kite was wary of.

'My first time. I'm here with friends.'

'What friends, my friend? Where they from? Scotland too?'

Kite suspected that the man knew who he was and had followed him from the beach. He pulled his café au lait towards him and said: 'Tell you what. What can I do for you? I just came in here for a quiet cup of coffee.'

'You are friends with Ali Eskandarian, yes?'

The blood must have drained from Kite's face because the man smiled reassuringly and offered to shake his hand.

'It is OK, my friend. I am not here to harm you. My name is Bijan. I am an Iranian. I live here in Cannes. France is my home.'

'How do you know Ali?' Kite looked around the café to see if anyone was watching them. *It's always the person you least expect*, Peele had told him.

'I recognised him. Let us just say that. And I wonder what a nice Scottish man like yourself is doing with this person. He is a friend of yours, you say? Of your family?'

Was this a game? Was Strawson orchestrating another test of Kite's nerve? Kite again scanned the café. A young family were eating ice creams two tables away. A workman was drinking a balloon of cognac at the bar. An elderly man and woman were playing cards in the corner. Out on the street, pedestrians were walking past carrying beach towels and bags of groceries, a drop-kick terrier yapping on the end of a leash. Kite tried to assess if anyone was standing around, someone who looked edgy or out of place. There didn't appear to be anybody. Peele had taught him how to remember repeating faces, how to recognise unusual behaviour on the street, but Kite hadn't taken much notice of the lessons because he had been reassured that his work in France wouldn't involve anti-surveillance of any kind.

BOX 88

'Ali is a friend of the family I'm staying with,' he replied, wondering if he had already admitted too much. 'I don't really know him. We only met two days ago.'

Without being invited to do so, the Iranian drew up a chair and sat opposite him. He squinted slightly against a beam of bright afternoon sun flooding in through the window and moved his head into a patch of shade. Only when he was satisfied with his position did he say: 'May I join you, please? This is permitted?' and signalled to the waiter to bring him a coffee. Kite was now too intrigued to object. He wanted to know why the man had cornered him and what he knew about Eskandarian.

'That's fine,' he said.

'You really do not know him,' Bijan replied, touching the scar on his lip.

'Excuse me?'

'If you did . . .' He reached for the copy of *Papillon* and turned it in his soft, unmarked hands. 'If you did know who he was, you would not spend time with him. You would not eat with him or allow your sisters to be in such a man's company.'

Kite was going to say: 'They're not my sisters' but thought better of it. Instead he took out a cigarette, offered one to the Iranian, and for reasons which he afterwards could not properly explain, gave Bijan a false name.

'I'm Adam.'

'Adam who?'

'Let's just leave it at Adam. What do you want from me?'

'How much do you know of life in Iran today, Adam?'

'Not much.'

'Don't you think that an intelligent young man like yourself should know more about my country when you are spending so much time with one of its most influential citizens?'

Kite wondered what he meant by the term 'influential citizen', but said: 'I'm not spending all that much time with him. I'm just on holiday.'

Bijan shook his head, thanked the waiter as he put an espresso in front of him and said: 'So you would like to know more?'

It sounded like a sales pitch, though there was a sudden emptying out of Bijan's eyes, the appearance of a profound disquiet. Kite felt that he had no alternative other than to say: 'Sure. Why not?'

'Do you know what kinds of corruption your friend Mr Ali Eskandarian presides over? The nature of the government in Tehran? The 1979 Revolution, in which your friend played a willing part, promised peace and stability to a generation of men who welcomed the arrival of Khomeini in Iran. Instead what did we get? The mujahideen have torn our peaceful country apart with a war against Saddam Hussein, a man supported and armed by the West. Did you know this, Mr Adam? That your government and the administration in Washington gave credibility to a man who used mustard gas, sarin gas against the Iranian people? Why did a million of my brothers and sisters have to die for this regime? Tell me.'

Kite saw that he was dealing with a fanatic. He wondered if he was compromising or in some other way undermining his own mission by agreeing to sit with an individual so opposed to Eskandarian.

'I really should be going,' he said, reaching for the book. 'I'm just a friend of the family. You've confused me with somebody else.'

'Have I? Have I confused you, kind sir? Do you not care that gangs of men roam the streets of Tehran at night carrying sticks and chains with which to attack anyone who does not share their belief in Islam? Do you not care that Rafsanjani and others of Ali Eskandarian's friends do nothing to stop this? You cannot wear shorts in Iran like you are wearing today in this nice quiet café. You cannot drink the alcohol such as you and your friend Mr Eskandarian enjoyed today at lunch. Perhaps you like to go to parties with the women in your group on the beach? There is

BOX 88

nothing wrong with this. But if you were a young man living in Iran today, you would be forbidden to attend such parties. Your sisters cannot wear make-up, they cannot own perfume. Is one of them your girlfriend? She could not be seen with you in public or she would be whipped, humiliated, while you, Adam, would be made an example of. Even western music, such as we can hear now in this café, is outlawed. People must listen to Madonna or Bruce Springsteen or Elton John with headphones, in the privacy of their houses. And they must hope that their records and tapes are not discovered by the Revolutionary Guard.'

Kite was still processing what Bijan had said about alcohol. *Such as you and your friend enjoyed today at lunch.* He must have been sitting in the brasserie and watching them on the beach. Bijan might now follow him back to the villa in order to discover where he was staying. Christ, maybe he was part of an exile group targeting Eskandarian.

'How would you feel if you were taken from this place, right here and now, and whipped in public, in front of all these people, just for sleeping with an unmarried woman or for wearing the clothes you are wearing, that T-shirt?' Bijan grabbed Kite's wrist and gestured outside at the crowded street. 'Would you like to be stoned to death in public? Your dead naked body hung from a crane for your friends and family to see? To serve as a warning to others?'

Kite said: 'Of course not' but Bijan was only listening to himself.

'This is the reality of modern Iran, my friend. This is the reality of the regime Mr Eskandarian serves, enriching them, enriching himself. There is no democracy.'

Kite still had most of his coffee to drink and a half-smoked cigarette tilted into the ashtray in front of him. He wanted to stand up and leave but had to be sure that Bijan would not follow him.

'Let me tell you, Adam,' the Iranian continued. The scar on

his lip seemed to have become more pronounced as he spoke. 'Then you can decide whether to believe me or not. Perhaps you think I am a mad person walking the streets of Cannes, stopping Scottish tourists in cafés and holding them prisoner with my tongue.' Bijan flashed him a gap-toothed grin, a strip of silver fillings visible in the lower recesses of his mouth. 'I myself am a marked man. Why? Because I oppose the regime. These men of God in Tehran, these supposed men of peace, send their Revolutionary Guards to France to hunt down and kill men like me. We are not allowed to organise peaceful opposition to our own government. We are not allowed to wish for a better country. This is the extent of their paranoia, of their murderous intentions. Bombs have been planted in cars in France. My comrades have been beheaded. Think about this, Adam. A man in his own home forced to kneel by the scum of the Revolution, sometimes in front of their wives, their children, and their heads taken off by a sword.'

Kite wanted to believe that what Bijan was telling him was pure fantasy, but there was such intensity, such range and detail in his accusations, that he could only assume that at least part of it was true.

'That sounds horrific,' he said, because there was a look in Bijan's eye which demanded a response. 'I'm so sorry.'

'I am sorry, too, my friend. Any former servant of the shah is a legitimate target, yet Ali Eskandarian, and scum like him, can take their vacations in France, drink alcohol, sleep with young women, and they will not be touched. Why? Because they help to make secret deals with America, they buy their arms and their weapons. In return, the regime gets rich and turns a blind eye. You know of your writer, Mr Rushdie?'

'Of course,' Kite replied, not wanting to talk about Rushdie but to hear more about the nature of Eskandarian's relationship with the American government. Was Bijan referring to Iran-

BOX 88

Contra, which Peele had spent a morning explaining to him in Hampstead, or to something else entirely?

'Rushdie also faces death, but at least he has the protection of the British government. At least he has the SAS or the MI5 to watch over him, to move him safely from house to house. We, on the other hand, can do nothing to escape the executioners sent to kill us. We can be abducted and tortured by agents of the Iranian government and not a soul will notice. The last person to be killed here on French soil, whose death merited a column in the newspapers of New York and London, was Gholam Oveissi, the commander of the shah's army, shot dead on the streets of Paris beside his brother, five long years ago. People noticed this because the general was the last hope for the opposition groups who planned to overthrow the ayatollah, may he rot in hell. Oveissi was assassinated two days before he was due to fly to Turkey's border with Iran and to lead our counter-revolution. Who tipped off the assassins? The Americans! MI6! Will they do so again, so that Shahpour Bakhtiar is also taken from us? You tell me, Mr Adam. You tell me.'

In a moment of distilled paranoia, Kite wondered if Bijan suspected that he was working for British intelligence. He was not familiar with the name Shahpour Bakhtiar, nor did he understand why Bijan assumed that he might be. The idea that MI6 were secretly siding with the government in Tehran *against* the exile community struck him as illogical, but he supposed anything was possible in the looking-glass world into which Peele and Strawson had thrust him.

'I don't know anything about any of this,' he said.

'Of course you don't,' Bijan replied, swallowing his espresso with a concise, practised flick of the wrist. 'How could you know? But be assured, this is also happening in London. You are an intelligent person who lives his life with people who can eat at the best restaurants, who can afford to take their holidays in the South of France.'

'With respect, you don't know anything about me.'

'Perhaps,' Bijan replied. 'And perhaps you do not care, Adam. But maybe you also want to help me.'

Kite realised that an offer of this kind had been brewing for some time, yet the question still caught him off guard.

'*Help* you?' he said. He experienced the disorientating sensation of falling into a trap. If Eskandarian or Abbas had grown suspicious of him and sent Bijan as a test of his loyalty, he must on no account agree to do anything for this man. He must leave the café as soon as possible and return to the beach.

'I'm sorry,' he said. 'I just came here to read my book and have a coffee. I have to be getting back. My friends will be worried.'

To his surprise, Bijan raised no objection and pulled back his chair, allowing Kite the space in which to stand.

'Of course, Adam,' he said. 'I understand. I will pay for your coffee.'

Kite readily accepted the offer, pleased to be released from the conversation, and watched as Bijan secured a ten-franc note under the ashtray.

'You really don't need to do that.'

'It is my pleasure. I just wanted you to know the reality of what is going on in Iran, the reality of the man you play Frisbee with in the sunshine. Thank you for listening to me.'

'You've certainly taught me a lot.'

Kite was almost at the door.

'Please . . .'

He turned. Bijan was holding out a piece of paper.

'Take this.' The Iranian tried to stuff the piece of paper into Kite's hand. 'It is my telephone number. You can call me if you ever want to discuss these matters. I would like the opportunity to speak with Mr Eskandarian. You can make this possible, yes?'

BOX 88

Kite knew that he should keep the telephone number so that Peele could have it checked, but also that he should reject outright any possibility of a meeting or conversation ever taking place. There was still a chance that the whole thing was a charade orchestrated by Abbas to analyse his character, a test cooked up by BOX 88 to make sure that their golden boy was still on the right track.

'I think it's very unlikely,' he said, pocketing the number. 'I hardly know Mr Eskandarian. He's friends with my hosts.'

'Ask him,' Bijan urged.

'It was good to meet you,' Kite replied, backing out of the door. 'Thank you for the coffee. There's really nothing I can do for you. I wish you good luck.'

41

Luc had given Jacqui money for a taxi. All the way back to the villa, Kite kept turning around to see if the same cars, the same number plates, kept repeating. If Bijan was following him, he was in trouble.

'What's the matter?' Jacqui asked. It was cramped in the back seat. Xavier was in the front chatting to the driver about Mitterrand. 'Why do you keep moving around?'

'Sorry,' Kite told her. 'Got a pain in my back. Helps when I twist it out.'

Martha was beside him. She was wearing denim shorts and a T-shirt and smelled of sun cream. There were tiny flakes of dried sea salt on her tanned thighs.

'How did you hurt it?' she asked.

'Frisbee.'

He realised with frustration that the lie would prevent him from going for a run when he got back to the villa. Kite stared out of the window, working out his next move. Abbas already knew that he only ever went for a jog in the morning, not after several hours of swimming and playing Frisbee on a beach. Instead he would write a note to BOX, insert it in a packet of

BOX 88

cigarettes, go for a smoke when he got back to the house and dead drop the packet on the wall.

As the driver indicated off the autoroute, Kite again turned in the back seat. Jacqui clicked her tongue. No car had followed them up the ramp. Two miles later, on the access road to the villa, Kite looked again. For theatrical effect, he winced slightly as he twisted. Martha said: 'Poor you.' Again there was no sign of a following car. If Bijan, or one of his associates, had attempted to follow the cab, they had surely failed.

'Have a swim when you get back,' she suggested. 'Stretch it out. You'll feel better.'

'There's no time,' Jacqui replied. 'We're all going out. Dinner in some fancy nightclub Dad knows in Antibes. Mum said on the phone we have to get changed before seven. Apparently it's a famous place, Kirk Douglas goes there.'

Back at the house Kite took a shower and had time to think more clearly. Perhaps reporting the details of his conversation with Bijan was not as pressing as he first thought. It could surely wait until morning. If he walked all the way to the bottom of the garden to have a smoke, it would look suspicious. Best just to hide Bijan's phone number among his belongings and show it to Peele in the morning.

'What are you wearing?' Xavier shouted.

'Fuck knows,' Kite replied, coming out of the bathroom.

'Language, Lockie, *please*.'

Rosamund had emerged from her room wearing a brown pencil skirt, two-inch white heels and a bright pink blouse bolstered by shoulder pads. He had never encountered a woman of his mother's generation with so much money and such good looks who dressed so disastrously. Behind her, enjoying his reflection in a floor-length mirror, was Luc, his Gekko hair oiled back, a pale blue shirt opened to the solar plexus. Kite turned around. Xavier was making the final touches to his Mud

Club uniform of ripped blue jeans, white T-shirt and black leather jacket.

'I see George Michael will be joining us again tonight,' he said.

'Yeah, yeah,' Xavier replied. 'Very funny.'

'You gotta have faith,' Kite sang, and went into his room singing the chorus of the song, Xavier's protests a faint murmur behind the closing door.

Kite dressed quickly, conscious of the meagreness of his own wardrobe, tonight comprised of a pair of Levi 501s, a navy blue sports jacket and a paisley shirt which had the potential to put Martha off him for the rest of her life. Flinging it back into his suitcase, he played it safe, recycling a button-down shirt from Gap which he refreshed with a spray of Right Guard after a quick sniff of the armpits.

'Leaving in five minutes, everyone!' Rosamund called out from the hall. 'Wheels turning.'

Kite heard the same clatter of ice cubes which had heralded the arrival of Eskandarian two nights earlier. He quickly dried his hair on a towel, reaching for a tub of radioactively green Boots hair gel which he applied in a dollop to the fringe. By the time he had left his room, his hairstyle could be plausibly compared to a photograph Kite had seen of River Phoenix in *Arena* magazine. This was suddenly all that mattered. He wanted to look good for Martha.

She was already outside, waiting to get into the Mercedes wearing an off-the-shoulder blue dress that caused Kite almost to lose his footing when he saw her. She must have been aware of the effect she was having because even Luc and Eskandarian were staring at her in barely suppressed awe. Rosamund knew it too and offered Martha a pale pink pashmina 'to cover your shoulders, darling'. Xavier emerged from the house smoking a cigarette and holding the black leather jacket over his shoulder like a male model prowling on a catwalk.

'Will you be my father figure, Xav?' Martha asked. Hana

BOX 88

came out seconds later in a vanishingly tight black miniskirt, received the gasps she had doubtless been hoping for—including a gobsmacked 'Jesus' from Xavier—and climbed into Eskandarian's Audi. Within a few minutes they had all left the house, Alain waving them off with a rake in one hand and a Gitane in the other.

'What's the deal with Hana?' Xavier asked his father from the back seat of the Mercedes.

Kite was in the front trying to find a decent song on French radio.

'Which one of your hits do you want to hear tonight, George?' he asked. '"Careless Whisper"? "Club Tropicana"?'

'She's not allowed into Iran,' Luc replied in French, talking across Kite's joke. 'Not dressed like that, anyway!' He laughed as he indicated onto the autoroute. 'They meet up when Ali is travelling. She's nice, no?'

'Bit young for him?'

Kite knew that Xavier was interested in her. At the beach his friend had said that Hana kept flirting with him whenever Eskandarian's back was turned.

'Seriously, man. By the pool, over dinner. Always catching my eye. She's trouble. Not getting enough attention from the ayatollah. What am I supposed to do? *Ignore* that?'

'Yes!' Kite had told him firmly, and not solely because Xavier getting off with Eskandarian's girlfriend had the potential to jeopardise his mission. He didn't want his friend landing on the wrong side of Ali or, come to that, for Hana to be found at the bottom of the Mediterranean wearing a pair of cement boots fitted for her by Abbas. 'That's exactly what you're going to do. *Ignore* that. She's taken. You mess with her, you're messing with the Iranians. Look what they did to Rushdie and that was just for writing a book.'

The Antibes nightclub was another place to which the Bonnard family had taken Kite—like the Farm Club in Verbier, the Royal

Opera House for a performance of *Swan Lake*, the dining room at Claridge's for Xavier's eighteenth birthday—which he would never otherwise have experienced without their generosity. Luc had reserved a table in a lavish upstairs restaurant where, for the second time that day, his guests were treated to superb wines and exquisite French cuisine. It was Kite's habit to compare the dishes on the menu—*Poitrine de Veau Confite et Farcie aux Légumes du Soleil, Poupetons de Fleurs de Courge au Saumon Nappés, L'Abricot des Vergers de Provence*—with their feeble equivalents on the menu at Killantringan: *Soup of the Day, 'Skipper's Choice' Seafood Pancake, Apple Crumble*. Spending time in the South of France, shuttling between his bedroom and the swimming pool, drinking wine at outdoor cafés and flirting with Martha in five-star restaurants—he had begun to worry that he was being offered a final glimpse of a life which would soon be torn away from him. Xavier was going on a gap year and they would likely lose touch for a while, particularly if Kite went to Edinburgh or continued to work for BOX 88. Neither of them were enthusiastic letter-writers and it had never been Kite's style to telephone his friends when he was at home in Scotland. As for Martha, she had another year at school in London: whatever happened between them in the next few days, if anything, would likely only be a summer fling before she returned to her older men with their credit cards and Alfa Romeo Spiders, old Alfordians with trust funds who could afford to whisk her away to cosy country house hotels or to New York for a dirty weekend. He *had* to make some money; not just to impress Martha, but so that he could continue to enjoy the life-style to which the Bonnards had introduced him.

The nightclub beneath the restaurant was an even starker demonstration of a world Kite had only dreamed about or seen in Hollywood movies. Extraordinarily beautiful women were seated at tables with impeccably turned out French and Italian plutocrats treating them to flutes of champagne and bottles of Bandol rosé. Although nobody in the Bonnard group looked out

BOX 88

of place in such an environment, Kite accepted that his button-down Gap shirt and scruffy denim jeans were the clothes of an impoverished interloper. It was Eskandarian, of all people, who seemed to sense his discomfort, approaching Kite at the bar and offering to buy him a drink while Abbas looked on.

'I feel as amazed as you look, Lockie!' he said. 'Can you believe this club? In Tehran we do not have such places.'

Kite thought of Bijan's words—*If you were a young man living in Iran today, you would be forbidden to attend such parties*—and tried to hide his disquiet. He could not square what Bijan had told him with the ebullient, liberal, westernised man now buying him a vodka and tonic in an exclusive Antibes nightclub. Surely if he was seen in this place—if Abbas, for example, reported him to whoever it was that policed the moral behaviour of Iran's citizens back home—he would be denounced by Rafsanjani and the new regime? Or was it simply a case of rank hypocrisy, that Eskandarian was part of an elite who behaved as they pleased, creaming off the top of a corrupt society while millions of others existed in miserable poverty?

'Are you enjoying your holiday, Lockie?'

It was hard to hear Eskandarian's question over Grace Jones singing 'La Vie En Rose', but Kite nodded enthusiastically and said: 'Yeah, *oui*, yeah', telling himself that this was his first proper opportunity to make an impression on Eskandarian. 'It's my first time in Antibes. Yours? Luc said you've travelled quite a lot . . .'

'You are right, Lockie. This is correct. I have travelled widely. I was living in France twelve years ago. I still get to go to a lot of places because of my work.'

Kite wanted to say, or if necessary shout: 'What work exactly?' but it was too direct. Instead he allowed Eskandarian to question him about his own background, describing life at the hotel and his mother's career as a model in the 1960s.

'And your father? What does he do?'

Eskandarian was standing with his back to the dance floor

holding a glass of champagne. Kite was leaning against the bar with his vodka and tonic. He had no hesitation in using his father's death to win Eskandarian's sympathy and told him that he had died several years earlier. His words had an immediate impact on the Iranian, who placed a hand on Kite's shoulder and offered his sincerest condolences.

'I also lost my father some time ago,' he said. 'To the SAVAK, the shah's secret police. But we will not talk of this now, not on this happier occasion. All that I will say is that you seem to be a very polite, very intelligent young man and that your father would be proud of you.'

Kite was buoyed by the compliment and felt his fondness for Eskandarian growing ever stronger, even as he made a mental note to tell Peele that the SAVAK had killed his father. *I am not who you think I am*, he thought. *You shouldn't trust me or compliment me.* He was surprised to feel exhilarated, rather than ashamed of his own duplicity, and thanked Eskandarian for his kind words.

'So you don't go dancing in Tehran?' he asked.

The Iranian cast his eyes out onto the packed dance floor. Jacqui and Hana were standing opposite one another, drunkenly miming the playing of trumpets at the start of 'Sledgehammer'.

'It is a religious society,' he replied, turning back to face Kite. 'Or rather, I should say it has *become* a religious society. The government does not tolerate western music like this, however much some of us may enjoy it.'

Eskandarian conveyed with an expression of wry amusement that he counted himself among this group of people. Out of the corner of his eye, Kite saw Xavier sidling onto the dance floor.

'I don't understand,' he said, shouting over the song.

'Let's discuss it another time,' Eskandarian replied, placing the same hand on the same part of Kite's shoulder. Kite was worried that he was being brushed off. 'These things are too

BOX 88

complicated for nightclubs. Isn't this the Peter Gabriel song with the famous video? On MTV?'

'Yeah, that's right,' he replied, intrigued that Eskandarian should know such a thing. 'Brilliant video. So are you going to dance?'

Eskandarian shook his head, stepped across Kite and tried to attract the barman's attention. As he did so, Kite saw to his horror that Xavier had put his arm around Hana's waist and was pulling her close. They looked sensational together: the handsome young man in jeans and a crisp white T-shirt, the beautiful Vietnamese woman moving sinuously beside him. Kite could lip-read both of them singing 'I wanna be your sledgehammer' and noted the delight in Hana's face as Xavier spun her around. If Eskandarian turned from the bar, he would see them. Doubtless Abbas, sitting alone in a booth by the entrance, was clocking the whole thing. With Eskandarian ordering another bottle of champagne, Kite somehow managed to catch Xavier's attention and warned him with a glance. His friend instantly moved towards his sister, leaving Hana dancing alone. She waved towards Eskandarian, shouting 'Join me, baby!' as the Iranian at last turned to face her. The disc jockey eased into 'Don't You Forget About Me' and Kite tapped Eskandarian on the shoulder.

'Scottish band!' he shouted.

'What's that, Lockie?'

'Simple Minds. The band playing this song. They're Scottish. You should dance.'

'You should too!'

They clinked glasses. Kite caught sight of Martha standing close to the stairs at the entrance to the nightclub. He gestured towards the dance floor and mouthed, 'Dance?' She shook her head and pointed upstairs, miming with her fingers that she wanted to go for a walk.

'You go ahead!' he shouted at Eskandarian. 'I'll be there in a minute.'

The Iranian looked up and saw Martha, understanding instantly what was going on.

'Good luck!' he said and sashayed towards Hana without rhythm or skill as Kite made his way to the entrance.

'Having a good time?' Martha asked him. 'Ros has gone home. Told me to tell you she says goodnight.'

'Why did she leave?'

'Had an argument with Luc. He's such a wanker. You notice how he's always putting her down? Criticised her outfit, they had a blazing row upstairs, she went off in a taxi.'

'Jesus.' Kite turned and saw Luc talking to Jacqui. 'He seems to have got over it.'

'He doesn't care. Only thinks about himself. Vain prat.'

Kite was startled by Martha's outburst, but impressed that she had spoken her mind. He told her that he had his own reservations where Luc was concerned, not least because Xavier often seemed so angered and frustrated by him.

'I don't know as much about Xav as I do Jacqui. Daddy spoils her, so she can't see it. You ask me, Ros is a saint for putting up with him. Classic bully. Puts people down so he can feel superior.'

Kite realised what it was about Luc that had always irked him: he took Ros for granted, taking little potshots at her background and class, needlessly picking fights and contradicting her when it would have been easier simply to let things go. Why had he never admitted this to himself? Was it because Luc's behaviour sometimes reminded him of his own mother?

'You going for some fresh air?' he asked.

'Nah,' Martha replied. 'Changed my mind. Let's dance.'

Abbas and Luc drove them back. They reached the villa just before three o'clock in the morning. Luc and Jacqui went straight

BOX 88

to bed. To Kite's surprise and pleasure, Eskandarian announced that he was in the mood to keep drinking and encouraged the others to join him on the terrace.

'We need music!' Xavier shouted.

Hana put a finger to her lips and ushered him away from the stairs. As Eskandarian led them through the sitting room he agreed that it would be a good idea to 'play some ABBA' as long as they kept the volume down.

'*ABBA?*' said Martha contemptuously, as if Eskandarian had suggested putting on Mozart or Perry Como. 'Who listens to *ABBA*? You must be joking.'

'I'll go and get the stereo from the pool,' said Kite, miraculously provided with an excuse finally to bring the ghetto blaster up to the house and to plug it in behind the sofa.

'I'll come with you,' Martha replied.

Leaving Xavier with Eskandarian, Hana and a bottle of Johnnie Walker, Kite led Martha away from the terrace into the darkened garden, following the twisting, narrow route to the pool by the light of the moon. As they approached the branches of the palm tree which had fallen across the path, it felt like the most natural thing in the world for Kite to reach back and take Martha's hand. They ducked beneath the fronds and emerged in front of the swimming pool. Kite pulled her towards him and kissed her. To his amazement it was not like the kisses he had known at parties back home—mouths wide open, tongues moving furiously with lust—but a slow, tender contact, almost motionless at first, so intense and pleasurable that Kite never wanted it to end.

'Jesus,' she said. 'You took your time. I've been waiting ages for you to do that.'

'More,' he said, and they were soon lying on the grass near the pool. It was still warm from a hundred summer days. Kite's hands were on Martha's waist, her hips, the small of her back, his mouth tasting the skin on her shoulders and the tops of her breasts. He unzipped her dress. They became reckless in the warmth of the night. Martha loosened the belt on Kite's trousers and unbuttoned his shirt as the cicadas continued their ceaseless chatter. Her lips and hands were everywhere at once, so quick and experienced, taking him into her mouth then rolling onto her back and urging him to be inside her. Kite lost all track of time, of place, of any sense that he should be on the terrace with Eskandarian doing his duty for Queen and country. He had never known passion like this, an experience at once so new and so intimate that it took him a long time afterwards to come to his senses.

'We should go back,' he whispered, holding Martha's naked body on the grass. Neither of them had spoken for what felt like ages. 'They'll wonder what happened to us.'

'They'll be playing backgammon,' Martha replied, kissing his neck and rolling away from him. She stood up and pulled on her dress, grinning with the mischief of what they had done. Kite's clothes were all over the grass. Martha picked up her knickers, a bracelet, his boxer shorts and shirt and they dressed separately in silence, moonlight reflecting on the motionless water of the pool.

'I think I've been bitten by a mozzy,' she said, but did not seem to mind.

Kite fastened his belt. Blades of grass were still stuck to his knees and the back of his shirt. The ghetto blaster was inside the swimming hut and he went to fetch it. When he came back, Martha kissed him again, grabbing the back of his head and pulling him towards her. He couldn't put his right arm around her because he was carrying the stereo and had to lower it carefully to the ground, aware of the fragile technology inside, so that he could kiss her properly.

'OK, enough,' she said after a minute. She touched her lips and smiled at him. 'You're such a good kisser, Lockie. Jesus.'

BOX 88

'You too,' he said.

'How do I look? I feel like a complete mess.'

'Fucking amazing,' he said.

Xavier and Eskandarian were indeed playing backgammon, their low conversation, the rattle of the dice and the soft wooden tap of the checkers audible as they made their way back through the garden. Kite was in a state of dizzied euphoria, completely smitten by Martha, elated finally to have been with her and pleased not to have messed it up. As they emerged onto the terrace, he triumphantly raised Strawson's ghetto blaster above his head, like Perseus with the head of Medusa.

'Music!' said Hana, coming outside with a cafetière of black coffee and some small blue cups on a tray. 'At last!'

'Where the fuck have you two been?' Xavier asked drunkenly. 'Or shouldn't I ask?'

'Lockie was showing me how the pool filter worked,' Martha replied. 'It was really interesting.'

Eskandarian smiled and stood up, stretching his arms above his head and letting out a deep, satisfied sigh. He knew exactly what had been going on and even slipped Kite a little sideways look of congratulation. Kite thought of Bijan, of all the women in Iran denied make-up and lipstick and lovers outside of marriage. If he and Martha had been caught doing what they had just done in a Tehran public park, would Martha have been whipped and Kite's dead body hung from a crane? Surely not. He snapped out of it and poured both of them a drink. Half of the Johnnie Walker had already been consumed and there was now a bottle of red wine on the table. Kite plugged in the stereo, positioned it so that the speakers were facing Eskandarian's chair, and pressed play on the tape deck. Strawson had promised that the Turings would have the ability to strip out any music on the surveillance tapes so that the recorded conversations remained intact, but as soon as Bob Marley started singing

'Is This Love?' Kite wondered how the hell they'd be able to hear anything at all.

'Who's winning at backgammon?' he asked.

'Who do you think?' Eskandarian replied. 'You have no faith in me?'

'Lucky dice,' said Xavier. 'He's just had lucky dice.'

Eskandarian was smoking a Cuban cigar. Hana was standing behind him, massaging his shoulders. She had changed out of her miniskirt and was wearing a sari which reminded Kite of adverts for Cathay Pacific featuring impossibly beautiful Asian stewardesses serving glasses of champagne in first class. It was very obvious that she was looking down at Xavier and trying to catch his eye. Kite began to worry. Drunk as they both were, surely Hana wouldn't cheat on Eskandarian and risk a fling with her hosts' eighteen-year-old son? Surely she was just an Olympic tease playing with the feelings of a boy who very obviously lusted after her? Maybe Eskandarian was in on the joke and they laughed about Xavier every night when they went to bed. Martha poured the coffee, then went inside to change. Kite offered to take on the winner of the next backgammon game and found himself playing—and losing—to Eskandarian, despite practising against Peele night after night in Hampstead.

'You're right,' he said to Xavier. 'He gets lucky dice.'

They stayed on the terrace for another hour, finishing the coffee, the wine and the whisky and trying out one of Eskandarian's cigars. Kite had never smoked one before; he told Ali that he liked the smell but not the taste. He judged that nothing Eskandarian said would be of any consequence to BOX 88, though perhaps his relaxed attitude to western music, his habit of enjoying the company of people half his age, as well as his heroic consumption of alcohol would help them to form a more detailed picture of his character. At four-thirty, the Iranian announced that he was going to bed and

BOX 88

bade everyone goodnight. Hana said that she would be up soon, after helping to clear the terrace. Ten minutes later, she failed to come back to say goodnight after ferrying a tray of glasses and coffee cups to the kitchen. Xavier lit a final cigarette and said he was going for a wander in the garden, leaving Martha and Kite alone.

'Let's go back to the pool,' she said. 'I want you again.'

'Give me five minutes,' Kite replied, amazed that he was going to be given another opportunity so soon to relive the bliss of their earlier encounter. 'Just going inside.'

He went upstairs, brushed his teeth and put on a fresh T-shirt. The lights in the attic were all out. The door to Abbas's room was closed. Kite could hear the sound of the bodyguard snoring. He tiptoed down to the ground floor, where he and Xavier had hung their jackets after getting back from the club. Kite walked across the hall to fetch them, only to find that Abbas had also left his jacket hanging next to Xavier's. Kite knew that he should search it; if he was caught, it would be simple to claim that he was looking for cigarettes.

Without removing it from the hook, he reached into the inside pockets of the jacket. They were empty. The material was heavy and smelled strongly of tobacco. Kite patted the sides of the jacket. There was a document of some kind in the left hip pocket. He took it out. It was an envelope which had already been opened.

A creaking noise behind him. Abbas? Eskandarian? Kite didn't want to risk being discovered so he walked to the downstairs bathroom, switched on the light, locked himself inside and searched the contents of the envelope.

There was a letter, written in Farsi on what appeared to be official government stationery. Two names were written in the text of the letter in English: ASEF BERBERIAN and DAVID FORMAN. With it, folded in half, was a return Air France airline ticket from Paris to New York JFK dated 22 August. The ticket was made out in the name 'Abbas Karrubi'. Kite committed the names and the flight numbers to memory, then opened up a third document, a letter from the Grand Hyatt Hotel in Manhattan confirming that Abbas had a room reservation for a five-night stay in New York.

It felt like a smoking gun. Kite hurriedly put the documents back as he had found them, unlocked the door, switched off the light and returned the envelope to the left-hand hip pocket of Abbas's jacket. By the time he got back to the terrace, Martha was wondering what had happened to him. Wordlessly she took his hand and they walked into the garden.

The first glow of the dawning sun was visible as a pale strip of light on the hills around Mougins. Kite was confused. The dates for the trip to New York coincided with a business conference Eskandarian was scheduled to attend in Lisbon. Was he planning to cancel his visit to Portugal so that Abbas could accompany him to the United States? Or was Abbas going solo, potentially meeting a contact in New York to discuss the subway attack? Martha suddenly stopped walking. They kissed beneath an olive tree. She tasted of cigarettes and wine. Kite wondered if it had been a mistake to brush his teeth.

'What was that?'

A noise near the pool. Perhaps an animal of some kind. They stood stock-still, listening out. Kite heard the movement again.

'Xav?' he mouthed with a shrug.

He walked ahead of Martha, along the moonlit path, reaching the palm tree with the fallen fronds. There was a gap through the trees towards the poolhouse. Kite gestured at Martha not to make any sound.

Pressed up against the side of the hut, his trousers round his ankles, his naked, untanned buttocks glowing white in the moonlight, was Xavier. On her knees in front of him, only yards from where Kite and Martha had earlier been rolling on the grass, was Hana.

BOX 88

'Jesus,' Kite whispered and gestured at Martha to tiptoe back-wards.

'What?' she said, heading back in the direction of the house.

'It's Xav and Hana,' he told her when they were far enough away, barely able to believe what he had just seen and convinced that the less Martha knew, the better. 'They're getting off with each other by the pool.'

42

The man who walked into the house was in his early thirties. He was tall and physically fit, wearing a white shirt, dark trousers and black shoes. He moved with a pumped-up swagger. His most striking feature was his facial hair: a thick, carefully tended moustache and goatee, without sideburns, which gave him the appearance of a thug biker or religious zealot. Isobel was immediately afraid of him.

Two of the men guarding her went to the door to greet him. They spoke in hushed tones in Farsi. Isobel thought that she heard one of them calling the man 'Hossein'. They were both subservient towards him. In due course the newcomer walked into the living room and stood in front of her.

'You don't look sick,' he said in English.

'Who are you?' Isobel replied.

Hossein snapped a remark at Karim, admonishing him for what Isobel assumed was weakness or stupidity. Karim looked ashamed.

'How pregnant are you?' Hossein asked.

'Five months. I need to go to hospital. I'm bleeding, it's not—'

The man did not let her finish. He shouted at her: 'You're not

BOX 88

bleeding!' and looked at the others with contempt. 'You fell for this act?' he said in English. 'She's not in pain. She's not bleeding. Why the fuck you stay here and not move her?'

None of the men answered. They were too cowed.

'Your husband,' Hossein continued, looking at Isobel. 'He's also making a lot of trouble for us. What is it with you two?'

Hope surged in Isobel at the mention of Lockie. He was alive. He was fighting back. She said: 'Good. I'm glad he's not giving in to you,' and showed him a defiant smile. It was a mistake.

Hossein struck Isobel across the face with the back of his hand. She cried out. The pain was excruciating. Tears sprang to her eyes. She tried to blink them away before the men would notice them.

'You are monsters,' she said. Karim looked to the ground. The guard with the narrow chin turned and walked out of the room.

'Maybe, maybe not,' Hossein replied, before speaking again to Karim in Farsi. Isobel dabbed at the tears with a tissue while they were looking away. She was too frightened to risk more play-acting. Rambo kicked, as if to ask his mother what was happening. She almost burst into tears.

'The last man to hit me was my father,' she said. 'That was the last time I ever saw him.'

It was meant as a statement of defiance, but Hossein did not react. There was a plate of chocolate biscuits on the table beside them. He leaned down and took one, sliding his eyes towards Isobel as he took a first bite. She noticed that the backs of both of his hands were bruised. She wondered if he had hit Lockie. There was a ring on his right hand. It must have been what had cut her face.

'You have an hour left,' he told her, chewing the biscuit.

'Excuse me?'

'One hour.'

'I don't understand. An hour for what?'

'If your husband doesn't give my boss the answers he wants, I have orders to kill you. So make yourself comfortable, enjoy these last few moments with your child.' Hossein nodded at her belly. 'Lachlan is the sort of person who values his own skin more than he values his family. I don't have much hope for you, Mrs Kite. Let's wait here and see what happens.'

43

Kite and Martha went to separate rooms. Martha was worried that they would sleep late and Jacqui or Rosamund might find them in bed together in the morning. Kite set the alarm and had the drunken idea of putting the clock under his pillow so that it would be inaudible to anyone in the house when it went off. As things turned out, he woke naturally just before nine and switched it off. Groggy and dazed, he went into the bathroom, splashed cold water onto his face and brushed his teeth, remembering how much he had smelled of booze and tobacco on his first visit to the safe house. The door of Abbas's bedroom was open and there was no sign of him. The rest of the house was silent. Kite changed into his running gear, put the piece of paper on which he had written Bijan's phone number in the back pocket of his shorts and walked downstairs.

Rosamund was dressed and drinking tea in the kitchen.

'Another run?' she said, feigning astonishment. 'Is there no stopping you, Lockie? I thought I heard someone going out a moment ago. Must have been Abbas.'

Kite told her he would be back within the hour, stretched under the lime tree and jogged down the drive. Abbas was indeed sitting in the Audi in his regular parking spot. He wound down the window when he saw Kite.

'You missed your friend,' he said.

For an awful moment Kite thought he meant Billy Peele. Then he looked down the road and saw Martha walking alone towards Mougins. A strong smell of sweat and unwashed clothes wafted out of the car. Abbas was wearing the suit jacket. The envelope was on the passenger seat beside him.

'Where's she going?' he asked.

Abbas summoned the energy to shrug, reached for the automated button and closed the window without responding. Kite called out to Martha just as she was about to pass out of sight of the house.

She stopped and turned. They were three hundred metres apart. A car came down the road, forcing her onto the verge. Kite walked towards her, she towards him.

'What's going on?' he said. They did not kiss but briefly held one another's hands. Kite was conscious that he was already late for his meeting with Peele. 'Where are you going?'

'Got to go into town,' she replied. She looked tired, but appeared happy to see him.

'Why? What's happened?'

'We weren't very careful last night,' she said, touching her stomach. 'I need to go to the chemist, see if I can get a morning-after pill.'

Kite was confused. At the time Martha had told him it was safe, that they didn't need to use protection.

'I thought you said—'

She looked at him sheepishly. 'I checked my pill. I've missed two in the last week. I'm a bit hopeless. I'm not on it for the normal reasons. It's not because I'm seeing anyone in London. Does that make sense?'

It didn't make complete sense, but Kite nodded as if it did, relieved that Martha didn't have a boyfriend but worried that

BOX 88

she was now going to have to suffer feeling sick after taking the medication. Des had slept with a girl at a party who had taken the morning-after pill. She had been laid up in bed for three days.

'Why didn't you tell me?' he said. 'I would have come with you.'

'It's fine, Lockie. Not your fault.' She tried to shake off the awkwardness with a friendly smile. Kite was worried that he had embarrassed her but determined that she should not go into Mougins alone.

'I can go back to the house and change,' he suggested. He did not want to do that but was prepared to put Martha's needs ahead of BOX 88. 'Or I can just come with you now.' He thought about Peele waiting for him along the road. If he didn't report today, there would be hell to pay. 'Or come back. Let's have breakfast. I'll go for my run. Then we can go in later on the Vespa and—'

'I don't want the others to know.'

'They won't. It'll just be you and me. Don't go on your own, Martha. That's miserable. It's my fault. I should have had a condom or—'

'Where? In your wallet? Whipped it out by the pool? Classy.'

He liked it that she was so easy-going with him, forgiving and quick to laugh. They decided that they would go into Mougins later, after breakfast, and walked back together towards the house.

'Give me half an hour,' he said within earshot of Abbas as they reached the gate. 'Save me a croissant.'

Kite was outside the safe house three minutes later. He turned to check that the coast was clear, then ducked into the garden. Peele opened the front door and welcomed him inside. He was wearing shorts and looked characteristically dishevelled. He appeared to be alone in the house.

'Where's Carl?' Kite asked.

Peele's eyes went up to the ceiling. 'Sleeping,' he said in a quiet voice. 'He was up all night transcribing conversations from the villa.'

'So the tentacles are working?' Kite asked.

Peele nodded. 'Lots of interesting material. The Cathedral is sitting up and taking notice.'

The Cathedral had become a mythical place in Kite's imagination. BOX 88 was headquartered in a small residential block somewhere in central London. The buildings could be accessed both from the street and via a church where the incumbent vicar, a former Royal Marine, had been discreetly placed on the payroll. Kite had been told that he would be taken to The Cathedral once the operation against Eskandarian was concluded. For this reason, it had always felt as though he was on a period of probation and must prove himself over the summer if he was to be granted access to BOX 88's inner sanctum.

'What kind of things are they saying?' he asked.

'You can't know what you shouldn't know,' Peele replied. 'If I tell you what Eskandarian is concerned about, the sorts of things Luc is saying on the telephone, we'd be leading the witness. It's best you're left in the dark. You'll behave more naturally that way.'

'What's Luc go to do with it?' Kite asked.

He recognised the sudden look of regret on Peele's face. He had seen it before, at Alford, when Peele had told him that Lionel Jones-Lewis was refusing to recommend Kite for a place at Oxford.

'We're now looking at Xavier's father just as much as we're looking at Ali. That's all I can say.'

Kite was stunned. 'At *Luc*? Why?'

Peele turned the palms of his hands towards Kite, indicating that he had just asked the sort of question he had been told was out of bounds.

'Don't worry about it,' he said. 'You're doing a great job.'

BOX 88

'I don't want to do a great job if it gets Xavier's dad in trouble,' he said.

Peele deliberately, and very obviously, switched the direction of the conversation.

'We don't have much time,' he said. 'Coffee?'

'Of course I worry about it.'

'If Luc's father gets into trouble with the law, that's his fault, not yours.'

'In trouble how?'

'*Coffee?*' Peele repeated.

'Fine. Black. Two sugars. Yes, please.'

Kite was still slightly out of breath from the run, but not as exhausted nor as hungover as he had felt on the first morning. There was a bottle of Volvic on the table in front of him. He drank two glasses in quick succession while Peele fetched him a mug of coffee from the kitchen. It was lukewarm. He hadn't added any sugar. Kite drank it without complaint, remembering Xavier's stoned, drunken words on the first night: *Luc Bonnard is a good man, not a bad man. Daddy never puts a foot wrong. My father does business with Ali Eskandarian.*

'So, Lockie!' Peele rubbed his hands together expectantly. 'What's the news across the road?'

Kite immediately told him about Abbas's trip to New York. Peele wrote down the flight details, the names of the men mentioned in the letter and the information about Karrubi's hotel. He checked the spelling of 'Berberian' with Kite and said he would pass the information to Rita.

'Isn't Ali supposed to be in Lisbon at the end of August?' Kite asked.

'Absolutely,' Peele replied. 'Either he's going to have what looks like a last-minute change of heart and get on a flight to New York or Abbas is going alone.'

'You think he could be scouting the place out, meeting these people to discuss the next steps?'

Peele indicated that he didn't want to speculate, but Kite judged from his reaction that he was concerned about what Abbas was up to. He finished his coffee and, prompted to move on, recounted the meeting with Bijan, relating in as much detail as possible the content of their conversation, as well as Bijan's manner and appearance. Peele listened very carefully, occasionally taking notes on a lined yellow pad, but appeared to be less interested in Bijan's views on life in modern Iran than in his remarks concerning the Bonnard party's movements around Cannes.

'He said that he'd seen you eating lunch? Were you aware of anyone watching you?'

'No. I assumed he'd somehow recognised Eskandarian on the beach and followed us into town, or vice versa. Maybe he saw us in the window of the restaurant and waited.'

'And he was alone?'

'As far as I'm aware. He said he lived in Cannes. That France was now his home. He implied that he was part of an opposition to the ayatollah, or whoever is in charge now.' Peele said 'Rafsanjani' and underlined something on the pad. 'He said that he lived in fear of his life. That his friends had been abducted and tortured by associates of Ali Eskandarian.'

Peele looked up. 'He used that exact wording?'

Kite paused and tried to remember precisely what Bijan had told him.

'No. It was more of a general attack on Ali. He's friends with the Iranian government, therefore he's responsible for making this guy's life miserable.'

Peele crossed something out. 'Go on,' he said.

'He mentioned that somebody, an Iranian general who worked for the shah, had been assassinated in Paris, his brother as well.'

'Gholam Oveissi,' Peele replied instantly. 'That was years ago.'

'Yes. Him.' Kite had grown so accustomed to the depth of Peele's memory that he was unsurprised he knew Oveissi's name.

BOX 88

'He said the Americans or the British tipped off the Iranians who carried out the assassinations. Is that true?'

'Highly unlikely,' Peele replied. 'On what basis?'

It didn't look as though he expected Kite to have an answer to this question. Peele turned a page on the pad as a telephone rang upstairs. Kite had yet to see any of the rooms on the upper level of the house. He knew that one of them had been turned into a listening post.

'Boss?'

It was Carl, shouting from the top of the stairs. Peele called out: 'Lockie's here, is it urgent?' and apologised to Kite for the interruption.

'Sorry,' Carl replied. 'Didn't realise. I'll tell her to call later.'

Peele rolled his eyes and indicated that Kite should resume. Kite longed for a cigarette but knew that he couldn't return from his run stinking of smoke.

'Bijan said he was worried about another guy in France,' he said. 'I can't remember his name off the top of my head. Another Iranian who worked for the shah. Surname sounded a bit like "baksheesh".'

'Shahpour Bakhtiar?' Peele summoned the name with the same speed with which he had retrieved Gholam Oveissi from the vault of his memory. 'Yes, he's a marked man. Why do you think he was telling you all this?'

Kite shrugged. He could feel the sweat on his back cooling beneath his shirt. 'I dunno. It was like he was lonely or wanted somebody harmless to have a rant at. At the end he gave me his number.'

Peele grinned. 'Oh *good.*'

Kite reached into the back pocket of his shorts and pulled out the piece of paper. It was crumpled and slightly damp. Peele straightened it out, immediately made a note of the number on the yellow pad and passed it back.

'Strange,' he said, a remark Kite interpreted as a question about Bijan's intentions.

'I thought maybe it was a test,' he replied. 'Either you'd sent him to make sure I wasn't going to panic and everything was still OK, or maybe Ali or Abbas had paid him to check me out.'

'None of the above.' Peele ran a hand through his hair. 'We've heard plenty of conversations between Ali and Abbas. Falcons wired the Audi while you were in the restaurant in Cannes. There hasn't been a squeak on the lamp or the Gameboy. Eskandarian has been concerned about activity from exiled opposition groups more or less since he arrived. Has told Abbas to keep an eye out.'

Kite craved the transcripts of their conversations, to know what was being said, to understand why Luc had fallen under suspicion. Xavier might even know what Peele now knew; that Luc was involved in a corrupt business relationship with Eskandarian, perhaps by default with the Iranian government itself.

'Before I forget,' said Peele. 'The batteries on the Gameboy have died. Can you get it back and replace them?'

Kite nodded. Retrieving the Gameboy, replacing the batteries and putting it back behind the chest of drawers would be difficult, even hazardous, but he didn't want to admit this. BOX 88 had hired him because they knew that he wouldn't shirk a challenge.

'There's also your Walkman. Don't forget that. Why isn't it in play? You took three days to get the ghetto blaster where we wanted it, we still haven't had a squeak out of—'

It occurred to Kite that from Peele's point of view it might have looked as though he wasn't doing very much to keep up his end of the bargain. Two late nights, a lot of time spent by the pool, expensive meals in restaurants, dancing and drinking in nightclubs. 'There just hasn't been the right opportunity. I don't

BOX 88

know which rooms you want covered. I can't get up to the attic and leave the Walkman there. If Ali finds it, I'm screwed.'

'You certainly are,' Peele concurred. He waved a hand in front of his face as if he regretted putting Kite under unnecessary pressure.

'Don't worry,' he said. 'You're doing marvellously well.' He flashed him a reassuring smile. 'Tell me about Eskandarian in general. Your impression of him as a person now that three days have gone past. No right or wrong answer. Just what comes to mind.'

Kite had prepared one or two things to say and began by remarking on how relaxed Eskandarian seemed. The Iranian was far more westernised than he had expected. He repeated what Ali had said to him at the bar of the nightclub: *Iran has become a religious society. It does not tolerate western music, however much some of us enjoy it.*

Peele picked up on this.

'*Become* a religious society? He stressed that? As if it was unexpected or something that he didn't like?'

'Definitely the second one.' Kite craved more coffee. 'He seemed frustrated that things were as strict as they are out there. When he said that people liked listening to Peter Gabriel, Elton John, whatever, he was including *himself* in that. Christ, his girlfriend was dancing to Simple Minds and he went out to join her.'

'In front of the bodyguard?'

'Yeah.' Kite registered that Peele had asked about Abbas. 'Then last night we got back and he was listening to U2, Queen. Loves that stuff. Tucked into the whisky. If I didn't know him, I'd say he was just a normal guy, a businessman from London or Paris who knows Luc, not some close ally of radical Muslim madmen who want to knife Salman Rushdie.'

'Well, he was never going to be that,' Peele replied, with a very slight note of condescension. 'You should go in a minute.' Then suddenly: 'How's the girl?'

Kite felt his cheeks reddening. He could not look his former schoolmaster in the eye. For an awful, paranoid moment he wondered if BOX 88 knew everything that had gone on beside the pool just a few hours earlier. Christ, maybe Carl or Peele had seen what had happened between Xavier and Hana.

'She's great, thanks.'

'You two involved?'

It was a trick question, a test. Kite felt cornered, reluctant to lie but unwilling to give up a precious part of his privacy.

'We like each other,' he said. 'It won't interfere with my work.'

'Never said it would! She's a lovely girl, Lockie. You're a lucky man. And Hana?'

Kite had no intention of telling Peele about her involvement with Xavier. It was relevant to the operation, but only in as far as it would put Hana in hot water if she was found out. Instead he said: 'She's fun. Very sexy. Doesn't say much. Gets on well with Jacqui.'

'How is Eskandarian around her? Treats her like a bit of crumpet or is it more serious?'

Kite had a flash memory of Xavier's ivory hips thrusting in the moonlight, Hana transporting him to heaven and back on bended knee.

'Big age gap,' he replied. 'I haven't heard her say anything political, anything about Iran. They've been into Mougins together. Abbas looks at her like she's dipped in shit. Very disapproving.'

'Really?' Again Peele seemed interested in the bodyguard's reaction. 'Why's that?'

'Can't be easy for him watching his boss sleeping with a Vietnamese supermodel every night, then Martha and Jacqui and Rosamund lying by the pool in their bikinis while he gets sweaty

BOX 88

in a suit and has to mind his own business. Martha says she catches him eyeing them up the whole time.'

'Can't blame him,' Peele sighed. Kite resented the remark without saying anything. 'So listen . . .'

'Yes?'

'I want you to do something for me.'

'Shoot,' said Kite.

'Go to Eskandarian. Find an appropriate moment. Tell him you need to speak to him in private, away from Luc, away from Abbas, away from Hana. He's bound to agree. He obviously likes you, he'll be concerned. Then tell him, word for word, about your encounter with Bijan. Don't say he gave you his phone number. Make out that you were appalled to hear some of the things that go on in Iran and can't believe they're true. You felt obliged to tell Ali about the approach. Play the innocent public schoolboy. Butter wouldn't melt, etcetera. See if he confirms or denies what Bijan told you or lands somewhere in the middle. Either way, he'll start to trust you. Do you think you could do that?'

It sounded easy. Kite said that he was looking forward to it. Peele consulted the yellow pad.

'Did you have the sense that Bijan knew where Eskandarian was staying?'

'None. And I kept looking behind our taxi on the way home for a tail, but there was nobody there.'

'Good. Well done.' He tapped the pen on the lined yellow paper and conjured a further plan. 'After you've spoken to Ali, go into Mougins, use the phone box at the supermarket and call Bijan. We've got it covered, we'll see you going in. Tell him you want to meet up. Make him feel like you're on his side, that you can't stop thinking about what he told you in Cannes, that you want to help broker a meeting with Eskandarian.'

Kite recalled his promise to take Martha into Mougins after

breakfast on the back of the Vespa. He couldn't tell Peele that, but it would look suspicious if he made two trips in one day.

'Where would a meeting take place?' he asked.

'Get him to suggest somewhere. He won't want to come to the house, he might give you an address in Mougins or back in Cannes. With any luck, it'll be his apartment or somewhere used by opposition groups. Write down the address in case there's a problem with the line and the Falcons don't catch it. If he says he needs more time, tell him you'll try to call back later. If he asks for the number at the house, tell him you don't know it. If he asks why you're calling from a phone box, tell him you didn't want anyone listening in. OK?'

It sounded straightforward. Kite shrugged and said: 'Sure.'

'Good man.' Peele set the pad on the table and stood up. 'Come and have a quick look at something.'

He showed Kite upstairs. The largest of four bedrooms had been turned into a listening post. Carl was seated at a desk with a pair of headphones clamped to his ears. There was a two-reel tape recorder in front of him, a word processor and a car phone resting on a charging block. A cigarette was burning in a Michelin ashtray next to a half-eaten bowl of cereal. The milk had already started to separate in the heat. Carl took off the headphones, looped them round his neck and said: 'Hey, Lockie. Good work. Getting lots out of the lamp.'

'Do you think if Hana rubs it, she'll be granted three wishes?' Peele asked.

'Master Aladdin,' said Carl, putting on a Vietnamese accent. 'Stop my boyfriend snoring. Send me Chanel handbag and diamond necklace so I go back home to Nice.'

'Is she a prostitute?' Kite asked. The question sounded more prurient than he had intended.

'That's what we're keen to find out,' Peele replied. 'We still don't know where she came from or how he found her. Hasn't made a phone call since she arrived. Doesn't seem to know Ali

BOX 88

very well and is astonishingly incurious about his life and times. We wondered if she was DST, but the behaviour doesn't fit.'

It hadn't even occurred to Kite that Hana might have been planted by French intelligence. This was the moment to tell them about the pool hut; surely no French spy would do what she had done. Yet Kite couldn't bring himself to betray Xavier's trust.

'Let me see if I can get her passport details,' he said, scrabbling around for an answer. 'I've kept trying but no dice. She doesn't act weirdly. There's nothing suspicious about her except for the fact that she's sleeping with a man twice her age.'

'We should all be so lucky,' Carl muttered. A bird started singing in the garden. 'What *is* that fucking noise?' he said. 'Never stops, day and night, on and on and on.' He did an impression of the sound. 'Is it a cuckoo? Some sort of French tit?'

'Wood pigeon,' Peele replied decisively.

Kite was looking behind the door of the bedroom. Several black-and-white surveillance photos had been laid out on a small table.

'Who took these?' he said, picking them up.

The first showed Eskandarian getting out of the Audi in Cannes. The second was a shot of Abbas sitting in his suit on the beach. Others were random long lens shots of Luc, Rosamund, Eskandarian and Abbas in various locations, including Mougins and the gardens of the villa. There were two blurred images of Martha, several of Xavier talking to Eskandarian by the pool. Kite realised that it was possible to see almost every corner of the swimming area, including the hut, from at least two vantage points in the hills.

'Just for background,' Carl explained.

'Big Brother is watching you,' Peele added, giving Kite a nudge.

Kite didn't know how to respond. Naively, he hadn't realised that the house would be under such tight surveillance.

'Talking of pictures,' Peele continued. 'Is Martha still snapping away?'

'All the time,' Kite replied. 'Why?'

'Just good to have a third eye.'

Before Kite had a chance to ask Peele what he meant by that, Carl looked up at a clock on the wall and said: 'Guys, keep an eye on the time. If Lockie's on a run, he should be going by now.'

'Good point.' Peele put his hand on Kite's back. 'The fragrant Abbas will be waiting.'

'I counted them all out and I counted them all back,' Carl declared, typing something into the computer keyboard. Kite didn't know what he was talking about. It was as if the two men had developed their own rhythms, their own secret language during the long days and nights running the operation. Kite suddenly felt like an outsider. Perhaps that was their purpose.

'Chop-chop,' said Peele. 'Or "wheels turning", as Lady Rosamund would say. Carl, get out on the road and give Lockie the all-clear, will you?'

They all went downstairs. Carl did as he had been asked. Peele surprised Kite by enveloping him in a bear hug on the porch, saying: 'Well done, keep going, well done.' As Kite walked off, he said: 'Don't forget now. Talk to Ali. Call Bijan. Use the Walkman,' and waved him onto the road.

'Cheers,' said Carl as Kite passed him at the gate. 'Houston, you are cleared for take-off.'

Within ten minutes, Kite was back at the house. Martha was talking to Rosamund in the kitchen. Luc came down the stairs with slicked-back hair and an attitude of isolated indifference. He smelled of eau de cologne. All the way home Kite had felt that he was carrying Peele's suspicions about Xavier's father like a set of rocks on his back. There and then he decided to do nothing about changing the Gameboy batteries. To revive the microphone in the study was to drive another nail into whatever

BOX 88

coffin BOX 88 were preparing for him. Kite had agreed to operate as an agent targeted against Ali Eskandarian, not against Luc Bonnard. He would never have agreed to betray Xavier's father, no matter how much he disliked and distrusted him. He took a shower, changed into shorts and a T-shirt, ate breakfast downstairs and asked Luc if he could take the Vespa into Mougins.

'Of course,' Luc replied. 'What do you need?'

'Just a few postcards to send home.' He caught Martha's eye. She smiled as she bit into a croissant. 'Need anything for the house?'

Rosamund immediately thanked Kite for his kind offer and asked if he could pick up some toothpaste from the supermarket.

'Can I come with you?' Martha asked.

'Sure,' Kite replied, acting surprised. 'You need postcards too?'

'Promised my mum I'd send one,' she said. 'Shall we go in the next five minutes?'

44

Kite took Martha into Mougins on the Vespa. The young woman behind the counter informed her that she had to wait to speak to the pharmacist. Martha told Kite that she would prefer to be on her own, so he offered to pick her up half an hour later.

It was the perfect window of time. He walked outside, climbed back onto the Vespa and rode up to the supermarket. He bought a card for the public telephone and dialled Bijan's number. It rang out for almost a minute before a man picked up and said 'Oui?'

'Hello,' said Kite. He was speaking in French. 'Is that Bijan?'

'Bijan isn't here,' the man replied. From his accent it sounded as though he was also Iranian.

'Do you speak English?'

'Yes.'

'When will Bijan be back?'

'I am not certain.'

'Can you give him a message?' Kite asked.

'OK.'

'Tell him La . . . tell him Adam called.' He had almost blown the call, forgetting until the very last moment that he had given

BOX 88

Bijan a cover name. 'I met him yesterday in Cannes. He will know who I am.'

'Adam?'

'Yes. The British guy.'

'British guy,' the man repeated. Kite couldn't tell if he was distracted by something or conscientiously writing things down. 'You have a number?'

'No. I'm calling from a phone box in Mougins. I'll try again tomorrow.'

'Wait, please.'

Kite had been about to hang up. Two very tanned, very blonde young girls with pigtails raced past the phone booth and disappeared into the supermarket. A woman was running to catch up with them, shouting something in what Kite presumed was a Scandinavian language. She was frantically pushing a shopping cart with a baby strapped across the handlebars. She looked exhausted. Kite wondered if the Turings had picked up the call. Presumably somebody at the safe house had seen him going into Mougins and was listening on the line.

'Hello? Adam?'

It was Bijan.

'Bijan, hi. I didn't think you were there.'

'I was sleeping.'

'I'm sorry to have woken you.'

'Not at all. It's good to hear your voice. I'm glad that you've telephoned. How are you?'

'I'm well, thank you.'

'You are in Mougins?'

'Yes,' Kite replied. Had it been a mistake to reveal his location?

'That's where you're staying?'

He avoided answering the question.

'I'm just at the supermarket. There may not be much credit left on my card.'

'I understand.'

'It was just that I've been thinking a lot about our conversation.' *Make him feel like you're on his side, that you can't stop thinking about what he told you.* 'To be honest, I was really shocked by some of the things you said.'

'Yes. It's a very difficult situation, Adam.'

'And I'm sorry that it's so dangerous for you.'

'It's considerate of you to say that. I knew as soon as we started talking that you were a good person, Adam.'

Kite waited, took a breath.

'I'd like to help if I can. You said you wanted to meet Ali. Mr Eskandarian. What would you like me to do? How can I be helpful?'

'Don't worry about it. I think this might be dangerous for you. We have other tactics, other ideas we can explore.'

Kite was confused. He had assumed that Bijan would leap at the chance of a meeting.

'I see. OK. What's changed?'

There was a delay. It sounded as though Bijan had covered the handset and was speaking in Farsi to someone in the room. After about five seconds he returned to the call.

'The situation is complicated. You say you are in Mougins? It is very beautiful up there. Not spoiled, like so much of the coast.'

'Yes, very beautiful.' Kite had the dismaying sense that he had played the wrong hand. The Scandinavian woman emerged from the supermarket, looking around the busy car park for her daughters. She was evidently distressed.

'Thank you for ringing, Adam. I enjoyed our talk the other day.'

'Me too,' Kite replied, only to hear the line go dead. He stepped out of the booth and shouted at the woman: 'I saw them go inside. Your daughters are inside the supermarket!' and she thanked him with a grateful wave. Why had Bijan hung up so abruptly? If the whole encounter had been set

BOX 88

up by Abbas or Eskandarian to test his loyalty, had he now fallen into a bear trap?

Kite retrieved his phone card and walked back to the Vespa. Peele had been completely wrong in his assessment of the situation. There had been no address to write down, no possibility of a second meeting in Cannes. The Iranian had not even asked Kite for his number. Why had he been so uninterested? *We have other tactics, other ideas we can explore.* Were the exiles planning a hit on Eskandarian? Kite rode back down to the pharmacy trying to work out what was happening but unable to untangle fact from speculation.

Martha was waiting for him on the road. She had already swallowed the pill. When she saw him, her expression changed from one of distracted anxiety to pleasure at his arrival. She swung onto the back of the Vespa, kissed Kite's neck and wrapped her arms around his waist. The joy of being with her and the complexity of his work for BOX 88 were like two pistons in some vast machine moving perfectly in time, pulling him one way and then the other. As they rode home, Martha told him that the pharmacist had been a 'judgemental Catholic with bad breath'. That made Kite laugh, though he was worried that she was going to feel unwell for the rest of the day.

'As soon as I'm better we must do it again,' she said, and Kite almost drove off the road. 'I loved what happened last night.'

'Me too,' he shouted over the noise of the engine.

He was grinning from ear to ear as he drove through the gates, tooting the horn as he sped past Abbas in the Audi. Martha kissed him and retired to her room with a copy of Paul Auster's *The New York Trilogy* which she had borrowed from Rosamund. She told Kite not to worry about her and put word out to the rest of the house that she was just feeling under the weather and would be fine by the evening.

Kite spent the rest of the morning chatting to Jacqui and Hana by the pool. He decided that he should stick to the plan to talk to Ali. If Bijan had been a trap, it was better to confront Eskandarian with his concerns about Iran, rather than to keep them to himself. That way he would look like less of a traitor. If Bijan was a genuine Iranian exile who regarded Eskandarian as his sworn enemy, then Kite had nothing to worry about. He could speak to Eskandarian as Peele had instructed, earning his trust in the process.

Xavier emerged just in time for lunch. Under orders from his father, he spent much of the afternoon marking and digging out an area in the south-eastern corner of the garden which Luc wanted to transform into a pétanque court. Kite helped them, but when Rosamund offered to drive father and son into Antibes at four o'clock to buy a set of boules, Kite seized his opportunity. He left them to it and went into the house to search for Eskandarian.

He was in the kitchen, making coffee.

'Lockie!' He had the charmer's habit of making everyone with whom he came into contact feel sought after and cherished. Even Kite, who knew that Eskandarian was potentially an agent of mass murder, could not help being seduced. 'How are you? Having a lazy afternoon? Is Martha OK? I think Hana is down by the pool.'

'She's fine. Just not feeling a hundred per cent.'

'OK, good.'

Eskandarian poured a small percolator of coffee into a yellow espresso cup. He offered to make more for Kite—'It's easy, will take five minutes!'—but Kite declined. Instead he said:

'Ali, this is a bit awkward, but could I possibly talk to you?'

The Iranian looked taken aback.

'Talk to me? Of course!'

His reaction suggested that he was flattered by the approach, rather than frustrated that Kite was going to be taking up his precious time. Kite was standing over a bowl of La Perruche

BOX 88

sugar and passed it to Eskandarian. He dropped a cube into the coffee.

'It's about something that happened in Cannes after you and Hana had gone home yesterday. Something about Iran.'

There was no microphone in the kitchen. Kite wanted Carl to hear. He tried to convey both with his body language and by his tone of voice that it would be better to hold the conversation elsewhere.

'Something about Iran?' Eskandarian looked confused. 'OK, so what happened?' He stirred the coffee with a matching yellow spoon. 'Shall we talk in the living room? In the garden?'

Kite had been hoping that he would suggest going up to the attic. As luck would have it, a lawnmower started up in a neighbouring garden.

'Might be a bit noisy outside.'

'The living room then?' Eskandarian suggested.

Kite glanced over his shoulder and grimaced slightly, as if to say: 'These walls have ears.' To his delight, Eskandarian took the hint. 'Or we can talk in my room if you're worried about something?'

'That's probably a good idea,' Kite replied. 'It's better that we don't get disturbed.'

With an expression of intrigue rather than concern, Eskandarian picked up his coffee and indicated that Kite should follow him upstairs.

'I wonder what it is,' he whispered as they passed Abbas's bedroom. The door was closed. Eskandarian pressed a finger to his lips, indicating with a mischievous smile that his bodyguard was enjoying a siesta.

'I'm sure it's nothing,' Kite replied, adopting the same stage whisper. They reached the bottom of the stairs. 'It's just something I thought you should know.'

He had not been back to the attic since the first frantic evening when he had switched the lamps. Eskandarian's study was now a melee of books and files, of French, American and British newspapers as well as letters and faxes strewn on the tables and the floor. Kite had not known that Eskandarian had received so much post and could only assume that he had brought much of it with him from Iran.

'Wow,' he said, registering the chaos. 'You've been busy up here.'

'Please forgive the mess.' Eskandarian set about clearing a space on the sofa so that Kite could sit down. It was like visiting a beak in his rooms at Alford. 'It is an exceptionally busy time for me. I am part of a team advising our new president, Mr Rafsanjani. There are a number of things I am doing for the new government over here in France. They never stop sending me faxes. Luc will soon start charging me for ink and paper! I wanted to use my holiday to catch up on correspondence. As you can see, I have not been able to make very much progress.'

It occurred to Kite that if Hana was an undercover DST officer, she was sleeping next to a goldmine of information. He thought about the Olympus Trip, wondering if he would get the chance to come back upstairs and photograph some of the more important-looking documents in the study. Time and again Peele had impressed on him the importance of not taking unnecessary risks, but to fail to take at least a roll of film in this Aladdin's cave of intelligence would be a dereliction of duty.

'So tell me.' Eskandarian sat at the desk and looked benevolently at his slightly nervous young guest. 'What is it you want to tell me, Lockie? What on earth happened in Cannes?'

Kite was sitting beside the lamp. Out of habit he committed Eskandarian's remarks to memory—*I am part of a team advising our new president, Mr Rafsanjani. There are a number of things I am doing for the new government over here in France*—just in case there was a problem with the technology.

He asked if he could smoke. Eskandarian offered him a ciga-

BOX 88

rette from a silver case on his desk and lit it with a gold lighter. It was a brand Kite did not recognise, far stronger than the red Marlboros he was used to. Settling back in the chair, Kite felt no need to embellish his story, to exaggerate what Bijan had said nor to imply that he was frightened or in any way feeling morally compromised by sharing a house with a man accused of such profound injustices. Instead he merely repeated, more or less verbatim, exactly what he had told Peele at their morning meeting. Throughout, Kite had the sense of talking to an exceptionally intelligent, emotionally sensitive man who was determined that Kite should know the truth about life in Iran. Kite quickly became convinced that Bijan was a genuine exile and that neither Eskandarian nor Abbas had used him to test Kite's loyalty. Eskandarian encouraged him to speak freely and at no point expressed any degree of anger or frustration with the things Bijan had said. Indeed, to Kite's astonishment, he admitted that many of them were true.

'We have become the wrong country,' he said. 'Iran today is not where I hoped she would be. It's strange that we are having this conversation when it is something Luc and I have also been discussing continually since I arrived in France. We both feel— looking at Iran from the inside and from the perspective of a foreigner—that my country has not yet emerged with full maturity from the Revolution of ten years ago.'

'What do you mean?' Kite asked. He did not want to seem too interested in what Eskandarian was saying, for fear of arousing his suspicion, but nor could he afford to appear indifferent. It was a question of balance. He knew that Eskandarian thought of him as a bright, intelligent young man, that he was intrigued by his Alford education and doubtless imagined that both he and Xavier would go on to lead interesting, fruitful lives. It was this that Kite needed to amplify, acting older than he was, playing the curious student sitting at the knee of the great man, listening intently as he imparted his pearls of wisdom.

'I mean that when I was living in France, when I first met Luc, Iran was a broken society. How much do you know of my country, its history, apart from what you hear about Mr Rushdie?'

'Very little,' Kite replied, remembering something Strawson had told him in London. *Eskandarian won't even notice you. You're too young to be taken seriously.*

'So I will tell you.' Eskandarian lit a cigarette of his own and briefly glanced out of the window. 'I lived in Tehran as a young man, when I was not much older than you are now. My friends and I went to discotheques, to cinemas. We could watch American films starring Clint Eastwood, Robert Redford, Faye Dunaway. She was my favourite. But I was one of the lucky ones. My family had money. They were what we call *bazaaris*, merchants. We lived well. My uncle drove an American car. He even owned a washing machine which had been made in West Germany!' Kite saw that he was expected to be amazed by this, so he said: 'Wow.' Eskandarian carefully tapped the ash from his cigarette. 'However, a great many people in the Iranian population did not live like this. They existed in poverty. Children went around in rags. Some survived on not much more than bread and a little salt. They watched the shah and his advisers, his foreign friends and American backers, gorging themselves on the best food, the finest wines, the most beautiful women, and they could do nothing about it. It was said that the shah was so ignorant of his country's many problems because he saw us only from the air, from an aeroplane or a helicopter. He never came down long enough to be with his own people. I came from this same world of privilege, Lockie, but in my youth I rejected it. I knew that Iran had to change. So I came to France, I followed the activities of the Imam in Paris, I was lucky enough to meet members of his circle. I trusted them, and they trusted me. You have heard of Gandhi?'

'Yes, of course,' Kite replied.

'So it is no exaggeration to say that I thought of the Imam as a man with the potential to be the Gandhi of Iran. The

BOX 88

Revolution, in which I played a willing part, a revolution in which I still believe, promised Iranians a total break with the chaos and injustice of the past. The shah had promised to make Iran the fifth largest economy in the world. He promised "Prosperity for All". Instead, he enriched himself on bribes and kickbacks while his people starved and suffered. The rural poor were illiterate. They lived in clay huts without electricity or running water where the only warmth—in a country rich in oil and natural gas!—came from burning dried cow manure. Can you believe such a thing, when other countries at this time could put a man in space, a man on the moon? We believed in freedom of the press, freedom of speech. A government of the people, for the people. Revenues from oil would pay for free electricity, free water, free telephone calls. These were our dreams! I knew that there were problems, that we were Persians, not Arabs, that we should not allow Islam to become too closely entwined with the business of government, but I was young like you and surrounded by men who convinced me of these things. I was a dreamer! Am I boring you, Lachlan?'

Kite almost jumped out of his seat, wondering how on earth Eskandarian could have reached such a conclusion.

'Definitely not!' he said, hoping to God, to Allah, to whatever deity Peele and Carl believed in, that the lamp was beaming every word of his conversation with Eskandarian to the listening post less than a mile from where they were seated.

'Good,' Eskandarian replied. 'You don't look bored! I just like to check. Sometimes the younger generation has no interest in politics, you know? Why would you want to listen to an Iranian businessman going on about the good and the bad things in his country? I have a habit of taking advantage of the young, trying out ideas on them that it would be—how can I express this—too risky to express to my friends and colleagues at home. I can only speak to the likes of you and Luc about it. Hana has no interest!'

'What kind of ideas?' Kite asked. He was aware that he was

slouching. He pulled himself up on the sofa. 'Does Luc have some ideas on Iran?'

It was the first slip he had made, demonstrating what might have been interpreted—both by Eskandarian and by Peele across the road—as an unusual interest in Luc's attitudes. Thankfully Eskandarian did not seem to interpret it as such. Indeed, in his response there was a faint suggestion of a disagreement between the two men which Eskandarian was keen to skirt over.

'We discuss a great many things. Luc, as you know, is a businessman with a wealth of experience.' Was he hinting at a darker, more complex relationship? 'We are old friends. We talk candidly.'

'What did you mean about Iran becoming the wrong sort of country?' Kite was trying to sound concerned and touchingly naive in equal measure. 'Is Bijan right? That the Revolution has ended up hurting people?'

Eskandarian hesitated. On the one hand he appeared to be in the mood to hold a frank and honest conversation, but on the other he was a citizen of the Iranian state, an adviser to its president, a government-sponsored official trained to avoid saying or doing anything that might be interpreted as treasonous, even if his only audience was a harmless eighteen-year-old boy.

'It is certainly the case that elements within the state wanted to sustain the Revolution, to give it a religious character, an Islamic character, and they have done this by limiting freedom of expression, to a certain extent.'

Kite knew that this was baloney and tried to extract a fuller answer.

'You mean women?'

'Women, yes. But this is hardly new in Islam, Lockie! I for one do not believe that women should be allowed to walk around the streets looking like Madonna!'

You hypocrite, he thought, wondering how Eskandarian squared this view with Hana's micro miniskirts, her figure-hugging black dresses, her suitcase full of lingerie and French perfumes.

BOX 88

Eskandarian must have sensed his surprise because he added: 'Of course over here it is different. In the nightclubs of Antibes, on the streets of Paris. In Iran it is preferred that such expressions of fashion be made privately, in the home.'

'Of course.' Kite smirked encouragingly. He thought of the faces of the young women killed on Pan Am 103. 'So what Bijan said is true? In fact you yourself even talked about this last night in the club. That you don't have discos in Iran. You can't listen to the sort of music we heard in Antibes or played on the terrace last night?'

Eskandarian smiled uneasily. Kite stubbed out his cigarette and wondered if he was being too pushy. He wanted to extract as much useful information as possible, but he was also keen to put on a good show for the Falcons. He recalled Peele's advice: *Play the innocent schoolboy. See if he confirms or denies what Bijan told you or lands somewhere in the middle.* How could he keep Eskandarian talking without seeming to be too critical of his political views? The idea was to get the Iranian to trust him, not to make him think that Lachlan Kite was a pious bore.

'Music is available,' Eskandarian replied. 'We can listen to it in our homes. But what this man Bijan said about people being stoned or whipped for these offences is nonsense.'

'Yeah, I thought so.' Kite made a face and rolled his eyes. 'He sounded a bit deranged. Said the ayatollah was assassinating exiles in Paris and London, that his life was in danger.'

'Such rubbish!' Eskandarian again looked out of the window, as if the distant hills would offer him respite from Kite's misapprehensions. A wood pigeon echoed in the garden. 'All revolutions take time to bear fruit,' he continued quickly. 'Look at France after 1789! In our case, the Iranian state has developed at the expense of the public. This is true. A battle of ideas is taking place between religious figures in Tehran and what you might call technocrats like myself, republicans who have a slightly different view of the country's future. But to say that my coun-trymen are murderers, well this is nonsense.'

Kite did not fully understand what Eskandarian had said about republicans and technocrats, partly because he was concen-trating so hard on what he might ask next. Peele and Strawson would be able to extract a fuller, more contextualised meaning from what Eskandarian was saying. Kite's job was just to keep him talking.

'Are you in danger here?' he asked.

'Me?!' Eskandarian inflated his chest, squared his shoulders and smiled broadly in a display of mock courage. 'No, of course not. Don't you worry, Lockie!' He picked up a sheaf of papers from the desk and tapped them into a neat, square pile. 'Of course there are allies of the shah, his followers and admirers, who wish to see Iran return to the bad old days. And why not? They were getting very rich while millions starved! Men like this Bijan hold men like Ali Eskandarian responsible for the collapse of their dreams. He saw me on the beach in Cannes—perhaps somebody in his network recognised me at the airport—and he decided to resort to desperate measures. I am sorry that he filled your head with lies and propaganda. I have also read *Papillon* and I can tell you it is a *much* better story than the one Bijan related to you!'

Kite smiled a crocodile smile, beginning to feel that Eskandarian was trying to wriggle off the hook.

'But you need Abbas,' he said, pointing towards Abbas's bedroom. 'You need a bodyguard.'

'This is just for show!' Eskandarian gave another puffed-up, sweeping gesture of omniscience. 'Who is to say that Abbas is not keeping an eye on *me*, eh? Protecting *me* from myself!' The Iranian broke into uproarious laughter. Kite played along, still as far away from knowing what, if anything, Eskandarian was up to in France.

'Well I definitely hope that no harm comes to you,' he replied.

BOX 88

'It's been so interesting meeting you and spending time with you here at the house—'

'Thank you,' Eskandarian replied. 'I have also very much enjoyed meeting you and Martha, seeing Jacqui and Xavier again after so long.' A sudden seriousness came over him. He leaned forward. 'He drinks too much, no?'

'Maybe.' Kite gave an equivocal shrug. He didn't want anything on tape that would make him sound disloyal or lead to concerns about Xavier.

'Tell me.' Eskandarian offered Kite another cigarette, which he declined. 'Did Bijan ask you to contact him? Did he give you a telephone number, an address?'

'No.' The lie sat as easily inside Kite as smoke from a cigarette. 'No number, no address.'

Eskandarian pondered this for a moment. 'So he just left you alone, you walked out of the café?'

'That's right.'

What was the exact nature of Eskandarian's concern? Was he worried that Bijan had followed the taxi back to the villa? Kite was hardly in a position to be able to put the Iranian's mind at rest.

They were interrupted by a noise on the stairs. Abbas appeared on the landing and peered into the room. He seemed both surprised and annoyed that Kite had penetrated the inner sanctum. Eskandarian said something to him in Farsi. Abbas stared at Kite, mumbled something and went back downstairs.

'He is in a mood today,' said Eskandarian.

'He seems to be in a mood every day.'

The Iranian laughed. 'Oh, do not mind Abbas!' He rubbed his hands together expectantly in a manner that reminded Kite of Billy Peele at the start of a history lesson. 'I must get back to work. Thank you for coming to me and telling me this. I appreciate that it must have been unsettling for you. I hope that I have at least put your mind at rest?'

'Absolutely,' Kite replied.

He stood up with the dismaying sensation that he had failed adequately to draw out enough information for BOX 88. What else could he have asked about? Lockerbie? Malta? The plane tickets to New York? It was all off limits. What else was left to say? Kite's mind was blank as Eskandarian started tidying the papers on his desk. He appeared to place them in order of importance, sliding certain documents to the top and moving others to the bottom, like a card dealer shuffling in slow motion. Kite made a private vow to return to the room and to photograph as many of the documents as possible.

'Hana is leaving tonight,' he said, as Kite turned towards the door.

Kite was stunned. He could only imagine that her departure was a direct consequence of what had happened with Xavier.

'Really? Oh no. Why?'

'It had always been her intention to stay only for a few days. She has a job to go back to in Nice. We may reconnect in Paris on my way home.'

Was he lying? Eskandarian smiled to himself, possibly at the thought of more miniskirts, more lingerie, more French perfume in Paris; the expression on his face might equally have been pleasure at the prospect of taking his revenge against Xavier. It was impossible to tell. 'Well, I'll be sorry to see her go,' he said. 'She's great company.'

Eskandarian took a moment to respond. It was not clear whether he agreed with Kite's assessment of his girlfriend's character or was distracted by something on his desk.

'You think?' he replied. 'How nice. Yes. I'll be sorry to see her go as well.'

45

The reason for Hana's sudden departure became clear the next day.

Kite made it to his morning meeting just before nine o'clock. Over lukewarm coffee, Peele and Carl told him that Eskandarian's former fiancée had been invited to lunch by Luc and Rosamund. When Hana had found out, she had reacted angrily and announced that she was leaving. Carl had heard the entire argument on the lamp microphone. Kite was relieved to have it confirmed that it had nothing to do with what had happened between Hana and Xavier, an incident which appeared to have escaped the attention of the otherwise eagle-eyed Falcons keeping watch on the house.

Peele also revealed that Bijan was a bona fide member of a large Iranian exile group in Europe targeting regime figures in France. Kite was pleased that he had not been duped but shocked to discover that the seemingly benign Bijan was potentially a man of violence. He was instructed to go back to the villa and to proceed as normal.

'You did brilliantly in the office yesterday, but we still need hard information,' Peele told him. 'Photographs. Documents. Anything and everything you can get your hands on. It might be impossible. You might get a window of opportunity. Improvise.'

Kite made it back in time to sneak into Martha's room. They had slept apart the previous night, but she had left a note on his bed telling him to join her when he got back from his run. They made love for the second time, silently and deliciously, Kite covering Martha's mouth as they moved, mindful that Jacqui was still asleep next door.

Just after midday he went downstairs to discover that Eskandarian's former fiancée had already arrived. Her name was Bita. She was a Frenchwoman of Iranian descent in her late thirties accompanied by two small children: a boy of nine named José and a little girl of three called Ada who clung to her mother's side at all times. Bita's Catalan husband had not come with her. She arrived in a hire car from Nice airport, having flown from Barcelona that morning. The other guests, appearing at intervals over the next hour, were a rotund, smartly dressed Frenchman in his fifties named Jacques and a younger French couple—Paul and Annette—who had two children of similar ages to José. Jacques worked as a banker in Paris, Paul in the film industry. Annette was a housewife. Kite had been exposed to the looking-glass world of espionage for long enough to suspect that at least one of them could be an intelligence officer investigating Eskandarian's alleged links to Lockerbie. On this basis, he had a responsibility to obtain as much information about the guests as possible. That meant finding out how they knew Eskandarian, what they wanted from him, why they had come to the villa, if they were friends of Luc's, of Rosamund's—or associates of Eskandarian's from Paris in the late 1970s. Kite decided to use the Walkman to record whatever conversations took place in the living room during the afternoon. The batteries supplied by BOX 88 would last up to eight hours. It was just a case of going up to his room, inserting the blank cassette provided by the Falcons, bringing the Walkman downstairs concealed among various personal belongings—a copy of Bruce Chatwin's *The Songlines*, a pair of swimming goggles, a bottle of suntan

BOX 88

lotion—and leaving all of them amid the general detritus which piled up during the day on a table near the doors to the terrace. Rosamund and Hélène tended to clear up at the end of every day, but Kite reckoned the Walkman would be left undisturbed until at least six o'clock. The only danger lay in someone picking it up, either to use it or to search for a tape. Xavier often did this when he couldn't find an album he was looking for or if he had left his own Walkman down by the pool.

Strawson and Peele would also want pictures. Kite had been taking photographs with the Olympus Trip more or less constantly since he arrived in France and snapped half a dozen shots of the group as they gathered for lunch on the terrace. None of them seemed to mind having their picture taken. Martha was also busily taking photographs, so much so that Rosamund jokingly asked if they were both thinking about taking it up as a career. Kite finally understood why Peele had been so interested in this aspect of Martha's behaviour: BOX were planning somehow to get a look at her photographs once they had been developed, either by asking Kite to obtain them or perhaps by intercepting the rolls of film at whatever chemist or laboratory Martha used to have them developed. Even if Martha never discovered that her pictures had been purloined and copied in such a way, the thought made him queasy. He made a note to tell Peele that her belongings were off limits, even though he knew that such a request would likely fall on indifferent ears.

When the guests had first arrived and were talking on the terrace with glasses of rosé and white wine, Kite had concentrated his attention on Bita and Eskandarian, knowing that BOX would want to know more about their relationship. There was clearly a deep fondness between them, both in the way that they spoke to one another and in their body language. Eskandarian was enormously attentive towards her children, but José quickly grew bored of the grown-up talk and tried to encourage his mother to go for a walk with him in the garden. Sensing an opportunity,

Kite offered to play with José and took him down to the pool, where Jacqui and Martha were doing their best to avoid joining the lunch party until the last possible moment.

'I want to swim!' José cried out in French when he saw the pool. The two girls instantly stood up from their sunloungers and started cooing over the divine Spanish boy. Moments later Annette, the young French mother who had also brought her children to the villa, emerged from beneath the fallen fronds of the palm tree holding her son and daughter by the hand. Kite found a spare pair of swimming trunks in the hut for José and they all jumped in the pool. Kite extracted Annette's surname—Mouret—and discovered that her husband knew Luc well but had never met Eskandarian before. When Annette began talking to Martha and Jacqui, Kite found out where José lived in Barcelona (a suburb called Sarrià), where he went to school and if he had ever been introduced to Luc or Eskandarian before (he had not). He also learned the boy's surname: Zamora. All this took place amid the general joyful chaos of an early afternoon swim: Kite and Martha ducking one another; Annette's children showing off how long they could hold their breath underwater; Xavier appearing from nowhere, bombing into the water to the annoyance of his sister but to the screams and delight of the children. Kite was aware that his deceptions had become so commonplace that he was spying almost without being aware of it.

In due course Rosamund called out, 'Lunch!' and the group gathered on the terrace to eat a three-course lunch prepared by Rosamund and Hélène. Kite was seated between Xavier and Martha, at the opposite end of the table to Jacques, Luc and Paul. He hoped that the ghetto blaster—which was still plugged in behind the sofa—would capture their conversation, but had a hunch that any potentially sensitive exchanges between them would take place behind closed doors in Luc's office, where the Gameboy had long since ceased to function.

The swim had forged a bond between Kite and the children,

BOX 88

particularly with Bita's son, José, who hung on his every word. After lunch, Luc invited his guests to join him on a walk around the property, an invitation taken up by all of the adults with the exception of Annette, Martha, Xavier and Kite. Ada, Bita's three-year-old daughter, was asleep in a hammock in the garden. Annette promised to keep an eye on her so that Bita could join the walk.

It was only as Kite was losing sight of Abbas and Eskandarian on the drive that the idea came to him. He had chanced on an opportunity to photograph the documents in Eskandarian's office. But how to do so without raising Xavier or Martha's suspicion? They were planning to watch a video with the kids. How to get away from the television room for long enough that his absence wouldn't be noticed? And how to do so without Martha wanting to come with him?

'I've got an idea,' Kite announced. They were all in the sitting room, helping Alain and Hélène to clear up lunch. Moments earlier Kite had taken his camera back upstairs and changed the roll of film. He turned to the children. 'Do you guys like playing hide-and-seek?'

Xavier groaned and said: 'Thought we were going to watch *Temple of Doom*?' But the children all squealed in delight. Annette agreed that it would be an excellent idea as long as they didn't wake Ada.

'Then let's play in the house,' Kite replied. The tactic had fallen into his lap, a moment of pure good fortune. He appointed Martha and Xavier as the chief hunters and divided the rest of the group into three teams: Annette would be with her son, Jacqui with Annette's daughter, and Kite with José.

'Fair?' he asked.

They all agreed that the teams were perfect. Xavier and Martha remained in the sitting room and said that they would count to a hundred. The garden and the pool were pronounced out of bounds, but every other area of the house was in play.

'Just don't make a mess in my room,' Xavier grumbled. Jacqui told him not to be so selfish.

As soon as Martha had closed her eyes and started counting, Kite grabbed José by the hand and sprinted up to the first floor. Momentarily leaving the boy on the landing, he grabbed the Olympus Trip from his room then ran up the stairs to the attic beckoning the giggling José to follow him, all the while urging him to be as quiet as possible.

Kite pushed open the door of Eskandarian's bedroom. He pressed his fingers to his lips and whispered in French: 'Hide behind the door. I'll be in the room on the other side.'

From two floors below he heard Martha shouting out: 'Three, two, one . . . coming!' as José froze in a tableau of excitement, stifling a delighted giggle. Kite showed him where to hide, willed him to stay where he was, and went back out onto the landing. He then closed the bedroom door and moved as quickly as possible into the office.

He shut the door behind him and took the camera out of his back pocket. There were several piles of correspondence on the far side of the office, some of it in envelopes, some of it open on Eskandarian's desk. Crossing the room, Kite held the lens over the desk as he had been instructed and took a photograph of the closest letter. The snap of the clicking shutter, of the reel winding on, seemed deafening. He had practised in the Hampstead flat and remembered Peele telling him not to think about the noise. Kite was aware that his hand was shaking slightly and his breath quickening as he lifted the letter, placed it upside-down on the desk beside him and photographed the document underneath. There were seven pieces of paper in all, some covered in Farsi, others in French. He kept the camera steady with his right hand and moved the pages with his left, putting them back as he had found them at the end of the process. One careless slip or sudden draught from the partly-open window and Eskandarian's corre-spondence would be scattered to the floor. Kite didn't look at

BOX 88

what he was photographing nor reason that one piece of paper might be more valuable than another. There was no time to take any letters out of their envelopes, only to photograph what was visible on the desk.

A sound from the opposite bedroom but—as far as Kite could tell—no noise yet from the floors below. He made sure that the desk looked as he had found it, then turned around. Eskandarian had scrawled a list of names and numbers on a piece of A4 paper which had been left on the sofa. Kite photographed it. As he lowered the camera, he looked closer at two of the names: *David Foreman*, several times underlined and now spelled with an added 'e', and *Asef Berberian*, after which Eskandarian had added two question marks. They were the same two names Kite had seen in the text of the letter from Abbas's suit pocket. What was the connection? He desperately wanted more time to comb the office for anything relating to New York, to the Air France flight or the Grand Hyatt Hotel. If Eskandarian was using the Lisbon conference as cover and planning to visit New York with Abbas under alias, BOX could follow him every step of the way. But why the question marks after Berberian? And why was Forman's name now aggressively underlined and spelled in a different way?

A scream from the first floor. At least one of the children had been discovered. Martha shouted: 'Found you!' There was an eruption of laughter. Kite knew that he had no more than twenty seconds before Martha or Xavier bounded up the stairs.

He looked around the office. What else might be of interest to BOX? He grabbed a diary from the desk, crouched down behind the armchair so that he would be plausibly out of sight if someone came into the room, and began to take photographs. He flicked through the entries for July, August and September. It was in weekly format. He took photos for every page as quickly and as steadily as possible. While holding down the pages for the second week of September, he heard a noise on the stairs and knew he must stop. He took the shot, stuffed the camera into his back pocket and closed the diary.

José was the first to be discovered. The little boy squealed in delighted frustration as Martha opened the door of the bedroom and said: 'There you are! Found you!' in English. Kite was next. Martha came into the room to find him cowering behind the chair.

'That's the worst hiding place I've ever seen,' she said. 'What are you *doing* down there? At least make an effort.' José was beside her, grinning. Kite held her gaze for a beat, sharing the moment with her. 'Come on then!' Martha said to José, taking him by the hand. 'Lockie's useless at hiding. Let's go and get the others.'

They left the room. Kite walked around the chair, put the diary back on the desk and followed them. In his hyped-up state, he half-expected to run into Eskandarian or Abbas on the first floor, but they were not yet back from their walk. He ducked into his bedroom, left the camera on the chest of drawers and headed downstairs to the hall.

Jacqui was the last to be found, huddled with Annette's daughter at the bottom of the garden in what Xavier described as 'a clear breach of the fucking rules'. Jacqui said that she couldn't remember Kite saying anything about not hiding in the garden, to which even Martha said: 'Oh come on, Jacks' and the game ended on a slightly sour note.

'Does this mean you were the last person to be found?' José asked.

'It does,' Kite replied, ruffling his hair.

The little boy leaped up and down on the sofa in the sitting room, shouting: 'Lockie won! Lockie won!' Martha looked at Kite and murmured: 'You've made a friend for life.' Moments later there were voices outside, the polite chit-chat of Rosamund, the booming laughter of Eskandarian. José, sensing that his mother was coming back from her walk, jumped down from the

BOX 88

sofa. At lunch he had eaten two bowls of Hélène's famously rich chocolate mousse and the sugars were kicking in.

There was a rug at the end of the room which was forever shifting on the varnished floor. Martha called out: 'Careful, José' but the hurrying little boy was oblivious to her warning. Shouting, 'Mama! Mama!' he ran at full pelt towards the hall, his body at a slight angle as he turned towards the door. His left foot landed on a corner of the loose rug which slipped beneath him. José lost his balance and careered sideways, striking his head on the doorjamb.

'José!'

The impact was an awful soft thud of bone and tissue. Bita was in the hall and could hear her son's screams. Martha covered her mouth and ran towards the stricken child. Xavier said: 'Bambi on ice' and went to fetch a tea towel from the kitchen.

Bedlam ensued. Bita was hugging the frightened, screaming boy. Luc demanded to know what had happened and looked embarrassed that the accident had occurred while guests were visiting the house. Annette apologised to Bita for not keeping a closer eye on her son while Jacques stood coolly by the front door wincing at the shrieks of pain. Kite felt wretched. Out of everyone, he had spent the most time with José. It was he who had suggested the extra bowl of chocolate mousse and the game of hide-and-seek which had wound the boy up into such a state of excitement. Now he was bleeding profusely from a deep gash on his forehead, just above the hairline.

'He'll need a doctor,' said Rosamund. 'He'll have to go to hospital and have it stitched up.'

It was at this point that Eskandarian appeared at the bottom of the stairs. He had gone up to his room after returning from the walk and had heard the pandemonium from the attic. When he saw that it was José who had been hurt, he cried out: *'Non!'* and rushed towards him, enveloping Bita and the boy in a desperate, protective hug.

Xavier looked at Kite and rolled his eyes, withdrawing to the sitting room. Kite followed him.

'What was that about?' he asked. He had been surprised by the intensity of Eskandarian's reaction.

'Didn't you realise?' his friend replied, as if Kite was being stupid. 'Bita was pregnant when Ali left for Iran. José is his son.'

46

Kite was alone with Torabi. He was seated in the chair, his hands tied behind his back. He repeated what Xavier had said to him in the sitting room. He told Torabi that Eskandarian had then accompanied Bita Zamora to the hospital in Cannes. The young José had received seven stitches in his forehead, just above the hairline.

'Seven stitches,' Torabi replied blankly. 'Yes, I know.'

There was a moment between them, a span of time in which Kite's understanding of what was taking place underwent a profound and sudden change. It was like one of those paintings he would occasionally see in galleries which looked from one angle like an abstract and from another, with just a minor adjustment of perspective, like a portrait or landscape. Torabi gazed at him, his eyes momentarily stripped of all malice, and the truth broke over Kite with a startling, euphoric clarity.

'You're José,' he said. 'You're the boy.'

Torabi's expression did not change. He pulled back a clump of hair, tipped his head forward and showed Kite a pale white scar running from the top of his forehead into the hairline.

'Yes. Bita is my mother. Ali was my father.'

Everything became clear in that moment: the uneven interrogation; Torabi's occasional moments of nervousness and uncertainty; his desperate desire to know anything and everything about Eskandarian. This wasn't a state mission authorised by MOIS. Torabi wasn't following orders. This was personal.

'Why didn't you say something?' Kite asked.

'Why should I? You would only have lied in a different way.'

It was necessary for Kite to say: 'For the last time, I am not lying,' but he knew that Torabi had set a trap for him. It was not at all clear to Kite how much the Iranian remembered of that distant summer afternoon. Was it possible that he had heard the eighteen-year-old Kite in the attic office taking pictures with the Olympus Trip, the click and roll of the camera audible across the landing? Did he know more than he was letting on about what had happened to Eskandarian? Not for the first time Kite wondered if Torabi had a line into BOX 88, access to an individual who was drip-feeding him secrets.

'I wanted to listen to your memories of that day and see if they matched my own,' he said.

Kite adopted an impassive manner. 'And did they?' He remembered what he had left out of the account—the questions he had asked José in the pool, the camera he had grabbed from his room with the little boy standing beside him—details which José might possibly have remembered.

Torabi reached for the gun. He moved his head from side to side, like an athlete warming up for a sprint, and rose from the sofa.

'I remember that you were kind to me,' he said, securing the gun in the waistband of his trousers. 'I remember swimming in the pool with Martha and Jacqui. I remember the long outside table covered in food, my sister sleeping in a hammock in the garden.'

'It was a beautiful house,' Kite replied, feeling the nail slip against his hip. Throughout his long account of what had

BOX 88

happened that summer, he had dared not look down and risk drawing Torabi's eyes towards the pocket. 'It was a beautiful afternoon. Do you remember going to the hospital with your mother and father?'

Torabi crossed the room and leaned against the door.

'I didn't know he was my father until many years later.'

'When you joined the MOIS?'

To Kite's surprise, Torabi did not deny that he had been recruited by Iranian intelligence.

'My mother died when I was twenty years old,' he said. 'My stepfather had betrayed her long before that. She told me shortly before she died that Ali Eskandarian was my biological father. I didn't want to stay in Spain. I wanted to live in Iran as an Iranian. It is true that I worked for the MOIS. I no longer work for them.' Torabi paused, as if he expected Kite to applaud him for his candour. 'I was recently able to obtain some intelligence files relating to my father, but they did not provide the answers I was seeking. I decided to find out what happened for myself. So: is it true my father insisted on accompanying my mother to the hospital?'

'Everything I told you is true,' Kite replied. He was still calculating what omissions he had made that Torabi might recognise as evidence of his duplicity. 'When Abbas insisted on going to the hospital with your father, he shouted at him and ordered him to remain at the house.'

'Why?'

'Because he wanted to be alone with you? Because he didn't want Abbas knowing that he had continued to visit your mother after 1979 and that she had borne him a secret child?'

Torabi bristled at this, as Kite should have anticipated. It had been a slip. The idea of his father concealing, even denying his existence, was clearly abhorrent to him.

'What about your friend?' Torabi asked. 'Xavier?'

'What about him?'

'He was with Hana in the way you described? Did they continue to see each other after the summer?'

Of all the questions Torabi might have asked, this was the one that Kite had least anticipated. The incident at the poolhouse had helped to burnish Xavier's legend as a ladies' man when he went up to Oxford the following year, but as far as Kite knew, he had never seen nor heard from Hana again.

'Didn't you ask Xavier that in Paris? Before you killed him?'

Torabi feigned mock outrage. 'I didn't kill your friend,' he said. 'Your friend killed himself. He was dying from the moment you betrayed him in France.'

'We've been over this.' Kite stayed in character, stung by the accusation and privately conceding that it was at least partly true. Everything that went wrong in Xavier's life went wrong from that moment onwards. He said: 'I was amazed by what happened between him and Hana. I told him he was crazy, that it was a stupid risk, but they were just drunk kids looking to have a good time.'

'But she was so much older than he was,' Torabi argued. 'It is Hana who should have been more discreet, no?'

'I agree.' Kite was baffled that Torabi was so concerned about the incident. By cuckolding his father, had Xavier somehow humiliated Torabi?

'Did my father ever find out?' he asked.

'Not to my knowledge, no.'

This, too, was true. Kite had never mentioned it to him. There was a knock at the door. Kamran entered holding a piece of paper and a small bottle of Volvic, both of which he passed to Torabi. Torabi read the note, scrunched it up and let it drop to the floor.

'Where's my wife?' Kite demanded. 'What's happening out there? Was that message to do with her?'

BOX 88

He was worried that the trail had gone cold. Wherever he was being held, MI5 had not been able to locate him. The Iranian unscrewed the Evian and drank the contents in four long gulps.

'Never mind about that,' he said, dropping the bottle at his feet. It landed within a few inches of the balled-up note. He ordered Kamran to leave the room then said: 'Why did you take me to the attic?'

'Excuse me?'

It was the single flaw in Kite's account, the one anomaly in what had otherwise been a watertight version of the afternoon's events.

'Why did you want to hide in the attic?' Torabi shrugged his shoulders and frowned mockingly, as if to suggest that he had finally cornered Kite in a lie from which there was no logical escape. 'There was the whole house—the ground floor, the upstairs bedrooms. Why did we go to my father's quarters?'

Kite gambled that Torabi's memory was not as detailed nor as vivid as his own.

'Because we were playing hide-and-seek! We wanted to win. Ali—sorry, I mean your father's—rooms were a mystery to everyone in the house. Martha had never been up there. I wondered if she and Xavier would even think to look in the attic. It felt like it was out of bounds. It seemed the perfect place to hide.'

'Then why did you leave me alone?'

'I didn't leave you alone! You were a nine-year-old boy. I was trying to make sure you had fun. There were two rooms up there so it made sense for us to split up. As I remember, you were excited by the idea of being on your own. Don't you remember that?'

Torabi ignored this. 'What did you do in the opposite room?' he asked. 'What was in there?'

Kite had to be careful. If Torabi had a memory of the noise

of a camera taking pictures, if the young José had come out onto the landing and pressed his ear to the closed door or even looked through the keyhole or a gap in the frame, he was finished.

'I've already told you. It was your father's office. I had sat with him the previous afternoon telling him about Bijan.'

'So it was not a mystery to you?'

Kite shook his head, as if to suggest that Torabi was twisting his words. 'I said the attic was a mystery to Martha and Xavier, not to me. I didn't think they'd come up and look for us. They'd assume it was out of bounds.'

'You did not take photographs?'

Kite summoned a look of outrage.

'What? *Photographs*? No. Why?'

Kite looked up. Kamran seemed to understand something vital about the nature of the conversation. It felt as though the two men were suddenly going to produce some ghastly rabbit out of a hat which would expose every lie and double-cross Kite had worked so hard to conjure.

'It is what a spy would do,' Torabi said quietly.

'Is it? Take a risk like that while playing a game of hide-and-seek with a little boy? An eighteen-year-old waiting for his A-level results? I don't think so.'

Kite still did not know with any degree of certainty whether or not José had heard the noise of the camera. Perhaps he had, but now had no recollection of it. Perhaps Xavier had told him something about Kite's mysterious, emerging passion for photography that summer which had led Torabi to draw the obvious conclusion.

'So you just hid in the room? Behind the chair? On your own?'

'No, I was in there with Bono and Meryl Streep. Yes! I was on my own. What else was I supposed to be doing? Making a cup of tea?'

To Kite's surprise, Torabi appeared to accept this. He

BOX 88

nodded at Kamran, issued an order in Farsi and the chauffeur left the room.

'When did you find out that Eskandarian was your father?' Kite asked. He wanted to try to regain control of the conversation.

'You don't ask the questions. I ask the questions.'

'Fine,' he replied. 'So go ahead and ask.'

'Was it true, your description of my father's reaction? When I cut my head? That he embraced me, he embraced my mother?'

Kite finally saw what it was all about. Absent fathers. Absent love. A missing life. Torabi was on a mission of revenge against the people who had betrayed Ali Eskandarian. If Kite could persuade him that he understood that, that he had played no part in what had happened to his father, he might yet survive.

'It's all true,' he said, playing on the Iranian's sentimentality. 'He loved you very much, Ramin. Should I call you Ramin or do you prefer José?'

'You call me Ramin. That is my name now.'

Kite continued, improvising: 'Knowing what I know about fathers and sons, he must have hated the fact that another man was raising you as his own. What happened to your mother's husband, by the way? Is he still alive? He didn't come that day.'

'Don't fucking patronise me.' Torabi's patience had suddenly snapped. 'You think I'm stupid? You think I can't see through you?'

Kite tried to respond, pulling at the bonds on his hands, but Torabi shouted him down, crossing the room.

'You're a trained liar. You pretend to be the innocent man, but you were the snake in that house, the rat betraying your friends. Does Martha Raine know who you are? When I get to her, when I find her in New York, will she tell me who Lachlan Kite really was?'

'You leave Martha alone.'

Torabi came to within a foot of Kite's chair and screamed

into his face: 'Who was my father?! Was he the man you say he was?!'

His spittle was all over Kite's face. Kite tried to wipe it off on his shoulder but could barely touch it with his jaw. He spat on the ground to clear the saliva from his mouth.

'What's the point?' he said. Torabi backed away. 'You think I'm lying. You think I'm making things up—'

The Iranian turned again, shouting.

'Was he a terrorist? Tell me!' Kamran burst into the room, but Torabi screamed at him to leave. 'Did he betray my country?' His face was flushed with angry despair. 'Was my father a murderer? Was he?'

'What are you talking about?' Kite was worried by how much Torabi potentially knew. Surely it wasn't possible that somebody had sold him the files on Eskandarian? 'Your father was the man I have described,' he said. 'How could he have been a terrorist? How could he have betrayed Iran?' He saw that Torabi's need for answers was not in any dimension political. It was personal, a question of family honour. 'Your father loved you,' he said. 'I saw it with my own eyes.'

'Did you know what was going to happen to him? To Luc?'

Again Kite thought of the files, of the deeper truth about Eskandarian, but he concealed this from Torabi, saying only: 'Of course I didn't. You're very confused, Ramin. Let me tell you what happened, at least from my point of view. Let me tell you what I came to understand after everything was over. Perhaps I can put your mind at rest.'

The Iranian was breathing heavily. He abruptly sat down on the sofa, looking around for more water.

'The note,' he said, indicating the balled-up piece of paper on the floor.

'What about it?' said Kite.

'Hossein contacted me when he reached your village. He will call again in one hour. You have this time to answer the last of

BOX 88

my questions and to tell me the truth about my father. Sixty minutes. No more.' Torabi tapped his head and nodded ominously. 'I have remembered everything you have told me so far. I am comparing it with what I already know. If anything else in your account is out of place, if I suspect again that you have misled me, you will not leave this room alive.'

47

The raid was on.

Jason turned towards CARPENTER, cocked his weapon to chamber a round and started jogging towards the road. Cara heard the order on comms.

'STONES, KAISER, we're mobile. See you in the house.'

She walked into the barn and stood behind Wal and Fred. Rita was beside her, staring at the laptop screens. Cara kept thinking about the photograph of Hillary and Obama watching the bin Laden raid in the White House. Their own surroundings seemed absurd by comparison: a filthy farmyard, a disused barn, drizzle falling in the English night.

People were going to die in front of her. The camera on Jason's helmet would be a second-by-second snuff movie playing out in real time. What she was about to see was what had been happening in Iraq and Afghanistan, in Syria and Somalia, since she was a young girl. It was just another operation to Jason and CARPENTER, just another gig for KAISER and STONES. To Cara, it was both shocking and extraordinarily exciting.

She could already make out the front door of the cottage,

BOX 88

the paint blue-black in the infra-red lens of Jason's camera. There was a sequence of clicks like Morse code. STONES and KAISER blew the back door with plastic explosives a split second after Jason and CARPENTER came through the front. Wal was feeding live positional information on comms as Cara heard a quiet burst of gunfire and saw a glowing body drop to the ground in the living room. Jason shouted, 'Isobel! Get behind me!' and a second figure, surely Kite's wife, moved forward and disappeared to the right of the screen. Simultaneously the helmet camera moved fractionally to the left and a second Iranian dropped to the floor in a slow, dayglo blur of gunfire.

'Two left,' said Rita, her voice preternaturally calm.

There was a gentle tap-tap, soft as a child blowing through a straw, and a third man slumped against a wall inside the house. He had been shot in the head and chest. The helmet cam on STONES showed a fourth Iranian coming down from the first floor, shouting threateningly, as all the others had shouted. STONES took him out and he fell to the bottom of the stairs.

It was already over. Jason continued to snap commands, the helmet camera showing doors opened, cupboards searched, rooms cleared of threats. STONES and KAISER went back up the stairs and did the same, kicking open the bathroom door and bursting into a second bedroom. Cara heard Jason say, 'Location secured,' but they all knew that it had ended once the fourth man had been killed on the stairs. CARPENTER had taken Isobel outside and was walking her towards the barn. Cara could see shaky footage of the lane from his helmet cam. Rita patted Wal and Fred on the back, said, 'Good job, lads,' and turned away from the screens. She indicated to Cara that she should follow her.

They went out onto the road. Cara was surprised by what

she found. Kite's wife was not shaking. She was not in tears. The American soldier was with her, but he was not supporting her on his arm nor calling for immediate medical assistance. Isobel looked tired, unquestionably, but there were otherwise no outward signs that she had been affected by the nightmare she had just endured. Her face was unmarked, and she was moving normally. If Cara hadn't known differently, she might have assumed that Kite's wife had gone for an evening stroll along the lane and was making her way back from the shops after buying a pint of milk.

'Isobel,' said Rita quietly. They embraced. CARPENTER looked at Cara and dropped his eyes, as if they were witness to a private moment that did not concern them. Cara could see that they knew one another well.

'Thank you, Rita.' Isobel wiped her mouth with her sleeve as she stood back. 'How long have you been out here? God almighty, that was horrible.'

Cara could see that she was in shock, but at the same time capable of functioning normally. She was beautiful in a healthy, big-boned, Scandinavian way, what her mother would have called a 'handsome woman'.

'This is Cara,' said Rita. 'She's been helping us.'

'Did they hurt you?' Cara asked.

'I'm fine,' Isobel replied, smiling warmly.

'And the baby?' Rita asked.

Isobel tapped her belly and said: 'He's fine. Where's Lockie? What's happening? Is he all right?'

Rita didn't dress it up, didn't say that everything was going to be all right and that Isobel had nothing to worry about. She told her the truth.

'We think he's being held by a group of rogue Iranian intelligence officers somewhere in Canary Wharf. They wanted to scare him, so they took you. You're free now. What do you need? Can we get you to a doctor?'

BOX 88

In normal circumstances, Cara reflected, the area would have been sealed off and the road swarming in cops and ambulances. But these were not normal circumstances. BOX 88 had barely made any sound, no song and dance, had raided the house and got the job done.

'I'm just tired,' Isobel insisted. 'We need to help Lockie.'

'That's what we're trying to do,' Rita told her. 'We're hoping the men in the house can lead us to him.'

48

The injury to José and the very public flare-up between Eskandarian and Abbas changed the atmosphere of the afternoon and brought the Bonnard lunch party to a premature end. Jacques left within ten minutes, Paul and Annette following soon afterwards.

'Is it true José is Ali's son?' Kite asked Luc. They were standing at the entrance to the terrace, within range of the Walkman.

Xavier's father cast a venomous admonishing glance at his son, as if he had breached a confidence by telling Kite. 'That's a private matter.'

Kite, duly reprimanded, picked up the Walkman and his copy of *The Songlines* and went upstairs to his room. He was carrying a packet of cigarettes in his back pocket. He took the tape out of the Walkman and put it in a drawer where it lay among several other blank cassettes and various Gameboy cartridges. In the morning he would take it to Peele, along with the rolls of film. He opened the shutters and laid a red T-shirt on the windowsill. Kite then grabbed a pen and a piece of paper and locked himself in the bathroom. He noticed that Abbas's door was closed and assumed that he was sulking after the dressing-down from Eskandarian. He did not give him another thought.

BOX 88

He sat on the toilet seat, tore the piece of paper in half and wrote the note using a Biro, balancing the Chatwin on his knee as a surface to lean on. Peele had taught him how to make his handwriting so small that it was almost illegible.

AE has son (9). José. Mother is 79. Fiancée: Bita Zamora.
Lives in Sarrià, with politician husband. Daughter Ada (3).
Other guests: Jacques (banker, Paris, c55). Serious, intellectual. Friend of LB.
Paul Mouret (film industry, Paris, c35).
PM didn't know AE or Jacques before today. Knows LB well. Not RB.
Wife Annette Mouret, also c35. 2 kids. Have photos.
Document in AE office mentions Forman/Foreman + Berberian. Have photos.

Kite wrote on both sides then folded the note twice so that it was the same size as a large postage stamp. He picked up the cigarettes and inserted the note behind the paper lining at the back of the packet. To the untrained eye, it would be impossible to tell that the packet had been tampered with. He threw the other half of the notepaper into the toilet, flushed it and went back to his room. Abbas's door was now open. There was no sign of him. Kite had been concentrating so hard on writing and concealing the note that he had not heard him leave.

He carried the Chatwin downstairs, passed Luc and Rosamund in the sitting room and walked outside with a lighter, the Biro and the packet of cigarettes in his back pocket. He could hear Xavier and Jacqui messing around in the pool. Kite's swimming trunks were on the table near the entrance to the terrace. He went back inside, picked them up, then walked through the garden in the direction of the pool. He was in a state of vivid concentration, akin to the feeling of batting against a moving ball, completely focussed and yet at the same time oddly free. Kite was drawing on his training but hardly aware of doing so.

Halfway to the pool, he turned sharply left and took the path towards the orchard at the northern end of the garden. Kite could still hear Xavier shouting and splashing around in the pool but had seen nobody else since leaving the house. He reached the wall which formed a boundary between the Bonnard villa and the access road, took out a cigarette and turned to face the house. There was nobody in sight. The wall was six feet high. It was covered in jagged, protruding shards of coloured glass sunk into a layer of weathered concrete. Kite had been here only once before, walking the gardens with Xavier on the first day. As casually as possible, he tossed the swimming trunks, the Chatwin and the packet of Marlboros on top of the wall, then turned around to light the cigarette.

He began to smoke in what he hoped would look to any passing member of the household like a moody teenager taking time out with his troubles, pondering the mysteries of the universe and the vagaries of solitude at the bottom of a French garden. As far as Kite could tell, he was alone, yet it felt as though he was being watched from some hidden corner of the garden, perhaps by Alain or the always suspecting Abbas. A gecko slipped up the wall a few inches from his feet, causing Kite to start. He stepped back. The tip of the cigarette brushed against the leaves of an olive tree and he had to relight it.

Kite continued to smoke the cigarette, telling himself that it was all just a question of hanging around near the wall, killing time, looking natural to anyone who might come past or spot him. The ground floor of the house was more than a hundred metres away, screened by trees. Kite could see the window of Xavier's room on the first floor, Eskandarian's attic bedroom above it. He reached up and took down the book, opening it halfway through. He leaned with his back against the tree, extinguishing the cigarette in a pile of loose earth and dried leaves. Kite could see ants on the ground and knew it would only be a matter of time before they climbed onto his espadrilles and started marching up his legs. Nevertheless he pretended to concentrate on *The Songlines*, reading the same paragraph several times and even marking a passage in the margin ('Life is a bridge. Cross

BOX 88

over it, but build no house on it.') for the benefit of anyone who might be watching him. After five minutes of this masquerade, he stood up, brushed off his legs and lifted the swimming trunks from the top of the wall. A corner of the material had snagged on the glass, but they did not tear as Kite pulled them free. He walked back towards the house, leaving the packet of cigarettes behind him as if he had forgotten it.

He had reached an enclosed, shaded walkway in the garden and was turning towards the swimming pool when Abbas suddenly appeared in front of him, blocking his path. Startled and afraid, Kite stepped back. There was a small, weathered bench to one side of the pergola on which Abbas must have been sitting.

'Jesus, you gave me a fright,' he said.

'Lockie,' Abbas murmured in acknowledgement.

Had he been watching him? Had he cottoned on to the ruse with the book and the swimming trunks?

'Having a siesta?' Kite asked. 'Sorry if I disturbed you.'

'You don't disturb me.'

'Is Ali not back from the hospital?' He knew that it was far too soon for José to have been treated, but couldn't think of anything else to say. 'That was a nasty cut.'

Abbas wasn't in the habit of speaking unless he had to. He merely grunted at Kite and sat down on the bench. His hair was greasy, the collar of his white shirt dirty and frayed. Kite had a sudden image of him creeping around the New York subway, weighing up which stations to target, checking out air vents.

'I'm going for a swim,' Kite told him.

'You have cigarette?'

It was as if Kite's heart had caught on a fragment of glass. He managed to say: 'Sorry, no, smoked my last one.'

Abbas patted the pockets of his suit jacket in a pantomime of frustration. Was he toying with Kite or was the request for a cigarette a genuine, if grim coincidence?

'Never mind,' he said.

'Xavier will have a Marlboro,' Kite told him. 'Come to the pool. Or I can fetch you one?'

His mind was racing. Should he go back to the wall and grab the packet, pretending to have forgotten it? No, he couldn't do that. It might already have been taken by Peele or Carl.

'It's OK,' the Iranian replied. 'I can wait.'

His words sounded loaded with menace. Kite knew that he should walk on, that it was pointless to hang around trying to act natural. Besides he could not be sure that Abbas was genuinely suspicious of him. Even if he had seen him reading and smoking by the wall, Kite was certain that he had carried off the dead drop with faultless precision. The cigarettes had been bundled in with the book and the swimming trunks. He had looked like someone grabbing ten minutes of peace and quiet at the end of a hectic afternoon. That was it. No reason to panic. He must hold his nerve.

'I'll leave you in peace,' he said. 'Watch out for mosquitoes.' Abbas shrugged, as if it was the mosquitoes who should watch out for him. 'See you later.'

Kite walked off clutching the swimming trunks and the Chatwin, reaching the pool to find Xavier and Jacqui in the water. Martha was sunbathing on the patch of ground where two days earlier they had made love. When she saw Kite, she sat up and waved.

'Where have you been?' she asked.

'Having a smoke, reading,' he said. He was sick with the fear that Abbas was already at the wall, pulling down the packet of cigarettes, finding the note. 'What's going on?'

Xavier surfaced in the deep end and said: 'Oh, hi. Fancy going into Mougins?'

'Sure.' Kite knew that his friend was low on alcohol and wanted to stock up. He turned to Martha. 'Come with us?'

BOX 88

'Love to,' she replied. 'I want to take more photos. But have a swim first, Lockie. The water's beautiful.'

Half an hour later, Xavier rode into Mougins on the Vespa. Rosamund offered to give Martha, Jacqui and Kite a lift. She told them that Abbas had made a phone call from the house, then driven off in the Audi, presumably to collect Eskandarian from the hospital. Kite could not help worrying that he had discovered the note and was raising the alarm. When he came back to the house, would Abbas and Eskandarian be waiting for him, Luc and Rosamund beside them, shaking their heads in stunned disbelief at the depths of his treachery? The thought made him feel nauseous.

They met Xavier at the café in the village square. He had already been to the supermarket and bought a Johnnie Walker and a replacement bottle of Smirnoff. Jacqui said nothing, even when the bottles clinked together as Xavier set them down on the ground.

'Well that was weird,' he said.

'What was?' Martha asked.

'Saw Abbas with a man on my way up to Carrefour. Acting strangely.'

A sensation of pure fear coursed through Kite.

'What do you mean "acting strangely"?' he said.

'Just that. He was sitting in a parked car with another bloke.'

'Maybe he's made friends in the local area,' Jacqui suggested. Both Xavier and Martha laughed at her apparent naivety. Kite was too shocked to join in.

'What were they doing?' he asked.

Xavier casually waved the waiter over and ordered a vodka and tonic. Waiting for him to answer was like watching a bullet travelling towards him in slow motion.

'I only saw them for a minute or two, at the traffic lights,' he said. 'Looked like they were having an argument, a heated debate about something.'

'Weird,' said Martha.

'Maybe Abbas is secretly gay,' Xavier suggested, lighting a cigarette. He put on a cod Middle Eastern accent. 'Are you friend of Dorothy, mister? Do you drop anchor in Poo Bay?'

'Xav, that's disgusting!' said Jacqui, and glanced over at Martha for support.

'What did he look like?' Kite asked. He felt completely removed from their joshing, as if Martha and Jacqui were sitting at a neighbouring table talking to someone else.

'I dunno,' Xavier replied. He was wearing Top Gun Ray-Bans. He took them off and polished the lenses on a napkin. Kite wanted to tear them out of his hands and plead with him to answer. Eventually he put the sunglasses back on, picked up his cigarette and said: 'About the same age as Abbas. Weird lip.'

'Weird lip?' Kite instantly thought of Bijan.

'Yeah. Why you so keen to know? Putting together a Photofit?'

Martha looked at Kite as though she also wanted an answer to that question.

'Sorry, I'm just wondering if it's the same guy who came up to me in Cannes after lunch.'

'What guy?' Martha asked.

'Nothing,' Kite replied quickly. He had only spoken to Peele and Eskandarian about his encounter with Bijan. 'Just this bloke who cornered me in a café in Cannes and started banging on about Iran. He was roughly the same age as Abbas. Had a hare lip.'

'Curly hair too?' said Xavier, intrigued.

Kite knew then that Abbas had been speaking to Bijan. It was as though he had been hit with an electric shock. He managed to say: 'Yeah, curly black hair. Must have been the same guy.'

Martha was staring at him. She could tell that Kite was distracted by something. She said: 'Are you OK?' and put her

BOX 88

hand on his arm. At the same time, Kite experienced a wave of relief, realising that if Abbas had found the note in the packet of cigarettes, he would surely have driven straight to Eskandarian, not into Mougins to meet Bijan. But why was Eskandarian's personal bodyguard arguing with a member of an exile group targeting Iranian VIPs in France? Had Bijan been setting a trap for him all along? Worse still, was Abbas conspiring to have his boss assassinated? Kite was bewildered. He felt that he could not answer these questions without speaking to Peele. Should he write a second note and leave it on the orchard wall or trust that BOX had witnessed the meeting and knew what to do?

'I'm fine,' he told Martha, but he could see that she was confused.

'Why would he be talking to you one day, then Abbas this afternoon?' she asked. It was the question to which Kite had no clear answer. Perhaps his initial theory had been correct: Abbas and Bijan were working together to investigate Kite. Bijan was not an exile, but part of Eskandarian's entourage. Yet that contradicted Peele's assertion that Bijan was a threat.

'God knows,' he replied.

'Is he following us?' Jacqui asked.

'Don't be stupid,' said Xavier. 'Of course he's not!'

Jacqui told him not to be so condescending and punched him on the arm. Xavier responded by grabbing her wrist and giving her a Chinese burn. The conversation collapsed as the siblings bickered back and forth, drawing disapproving stares from neighbouring tables. Martha put the fire out by asking Kite and Xavier when their A-level results were due. That took them into a ten-minute conversation about gap years and university applications, at the end of which Martha announced that she wanted to walk home and take some photographs. She picked up her camera bag, took the Nikon out and hung it around her neck.

'Come with me?' she asked Kite.

Xavier and Jacqui looked at one another but said nothing.

'You guys can go back together on the Vespa,' Kite suggested.

'It's OK, Mum's coming to pick me up,' Jacqui replied.

Kite put a fifty-franc note on the table for the drinks. Xavier immediately gave it back to him, saying it was far too much.

'My treat,' he said. 'You lovebirds enjoy yourselves.'

Jacqui made a noise at the back of her throat and their bickering started up again. Kite and Martha walked away, saying they would see them back at home.

As soon as they were out of sight of the café, Kite reached for Martha's hand and they kissed. Later, walking out of the village, he told her in more detail about the meeting with Bijan. She was appalled by many of the things Bijan had said, and they talked in general about their opinion of Eskandarian. Martha thought that he was fun and clever, respectful towards her and not sexist or patronising, which was often the default position of older men when they interacted with her. She found it hard to believe that charming, friendly Ali was an adviser to a regime that meted out the kinds of punishments and restrictions Bijan had described. Kite thought about Abbas in New York, of the rumours linking Eskandarian to the slaughterers of Pan Am 103. He wanted to tell Martha everything, not least because he was still bewildered by the nature of the meeting between Abbas and Bijan and would have liked to get her take on it. But that option simply wasn't available to him. Strawson's warning sounded in Kite's mind: *We sure as shit don't need you with your head up your ass the next two weeks.* To be with Martha was to find respite from the constant stress and double-think of his new existence. That morning, in bed with her, it was as though Strawson and Peele and the entire crazy operation had never been conceived. Kite had felt that he might somehow walk out of her room and it would just be a beautiful summer day in France, two people falling in love with nothing to worry about except what book to read, what clothes to wear, what music to listen to. Then he had been pulled back into duplicity,

BOX 88

deceiving Martha—deceiving all of them—with his ploys and schemes around José. Kite relished the adrenalising risks of his new existence, but had already recognised that it could not last forever. He would inevitably burn out. Either he would continue to see Martha and stop working for Peele and Strawson, or their relationship would have to end and he would dedicate himself to BOX 88. There was no alternative, no way to juggle his split lives if Martha was not to be compromised.

After half an hour they reached the access road, a mile or so from home. It was almost seven o'clock. A sudden cool wind came in from the south, rattling the leaves on the olive trees. The cicadas were briefly silenced.

'Vent du sud,' said Martha.

'What's that?'

'Means it's going to rain,' she said.

They looked up at the darkening sky. There were no clouds, no stars. Just the cool wind and the distant cry of a wood pigeon.

Then, a moped. At first Kite thought it was Xavier coming back from Mougins, but he saw the light of a bike coming down the hill towards them from the north. Martha was taking the lens cap off her camera. Kite had walked a few metres ahead of her. He reached into his back pocket for a cigarette and turned to see what had caught her eye. Martha was crouched down, both hands on the Nikon, pulling focus on something in the distance. The moped was about to pass them.

Kite stepped onto the verge to give it the road. He saw that someone was riding pillion behind the driver. Both were wearing helmets. From the size of the bike and the pitch of the engine, Kite understood that it wasn't a moped, but something larger, faster. The bike slowed down as it came towards him, as if the driver wanted to stop and say hello. But he went past—Kite was sure it was a man—then slowed almost to a halt beside Martha.

Her camera bag was on the ground. The passenger riding pillion leaned over and scooped it up, like a polo player striking the ball. Before Kite could react, the motorbike had screamed off, throwing up a spume of dust and stones.

'No!' Martha shouted.

Kite tried to give chase, but it was pointless. The driver was already fifty metres away, sixty, accelerating into the distance.

'Jesus Christ, that was all my films, my lenses, everything!'

Kite knew with sickening fury that BOX had carried out the theft.

'Every photo I've taken since I got to France. My other camera. Wankers!'

She shouted into the valley, stunned by what had happened. Kite put his arm around her, but it was no comfort. He knew they had wanted the pictures from lunch, from Cannes, from every moment Martha had been at the villa.

'We can call the police,' he said, fighting an urge to go straight to the safe house and to confront Peele face to face.

'Did you get a number plate?' she asked.

Kite was embarrassed to admit that he had not even thought to look. 'We should still go to the police,' he said.

'What's the point? I'll never get it back.'

'Maybe they'll dump the bag when they see there's no money in there. Nothing of value. Maybe they'll just take the backup camera.'

Even this was a lie, sowing false hope in Martha that would never come good. She was standing at the edge of the road in a state of dazed rage.

'Are you insured?' Kite asked.

'Fuck no,' she said contemptuously. 'Who has travel insurance, Lockie?' It was the first time she had lost her temper with him. 'No, it's done. They're gone. My whole summer holiday. Fuck.'

There was nothing for it but to walk back to the house and tell the others. Luc was incensed, said it was 'probably Arabs', and insisted on calling the police. They told him that Martha would have to come into Mougins to file a report. Martha said

BOX 88

that she was resigned to never seeing the bag or the rolls of film again. Kite didn't bother trying to change her mind. He made a promise to himself to buy her a new camera.

'I'm so sorry,' he said, touching her neck as they sat on the terrace before dinner. 'It's such bad luck.'

'Don't worry,' she replied, turning and kissing him on the forehead. 'It's not your fault, Lockie. It's not your fault.'

Kite knew differently. All night he privately raged at Carl and Peele. He wondered if Strawson had come back from wherever he had been and ordered the theft. From an operational perspective, Kite could see why Martha's photographs might be of value to BOX: she had taken dozens of pictures of Ali, of Abbas and Luc, of Jacques, José and Bita. They would be useful additions to the Eskandarian files and to the pictures Kite had taken in the office which he had yet to give them. But essential? Surely they hadn't *needed* the photos? Perhaps it was Strawson's way of reminding Kite that the operation was more important than Martha.

Eskandarian returned from the hospital at around eight o'clock, driven back by Abbas. Nobody said anything about seeing Abbas in the car with Bijan. José had been given seven stitches in his forehead and was now resting with his mother in a hotel room in Cannes. The accident and the theft of the photographs caused a veil of gloom to descend on dinner, until Martha reassured everyone that she was fine, that she was still having the best summer of her life and raised a glass to her hosts, catching Kite's eye as she did so. Still boiling with anger, Kite wandered down the drive with Xavier, ostensibly to smoke a cigarette, but in truth wondering if Abbas was parked in the lay-by and therefore blocking any chance he might have of later going to the safe house. Sure enough, the bodyguard was sitting in the Audi smoking a cigarette. Kite checked the walls on either side of the gate, as he always did, to see if they had been marked in chalk. There was nothing on them.

'All right, man?' Xavier asked, waving at Abbas.

The Iranian nodded, keeping the window closed.

'Miserable bastard,' Xavier whispered. 'Here's a question.' He turned back to the house. 'You're forced to live on a desert island with Ted Bundy, Jumpy Jones-Lewis or Abbas. Everyone else is dead. Who do you choose?'

'Ted Bundy,' said Kite.

It had occurred to him that his friend had no knowledge nor understanding of the threat from the exile community and therefore no concept of the seriousness of Abbas's meeting with Bijan. For the second time he wondered if he should write a note to Peele and leave it on the orchard wall. With Abbas in the car, there was less risk that he might be seen.

'Got any of that whisky?' Kite asked.

'Sure,' Xavier replied. 'Let's drink it down by the pool.'

They lit a mosquito coil and sat looking out at the mountains as a storm rumbled in the distance. Kite opted to wait until the morning before confronting Peele: there was no safe way to get to the orchard and leave a note without it looking suspicious to Xavier or Martha. Nor could he get past Abbas and visit the safe house. Best to deal with everything later. With Leonard Cohen on Strawson's ghetto blaster, they talked for almost an hour by the pool, Xavier finally asking Kite what was happening with Martha. Never happy talking about his private life, Kite ducked the question and said only that they were having a good time. Xavier reached for the bottle, poured himself another two inches of whisky and said: 'Nothing wrong with that.' It was perhaps his way of saying that he understood Kite's need for privacy.

Just when they were on the point of going back to the house to find the girls, Kite heard Luc and Eskandarian talking in the garden. It sounded as though they were fifty metres away, somewhere close to the bench where Kite had earlier been confronted by Abbas.

BOX 88

'Sounds like Ali and Papa,' said Xavier, turning around in his deckchair. He had been drinking steadily since the café in Mougins and was already halfway through the Johnnie Walker. 'Ali Papa,' he slurred drunkenly. 'Ali Papa and his forty thieves.'

The voices of the two men became louder, not because they were drawing closer, but because they were clearly having an argument. Kite heard Luc swear in French. He remembered what Eskandarian had said in the office: *Luc, as you know, is a businessman with a wealth of experience. We are old friends. We talk candidly.* It sounded as though the Iranian was trying to reason with him.

'The chickens are coming home to roost,' Xavier declared. 'This was bound to happen.'

'What do you mean?' Kite asked.

'Business thing,' he replied. 'Don't understand it. Something's happened.'

'What business are they in?' Kite wondered if the Falcons had a directional microphone aimed at the garden under cover of darkness.

'Import-export,' Xavier replied, sounding as if he knew more but didn't want to breach his father's confidence. 'More whisky?'

The argument continued for another minute or so. It sounded to Kite as though Eskandarian was apologising to Luc, but that his entreaties were falling on deaf ears. There was silence. He assumed that one, or both of them, had gone back to the house.

'Sounds like that's that,' said Xavier. 'Night night, sleep tight, don't let the bed bugs bite.'

'What's going on?'

It was Jacqui. She had emerged with Martha from beneath the fallen branches of the palm tree. Kite had been too distracted by the argument to notice their approach.

'Thought you guys were in bed,' said Xavier.

'We got stuck in the garden. Dad was having a massive row with Ali. Did you hear?'

'No, we're both completely deaf and couldn't hear a thing.' Xavier rolled his eyes. 'Of course we heard it!'

'All right, all right, smart arse,' said Jacqui and pulled her dress over her head. She was wearing a bikini. 'We're going swimming. Want to get in or are you too pissed?'

'Too pissed,' said Xavier. 'And knackered. I'm off to bed.'

'I'll come,' said Kite. Martha was stepping out of a skirt.

'Great,' said Jacqui. 'Leave me with the lovebirds.'

It began to rain. Grumbling about getting wet, Xavier left the bottle of whisky beside his chair, whispered a slurred 'Enjoy yourselves' and walked back towards the house. Jacqui swam for only a few minutes before announcing that she was 'freezing' and hurrying back to the villa in a towel.

'That's why I love her,' said Martha, the rain beginning to fall more heavily. 'She wasn't cold. She just wanted to leave us together.'

Kite lifted her towards him. He was amazed by her weightlessness in the water; it was the first time he had ever held a woman in such a way.

'You feeling a bit better?' he asked.

She scrunched up her face.

'Still annoyed,' she said. 'So sad to lose those pictures. Your breath stinks of whisky.'

'Have some then,' said Kite, and got out of the pool to grab the Johnnie Walker. They stood in the water up to their waists drinking from the bottle as the rain ran down their faces and bounced on the tiles around the pool. Later they slipped back into the house and went to Martha's bedroom. Only when she was asleep, almost three hours later, did Kite head back to his own room. Xavier's light was still on and his door ajar, so he knocked quietly and went inside.

His friend had fallen asleep in his clothes. A bottle of Smirnoff had tipped over beside him, soaking an old Turkish rug and a copy of the *Herald Tribune*. A cigarette had burned down to the

BOX 88

filter in his hand. Kite took the cigarette and threw it in the bin. The smell of alcohol on Xavier's breath was the smell of his father, passed out in the living room when Kite was still a child. The vodka bottle was half-empty. He prised it from Xavier's grasp, screwed on the cap and put it on the bedside table. Kite then pulled his groaning, mumbling friend out of his clothes, lifted him in his boxer shorts onto the bed and covered him with a sheet. He thought of his mother, of all the nights when she had put Paddy to bed in this way, the unutterable sadness and fury of dealing with a drunk.

Wrapping the newspaper and the bottle of vodka inside the rug, Kite opened the door and carried it back to his room, moving as quietly as he could. Abbas's door was open, but he was not inside. The sun was rising, the dawn perfectly still. Kite closed his bedroom door, stuffed the rug in the cupboard and set the alarm for nine. Knowing that he would be groggy when he woke up, he retrieved the rolls of film and the Walkman cassette from his chest of drawers, put them inside his running shoes and sat on the bed.

This is what happens to the people closest to me, he thought. *They become alcoholics.* He had been so distracted by his work for BOX 88 that he had not even stopped to notice that his closest friend was slipping deeper and deeper into addiction, drinking quantities of alcohol at eighteen that his father had drunk as a grown man of thirty-five. It felt like a double betrayal: not only to spy in Xavier's home, but to ignore his descent into misery.

Try as he might, Kite could not sleep. He lay on the bed, his mind turning over, until at last the clock ticked past eight o'clock and he knew that there was no time left to rest. Having showered and changed into his running gear, he put the rolls of film in the pockets of his shorts, then wearily slipped the cassette in his Walkman and looped the headphones around his neck like a noose.

Luc was waiting for him at the bottom of the stairs.

49

'Lockie!'

Xavier's father was wearing trainers, a pair of khaki shorts, a McEnroe headband and a plain white T-shirt. He looked like a man playing a role for his own private amusement. There was something profoundly unsettling at the sight of him.

'Thought I would join you on your morning run.' He tapped his stomach. 'Rosamund says that with all this food and no exercise, I am developing a beer belly. Is that correct? Is that what you call it?'

'A beer belly, yes,' Kite replied. It was clearly a lie. Xavier's father kept himself in exceptional physical condition and was probably fitter than half the boys at Alford. 'But you look well. You've been swimming a lot, working in the garden.'

Kite needed to persuade Luc out of joining him on the run; if he came, it would be impossible to visit Peele. But it was a forlorn hope: Luc was changed and ready, hopping up and down in the hall like a football player waiting in the tunnel before a big game. He knew something about Kite's hidden life. It was obvious. There was a constant glimmer of suspicion in his cheery gaze.

'So how far do we go?' he asked.

BOX 88

Kite had never been further than half a mile. He knew nothing of the surrounding countryside, no route around the hills.

'I usually just keep going until I get tired,' he said, moving towards the front door. Out of the corner of his eye he saw Abbas in the kitchen. He was eating breakfast, staring at them, listening to every word. 'Do you do much jogging back in London?'

'Sometimes in Paris,' Luc replied. Kite had a mental image of Luc running through the Bois de Boulogne alongside a pig-tailed, giggling mistress half his age. 'So let's go!'

Kite said that there was now no point in taking his Walkman. He went back to his room, threw it on the bed, put the roll of film in the drawer and returned to the hall. He did not know when, if ever, he would have the chance to get the film to BOX. Meanwhile, Luc was outside, doing squat thrusts beneath the lime tree. The idea of going through the motions of a forty-minute run, of passing the safe house and not being able to go in, was not just frustrating; it felt to Kite as though he was being led into a trap. He wished that he could turn round and go back upstairs, but desperately wanted to know what had motivated Luc to accompany him on his run.

'OK, let's go!' he said, as if Kite was a personal trainer and he was paying him by the hour. 'You lead the way!'

They set off down the drive. Kite hadn't warmed up properly and his knee immediately started to ache. At the gates he paused and told Luc that he needed to stretch.

Near the bottom of the wall, as clear as day, was a four-inch line drawn in white chalk, the signal from Peele to make contact.

They were back at the house within half an hour. There had been no sinister reason why Luc had decided to go for a jog, no hidden agenda in his desire to accompany Kite. Or so it seemed. Though Kite tried to talk to him, Xavier's father remained monosyllabic throughout, very obviously testing his fitness against a young man almost thirty years his junior. Back at the house, Kite leaning on his knees and gasping for breath, Luc made a point of drawing himself up to his full height, puffing out his chest and saying: 'I thought you did this every day?' Kite played the gracious, admiring underling, flattering Luc's vanity by telling him that he had the heart and lungs of a professional athlete. That seemed to satisfy him. He went back into the house preening like a matador taking the applause of the crowd after a kill. Kite stumbled back to his room, tired and paranoid, and decided that there was only one way left open to him to contact Peele.

After taking a shower and eating breakfast, he asked Rosamund if he could phone his mother to find out about his A-level results. She thought that was a marvellous idea and told Kite to send Cheryl her love. Dialling the number felt like an act of surrender. He pictured Carl at the safe house, beckoning Peele towards him as he listened on the line, drawing a hand across his throat to indicate that Kite had hit the wall.

The number his mother had given him rang out until it was picked up by an answering machine. Kite did what he had been trained to do.

'Mum, hi, it's me, calling from France. Just wondering if you've heard anything about my results? Also, have there been any letters from the University of Edinburgh? I'm waiting for them to write to me. Give me a call. Hope everything's OK with you. Lots of love.'

He would have liked to have spoken to her, to hear his mother's voice. She probably wouldn't have wanted to know much about France or Martha, but by speaking to her, Kite might at least have been able to forge some kind of connection with his old self, however briefly. He hung up and realised that he had said nothing about the holiday, hadn't given the number of the villa or any indication when he would be back home. Eskandarian, Rosamund and Luc had all been in the kitchen as he made the call, well within earshot of the sitting room. Kite wondered if he should call back and leave the number but didn't want to

BOX 88

sound amateur to the eavesdropping Falcons. Xavier came into the sitting room looking surprisingly well-rested and beckoned him onto the terrace.

'What happened last night?' he whispered, closing the door behind him.

'You passed out,' Kite replied.

'Did Mum see?'

'I don't think so. It was very late. They were asleep.'

'Did you take off my clothes?'

'Yeah, but nothing happened. You weren't in the mood.'

Xavier made a face. 'Very funny.' He grabbed Kite on the shoulder and squeezed the muscle. 'Thanks, mate. What happened to the bottle?'

'Stuffed it in the cupboard in my room with the rug. What do I do with them?'

Xavier looked perplexed. 'Maybe give them to Hélène?' It was the kind of thing a boy who had grown up with servants assumed was the easiest thing to do. 'Sorry to fuck up,' he said. 'Lost it a bit last night.'

'It's OK. I'm sorry you're drinking so much.'

Xavier stepped back, as if Kite had swung a punch and missed. 'I'm on holiday.'

'We're all on holiday, Xav.'

It wasn't in the nature of their friendship for Kite to admonish him. Xavier looked puzzled.

'What does that mean?'

Kite held up his hands as an indication that he wasn't going to press the point. He wanted Xavier to know that he was worried, but didn't want to come across as a prig.

'It's just that you seem upset about something. About your dad.'

'Forget that.' Xavier opened the door into the sitting room, escaping the conversation. 'I'm going into Mougins on the Vespa. Want anything?'

Kite thought about going pillion in the hope of running into Peele, or perhaps a random Falcon carrying a rolled-up copy of the *FT*, but not enough time had passed since he had flown the signal. Besides, Xavier didn't seem in the mood for company.

He went back to his room and lay down on the bed. He closed his eyes and quickly fell asleep, waking two hours later to the sound of the Vespa coming back and the noise of a car on the drive. Moments later Xavier was shouting up the stairs.

'Lockie!'

Kite rolled out of bed and opened the door.

'What?'

'Come down. Look who I ran into.'

Standing in the hall, a bottle of wine in one hand and a box of chocolates in the other, beaming from ear to ear beneath a crumpled Panama hat, was Billy Peele.

'Lachlan Kite, as I live and breathe,' he said. 'Fancy seeing you here.'

50

Peele had come prepared. He knew their A-level results—two As and a B for Xavier, the same for Kite—and gave a faultless account of running into Xavier 'quite by chance' in the back alleys of Mougins.

'I'm here with my girlfriend,' he explained to an enraptured Rosamund, who seemed delighted that a cultivated, charming, intelligent Englishman was visiting the villa. Jacqui and Martha were beside her in the sitting room, Luc and Xavier looking on. 'She's not been well, unfortunately. Ate some shellfish in Antibes and the blighters exacted a terrible revenge. I'd warned her—no oysters when there isn't an "r" in the month—but she wouldn't listen. So she's back at our hotel nursing the most ghastly stomach cramps and feeling wretched that she's left me all on my tod. But then who should I run into but the recently departed—and much-missed—old Alfordian Monsieur Xavier Bonnard, who very kindly asked me to lunch. I hope it's not too much of an imposition?'

It wasn't. Rosamund said that Hélène always prepared more food than the household could possibly eat and that laying another place at table would be the easiest thing in the world. As Xavier and Luc showed Peele around the garden, Kite tagged along, simultaneously impressed by Peele's chutzpah and anxious to know when they would have the chance to talk.

An opportunity finally presented itself after lunch. Eskandarian had gone back to his office after speaking to Peele only briefly, not about Rushdie or the ayatollah but—of all things—the laws of cricket. As usual, Jacqui and Martha were helping Rosamund and Hélène with the washing-up; Luc was firmly of the view that kitchens were for women or professional male chefs and sat with Peele, Xavier and Kite on the terrace drinking coffee.

'Fancy a game of pétanque?' Xavier suggested, swallowing the final triangle of a Toblerone he had bought at Charles de Gaulle.

Luc thought this was a great idea and immediately stood up, clapping his hands together and dividing the four of them into teams.

'The men against the boys,' he said.

'You're on,' Kite replied.

Throughout the ensuing match, just as had been the case at every moment since his arrival, Peele made no attempt to communicate with Kite about the operation. Every word they exchanged was all of a piece with Peele's job at Alford and his former role as Kite's tutor. There were no discreet looks, no indications that he was alarmed or frustrated, nothing at all to suggest that his relationship with Kite was anything other than that of a popular history beak and his former pupil. Only when Kite and Xavier had roundly defeated their opponents by five games to one, and Xavier had gone into the house to use the bathroom, did Peele make his move.

'So Lockie. It's been very good to see you. I want to hear all your plans. The A-level results are exactly where you must have wanted them. Congratulations indeed. Can I help with Edinburgh, with UCCA forms, with anything at all?'

Luc, who was standing with them, plainly wanted no part in the conversation. He went into the house to check on Rosamund

BOX 88

and Eskandarian, promising to dig out a French novel from his office which Peele had shown an interest in at lunch.

'Keep smiling,' Peele whispered as soon as Luc was out of sight. 'We're catching up, I'm happy to see you. Neither of us has anything to worry about.'

He was beaming at Kite, wholly in character, the tone of his voice and occasional bursts of laughter completely at odds with the words that were coming of his mouth.

'Listen carefully. I don't know why you haven't been able to come to the house, why the bloody Gameboy wasn't working, but not to worry. Things have moved on.'

'Xavier saw Abbas talking to Bijan in a car in Mougins yesterday. I think they're planning something.'

Peele seemed surprised that Kite should know this.

'We saw it. The Falcons have had Bijan's car for twenty-four hours. Abbas has sold out Eskandarian to the exiles.'

'Jesus Christ.'

'Smile, Lockie. Smile.'

Peele turned away from the pétanque court and began walking in the direction of the pool. Kite realised that their faces could now only be seen by someone on the access road. The villa was directly behind them.

'Abbas thinks you're sympathetic to Bijan. If he's been off with you, that may explain it. They discussed using you as a conduit to Eskandarian, but now the landscape has changed.'

'What do you mean?' Kite was trying to fathom why Abbas had betrayed Ali.

'If they can't get to Eskandarian in the open, their backup plan is to hit the house. Abbas will make himself scarce, Bijan and his merry men will come up the drive. They'll likely shoot Eskandarian in cold blood, wherever he happens to be.'

'Jesus.'

'Yes, he'll need some divine intervention.'

Kite was astonished by Peele's sangfroid. They turned towards the pool. Martha and Jacqui were sunbathing on loungers, listening to 'Every Time You Go Away' on the ghetto blaster. Peele had his arm around Kite and suddenly stepped back, saying: 'You're *joking*? That's not possible! He really *said* that?' with an accompanying laugh. It was like watching a film with the dialogue dubbed into the wrong scene. Kite saw that he was supposed to play along, so he said: 'Seriously. I'm not joking!' and grinned for the benefit of anyone who might be watching. Peele continued, sotto voce.

'There's something else, Lockie. Luc is not who you think he is.'

Kite struggled to maintain a poker face. The remark winded him, both because Peele had delivered it with such apparent thoughtlessness and because it spelled doom for Xavier.

'What do you mean?'

'French liaison is all over him. Your lunch guest Paul doesn't work in the film industry. He's DST. Befriended Luc in Paris over a year ago, suspecting that he was breaking Iranian sanctions. Pretended to be a scriptwriter, went whoring with him in Paris. Luc thinks he's the best thing since sliced baguette. Keep smiling.'

Kite did so. He wished that he had a cigarette to smoke so that his gestures and attitudes might appear more natural.

'He was arguing with Ali last night,' he said. 'They had a big row.'

'We know.' Peele turned towards the access road. 'Got the whole thing. Eskandarian has been working with Luc for most of the decade, importing dual-use components for military technology that explicitly break the sanctions. Now that Rafsanjani is in place, he wants to bring that relationship to an end. Ali is forward-looking, more angel than devil. Wants to help bring Iran in from the cold, engage with the western powers, change the economic dynamic, move away from the mad mullahs into a period of relative normality. Was decent enough to come to

BOX 88

France and tell Luc all this in person, but Bonnard hasn't reacted well. He was making a lot of money from their tidy arrangement and expecting to make a lot more. In April last year, shortly after the Halabja attack, Eskandarian and Luc discussed obtaining banned nerve agents so that Iran had some sort of answer to Saddam Hussein if he—or any other entity—launched further chemical strikes. All that's been consigned to the dustbin. Eskandarian is cleaning up his act. He knows that Iran is now self-sufficient in all the lovely things Luc used to arrange to have smuggled across the border with Turkey. What we're still trying to find out—and what we can't get from the Frogs—is whether Luc is in league with Abbas and the exiles.'

Kite could not have been more shocked if Peele had told him that Xavier's father was secretly working for BOX 88. Once again, Peele had to tell him to temper his reaction. Kite forced a smile onto his face but felt that he was grinding his teeth into a rictus.

'I took a few photographs in Ali's office yesterday. Letters. Documents. I was going to bring the roll of film to you this morning, but at the last minute Luc decided to join me on my run.'

Peele looked momentarily concerned. 'He did? Why?'

Kite shrugged. 'You saw my note? Forman and Berberian are mentioned in the correspondence.'

Peele nodded. They turned back towards the pétanque court.

'We're looking at the possibility that Eskandarian has been set up as a patsy. The more we look at Abbas, the more we see of Lockerbie. Too early to say, but your photographs will doubt-less prove very useful.' He put his arm across Kite's back. 'Whatever happens, we can step across the New York visit and shut down the threat to the subway. Well done.'

Kite absorbed the compliment, smiled naturally for the first time in several minutes, and sensed an opportunity to get some answers.

'Why did you have to steal Martha's photographs?'

Peele's mask dropped.

'Is that all you're worried about?'

Kite felt his disappointment as a personal snub and reframed the question.

'I'm just curious,' he said. 'What did she take that you needed? Pictures of Luc and Abbas?'

'We didn't steal the bag.' Peele's reply was emphatic. He nodded his head and grinned enthusiastically. It was like talking to a manic life-sized doll. 'Bijan was on the bike that passed you last night. He wanted the photographs so that the exiles can find their way around the house when they come for Eskandarian.'

'Can't you stop them?'

'It doesn't work like that.' Peele pointed into the distance, presumably to make it look as though they were discussing some aspect of the Provencal countryside. 'BOX are not supposed to be here, remember?'

'That's ridiculous.'

Kite pictured a bloodbath at the villa in which Martha and Xavier would be collateral damage. It had to be stopped. Surely BOX 88 had the power to apprehend Abbas and Bijan?

'Don't worry,' Peele reassured him. They were now twenty metres from the pool; when they turned around, Jacqui looked up to acknowledge them, pressing stop on the ghetto blaster after the first few bars of a Paul Young song she didn't like. 'The Frogs are taking this from us. You'll all be protected.'

'Are they going to arrest Abbas?'

'Don't worry about it. Your work is done. There's nothing left for you to do. You can stand down and feel very, very proud of what you've achieved. We wouldn't know half of this, and certainly wouldn't be able to plan for it, had it not been for your contribution.'

Of all things at that moment, Kite thought about his A-level results, and the absurdity of everyone in the house celebrating the fact that he and Xavier had managed two As and a B. There

BOX 88

had been chilled champagne and speeches at lunch. Peele had toasted 'the boys', describing them as 'the best of Alford' and joked that their 'B' grades would haunt them for the rest of their lives. How could he have been so calm, so blasé, knowing that at any moment there might be an attempt on Eskandarian's life?

'What are you planning?' he asked.

'Above your pay grade, I'm afraid,' Peele replied. 'Better that you don't know.'

They were almost back at the pool. Kite stopped walking.

'How did you know about Paul so quickly?' he asked.

Peele laughed again and threw his head back, almost to the point that Kite thought he was overplaying it. 'As you know, we've been working on Luc and Eskandarian for several months. Paul popped up in research a few weeks ago.'

'So you've always been suspicious of Luc? You just decided not to tell me?'

'Are you happy for your friend's father to be selling chemical weapons to the government in Tehran? To be passing Ali Eskandarian into the hands of an exile group so that he can continue to make money while Iran reverts to the Stone Age?'

Kite didn't know how to answer. All he was sure of was that Luc was corrupt. He wanted him to stop doing what he was doing so that Xavier could find faith in his father again. He didn't want Luc going to prison or the Bonnard name dragged through the mud.

'Xavier suspects that his dad is up to something,' he said.

'I'm not surprised.' Peele sounded glib. 'He's been around his father. He's probably picked up the scent of what's going on.'

Kite was trying to imagine how Xavier could have worked out the nature of Luc's arrangement with Eskandarian. Perhaps he didn't know the details; perhaps he knew a lot more than he was letting on.

'Have you passed on what you know about Luc to the French police?' Jacqui had put a new album in the ghetto blaster. The music smothered Kite's question. He felt suffocated, as though Peele and Strawson had taken advantage of his youth and inexperience to damage Luc. He could tell from Peele's reaction that BOX 88 had indeed been in contact with the French authorities. Peele made no attempt to conceal this.

'Don't be concerned,' he said.

'Of course I'm concerned. He's going to go to prison, isn't he?'

'Not necessarily.'

'Hey!'

It was Xavier, walking towards them wearing sunglasses and a smile. He was carrying a bottle of Kronenbourg without an apparent care in the world. Kite wished that he could say something. He could not remember why he had put the needs of BOX 88 ahead of Xavier's. To his despair, but not to his surprise, Peele instantly dropped back into the role of the cheerful, avuncular schoolmaster. They resumed a dismal small talk, Xavier completely unaware of Kite's despondency, Peele complaining about the quality of the food at Alford. They made their way back to the house.

'So your father tells me Ali is buying dinner for everyone in Vence this evening?'

It was the first Kite had heard of it. They were standing underneath the lime tree. Martha glided past wearing a towel and a pair of flip-flops, saying she was heading upstairs for a shower.

'Yeah,' Xavier replied. 'You coming?'

'Sadly not. I'll be looking after Charlotte.' Charlotte was the phantom girlfriend with oyster poisoning. Peele talked about her with expert conviction. 'But I know the restaurant. You'll eat very well. Has Ali arranged a table outside?'

'Dunno,' Xavier replied.

Kite realised why Peele was so interested. There was a risk of the exiles targeting the restaurant.

'Well, do have fun,' he said. 'It's been such a lovely surprise

BOX 88

seeing you both. I've got to be getting back. I'll pop in and say goodbye to your parents.'

As soon as Peele had driven off, Kite went for a swim in an effort to clear his head. Xavier had brought the backgammon board down to the pool and was playing with Jacqui. Eskandarian had not been seen since lunch. Kite assumed that he was still in his office.

He walked back through the garden on his own, entering the house via the terrace. Earlier in the holiday Rosamund had complained about people walking through the sitting room with wet feet. Kite had left a pair of espadrilles by the door and put them on. He was conscious that his swimming trunks were wet and might drip onto the floor. He picked up a towel from the table and wrapped it around his waist.

Luc came out of his office. All of the relaxed ebullience he had displayed with Peele had vanished. He looked drained of energy and intensely angry.

'Can I speak to you, please?' he said.

It took Kite a moment to realise what Luc was holding in his hand. It was the Gameboy.

51

Luc was holding the device as if it was a dead rat. Before he could finish saying: 'What was this doing in my office?' Kite jumped into a lie.

'You found it!' he exclaimed, striding confidently across the sitting room, beaming with relief. 'I've been looking everywhere for that. Where was it?'

'Behind a piece of furniture in my office. I was looking for the book for Mr Peele. What was it doing in there, Lockie?'

Luc's tone of voice was indisputably suspicious. He knew that a device of this kind could be used as a microphone. Kite saw that he was afraid.

'I've no idea,' he replied. 'It's not even working, is it? I smashed the screen but was going to get it repaired—'

There was a look of concentrated animosity on Luc's face.

'How did you smash it? When?'

Kite tried to look baffled by the line of questioning, even though he knew exactly what Luc was trying to establish.

'Just before I came to your house in London. Literally dropped it on the floor as I was heading out the door.'

Xavier's father turned and walked back into the office. Kite

BOX 88

had no choice other than to follow him. As soon as they were inside, Luc closed the door, sealing him in.

'So why did you not leave it behind?'

Kite shrugged and screwed up his face, as if Luc was asking ridiculous questions to which he had no plausible answers.

'I don't understand,' he said. He was so anxious it was as though someone was pulling at the skin on his chest. 'What's the matter?'

'I'm worried that this should not have been in my office. Why were you playing with it?'

'I wasn't.' *They find a microphone, you didn't put it there. They search your room, somebody planted whatever they found. Never confess. Never break cover.* 'I told you. It's broken. I think the power comes on, but you can't see any of the games.'

'So who took it?'

'Who took what? The Nintendo? I don't know. What's the matter? You seem really angry.'

Luc took a step towards him, teeth bared, as if he was about to strike. The loss of self-control was startling. At first Kite thought that he was watching a man unravel; then he realised that for the first time he was seeing Luc Bonnard for who he really was.

'I am not angry, Lockie. I am just concerned. I'm trying to find out the truth.'

'The truth about what?'

'Who put this in my office?'

Kite felt that he had no alternative other than to repeat what he had already said. He had to try to sow doubt in Luc's mind.

'I have no idea. I've been using Xav's Gameboy out here. Maybe José moved mine when we were playing hide-and-seek. It was on my chest of drawers until a couple of days ago.'

Never embellish the lie. Make it short and sweet and get out fast. Kite knew that he must not show that he understood the nature of Luc's concern. It would never have occurred to a normal eighteen-year-old that a Nintendo Gameboy could be converted into a tentacle nor that Luc would be worried about surveillance.

'José was in your room?'

Kite took a chance and said: 'Yeah.'

'And he took this downstairs?' Luc again held up the console like some kind of diseased animal. Kite shrugged his shoulders as if to say: 'How should I know?'

'It never worked?' he asked. 'You never played with it out here?'

'No,' Kite replied. 'Just used Xav's.'

Luc put the Gameboy down. Kite had the feeling that he was pulling clear of danger. He had brazened things out. Perhaps Xavier's father was starting to think that it was Abbas or Eskandarian who had planted the Gameboy. Then he walked over to his desk, opened a drawer and took out a screwdriver.

'Let us take a look, shall we?'

Kite's chest contracted. He thought of countless confrontations in the study of Lionel Jones-Lewis, his housemaster sadistically meting out yet another punishment to Kite for some minor infringement of the school rules. This was a different order of seriousness. If Luc opened the Gameboy, found the microphone and transmitter and showed them to Abbas or Eskandarian, he was finished.

'You're going to open it up?' he asked, trying to sound bewildered. 'Why?'

Luc ignored him. He tried to remove a screw in the casing. It was harder than he had anticipated. Xavier's father was a corporate animal of the boardroom and airport lounge, not a handyman. When the screw failed to move, he tried to prise the plastic apart.

'What are you worried about?' Kite asked because it was essential to keep playing the innocent. A new tactic presented

BOX 88

itself. 'You don't have to get it fixed for me!' he said. 'I can do it when I get back to London.'

'Not for that,' Luc replied contemptuously. 'Not to get it fixed.'

Again Kite was forced to say: 'Why then? What are you doing?'

'You know what I'm doing, Lockie.'

Luc flashed Kite a pitiless stare, as if to say: *I know who you are. I know that you have betrayed me.* There was a sudden noise in the sitting room, a door banging shut. Kite prayed that nobody would come into the study. To be accused of planting a bug in front of Xavier or Martha would sow a suspicion which he would never shake off.

'*Merde!*' Luc swore as the screwdriver persistently slipped off the surface of the plastic. To Kite's horror, he saw that Luc fully intended to smash the Gameboy on the side of the table. Just then, there was a knock on the door. Eskandarian walked in. When he saw Kite and Luc standing together, Luc's face flushed with anger, he frowned.

'What's going on?' he asked.

Kite knew that he was finished. The Gameboy would be opened up, the transmitter and microphone exposed. Yet to his astonishment, Luc set the device to one side, conjured an inno-cent, welcoming smile, and lied through his teeth.

'Ali! Poor Lockie. His Gameboy isn't working. We were just trying to fix it.'

At first Kite didn't understand why Luc hadn't come clean. Surely both men were vulnerable to the risk from surveillance? Then he put two and two together. By failing to uncover the Gameboy, Luc had exposed Eskandarian to risk. No matter that Luc was intending to cast his so-called friend aside in pursuit of greater profits; he had to continue to pretend that he had his best interests at heart.

'Oh,' said Eskandarian. It was obvious that he knew he was being palmed off. 'Rosamund is looking for you. I think she wants to leave soon. Maybe I can take a look at the toy if you both want to change for the restaurant?'

'No, it's fine!' Kite replied quickly. 'It's so kind of you to be taking us all out tonight.'

'My pleasure, Lockie.'

'Luc! Darling!'

Now Rosamund was calling to him from the hall. She walked into the study, bustling around like a hostess moments before the start of a party.

'What are you three talking about?' she said. 'Aren't you getting changed for dinner, darling? We have to leave in ten minutes.'

'Ten minutes?' Luc replied in a dazed manner. 'Why so soon?'

'The restaurant could only take all of us at seven,' she replied. 'Didn't you *listen*? Come on!' She looked briefly at the Gameboy in Luc's hand. 'You too, Lockie. This is no time to teach my husband Tetris. Wheels turning at half-past six.'

Luc waited until both his wife and Eskandarian had left the room.

'We can discuss this later,' he said.

'Discuss what?' Kite replied. 'I still don't understand.'

'Yes, you do,' Luc replied ominously. 'You know exactly what I'm worried about.'

52

All the way to the restaurant Kite sat in the back seat of the BMW listening to Martha, Xavier and Jacqui casually chatting to Rosamund without a care in the world. For Kite, it was like driving towards a public hanging. He knew that it was only a matter of time before they returned to the villa and Luc confronted him with his treachery. He could picture the scene. All the major players would be standing in the hall: the Bonnards, Martha, Abbas, Alain and Hélène. Luc would be holding the doctored innards of the Nintendo, explaining to Eskandarian that the Gameboy had been transformed into a voice-activated microphone with a radio transmitter relaying conversations from the office to a listening post somewhere nearby. By then Abbas would have checked Kite's bedroom, found the Walkman and brought it downstairs. Like some bit-part player in a country house murder mystery, Hélène would reveal to the assembled company that a lamp had been moved on the day of the Bonnards' arrival. She had come across Monsieur Lockie acting suspiciously in the attic. Abbas would duly fetch the lamp and break it open. Kite would be finished.

He worked through his options. He could call Peele from the restaurant and get somebody to go to the villa, remove the microphone from the lamp and replace his Walkman with a copy. But how would BOX have the time and the wherewithal to do that, especially with Alain and Hélène lurking around? Kite already knew what Peele would say: 'Stop worrying, Lockie. You're over-thinking things. If the shit hits the fan, your luggage was tampered with at some point between London and Charles de Gaulle. The Frogs took advantage of you. Nobody in their right mind would accuse you of being a spy.' Kite tried to believe that he had the nerve and the tenacity to keep lying indefinitely, but was worried that the longer he did so, the more doubt would be sown in the minds of Martha and Xavier. Above all, he did not want them ever to learn of his treachery. What he had done was for Queen and country, for the future of Iran, to prevent the attack in New York. He had never meant to hurt anyone.

Luc was alone with Eskandarian in the Mercedes. The two men had said that they needed to talk. Rosamund had encour-aged this, saying: 'Yes, you two kiss and make up after last night.' Kite suspected that Luc was going to tell Eskandarian about a possible intrusion in his office. Abbas had driven ahead to the restaurant, ostensibly to check security. Kite hoped to God there was a plain-clothes team of BOX 88 Closers in Vence who would protect Eskandarian, Martha and the rest of the group from any attack, if and when it came.

Their table, inevitably, was outside, at the edge of a busy square in the centre of Vence. Both Luc and Eskandarian emerged from the Mercedes in an upbeat mood, which Kite took as a small sign of encouragement. Abbas took up his post at a neighbouring table, smoking a cigarette and drinking a glass of water, without seeming to be unusually nervous or agitated. Nevertheless, when the time came for Eskandarian to seat his guests, Kite held Martha back so that she would not be next to Eskandarian during the meal. Instead, that honour fell to Kite himself, and to Rosamund, who was seated to the right of the Iranian.

It was a typically warm August evening. Several families with

BOX 88

young children were eating dinner at the outdoor tables, but it was still early enough for many of the locals and tourists still to be enjoying aperitifs and cups of coffee as the sun went down. Directly behind Eskandarian, a toddler in a high chair was having baby food spooned into his mouth by an exhausted mother with a Scottish accent. The toddler's slightly older brother was throwing pizza crusts onto the ground and screaming in frustration, much to his father's annoyance.

'I don't know why we didn't just feed them at the house,' he hissed as another chunk of ham landed on the square.

'Because I'm sick of cooking and cleaning up,' his wife replied, on the verge of tears. Kite wondered if a spoonful of baby food would soon flick onto the back of Eskandarian's shirt or plop into Rosamund's Kir. The thought made him feel slightly more relaxed and he tried to distract himself, concentrating on the back-and-forth chat at the table and occasionally joining in whenever he could think of something constructive to add to the conversation.

The attack, when it came, happened so fast that Kite was not fully aware of the threat when the van pulled up on the road and stopped in front of the table. For the first few seconds it felt as though a vehicle supplying food to the restaurant had perhaps gone to the wrong entrance or that the van was stopping only momentarily so that it could be loaded with flowers from a nearby stall. Looking back, Kite unconsciously took his cue from Abbas, who did not move from his seat as the van applied its brakes, emitting a burst of thick black exhaust fumes. Rosamund coughed and waved a hand in front of her face saying: 'Goodness, is that really necessary when we're all trying to eat?' Then the meal and the beautiful summer evening and the easy talk at the table came to an end.

The back doors of the van burst open and a man in a red balaclava jumped down. He was holding a handgun. Simultaneously a second armed man, his face concealed by a black bandana, leaped down from the passenger seat and moved quickly towards the tables. Later, giving statements to the French police, both Kite and Martha would tell them that the man in the black bandana deliberately targeted Abbas, not Eskandarian, so as to remove the possibility that he could prevent the attack. Before Eskandarian's bodyguard had so much as moved from his seat, the man had fired two shots at his chest from a distance of no more than three metres. In the ensuing panic, Kite instinctively moved to protect Martha, who had gone to Abbas to try to help him. At the same time the man in the red balaclava seized the back of Eskandarian's head, drove it forward twice onto the hard table, then dragged him, with the assistance of a third man, into the back of the van.

Seeing what was happening, Kite did what he could to prevent Eskandarian from being taken. Rushing towards the man in the red balaclava, he wrapped his arms around his waist, only to receive an elbow in the face which hit him with such force that he was knocked backwards onto the table, bringing plates and glasses and cutlery crashing down around him. Eskandarian himself was kicking out and shouting in Farsi, but the men easily overpowered him, and he was bundled into the vehicle.

Kite was on the ground trying to make a mental note of the number plate when he heard the gunshot. With Eskandarian safely inside the van, the man in the red balaclava had closed one of the rear doors and was trying to shut the other. With what life remained to him, Abbas fired and hit him in the chest as he was closing the second door. Somebody inside shouted a word Kite assumed meant 'Go!' in Farsi and the driver accelerated away, the rear door slamming shut as the van moved off. A moped, parked on the edge of the square, was knocked to one side and the flower stall smashed as the vehicle made its getaway. Within less than a minute, the men had come and gone, taking Eskandarian with them.

53

'Why do you think they shot the bodyguard?' Torabi asked. 'Why did they target Abbas?'

Kite had said nothing to Torabi about Peele's visit to the house or Abbas's betrayal of Eskandarian.

'I suppose they wanted to get rid of him because he was a threat. He had met Bijan, he had seen his face. Why let him live? The exile group wanted him out of the picture. They needed to sever the link so that Eskandarian wouldn't be found.'

'But Bijan was found dead only a day later. He and all his associates, killed when the French police stormed their apartment in Cannes.'

'I know,' Kite replied.

'But they didn't find my father.'

Kite shrugged. 'No, they didn't,' he said, concerned that Torabi's line of questioning suggested he knew more than he was letting on. 'I always assumed Ali was killed that night, at the very latest the next morning.'

'Why did they not shoot him in the restaurant?'

'You're asking the wrong man!' Kite replied. 'I have no idea. The Americans I spoke to after the attack said that it was possible they intended to ransom him, to put his face on television as a way of bringing the world's attention to what was happening in Iran. That he was being held at an unknown location when Bijan and his comrades were killed. Once that happened, the exiles cut their losses and murdered your father.'

Torabi nodded, as if this was a more plausible version of events. Kite had lost the feeling in his left arm and asked if Kamran, who was standing by the door, would release his hands so that he could move around and stretch. The request was ignored.

'You saw the three men in bandanas and balaclavas?'

'Of course. I tried to restrain one of them.'

'Yes. Xavier told me that. He told me you were very brave.'

Kite did not know how to respond. He felt that Xavier had betrayed him by speaking to Torabi, endangering Isobel's life in doing so. Yet he could not blame his friend for his anger and confusion. He was glad, at least, that Xavier had verified his account of the kidnapping. He had never known the full truth.

'Did you recognise Bijan?'

Kite lied and said: 'Yes, a part of me thought that the man who shot Abbas looked a bit like Bijan. The way he moved, his size, that sort of thing.'

'But he was not the man in the red balaclava. The one who was shot as the van was leaving?'

'No, not him,' Kite replied.

'Who was he?' Torabi asked.

Kite winced and said: 'I have no idea. I only ever met Bijan. The worst of it was that Luc didn't try to save his children, didn't do anything to protect Rosamund. As soon as he saw that Abbas had been shot, he panicked and a kind of fight-or-flight impulse kicked in. He ran inside the restaurant. Jacqui saw him go and shouted 'Daddy!' and followed him. The baby in the highchair toppled over and was crying on the ground. The other children were screaming. It was awful, the worst thing I've ever seen, still to this day. There was blood every-where, total panic, the realisation that Abbas had been shot,

BOX 88

that he was dying right there in front of everyone, and Ali had been kidnapped. It was horrific.'

Torabi sat down on the sofa.

'What else?' he said. 'What else do you remember from that day?'

Kite was concerned that Torabi was holding something back. Did he have access to a better source than Xavier, someone who knew the truth about Eskandarian? He knew that his time was running out. In his long and detailed version of events, this was the natural point at which Eskandarian's story came to an end.

'The truth is I've never looked back,' he said. 'I never wanted to know what they did to your father. It was too painful. Martha and I made a promise never to speak of it. After Luc was arrested, when Xavier and Jacqui had to go through the pain and public embarrassment of seeing their father exposed as a crook, when he was photographed in handcuffs being sent off to prison, well, all we were concerned about was looking after them as friends and giving them the support they needed. Xavier and I spent a lot of time together over the next ten years—'

Torabi interrupted him.

'He blamed you. He blamed the Americans. He said Bijan and his colleagues knew nothing about the restaurant in Vence. Their plan was to come to the house the next day and kill my father on sight. They weren't interested in *talking* to him. They were interested in sending a message.'

Kite knew that Torabi was close to the truth, but not close enough. He relied on the same lies, the same obfuscations that had seen him through the long hours on the ship.

'When we came home, and later during his time in prison, Luc became obsessed by the idea that the house had been bugged. He found a Gameboy in his office that belonged to me. The screen had been smashed. It was trapped down the back of a chest of drawers in his office.' It was the first time he had mentioned the Gameboy to Torabi. 'Luc accused Alain and

439

Hélène of being agents for the CIA who had given them the Nintendo and turned it into a bug, despite the fact that bugs in those days needed a power source, needed to be hooked up to a permanent electric current or they wouldn't work. Then he wrote a long memoir in prison saying that it was the *French* authorities who had made him a scapegoat. They didn't like the fact that Luc had been making money with your father while breaking the sanctions because it was Mitterrand's cronies who wanted to be filling their boots. You can see how this story has turned into a conspiracy theory over the last thirty years.'

'You are a good liar, Lachlan Kite. I will give you that.'

Kite shook his head with exaggerated impatience.

'For the last time,' he said, 'I am not fucking lying. Everything I've told you has been the truth. I just want to get out of here. I'm sorry about what happened to your father. I really am. I liked him. What happened that night scarred me very badly. But you'll understand that my priority now is my wife, my child. I want all of us to be safe. I want you to stick to your promise and let both of us go.'

'I'm not finished with you yet.'

Kite knew that he was doomed. He would never leave this place unless he fought his way out. MI5 weren't going to ride to the rescue. BOX 88 had not been able to isolate where he was being held. He would have to resort to desperate measures in order to get off the ship.

'But when you are finished, you'll release my wife?' he pleaded. 'At least promise me that. At least let my child survive.'

'When you murdered my father?'

'I didn't murder your father! How dare you say that? How dare you accuse me of such a thing?'

Torabi nodded at Kamran, who took out a knife, flashing the blade in front of Kite's eyes. Kite reared back, fearing that he would be cut. Torabi mumbled something in Farsi and the chauffeur moved behind him. He leaned down and sliced off

BOX 88

the plastic ties binding his wrists. Kite's hands fell free. He shook out the numbness in his arms, touching the line of dried blood on his wrist.

'I have a call to make,' said Torabi, nodding at Kamran. 'Give him water. Give him food.'

'I need to piss again,' Kite replied. He knew that the call would be to the team guarding Isobel. He hoped to God that by now it was over and the Closers had freed her.

Torabi addressed Kamran in English.

'Put a bucket in his room,' he said. 'He can piss in that.'

54

Jason was standing in the door of the cottage, making what Cara assumed was a call to his superiors at BOX 88. The American was talking in a jumble of code and jargon, the gist of which seemed to involve ordering in a team to remove the bodies and clean up the mess.

Rita had taken Isobel back to the farm, leaving Cara inside the cottage. The faces of the dead men had not been covered. KAISER and STONES had been through their pockets and searched every room, finding five mobile phones and two laptops which they had placed on a table in the living room. There was blood on the walls and on the ground, but not as much as Cara had been expecting. STONES had mopped up a pool of blood around one corpse using pages from a local newspaper; he was busy taking photographs of the dead man's face. Cara was allowed to walk around freely. She had the odd, slightly hypnotic sensation of being adopted into a cult, as if Kite's house, and what was going on inside it, was somehow sealed off from the normal world in which normal rules applied.

STONES moved towards the first Iranian that Jason had

BOX 88

shot. He had fallen forward. It was necessary to turn him to one side so that his face could be seen by the camera.

With a surge of excitement, Cara realised that she recognised him. A full beard around the mouth and chin, no sideburns. It was the man from the passenger seat of the white van. He was wearing the same white shirt, now soaked in blood.

'I've seen this guy before,' she said.

Jason heard her and stepped closer.

'Where?'

'He was in the front seat of the van which they used to transport Lockie from the car park.' It amazed her that she was already calling him 'Lockie'. 'This guy must have known where they were keeping him.'

'Well he sure as shit isn't telling us now,' Jason replied, checking the time on his watch. 'Which one was his phone?'

'Red one. Samsung,' STONES replied instantly.

'What's that smell?' Cara asked. It wasn't sweat or blood, it wasn't aftershave or any of the other odours she might have expected to encounter after such an attack. The smell was closer to diesel or engine oil. She sniffed again, drawing it into her nostrils. 'Like petrol,' she muttered, and looked down at the dead man's shoes. The edges of the soles were flecked with white paint. Cara bent down and removed one of them.

'Hey, what are you doing?' Jason asked.

Cara sniffed the shoe, the engine oil much sharper now and cut with an odd, low tide smell of the sea. The flat soles were spotted with white paint and flecks of rust like tiny pieces of gold leaf.

'He's been on a boat,' she said. 'Look at this.'

She turned the shoe towards Jason and showed him the little rust marks and the dots of paint. The strange seaweed smell had become even more pronounced.

'Seawater,' he whispered, realising that Cara had just identified where they were holding Kite. 'Good job,' he said, slapping her so hard on the shoulder that she almost fell over. On comms he said: 'I need live and archive satellite imaging of every dock and basin in Canary Wharf for the past twenty-four hours. Subject is on a boat, I say again, a boat. Recently arrived from the open sea. Look for anything bigger than a dinghy. People getting on, people getting off. We are moving to the helo. We will find Kite.'

55

Kamran stuck a gun in the small of Kite's back and pushed him down the corridor, steering him towards his cell. He told Kite to open the door then put his free hand on his back and shoved him inside.

'I need to piss,' Kite told him. 'I need the bucket.'

'Wait,' Kamran replied.

Walking backwards towards the bathroom, his eyes always on Kite, the Iranian opened a door on the opposite side of the corridor. A long-handled mop toppled out, brushing against his shoulder as it fell to the ground. In the second that it took Kamran to bend down and pick it up, Kite took the nail out of his hip pocket and concealed it in the palm of his right hand. Kamran looked at him, the gun still pointed at Kite's chest, then momentarily looked away a second time so that he could retrieve a blue plastic bucket from the cupboard. Kite adjusted the position of the nail.

'Wouldn't it be easier just to let me use the bathroom?'

'Shut the fuck up.'

Holding the bucket in one hand and the gun in the other, the chauffeur walked back down the corridor towards Kite's cell. Kite turned his back on him, feigned to miss a step then spun around as Kamran stepped into the room behind him. Pushing the gun away from his back so that it was pointed at the wall, he grabbed the Iranian's jaw, drove it backwards and rammed the nail into his neck so that it buried in the throat up to the palm of Kite's right hand. In the same continuous movement he slammed down onto Kamran's forearm in an effort to shake the gun from his grip. The Iranian was retching, gasping for air, blood spurting from his throat onto Kite's skin and clothes in thin, pulsing strands. He cried out, but his voice was muffled and strained. He doubled over and managed to fire the gun. The bullet missed Kite's foot by less than an inch, lodging in the carpet. In the cramped steel room the noise of the shot was deafening. It spurred Kite to greater speed and violence. Kamran was trying to fight back, at once clutching his bleeding throat and flailing at his assailant with the gun, but Kite drove his knee into his jaw, grabbed his hair and repeatedly smashed his head against the wall, forcing the gun from his grasp. It fell to the floor and fired. A second shot whistled past Kite's ear. He bent down, seized the gun, stepped back and fired two shots into Kamran's head.

He had no time to pause and assess what to do next. He was not avenged nor somehow purified by the act of killing Kamran. Kite had been planning how to get off the ship since the moment he had woken up in his cell. Stepping over the body, he ran down the corridor, away from the interrogation room, opened a heavy steel door and found himself in a makeshift gym. There was a television bolted to the wall above a treadmill and a weight-lifting machine. Kite crossed the room, opened another connecting door and entered a sleeping area with bunk beds three-high on either side. The beds were all neatly made up. He did not know how many more men were on the ship, but had not yet heard any reaction to the gunshots. With Kamran dead and Hossein on his way to the cottage, Torabi might be the last man on board.

BOX 88

Then the sound of a door slamming behind him and the voice of a man calling out in Farsi. It did not sound like Torabi. Kite opened the next door and found himself in a bathroom. He moved quickly across the linoleum floor, again with the impression that the room was not being used: the sinks and mirrors were clean, the tiling in the shower area dry. As he was pushing open a swing door leading out into a narrow passage, there was a crashing sound behind him. Kite turned to see a man stumbling from the sleeping area into the bathroom. He was brandishing a gun. Kite fired two shots, hitting the man in the chest and stomach. He fell to the ground.

'Put it down!'

Kite froze.

'Drop the fucking gun!'

Torabi was behind him. Kite had no choice but to comply, letting the weapon drop to the floor. If he made any sudden move, however quick, Torabi would shoot him. It was a miracle that he had not yet put a bullet in his back.

'Face me!'

Slowly Kite turned around, his hands in the air. Torabi's feet were wide apart, planted on either side of the narrow corridor. He was aiming a gun at Kite's chest.

'You fucking killed Kamran. You killed two of my men.'

'They were going to do the same to me.'

Torabi was slightly out of breath, as if he had heard the gunshots and run back to the ship.

'You're wrong,' he said. 'It's me who is going to do the same to you. On your knees, you fucking liar, hands behind your head.'

Kite sank to the ground. 'At least tell me that Isobel is free,' he said.

The Iranian looked at his watch and smiled.

'Hossein will be there now,' he said. 'Putting a bullet in her brain. I wish you could watch.'

'There's something you should know.'

Kite had one more card left to play. He felt extraordinarily calm, though he was about to break the one rule that he had vowed never to break.

'Yeah? And what's that?'

'Ali Eskandarian lives in London. He has been here for the past fifteen years. I can take you to him. He can answer all your questions. You were right. I did lie to you. Your father is still alive.'

56

It was after midnight by the time the French police had concluded their interviews and allowed the Bonnard family to return home. Vence was by then deserted. The entire square had been cordoned off, all restaurants closed, traffic prevented from entering the town. Jacqui, who was deeply upset, went home with Martha and Rosamund. Luc drove Xavier and Kite back to the villa.

Nothing was said on the journey. Xavier knew that his father had been a coward. Luc was wrestling with the inerasable shame of his inaction; he had run when he should have stood his ground. He had abandoned his wife, his daughter, his son just at the moment when they needed him most. Kite, by contrast, had tried to fight back and was nursing a swollen jaw for his efforts. The comparison was stark. The incident with the Nintendo seemed to have been forgotten. It felt to Kite as though it had taken place in a different dimension of time.

Luc followed Rosamund from Vence and they reached the villa only minutes apart. Jacqui immediately went to bed. She hugged her mother but not her father. She said nothing to Xavier but embraced Kite in the hall before going upstairs. Martha could see that she was needed and went with her, kissing Kite goodnight. Xavier found a bottle of red wine in the kitchen and was about to take it out to the pool when his mother told him that it was late, that everybody needed to get some rest and should go to their respective rooms. Kite and Xavier were suddenly children again and did as they were told. Xavier embraced him on the first-floor landing and held him for a long time.

'I'm sorry,' he said. The apology sliced through Kite like a cut to his eyes. 'It was meant to be fun. It was meant to be a good holiday for you . . .'

Kite could hardly stand what he was hearing.

'It's not your fault,' he said, stepping back and holding Xavier by the shoulders. He looked at him with as much sincerity as he could find. 'Nobody knew this was going to happen. We'll all get over it. We'll look after each other.'

'I've never seen a dead body before.'

'Me neither,' said Kite. Even this was a lie. He thought of his father laid out on a stretcher at the hotel, a sheet covering his face. The eleven-year-old Kite had pulled it back and seen the cuts on his cheeks, the skin chalk white, all the laughter and vitality withdrawn from his eyes.

'See you in the morning.' Xavier went into his room. 'Poor Ali. Mum's worried sick. What do you think they'll do to him?'

'I dread to think,' Kite replied.

He slept deeply, woke up before seven, put on his running shoes, a pair of shorts and a T-shirt and went out outside. He still had the roll of film and took it with him. This time there was no Rosamund drinking English Breakfast tea in the kitchen, no Abbas parked at the end of the drive. Kite jogged down the road, checked that nobody had followed him, then ducked into the garden of the safe house.

The Peugeot was not parked outside. Kite stood in the shaded porch and knocked gently on the door. Nobody answered. He remembered the smell of fried bacon on his first visit to the house, barely a week earlier. There was no breeze, only the trilling of cicadas and birdsong. The olive trees lining the whitewashed

BOX 88

wall were perfectly still. Kite knocked again, this time more loudly. Again there was no response.

He stepped towards the closest window and looked inside. No shoes in the hall, no keys on the table or jackets on hooks. He walked round to the living-room window, stood on a concrete ledge and peered through a gap in the curtains. The room looked as if it had been cleaned. The cushions on the sofa and armchairs were plumped up and the books on the coffee table divided into two neat piles. Peele and Carl had gone. Kite was sure of it. There was nobody home.

He returned to the front door and knocked again. He walked around to the back of the house, looked through the window and saw that the kitchen had also been thoroughly cleaned. It was like changeover day on a summer rental; the existing tenants had left, a maid had been in to wash the sheets and hoover the carpets, a new family would be arriving later in the day.

Kite jogged back to the house. He stopped at the gates and saw that the chalk mark had been removed from the wall. He felt utterly isolated, still in a state of shock about Abbas's murder and the kidnapping of Eskandarian, and now bewildered by the vanishing act of BOX 88. Peele had not written him a note, made a call to the house nor given Kite any indication that he was clearing out. Perhaps this was the way it would always be. At some point in the near future, when it was safe to do so, Peele would explain why he had left the safe house so quickly and without warning. It was undoubtedly because his mission had failed. He and Carl were most likely already on their way to The Cathedral, ready to face the music.

It was decided that Martha and Kite would fly home from Nice at lunchtime. Back at the house, with Luc eating breakfast alone and his children still asleep in their beds, Kite packed up his belongings and left a fifty-franc note in his room as a tip for Alain and Hélène. The Nintendo had been left on his bed, like an admission of defeat. Kite wondered what to do about the lamp in the attic, the ghetto blaster by the pool. He assumed that someone from BOX 88 would come to the house and deal with them as soon as the coast was clear. He felt that they were not his responsibility.

The police came as Martha and Kite were leaving by taxi for the airport. Three cars, six men, no sirens. Kite knew that they intended to arrest Luc. Martha was oblivious to the accusations against him and assumed that the police had come to the house merely to further their investigation into the awful events of the previous evening. They sat in the back of the cab holding hands, talking about Jacqui and Xavier, about who may or may not have been responsible for kidnapping Ali. Kite was of course obliged to feign ignorance, to claim that he had no more idea who was behind the attack than she did. He did not feel bad lying to her; he did not want to expose Martha to any more suffering. What troubled him was not being able to discuss his own very complicated feelings. He needed someone in whom he could confide. Kite felt that he was being forced to deal with the ramifications of what had happened without any support or guidance at all.

At Nice airport he telephoned his mother, using the operational number he had dialled in order to fly the signal a day earlier. The same answering machine picked up. Kite left a brief message saying that he was flying home early, giving the number of the British Airways flight and the time it was scheduled to land. He hoped that the Falcons were listening, but could not shake the feeling that he had been used by BOX and now abandoned. Martha told him that her brother was coming to pick her up and that they could give him a lift into town if his mother wasn't available. She asked where Kite was going to stay. He lied and said that his mother had rented a flat in Chelsea. He bought Martha lunch at a café in the airport, picked up a carton of cigarettes and a bottle of Jim Beam in Duty-Free, and slept most of the way to Heathrow.

There were no delays at Passport Control. They collected their

BOX 88

luggage and made their way out of the baggage hall. Martha's older brother, a tall, dark-haired Morrissey clone in black jeans, Doc Martens and a moth-eaten turtleneck, was waiting for her in Arrivals wearing a look of studied apathy. Kite assumed that he knew what had happened in Vence, but he offered no evident signs of sympathy nor showed any interest in his sister's well-being.

'Jack, this is Lockie. He was staying at the house. Can we give him a lift?'

Kite shook Jack's clammy, indifferent hand and looked around for his mother. There was no sign of her. All around them people were hugging, yelping and kissing. A few bored taxi drivers were leaning on a metal rail holding up signs with names scrawled on them in marker pen. *ANDREW & JAMES RAMSAY. MR V. BLACKETT. DYLAN PATHMAN SPENCE.* Kite looked along the rail. Beneath a poster advertising Concorde flights to New York, a Sikh man in his mid-fifties was reading a copy of the *Financial Times.* When he looked up and saw Kite, he produced a small rectangular card on which he had written: 'MR L. KITE'.

'Ah, my mum's sent a taxi,' he said, his spirits instantly lifted. He waved at the driver and indicated that he would come over as soon as he had said goodbye to his friends.

'I'll call you tonight,' he told Martha.

'Or I can ring you,' she said. 'What's the number at the flat where you're staying?'

Kite said that he didn't know. They hugged one another and kissed briefly, aware of Martha's brother standing only feet away moodily smoking a roll-up and clicking his tongue to the rhythm of a song in his head. Kite waved Martha off in the hope that he would see her within a few days, as soon as BOX 88 had concluded their debriefing. He made his way over to the driver.

'Master Lachlan?'

'Lockie, yes.' He didn't like being called 'Master'. It reminded him of flying south from Scotland as an unaccompanied minor,

British Midland stewardesses fussing over him at the end of the school holidays.

'I am Janki. The *Financial Times* is a very interesting newspaper. My car is this way.'

Kite had the good sense not to enquire how Janki had known what flight he was on; BOX 88 would have heard Rosamund booking the tickets on the phone. Instead he asked where he was being taken.

'The Cathedral, of course,' Janki replied, turning and catching Kite's eye. 'I understand this is to be your first time?'

57

If Kite had been entertaining any thoughts of quitting in the aftermath of Luc's arrest, they evaporated as soon as he learned that he was to be welcomed into the inner sanctum of BOX 88. The unmoored, rootless feeling that had dogged him all summer vanished. His period of probation was over; he had finally been accepted as a bona fide intelligence officer. The operation in France may have ended in chaos, but his own role in it was surely blameless. Peele and Strawson had seen what Kite could offer. He had done what had been asked of him. That Eskandarian had been kidnapped by the exiles was the fault of Carl and Peele and their associates, not of Lachlan Kite. If they had been given advance warning about the kidnapping and alerted him, perhaps Kite might even have been able to do something to prevent it.

'Do you know this part of London?' Janki asked as they were coming off the A4 at Hammersmith.

'Not really,' Kite replied. 'I'm from Scotland. Whenever I stay in London, it's usually further east, in Kensington and Chelsea.'

'Ah yes, of course,' he said. 'Where the Alford boys live.'

They parked in front of a church in a square that Kite did not recognise. He got out of the car and looked around for a street sign, but couldn't see one.

'Just in here,' said Janki, locking the car and leading him towards the church.

They walked up a short flight of steps and the driver knocked on the door. Without waiting for a response, he turned the handle and indicated to Kite that he should go inside. Kite moved forward, waiting for Janki to join him. It was dark and cold in the vestibule. To his surprise, he saw that the driver had turned around and was already walking back in the direction of the car.

'I just wait here?' he called out.

Janki did not respond. Kite turned and peered down the aisle, wondering if Peele or Strawson were waiting for him in one of the pews. There appeared to be nobody in the building save for a rotund, middle-aged vicar standing at the altar within touching distance of a vast silver cross. He was wearing clerical robes and shifting from foot to foot.

'You must be Lachlan,' he said as Kite approached him. He had a cut-glass English accent and an open, friendly manner. 'Anthony Childs.'

'Lockie,' Kite replied, shaking his hand.

'Good flight? Everything OK at Heathrow?'

'Everything was fine, thank you.'

Kite felt a sense of unease, as if Childs was going to sit him down and explain that, regrettably, BOX 88 had decided to dispense with his services. Instead he said: 'I'm to show you the way,' and put his hand on Kite's arm, guiding him towards a door in the side of the church. 'Forgive all the cloak and dagger. There are a number of ways in and out of The Cathedral, but all first-timers get the full Monty. Bit of a tradition. Everything will make sense in just a moment.'

Childs unlocked the door using two separate keys, invited Kite to step forward, then studiously bent down to secure the locks again before continuing. They were now in a short corridor leading to an office. Inside the office Kite could see an antique wooden desk piled high with coloured booklets and magazines.

BOX 88

There was a typewriter on the desk and a half-finished jug of orange squash next to some plastic mugs of various colours. Kite was reminded of Sunday school classes at the church in Portpatrick. Instead of going into the office, Childs unlocked a second door, again using two keys, and beckoned Kite to follow him.

They walked down a flight of stone steps into what Kite assumed was the crypt. The walls were constructed of grey breeze-blocks. There was no carpeting on the floor.

'This way please,' he said, walking towards a third locked door. The vicar knocked three times in quick succession, paused for a moment, then three times again. Kite now wondered if he was the object of an elaborate practical joke.

The sound of a bolt being drawn back. Kite waited as the heavy steel door was opened by someone on the other side.

'You'll be looked after from here,' said Childs as a man of at least sixty wearing denim jeans, a collared shirt and tweed jacket appeared on the other side of the door, nodded at Kite and said: 'Welcome.'

Like Janki before him, the vicar turned swiftly around and walked back in the direction from which he had come. Kite was lost for words. He simply said: 'Bye then.'

'This way, son,' said the man. He had an Arthur Daley accent and a twinkle in his eye. 'I'm Jock. Look after the place with my wife. They call her Miss Ellie, like the Ewings. Gettit? Only a short walk from here.'

'Jock' was the nickname Kite had been given in his first days at Alford. He wondered what ties this cheerful, sixty-something Cockney had to Scotland. They were now standing at one end of a long, underground bunker, presumably a relic of the war. The area was dimly lit but again neither cold nor damp. Kite was so bewildered by what was happening that he struggled even to respond to Jock's greeting.

'All this must be very unusual for you,' he said, sensing Kite's confusion. 'Did the Reverend explain? We don't always come in this way. Just on special occasions, star guests. Anthony as gatekeeper.'

They reached the far end of the bunker. Jock unlocked another steel door and Kite was shown into a well-lit, furnished foyer in what was presumably the basement of a building on the opposite side of the square to the church. Two men in suits were waiting for him. They did not introduce themselves, they were neither of them particularly welcoming nor cheerful. To break the tension, Kite said: 'Doctor Livingstone, I presume,' but he had misjudged the moment; they looked at their shoes. He stepped into a lift with the three men and stood in the corner, his face flushed with embarrassment, wondering why Peele or Strawson had not come to meet him. When the doors eventually opened, he was invited to make his way along another long passage in what was evidently a modern multi-storey office block. Each of the rooms on either side of the passage was a large glass-fronted office with slatted blinds. There was a smell of instant coffee and cigarette smoke. Kite could hear the ringing of telephones and the chatter of a Telex. In one of the offices he glimpsed a map of the Middle East; in another, people were standing up and watching CNN on a colour television. By the time he had reached the door, Jock and the younger of the two men were no longer with him.

The older man knocked and walked straight into the room without waiting for an answer.

'He's here,' he announced.

Seated in a chair by the window, looking out through a partially open Venetian blind, was Michael Strawson. Kite had expected as much. He felt that he was always walking into strange rooms in which the American was waiting for him.

'Lockie,' he said. He looked tired and distracted, as if Kite's arrival had shaken him from deep contemplation. 'How was your flight?'

'Fine, thanks. Good to be here.'

BOX 88

'So you met Sebastian?'

Kite was keen to claw back some of the face he had lost in the lift and said: 'No. Actually, he didn't introduce himself.'

Strawson seemed surprised by this and cut the man a look.

'Oh. This is Sebastian Maidstone, my number two here in London. Sebastian began life in SIS, he's across what's been going on in France.'

'What's happened to Luc?' Kite asked him. He was shaking Maidstone's hand and had the sense of a controlling, calculating man who did not approve of him.

'I'll let Michael discuss that,' Maidstone replied. He forced a smile onto his face which managed to be both inauthentic and powerfully condescending.

'Give us five minutes, will you?' Strawson told him.

Kite was relieved to see Maidstone leave the room. He had reminded him of a particularly starchy beak at Alford who had several times taken pleasure in sending Kite to see the headmaster for some minor infraction of the school rules. Strawson went back to his chair and invited Kite to sit with him by the window. In his eyeline, Kite could see the same framed photograph of Strawson's wife which had been beside his bed at Killantringan. There was a word processor on his desk, two telephones and several in-trays filled with paperwork.

'To answer your question. Luc has been taken into custody by the French police. You want something to drink?'

'Nothing, thank you,' Kite replied, confused by Strawson's matter-of-fact tone.

'I want you to know that it was never the objective of this organisation to gather intelligence on Xavier's father with the purpose of bringing him to trial. Anomalies arose in connection with his relationship to Eskandarian which we were powerless to ignore.'

If Peele had said such a thing, Kite would have challenged it. With Strawson, he always felt that it was unwise to argue.

What was done was done. Strawson could be lying to him; Strawson could be telling the truth. Either way, someone as junior as Kite was never going to be allowed to get to the bottom of it.

'OK,' he said. 'What have they charged him with?'

He thought of Xavier at the villa, alone with his mother and sister, the family cracked open.

'Breaching the Iranian sanctions. Supplying illegal dual-use materials to the regime in Tehran. They're also looking at the possibility Luc was facilitating the production of chemical weapons.'

'With Ali's help?'

Strawson's mouth puckered. 'No. I don't know if Billy . . .' He hesitated, seemingly choosing his words carefully. 'If Billy told you, but that was one of the issues on which Luc and Ali disagreed. We captured at least one conversation between Luc and Abbas in which they discussed finding a new Iranian government source for the nerve agents.'

Kite was poleaxed. He said: 'Billy mentioned that you were suspicious of Luc's relationship with Abbas. You suspected he was going behind Ali's back.'

'Certainly seems that way.' Strawson looked out through the slats of the Venetian blind.

'Where am I?' Kite asked. The slats were open, but he could not see the square nor the steeple of the church in which the vicar had been waiting for him.

'Well, as you know by now, we call this The Cathedral,' Strawson replied. 'Largest of three buildings in London owned and controlled by us, in effect BOX 88 operational headquarters in the UK.' There was still something oddly flat about his mood. Kite had expected greater enthusiasm, more of Strawson's characteristic ebullience. He put it down to the American's disappointment over Eskandarian. 'Jock brought you in via the church, where Anthony is pastor. Used to be one of us and, as

BOX 88

you can see, he continues to help out from time to time.' Strawson parted two of the slats in the blind and pointed downwards. 'We're in what appears to the outside world to be a residential and commercial compound consisting of houses, this office block and a small recreational area. Several of the staff live here full time in order to give an appearance of ordinary day-to-day activity to whoever might be passing by or giving too much thought to what goes on behind the gates.'

'The gates,' said Kite.

'There are standard In-Out security lanes on the square for vehicles, another to the east, also access via the air-raid shelter you passed through just now. The office itself—this building we are in—faces out onto a residential street.' Strawson pointed around the corner to a spot Kite could not see. 'You'll see a list of shell companies on the wall as you walk in, travel bureaus, advertising agencies, that kind of thing. All of it designed to give the impression of nothing much in particular going on. Everybody who works here is known to security. You show a face, you show a pass, you get in.'

Perhaps it didn't interest Strawson to talk about The Cathedral in this way, but Kite had the strong sense that he was distracted by something and wanted to move on. Clearly he had been admitted to the inner sanctum to discuss what had happened in Vence. As an eyewitness, Kite's testimony would be vital.

'Look, kid . . .' Strawson turned to face him. He took hold of Kite's arm. There was suddenly an awful, avuncular softness both to his words and to this simple gesture which filled Kite with dread. 'I have to tell you something. It's not good. It's not good at all.'

Nothing could have prepared Kite for this moment. He somehow knew what Strawson was going to tell him before he said it.

'We lost Billy last night. He was shot in the van. He was killed.'

It was as if Kite had been overcome by a fever, the building beneath him falling away, the floor and the walls slipping to earth and a young man emptied of all that was hopeful and good in him.

'What?' he managed to say. 'How?'

'It was us in Vence, kid. We had to get Eskandarian. We have him now. The shot that was fired, the man that was hit in the van, that was Billy. Your friend and mine.'

Through his consternation, Kite replayed the moment in his mind like a sickening home video. He remembered rushing towards the man in the red balaclava, trying to stop him hurting Eskandarian. It had been Peele's elbow that had sent him backwards onto the table, bringing plates and glasses crashing down all around him. He could still feel the pain in his jaw where his friend had struck him. Why hadn't he told him they were going to be in the van, that this was what BOX had planned all along?

Kite was numb with shock. He did not want to show weakness to Strawson, did not want to fail in front of him, but he lost the strength in his legs and slumped back into a chair. Strawson steadied him, saying: 'I'm so sorry, Lockie. Really, I'm so sorry.' The dreadful thought occurred to Kite: *If I hadn't interfered, would Peele still be alive?* By grabbing him, by trying to be the hero, had he delayed his escape by the few seconds it took Abbas to summon the last of his energy and fire the fatal shot? Kite found that he was hardly able to breathe. Tears welled in his eyes. He did not want Strawson to see him crying and looked away. He remembered the bullet hitting Peele in the chest, the flower stall burst apart by the van. It was his fault. His failure.

'We're all devastated, as you can imagine,' said Strawson.

Kite could not believe that anybody in that strange, secret building was as devastated as he was. Nobody had known Billy Peele in the way that he did. Nobody had believed in Lachlan Kite in the way that Billy Peele had believed in him. Everything that had happened in France had only happened because of this

BOX 88

man who had trusted him, taught him, taken him under his wing. That man was now lying dead, somewhere in France, somewhere in London, with a bullet in his heart.

'Where is he?' he asked. He was extraordinarily cold. 'Is he here? Did you bring him back? Can I see him?'

Kite began to sob uncontrollably. It was the first time that he had cried since his father's funeral. He was ashamed of himself but completely powerless to stop it. Strawson, to his amazement, crouched down and held him, whispering: 'I'm so sorry, kid. It's OK. Let it out. I'm so sorry.' Kite had the wild, awful thought that Sebastian Maidstone was going to walk in and laugh at them. Strawson produced a pale blue handkerchief from his pocket which Kite used to mop his tears. It smelled of the same cologne Luc had worn in France. 'We haven't lost a man in five years. It's just one of those things.'

'One of those things?' Kite repeated, sitting up and looking at Strawson. He could feel that his tears were stopping, as if the initial shock of hearing that Peele was dead had been expelled from him. 'What were you doing in the van? What happened to Ali? I don't understand.'

'When you're ready, I can tell you. I'll explain everything, OK?'

Kite nodded mutely. The American touched his face as he might have touched the face of his own son.

'It will take time. Everything is going to be all right. I'm going to take care of you. We all will. We're going to make sure that you never have to go through anything like this again. You're one of us now, Lockie. Part of the family.'

58

'How is it possible that my father is still alive?' Torabi asked.

Kite could see that he believed him. The Iranian had read enough files and spoken to enough people to have doubted the official version of the kidnapping; they had fed his obsession. He continued to point the gun at Kite's chest, but appeared to be deep in thought. Perhaps he was allowing himself a moment of quiet celebration. He started nodding his head in a kind of warped daze, like someone listening to music through headphones, losing themselves to the beat.

'It's possible because you were right about the Americans. It was CIA in the van, not the exiles. The CIA shot Abbas and kidnapped your father. Bijan and his comrades were assassinated on the orders of MI6. They both wanted Eskandarian for themselves.' Kite was as close to the truth as he would ever go; it was unthinkable that he would tell Torabi about Peele or BOX 88. 'He lived in Maryland under witness protection for the next fifteen years. Since then he's been resident here in the UK.'

'How do you know this?'

Never confess, never break cover, never admit to being a spy.

'I know this because I am who you thought I was. I'm not

BOX 88

an oil trader. I work for British intelligence. I can take you to your father if you call off Hossein.'

There was no discernible reaction to Kite's revelation: no shock that Eskandarian had resided in the United States, nor any visible acknowledgement that Kite had at last confessed the truth. Torabi said only: 'Explain it to me.'

'There isn't time.'

'My father was a traitor?'

'Your father was a hero. He was seized because the Americans made a calculation that he would be more useful to them in Washington than he would have been in Tehran. He did more to heal the divisions between Iran and the West than a thousand diplomats, a thousand politicians. There's a reason we were able to do business with Rafsanjani and Khatami in the nineties. That reason was your father.'

'I don't understand,' said Torabi, too astonished fully to acknowledge what Kite had told him.

'Your father believed that the Iran which had been promised to the children of the Revolution was not the Iran which has materialised. He wanted to do something about that, to bring your country in from the cold. After 9/11, there was less any of us could do. We went into Iraq, Ahmedinajad came along, Netanyahu, and the whole mess started up again. But Ali played a pivotal role in the long negotiations which led to the nuclear deal.'

Kite paused, knowing that he had left out the salient fact that Eskandarian had died in his bed in 2014. He had not lived long enough to see the deal on which he had worked so hard signed into law, nor to watch it being pulled apart two years later by the Trump administration. By an extraordinary twist of fate, Luc Bonnard had passed away on the same day at a hospital in Paris, nine years after his release from prison.

'And Lockerbie?' Torabi asked.

'What about it?' Kite calculated that there would be no harm in telling his captor a little more of the truth. 'Abbas Karrubi was the channel to the PFLP, not Ali. We got our wires crossed. The regime in Tehran was using Abbas as the linkman to Jibril and al-Megrahi. They set your father up as a patsy. Before the end of the month, the FBI had arrested four members of an Iranian terrorist cell in New York, all of whom were shown in court to have had links to Abbas Karrubi. One of them was called Asef Berberian. The other was using a pseudonym: David Forman. They would have killed hundreds on the subway using sarin gas, a terrorist nightmare in Manhattan more than a decade in advance of 9/11. You must have read about that at MOIS?'

Torabi ignored the question. He was still pointing the gun at Kite, although his forearm was now shaking very slightly. Kite knew that his best chance was still to get both of them off the ship. It was too risky to try to overpower him.

'We should move if you want to see your father,' he said. 'Somebody will have heard the gunshots. The police will be here at any moment. I'll be dead, you'll be arrested, and you'll never get what you want. No answers, no contact.'

'Maybe,' Torabi replied.

'I'm offering you a trade. My wife's life and the life of my child for your freedom and a chance to see your father again.'

To Kite's surprise, Torabi lowered the gun. 'You know where he lives?' he asked. 'You know his address?'

'I went to see him eight months ago. He lives in Marble Arch. That's all I'm going to tell you.' Torabi was never going to get the closure he craved. Kite's lies would see to that. 'No address, no details,' he said. 'We go together or we don't go at all.'

'How can I trust you? As soon as we step through the door, I will be arrested.'

'Not if I tell them to leave you alone. Not if you contact Hossein and call off your dogs. I have that power. You know I do.'

BOX 88

Torabi beckoned Kite to his feet. He looked like a pharaoh bestowing forgiveness on an errant subject. As he stood up, Kite had a sudden flash memory of the bullet hitting Billy Peele in the chest. He saw the flower stall burst open, heard the children crying in the square. He briefly closed his eyes, remembering the long sickness of his grief.

'Do we have a deal?' he asked.

Inhaling deeply, as if suppressing the last of his doubts, Torabi appeared to calculate that his chances of survival were strong.

'We have a deal,' he replied, powerless to resist Kite's inducement. He looked at his bloodstained clothes. 'You will need to change your shirt,' he said. 'I have one inside. Then you'll take me to him. If we reach my father's house unharmed, I will call off Hossein.'

59

The chopper carrying Jason, Cara and two of the Special Forces soldiers had taken off from a field a quarter of a mile from the cottage. Rita had insisted on taking Isobel to hospital, telling Cara to do as she was instructed by Jason and not to get in his way. It was the first time that Cara had flown in a helicopter, weightless in the air with an electrifying, God's-eye view of London. The chopper was over Greenwich within half an hour and they landed at City Airport soon after. Three cars were waiting for them on the tarmac. Less than fifteen minutes after touching down, Cara was in Canary Wharf.

It had been agreed that they would split into four. KAISER, now in civilian clothes and carrying only a small firearm, was to be dropped off at Millwall Outer Dock, the body of water closest to Spindrift Avenue. There were five vessels moored on the dock, three of which were believed to be possible locations for Kite. Jason, also out of battle rig, was to take West India Docks, closer to the centre of Canary Wharf, where seven boats had been identified. One of them was a multimillion-dollar superyacht belonging to a Lebanese industrialist which was available for private hire; Cara had suggested it might have been

BOX 88

chartered by the Iranians. Jason instructed STONES to sweep West India Quay, the area immediately to the west of Billingsgate Market where other possible vessels had been identified.

'What about me?' Cara asked.

'We can use your eyes,' Jason replied, equipping her with an earpiece that linked her on comms to the rest of the team. 'Take Heron Quays, make your way east towards me. You see anything, you holler.'

'Right.'

'Ever fired one of these?'

He held up a pistol. Cara almost laughed.

'Fuck no,' she said. 'Only on a staff bonding weekend.'

'But you know how they work, right? Safety catch, trigger, a bullet flies out one end and hits the other person?'

Cara wondered if he was flirting with her.

'You Americans and your guns,' she joked, slipping the weapon into her coat. 'Fine. How many shots do I have?'

'Enough to take out a couple of hedge-fund managers if you have any left over,' Jason replied. 'Just don't shoot anywhere close to Lockie.'

They dropped her at a roundabout at the western edge of Heron Quays. From there, Cara made her way east, following the route of the Docklands Light Railway. She saw only three boats, none of which struck her as plausible locations for Kite. The first two were houseboats with hipsters on deck eating organic crisps and necking craft lager; the third was a 'party boat' hosting a corporate shindig. Music was booming out into the night and there were disco lights flashing in the windows.

She passed a Hilton hotel, heading for a small area beside South Quay station where satellite imaging had identified three possible vessels docked on either side of a narrow harbour. Jason was in her ear telling STONES and KAISER that the Lebanese superyacht was 'a dead end'. KAISER said he was going to take

a look at a large ship moored opposite a branch of Burger &
Lobster in West India Quay.

Cara had reached the entrance to the station and crossed the
road when her phone rang. She looked down and saw that Vosse
was trying to reach her. She picked up, mentally preparing herself
for a blast of invective.

'Sir?' she said tentatively.

That was when she saw Lachlan Kite.

60

Torabi had led Kite to the entrance of the ship. He pulled a warped wooden door towards him, struggling as it jammed. Feeble street light filtered in from outside as the door finally opened. A sudden burst of fresh air kindled a fire inside Kite; once he was away from the ship, his options would multiply. Torabi climbed a short flight of steps, ducked down and unzipped a canopy; it was as if they were inside a tent. There was a strong smell of paint thinners and diesel. Torabi told Kite to wait behind him on a section of deck which felt sticky and uneven underfoot. When the Iranian was certain that the coast was clear, he waved Kite forward saying: 'It's fine. Let's go.'

They emerged into the night. Kite looked up and was astonished to find that they were on the Isle of Dogs. Sixteen years earlier, the headquarters of BOX 88 had been moved from west London to an anonymous high-rise in Canary Wharf. The new Cathedral was almost within sight of the barge where Kite had been held prisoner. Across an expanse of blackened water was a glittering skyline of towering apartment blocks and corporate towers. Judging by the full illumination of the buildings and the density of passing traffic, Kite guessed that it was no later than nine o'clock in the evening. He had been on the barge for about thirty-six hours. That MI5 had failed to find him in that time was both a tribute to Torabi's professionalism and proof that even the most sophisticated state-of-the-art technology would buckle in the presence of old-fashioned tradecraft.

'Where are we?' he asked, feigning ignorance. The barge was moored opposite three other vessels in a narrow rectangular inlet. A vast tarpaulin had been hauled across it, heavy enough when combined with the noise in the local area to have smothered the sound of the gunshots. 'Is that Canary Wharf?'

'South Quay,' Torabi replied, securing the door. 'The station is just over there.'

He indicated a Docklands Light Railway line running overhead a hundred metres to the south. Kite assumed that Torabi wouldn't risk the CCTV on a train and instead had a car waiting for him on the road. To get to it, he was going to have to move from the relative seclusion of the inlet onto a pedestrianised walkway, risking exposure and possible attack in the open.

'How many of you are left?' Kite asked.

'Enough,' Torabi replied.

'Are you all registered with the Iranian embassy?'

Torabi looked at him as if he had lost his mind.

'Why?' he said.

'You know why. I can arrange immunity. You release Isobel, you see your father, you can all be on a plane to Tehran in twelve hours.'

'We no longer work for the Iranian government.'

Kite had not expected such a candid reply, but it matched his assumption that Kamran, Hossein and the other goons in Torabi's employ were hired mercenaries, not operational MOIS.

'So it's just you and me out here?' he asked.

The fact that Torabi ignored the question made Kite certain that he was working alone. Nobody was waiting for him on the outside, nobody else had emerged from the ship. All the Iranian seemed to care about was seeing his father. In that respect, he

BOX 88

was going to be bitterly disappointed. They were standing beside a chain-link fence separating the barge from the walkway. Torabi had put the gun in the waistband of his trousers and was calling someone on a mobile.

'Is that Hossein?' Kite asked.

Torabi ignored him. It looked as though he was waiting for somebody to answer the call. After thirty seconds he gave up. He wore a look of concentrated frustration.

'Was that Hossein?' Kite asked again. 'Was that the cottage?'

'Not your business who it was.'

'They're not answering, are they? You can't get through.' Was that good news or bad? 'We don't go to see your father until Hossein knows we have a deal.'

'We are going to Marble Arch,' Torabi told him. 'We are going to see my father.'

Then confirmation at last that MI5 had closed the net. As Torabi indicated that they should walk towards the station, Kite caught sight of 'Emma', the woman who had approached him at the funeral. She was standing seventy-five metres away on the road, holding a mobile phone. It wasn't immediately clear that she had seen him. When she did, Kite hoped to God that she would know what to do.

61

'This is Jannaway. I have positive ID on Kite. I say again, positive ID on Kite.'

Cara had immediately hung up on Vosse and activated the commslink in her jacket. Her breathing had quickened. Kite was on the western side of the narrow harbour, clear as day, standing next to the Middle Eastern man from the funeral.

'Seven zero metres from South Quay station, western side of the dock near a barge, possible enemy alongside.'

'Copy that,' said Jason.

'Moving to you,' said STONES.

Cara heard a crackle of feedback in her earpiece—then the link went down.

'Jason? KAISER? You there?'

No response. She tried again.

'He's with the Middle Eastern guy from the funeral. The one in the car.'

Nothing. The connection was down. Pulling the earpiece free, Cara looked to her phone, turning back to face the station in case the Iranian had spotted her. Vosse was trying her again. She rejected the call and pulled up Fred's number. He answered on the first ring.

BOX 88

'It's Cara. My comms are down. I'm on the road beside South Quay station. Kite is below me on the dock with the guy from the funeral. Looks like it's just the two of them.'

'OK.' Fred sounded very calm, very controlled. 'I can see your position. I'll let the others know. Stay on the line.'

Cara heard a quick exchange between Fred and Jason on comms. Kite and the Iranian were moving towards her.

'It's just the two of them,' she said. 'They're heading this way. There's a kind of switchback ramp beside me leading down to the quay. They'll be on the ramp in twenty seconds.'

'Weapon?' Fred asked. 'Jason in one minute. He sees you.'

'Not clear on weapon,' Cara replied. 'I'm going to bump him.'

'You're going to *what?*'

She had no sense where the idea came from, no thought that she might be taking an unnecessary risk or endangering Kite by approaching him. Cara intuited that Isobel was the key to the Iranian's influence over Kite. He needed to know that she was safe.

'Cara, there could be a weapon. Enemy could panic. Do not engage. I say again, do not engage.'

Kite and the Iranian were now less than ten metres away at the bottom of the ramp. Cara began to walk towards them. She moved along the first section of the ramp, turned at a concrete wall and continued until Kite was passing her on the opposite side of a thin dividing rail. She was still connected to Fred on the phone.

'Hang on a minute,' she said, flashing Kite a startled smile. 'I've just run into a friend.'

62

'Emma' was standing at the top of a switchback ramp fifty metres ahead of Kite. As the only member of the Security Service who could positively identify Ramin Torabi, she had evidently been sent to look for him. She appeared to be looking down at the line of barges moored on the eastern side of the inlet.

'Where are we going?' Kite asked.

Emma was speaking to someone on the phone. She turned her back and faced the station. Kite was certain that she had spotted him.

'To the street,' Torabi replied.

There were two ways to reach the road: by walking up a flight of steps fifty feet to the west or via a ramp directly ahead. Torabi was heading for the ramp. As they reached it, Emma turned and began to walk towards them, still talking animatedly on the phone. Kite looked around for surveillance personnel but could not tell who else was on him. There were at least forty pedestrians on the walkway, more on the road above. Emma was chatting away, as if to a friend or colleague, but it was surely just cover behaviour. When they were no more than a metre apart, on parallel sections of the ramp, she suddenly stopped and flashed Kite a stunned, fancy-seeing-you-here smile. He heard her say:

BOX 88

'Hang on a minute, I've just run into a friend.' Then she lowered the phone.

'Lachlan?'

Kite stopped beside her. 'Yes?'

'It's Cara. From the funeral yesterday. Do you remember?'

She was very good—surprised, lively, making apologetic eye contact with Torabi—but the Iranian would surely know that the meeting was not a coincidence. He looked at both of them quickly.

'Oh yes! Cara.' Smart of her to have dispensed with the Emma alias. 'How are you?'

'Fine,' she replied. Kite could see that she was trying to work out if Torabi was carrying a weapon. 'Do you live around here?'

Kite shook his head and put a hand on Torabi's shoulder, as if to reassure him that there was no need to panic. 'This is my friend, Ramin. Ramin, this is Cara.' Kite tried to indicate with his eyes that Torabi held all the cards, loading his next remark with what he hoped would be an obvious code. 'We're actually in a bit of a hurry, shooting off somewhere.'

'Oh.'

It worked. Cara understood what he was trying to do. As they were passing one another she found a way to bring everything to an end.

'Well it was nice to bump into you again,' she said. 'Weirdly I've just come from seeing your wife. We had a meeting in Canary Wharf. She was in a really good mood. Are you on your way to see her?'

It was all Kite needed. No sooner was the question out of Cara's mouth than he slammed his elbow into Torabi's chest, striking him with such force that the Iranian doubled over, gasping for air. Two young runners were coming up the ramp behind him, iPads strapped to their biceps. When they saw what Kite had done, they immediately turned around and jogged off in the opposite direction. Kite reached behind Ramin and seized the gun from the waistband of his trousers, pocketing it with the speed and dexterity of a close-up magician. He then grabbed the panting Iranian around the chest, whispering: 'It's all right, you're OK, Ramin. Take a deep breath' while pushing a thumb into the pressure point at the base of his neck. Cara moved closer as Kite shuffled Torabi towards the wall. The Iranian was still trying to catch his breath. It sounded as though he was choking.

'Is he all right?' An old woman had passed them on the ramp.

'He's fine,' Cara replied, beaming her widest smile. 'Too much to drink.'

Kite made a face at the old woman, as if to confirm this. She looked at Torabi. His frightened eyes were so dizzied, so shocked, that it might almost have been the truth. She walked off.

'We all OK here?'

Jason Franks was beside them. Kite wondered how the hell Jason and Cara had got together.

'We're fine, Jase,' he replied. 'We need to move.'

'Vehicle on the road,' the American replied, pulling Torabi's hands behind his back and cuffing his wrists. 'Let's go.'

On the road above them, somebody leaned on a horn. Kite encouraged Torabi to come with him and they walked back up the ramp.

'My father,' he groaned, breathing more easily. 'You promised me.'

Jason was on one side of him, Kite on the other. A pedestrian passed them on a Boris bike, weaving from the pavement onto the road to avoid hitting them. Kite recognised a BOX 88 driver—Pete Thompson—at the wheel of a Jaguar parked illegally in front of the station. There was a Mercedes immediately behind it with STONES at the wheel, KAISER standing alongside. Cara opened the back door of the Jag and they bundled Torabi into the back seat. Thompson had activated LED lights in the front and rear so that it looked as though two plain-clothes police officers were putting a suspect in the back of an unmarked car.

BOX 88

Kite glanced up towards the station and saw someone filming what was happening on a mobile.

'Phone across the street,' he said to KAISER. 'Two o'clock. Get it.'

KAISER immediately crossed the road, flashed a badge ID and took the phone from the startled pedestrian. Cara sat in the front seat.

'Where's Isobel?' Kite asked, closing the back door.

'She's fine,' Cara replied. 'Rita is with her. Everything's cool.'

Kite looked at Jason as if to say: *How the hell does she know Rita?* Thompson was already on the move, the Mercedes tucking in behind them.

'The baby?' Kite asked.

Torabi tried to free his hands, swearing in Farsi. Jason put him in a headlock.

'Also fine,' said Cara. 'We can call them.'

'Who do we have here?' Jason asked, squeezing Torabi's neck as the Jaguar made a fast turn in the road. 'His friends made a mess of your house.'

'His name is Ramin Torabi,' Kite replied. He indicated to Cara that he wanted to speak to Isobel. She passed him the phone, redialling the number she had used to speak to Fred.

'This will connect you.'

Kite sat back in the seat, listening to the number ringing out. He turned to see if the Jaguar was being followed. Thompson reassured him they were clean.

'And where are we taking him?' Jason asked, releasing Torabi so that he bounced back into the centre of the seat like a crash test dummy.

'Cathedral,' said Kite.

63

Ramin Torabi was put into a secure, soundproofed room at The Cathedral and left alone. He was given food and water. The Iranian was still under the impression that his father was alive and well and living in Marble Arch and was therefore not considered a suicide risk.

Rita drove Isobel to London from the hospital in Sussex where she had received a clean bill of health. Kite was reunited with her shortly after midnight at a BOX 88 apartment in Canary Wharf. Rather than talk long into the night, they both fell into a deep sleep, Kite slipping away at dawn so that he could return to The Cathedral and begin to address the myriad problems which had arisen as a consequence of their respective ordeals.

He left his wife a note, trusting that she would understand why he could not spend the day with her.

Thank God you are safe (and Rambo). You mustn't worry about the future. I promise you'll both be safe. What happened will never happen again. I'll make sure of it.

I've gone to the office. Back this evening. Let's have dinner at Gaucho and talk. Call me if you need anything. There's a woman in the flat next door, Catherine, who works for us.

BOX 88

Dial 12 on the phone. Food, clothes, books, newspapers—what-
ever you need, she'll get it. You just have to ask.

I'm sorry you've had to take time off work. There are people
fixing the cottage, they'll be finished by tonight. Let's talk about
all that over dinner.

I love you.

L x

Kite was aware that his actions might seem reckless or even uncaring, but he calculated that his wife and the baby were both fine and that his own injuries were negligible. He felt justified in leaving Isobel in the flat. What mattered now was the security of BOX 88. He compartmentalised his life in this way, dividing work from family. He had done so for years.

Rita had left a report on his desk. As far as Kite could deduce, there were two areas of immediate concern: the MI5 investigation, which needed to be shut down as quickly as possible, and Ramin Torabi's access to sensitive information relating to Ali Eskandarian. The murder of Zoltan Pavkov, the bodies on the boat, the fracas in South Quay were of secondary importance. With time, and a little imagination, they could all be explained away and, if necessary, covered up. A team from BOX 88 had already visited the ship and taken wallets and phones from the bodies of the slain men as well as a laptop belonging to Torabi. Turings had wiped forty-eight hours of CCTV from the dock and were working on a Transport for London camera which had recorded the vehicles while they were parked outside South Quay station. Vetting requests had been sent to BOX personnel in New York and Dubai for information relating to Ramin Torabi; the London office was in the process of analysing the laptop and phones with a view to piecing together Torabi's movements in the weeks leading up to Xavier's funeral.

Kite decided to deal with MI5 first. Rita had left a number for Cara Jannaway, with whom Kite had spoken only briefly the previous evening. His assistant caught her on the way to work and asked her to ring back from a telephone box so that she could speak to Kite without Five scooping the call. It took Cara less than two minutes to do as she had been asked.

'Mr Kite,' she said when she was put through.

'Call me Lockie. I just wanted to thank you again for everything you did yesterday.'

'Don't mention it,' she replied. 'How are you feeling?'

'Absolutely fine.'

'And your wife?'

'Left her sleeping.' On his desk, Kite kept the small silver box given to him by his father in 1971 as a christening present. He lifted the lid and read the inscription inside: *To Lachlan, from Da.* He twisted the box in his fingers as he weighed his next remark. 'You could be very useful to us, Cara.'

'Us?' she said.

'You know who we are.'

'Do I?'

Kite liked it that she wasn't deferential. Her voice sounded confident, even slightly amused. In her report Rita had described her as 'sassy, quick on the uptake, not easily panicked'.

'Tell me about Robert Vosse.'

'What do you want to know?' It was the reaction Kite had been hoping for: Cara was instantly suspicious of the motive behind Kite's question, instinctively loyal to her boss. 'He's a good guy. Experienced. Decent. Thorough.'

'Tessa Swinburn?'

'Tess is lovely.'

'Matt Tomkins?' Kite asked.

'Honestly?'

'Honestly.'

'Bit of a prat,' Cara replied.

Kite suppressed a laugh. 'And how much do they know about what went on yesterday?'

BOX 88

'Not much.' There was a momentary silence. 'Rita asked me not to tell them.'

'I'm assuming you spoke to Vosse last night.'

'I did,' Cara replied. 'Told him there was nobody at the cottage. He still thinks you're kidnapped.'

Kite put the silver box back on the desk and tapped out an internal message to his assistant: *Get me a number for Robert Vosse.*

'What's the scale of your investigation?' he asked.

'Small. Internal. Far as I know, just us and the DG.'

'Far as you know . . .' Kite picked up the box again and opened it. 'I'm going to have a word with Vosse about shutting your unit down.'

'OK,' Cara replied evenly.

'And I'd like you to hand in your notice.'

Silence on the line, then: 'My what now?'

Kite smiled. 'You have a choice, Cara,' he said. 'Walk off into the sunset, keep quiet and nobody will ever bother you again. Or meet me in Canary Wharf this evening with Robert Vosse to discuss your future.'

'Our future where?'

'At BOX 88.'

There was method to Kite's madness. Cara's potential was plain to see: she was young, brave, quick on her feet. As for Vosse, he could join the handful of serving officers inside MI5 who were already active in support of BOX 88. With Vosse's assistance, Kite intended to find out the identity of the whistle-blower who had tipped off the director general, setting in train the investigation.

'I'm flattered,' Cara replied. 'Thank you. What about Matt and Tessa?'

'Don't worry about them.' If it came to it, BOX 88 had ways of making sure that people like Matt Tomkins and Tessa Swinburn kept their mouths shut. 'Just go back to work this morning. Charge up my mobile. I'll call it around midday, that way your team will know I'm back in circulation. When you have the chance to speak privately to Vosse, tell him I want to meet up. He'll agree.'

'You sound confident.'

Kite didn't have the opportunity to reply because Rita had appeared outside his office, knocking on the glass door, gesturing Kite to let her in.

'I have to go,' he said.

'What about your wallet and shoes?' Cara asked. 'We found lots of your stuff in a skip at the car park. Suit jacket, keys, your watch.'

'Bring them tonight.'

64

Everything was resolved as Kite had planned it. With a skill and subtlety that surprised both Kite and Cara, Robert Vosse persuaded the director general of the Security Service that Lachlan Kite was an oil executive working under non-official cover for MI6, that the whistle-blower was a fantasist and the internal investigation into BOX 88 a wild goose chase.

Matt Tomkins, still rattled by the Pavkov murder, gratefully seized the opportunity to join a new MI5 team investigating a Russian money-laundering operation in Manchester. A week before announcing that she was pregnant, Tessa Swinburn was promoted to run a counter terrorism unit inside Thames House, taking Kieran Dean with her. All three filed reports detailing their experiences on the BOX 88 investigation. These were intercepted by Vosse en route to the DG and redrafted to remove what was euphemistically described as 'unnecessary content'. Any record of the kidnapping of Lachlan Kite, the murder of Zoltan Pavkov and the arrest of Ramin Torabi was wiped from the historical memory.

It remained only to deal with Torabi. Kite had neither the time nor the inclination to spend days interrogating the Iranian in his cell. What he needed to know could be disinterred by colleagues, all of whom would leap at the chance to work Torabi over. There was no belief in torture at BOX 88, only in a forensic study of intelligence and the steady accumulation of facts. If it took weeks for Torabi to break, so be it. Kite would wait. If he was ready to spill his guts, so much the better. Either way, his life as he had known it was over.

Kite had made a comprehensive list of subjects on which to question Torabi—How had he known the location of the cottage? Why had Torabi referred to Cosmo de Paul as an 'associate' of Kite's? Was he responsible for the death of Xavier Bonnard?—and discussed them at length with the interrogation team. As they embarked on several days of initial questioning, Torabi began to show signs of depression. The humiliating failure of his operation had settled on him. He spoke constantly about Kite's promise to take him to Marble Arch and demanded to know when he would be released so that his wife could be reassured that he was safe from harm.

'Pity you didn't extend the same courtesy to me,' Kite muttered, watching the interrogation on a live feed.

On the subject of Xavier's murder, Torabi pleaded innocence. A technical analysis of the Iranian's movements in the days leading up to his death, coupled with a report obtained from a BOX 88 source in French intelligence, persuaded Kite that Torabi had indeed left Paris two days before Xavier had taken his own life. It was scant consolation: to imagine his oldest friend in a suicidal despair, alone and broken in a Paris apartment, was hard to take. Kite knew that there was nothing he could have done to help Xavier in his hour of need, just as he had been unable to help him in any meaningful way throughout their twenties and thirties. He had long believed that it had been right and just to put Luc Bonnard behind bars. Nevertheless, he shared the widespread view that Luc's disgrace, the public exposure of his crimes and venality, had accelerated Xavier's descent into addiction. In this respect, Kite bore partial responsibility for the way

BOX 88

that his friend's life had turned out. He had betrayed him in France. There was no getting away from it.

Ten days after his release from captivity, Kite finally paid a visit to the gallerist in Mayfair who had obtained the painting by Jean-Paul Riopelle which he had intended to view on the afternoon of Xavier's funeral. Ever since he had bought a small brush and ink Pierre Soulages in 1993 with his earnings from a job in Russia, it had been his habit to buy a picture at the end of an operation. But what had happened with Torabi did not feel like an operational success. Kite had not bid for the Riopelle, instead offering the Soulages to the dealer. He had paid 30,000 francs for it in 1993 at a gallery on the Rue de Seine, the equivalent of about £3,000. For its current market value of around £90,000, Kite could set some money aside for Rambo and take Isobel to the Caribbean. She would need time to recuperate from her ordeal. Kite knew that keeping his past a secret from her would no longer be possible: his wife would want answers. They had a lot of conversational ground to cover.

Coming back to BOX 88 headquarters at around five o'clock, he caught sight of a bearded man standing alone outside Canary Wharf station. The man appeared to be waiting for someone. Nothing unusual about that at the start of the rush hour, but Kite did a double-take. It was John, the American with whom he had smoked at the funeral. He looked up as Kite came towards him.

'Lachlan.'

'I get the feeling this isn't a chance encounter.'

'Was told you would pass this way.' The American extended a huge, hairy hand and clasped Kite in a vigorous handshake. 'Ward Hansell. I'm over from the Stadium.'

The Stadium was the Service nickname for BOX 88 headquarters in the United States, so called because of its proximity to the home of the New York Giants. Kite was astonished that

Hansell was a colleague: he had been convinced that the bearded, unkempt 'John' at the Oratory was a bona fide addict and friend of Xavier's.

'Sorry I didn't introduce myself at the funeral. When you approached me asking for a smoke, I thought it was a bump. Didn't know who you were until I put two and two together.'

'That's all right,' Kite replied, conscious of the extent to which his guard had been down on the morning of the funeral. Was he getting sloppy? Were his sharpest days behind him? 'What are you doing in London?'

'Let's walk.'

It transpired that Hansell had taken an interest in one of the mourners at Xavier's service: Cosmo de Paul. That Kite's nemesis and sparring partner should again pop up on his radar struck him as an eerie coincidence: Torabi had twice brought up de Paul's name on the ship.

'How long have you been watching him?' he asked.

'Three months.'

De Paul had been recruited by MI6 out of Oxford in 1994, eventually leaving the Service in 2008 to take up a position in the private sector. As someone who had known de Paul both operationally and personally over a period of thirty years, Kite assumed that Hansell wanted to speak to him on background.

'We think he may be a security risk.'

'To BOX or the wider population?' Kite asked.

He hadn't intended to make a joke, but Hansell chuckled. Evidently, he had already spent enough time around de Paul to know that he was a disruptive, unpredictable opportunist.

'You guys getting any heat from Five?' the American asked.

'You could say that.'

Kite wondered how much or how little Hansell knew about the Vosse unit.

'De Paul has been talking to Rebecca Simmonds, saying things he shouldn't be saying.'

BOX 88

Of course. Suddenly it all made sense. Simmonds was the director general of MI5. De Paul was the DG's whistle-blower. He had known of Kite's involvement in BOX 88 for more than twenty years and had long resented his own exclusion from that most elite of clubs. But why choose this moment to pour poison in Simmonds's ear?

'What sort of things?' he asked.

'Well that's what I don't fully understand,' Hansell replied. 'You have an old girlfriend living in New York, right? Martha Raine?'

Kite came to a halt. Of all things, he had not expected this. He felt the tide of the past rushing up to meet him, the bitter memories of Martha's years at Oxford, the spectre of de Paul's bizarre, private obsession with Kite, incubated at Alford and continuing to the present day.

'Martha?' he asked, as if Hansell had made a mistake. 'What does she have to do with any of this?'

There was a corporate bar across the square filled with office workers grabbing a drink before heading home. At the church, Hansell had possessed the wild, dishevelled appearance of an Old Testament prophet; now, in the pale evening light of Canary Wharf, his beard trimmed and hair neatly cut, he could have passed for one of the mid-level executives queuing for a pint at the bar. He nodded towards the entrance, laying a heavy hand on Kite's back.

'Let's get a drink,' he said. 'You and I need to talk.'

Acknowledgements

With thanks to: Julia Wisdom, Kathryn Cheshire, Finn Cotton, Ann Bissell, Roger Cazalet, Kate Elton, Liz Dawson, Anne O'Brien and everyone behind the scenes at HarperCollins. To Will Francis, Kirsty Gordon and the team at Janklow & Nesbit. To Harriette Peel, Perdita Martell, Christopher de Bellaigue, Sarah Gabriel, TC, Nick Green, Natasha Fairweather, Boris Starling, P, Benedict Bull, JF, Olivier Bonas, Laila D, KS, Dr Charlotte Cassis, Angus Maguire, Ben Barrett, JJ Keith, Nick Lockley, Christian Spurrier, Ben Higgins, Charlie Gammell, Nicholas Griffin, Peter F, Nick S, Rupert Harris, Debbie Winfield, Ian Cumming and Caroline Pilkington. Jamie Blackett's 'The Enigma of Kidson', Ryszard Kapuscinski's 'Shah of Shahs' and Reza Kahlili's memoir 'A Time to Betray' were all very helpful.

C.C. London 2020